RUPE

An expression of rage swept over Cade's face and for the first time Lauren saw the true danger in the man. If she showed any weakness, one of them would die. Either she convinced him that she was serious or she would have to kill him. The thought was compelling. *Kill him now,* the trees seemed to urge.

She aimed at the sky and squeezed the trigger. The sound roared through the forest, startling ravens and magpies out of trees to squawk in alarm.

As if that was the signal he'd been waiting for, Rupe launched himself at Cade's throat, his lips drawn back in a snarl.

"Rupe!"

Cade raised a massive fist and in a movement that was so fast it became a blur, struck Rupe down in mid-air. The dog landed heavily five feet away and lay still.

All the air seemed to leave her lungs while she waited for Rupe to get up again. As the slow seconds ticked by and he didn't move, she deliberately brought the muzzle of the Winchester to bear on Cade's solid chest.

NOVELS BY MARCELLE DUBÉ

Mendenhall Mystery Series:
The Shoeless Kid
The Tuxedoed Man
The Weeping Woman
The Untethered Woman
The Forsaken Man
The Wronged Woman

A'lle Chronicles Series:
The A'lle Murders
The A'lle Mutation

Standalone:
Ghosts of Morocco
Identity Withheld
Jilimar
Kirwan's Son
Obeah
On Her Trail
Shelter

A Little Strangeness (collection)

OBEAH

by

Marcelle Dubé

FALCON
RIDGE
PUBLISHING

OBEAH
Copyright © 2013 by Marcelle Dubé

First published as an e-book in 2012
by Falcon Ridge Publishing
(As written by Emma Faraday)

Cover image © M. Cornelius
Via Shutterstock
Book and cover design copyright © 2013
by Falcon Ridge Publishing

ISBN: 978-0-9918746-7-5

Falcon Ridge Publishing
www.falconridgepublishing.com

OBEAH

MONTREAL, QUEBEC, CANADA
AUGUST 2041

S ILAS walked stiffly down the middle of the dark, cobble-
stone street toward the New Montreal Library. He kept
his head down to let the rain run off his hat brim, away
from his eyes. The downpour released the pent-up odors of the
day—fried fish, wet garbage, outhouses—and his sensitive gaians
nose wrinkled in protest.

He took a circuitous route to avoid the worst of the puddles.
The only light on Rue St-Clément shone above the library door,
half a block away, where a solar cell lamp reflected wetly on the
cobblestones. Inside, he knew from experience, beeswax candles
would be the only source of light in the reading room. It always
reminded him of his early days in this city, before electricity came.
And went.

A few latecomers emerged from the darkness on the far side of
the library and hurried for the door, their feet splashing. With their
sapiens eyes, they didn't see him in the dark and they disappeared
into the library, leaving the street deserted once more.

The poet reading tonight was a Montreal favorite. Silas sighed.
If he didn't hurry, he'd have to stand. His knees already ached
enough. Of all the things to have in common with sapiens, arthritis
seemed like a particularly cruel irony.

He was getting foolish in his old age. Coming out on a wet night would mean pain for the next few days, all because he admired the way some sapiens could string words together.

A familiar tingle in his belly warned him as he approached the lit library door and he stopped in the middle of the street, his mind blank with surprise. There was another obeah nearby.

As if conjured, a shadow pulled away from the recessed doorway of the Boulangerie St-Clément. Silas saw the man clearly, his gaians eyes compensating for the distracting light.

The man was big, judging by the way he narrowed the doorway, but it wasn't his size alone that left Silas staring. The entire gaians species was of one genotype: small, dark, and wiry. This stranger's hair was white blond in the reflection from the lamp next door. He was part sapiens.

The stranger stared back at Silas, his expression unreadable.

Silas forced himself to breathe. The man was here for the reading. There was no reason for alarm. It wasn't unusual to find two gaians living in the same city, especially a big one like Montreal.

But two obeahs? Obeahs were so rare that the likelihood of two of them being in the same area, let alone the same city—

Then a breath of warning from the ancestors reached him, cool on the back of his damp neck.

The obeah had been waiting for him.

Silas finally found his voice. "My name is Silas."

"I know who you are," said the stranger. He stepped onto the street and walked to within ten feet of Silas, where he stopped.

Silas grew still as he realized that he now knew who this man was, too. He had heard rumors about a young obeah seeking out other obeahs. Of the eight obeahs the man had found, two were dead and three were crippled, their link with the underworld severed. No one knew what had happened to the last three.

The younger man stood in the middle of the street, feet apart, hands in his pockets. Insolent. Or nervous? Rain plastered that pale hair to his skull.

A gust of wind swept rain over Silas' face. He took strength from the cleansing and from the strong thread of contact to the ancestors. He steeled himself for an attack.

Just then a woman turned the corner and ran head down toward the library, only seeing them at the last minute. She looked up, startled, and scurried inside, to Silas' relief. He didn't want any sapiens hurt.

"You're wrong to protect the saps," said the young man, reading Silas as clearly as if he had spoken. His voice was deep and edged with bitterness.

So much anger in this one. It made him dangerous. "Don't hate them," said Silas gently. "We can teach them—are teaching them. They are our cousins, after all."

But the young obeah shook his head.

"They're rats, feeding on our dying world. They should be exterminated before they can destroy us all."

Without warning, the young obeah closed his eyes, reached, and wrenched Silas's awareness out of his body and into the underworld. The street disappeared as darkness swooped over Silas. His unprepared body crumpled to the hard cobblestones and his untethered mind reeled. He couldn't find his bearings.

Then something hard clamped onto his ankles, pulling him downward so fast that a cold wind whistled past his ears and snatched his breath, slashing his unprotected face and hands like tiny knives.

Voices gibbered in his ears and invisible hands clutched at him. When the hands turned into claws and sharp teeth nipped at his calves, he flailed in horror, trying to drive the creatures away.

For the first time in over a century, Silas was afraid.

❧ ONE ❧

SOUTH CENTRAL YUKON, CANADA
SEPTEMBER 2041

THE ANCIENT Ford pickup rumbled a deeper note as Lauren downshifted near the intersection of the Alaska Highway and the Carcross Road. The morning sun had finally climbed over Mount Lorne, and sunlight glittered on a dusting of snow covering the disintegrating asphalt. Winter was early.

She scanned the road out of habit, trying to catch the stealthy movements of men waiting in ambush between the frost-covered aspen and pine trees that grew right up to the road. A flicker in the trees sent adrenalin pumping through her muscles but it was only a coyote slinking from a lodgepole pine to a spruce tree.

On the seat next to her, Rupe whined softly, his dog smell competing with the smell of burning oil and exhaust.

"It's okay, boy." She scratched the black Lab's head and he licked her fingers in sympathy. It wasn't fair to infect him with her uneasiness.

The Alaska Highway was up ahead. Lauren's shoulders tightened under the parka and she slowed even more, ready to speed up in the turn. Rupe's ears pricked up and the peppery smell of his tension filled the cab.

She hadn't come to a full stop at this intersection since a gang of punks had swarmed Geraldine Somner's Ranger. Their hammers and axes had punched through the Ranger's windows and doors like cardboard. It was three days before they found Geri's body.

But that was over ten years ago, in the bad time when strangers poured into the territory hoping to escape the epidemics sweeping the south. She had been ten then, and it had seemed as if the whole world was going to hell.

Things were different now.

It wasn't really the intersection that bothered her and she knew it. It was market day. She scowled at the cracked windshield. She resented market day more with each turn of the wheels. Each time she drove the ancient Ford brought it that much closer to its final breakdown. One day she wouldn't be able to fix it or find replacement tires. Besides, the price of gas—when it was available—was climbing out of her range. She glanced at the gas gauge. Just under half full. She would fill up at Jimmy's at the corner. He was expensive but he usually had gas, sometimes even kerosene.

There was a time when Jimmy kept guards to watch over his supply of precious gasoline and protect his customers. Now he worked alone with his sons... but he still kept a loaded rifle under the counter.

There was no help for it. This was likely the last market day before winter closed down the roads. If she didn't get the wire for her snares now, there would be no rabbit stew this winter and no wolverine fur to trade next spring.

And she had to make sure Mary and Charlie were set for winter. Her foster parents were getting older. One of these days she was going to have to move closer to them. The thought left her in a cold sweat and she quickly shifted her attention back to the road.

She took the turn onto the Alaska Highway too fast on her bald tires and Rupe scrambled to keep his footing, barking reproachfully.

Maybe Jimmy would have coffee today. Maybe he'd trade her a pound for a marten pelt. Of the things she missed from her childhood, only toilet paper ranked as high as coffee. Stupid. She didn't even like coffee—and it was more expensive than gas—but the smell always brought her back to the safe time before Dad died. Back then, Mom used to cook a fancy breakfast on Sundays and always brewed real coffee. None of that instant crap. She could always give the coffee to Mary and Charlie.

Movement.

Her foot slammed down on the accelerator before her brain registered what her eyes had seen. Caught off balance, Rupe fell into the seat back.

Two men were walking toward her on the side of the road.

Not walking. Striding. She had an impression of size—a big man and a smaller one, with packs on their backs—then she was past them.

Regaining his balance, Rupe stood looking out the rear window, growling, the hair on his back standing straight up. With a chill crawling up her spine, Lauren glanced at her cracked rearview mirror. The men had stopped and were staring after her.

As she drove past Jimmy's place, she felt under the passenger seat for her Winchester. She'd stop for gas on the way back. When the strangers were long gone.

* * *

Market day at Shipyards Park on the banks of the Yukon River. Frenzied in the summer, pathetic in the fall. Always too many people.

Lauren stopped at the gate for the guard to identify her. It was Charlie.

"Lauren." He didn't look at her at first but glanced inside the cab, then into the truck's bed, brown eyes missing nothing. "Got some pelts."

She nodded. "A few marten and a bunch of rabbit." She pulled out the top beaver she had been saving. "This one's for Mary." The old woman had a gift with a needle. She could make a flap hat and a child's vest out of one good-sized beaver pelt. Lauren still had the hat Mary had made her when she first came to live with the couple, after her mother disappeared. Warmest hat she owned.

Charlie finally looked at her and his brown face crinkled up in a smile. "She'll like that."

Lauren looked away, embarrassed. He didn't say that it was two months since she'd last seen him and Mary but the thought hung between them. She had lived with her parents' friends for six years after her mother's disappearance. By the time she was sixteen, Lauren couldn't wait to get away from their benevolent smothering.

Still. She met his gaze. "Where is she?"

He started to speak then hesitated. "She stayed home today. Knees bothering her again."

Lauren looked at him for a long heartbeat, her stomach knotting. "I'll drop by after market. We'll have tea and bannock."

With a crooked smile, Charlie patted her cheek with his free hand then reached in to tug gently on Rupe's ear. "Hi, pup." The black Lab licked the old man's hand, tail thumping on the cracked leather seat. Charlie straightened. He looked tired. "Shotgun under the seat, Lauren." Then he turned away to meet a small group of riders.

Lauren stared at his back. The acrid smell of wet ashes trailed after the old man—the smell of sadness. Her belly tightened in dread. What wasn't he telling her? She looked at Rupe. "Whatever it is, Mary will tell us."

Rupe barked once in agreement.

There were only two other trucks in the parking area, one a big flatbed that had once been green but was now covered in splotches of rust. It was filled with bales of hay. She parked next to it. At the far end of the parking lot, thirty horses waited at various hitching posts. In summer the hitching posts were crowded and there were even a few carts. Shipyards Park nestled between the river and a berm, on the other side of which was the parking lot. She used to slide down that berm on her toboggan when she was little.

"Stay with Charlie," she told Rupe. With a happy bark, he launched his eighty pounds of solid muscle at Charlie, stopping just short of the old man. Charlie laughed, revealing yellowed teeth, and rubbed his knuckles over Rupe's skull.

As Lauren hauled her bundle of pelts out of the back of the pickup, she noticed Charlie watching her, making sure she wasn't bringing the Winchester into the market. No dogs or firearms allowed. Only knives. Only a fool parted with her knife.

She walked around the flatbed, pelts balanced precariously on her left shoulder, and stopped short.

On the other side of the flatbed, hidden by the big truck's bulk, was an all-terrain vehicle. It was short and squat, and bright red. Its fenders were a little banged up but its tires looked almost new, with lots of tread on them. The ATV brought back memories of hanging on to her father's waist as they rode the trails around their cabin. She hadn't seen one in years.

She hadn't seen tires that new in years—hadn't known that the outside world had recovered enough to start producing them again. She certainly didn't know anyone who could afford them. The tires alone were more valuable than the ATV.

She glanced over at Charlie, but he faced away from her and was talking to a young couple with heavy packs on their backs. She'd ask him later who owned the ATV. Shrugging the pile of furs into a more comfortable position, she headed for the opening into the park. It was time to do some trading so she could get back home.

The park teemed with people. Folks called to each other from behind tables heaped with the last potatoes of the season, dog-hair wool, moose-hide moccasins, and felted wool hats and mitts. Lauren glanced at her cold-chapped hand. Maybe she would make herself lighter mittens for spring and fall. It wasn't cold enough yet for her sheepskin mitts.

At the river edge of the park, Don Buchanan sat at his stone wheel, sharpening a hunting knife. He pumped the pedal with one foot, his whole body moving in time to the pumping, while the wheel whooshed through the water trough in time to his pedal. Sparks flew as he worked the knife on the wheel. Five people clustered next to him, chatting and waiting their turn.

Lauren breathed deeply. Someone was cooking caribou.

As she walked by, people looked up at her and nodded politely. Then they looked away quickly, as if afraid she would talk to them. She had lived in this area for almost twenty-one years, her whole life, and still they treated her like an outsider.

She steeled herself against the familiar hurt. It wasn't all of them. To Charlie and Mary, she was family.

From the tattered wall tent at the far end of the park came raucous laughter, distracting her. The beer tent. Nothing stronger was allowed in the park, although occasionally a man slipped out the back and to the riverbank for a quick nip of potato moonshine.

Aside from the beer tent, there was no shelter from the north wind. Half a dozen rusted and pitted oil drums glowed with fire. Folks clustered red-cheeked around them, warming their hands and backsides before going back to their tables.

"Lauren!"

Lauren looked up to see Emily Pounder waving at her. Her closest neighbors, Emily, Stan, and their three kids, lived five miles up the road from her. Too close to the intersection for safety. Too poor to move anywhere else.

Stan nodded acknowledgment, his eyes hooded.

"There's room at our table," said Emily cheerfully. She ignored the look her husband gave her and waved Lauren over.

Lauren hid a smile. Emily Pounder was a practical woman. Sharing the table meant sharing the rental cost. It also meant Stan and Emily didn't have enough to fill the table. Lauren set her bundle down on the cleared space and spread out her pelts. Her trapline wouldn't be producing for another few weeks, but last winter had yielded more pelts than she needed.

"When did you get back?" asked Stan politely as he finished setting out his tins of marijuana sticks. Emily added her eggs and dried herbs next to the marijuana. Lauren tried not to stare. The dope was a luxury few people could afford, and most folks had their own chickens, or at least an arrangement with neighbors who did. Nobody traded for eggs at market. Stan and Emily couldn't feed the kids, let alone themselves, on what was on the table.

She'd be sharing her meat with them again this year.

"A couple of weeks ago," she finally remembered to reply.

"Where did you go this time?" asked Emily.

"Kluane."

Emily and Stan looked at her in bewilderment.

Every summer, Lauren set out with Rupe on a walkabout. She picked a direction and started walking. Sometimes she came back in a couple of weeks, sometimes longer. This year she had been gone over a month, but she had made it as far as Kathleen Lake, in what used to be Kluane Park. She had spent long days fishing with Rupe and lazing by the frigid mountain lake. It was beautiful.

Next summer she planned to cross the White Pass and head for the Alaskan coast. She had never seen the ocean.

Even Mary and Charlie thought she was crazy.

"Do you ever find what you're looking for?" asked Stan, surprising her. It was the first genuine question he had ever asked her.

"Oh, Stan!" Emily slapped his arm playfully but Lauren saw the bafflement in his eyes and looked away. No, she never found what she was looking for. She didn't even know what she was looking for. Maybe she was looking for where she belonged.

It certainly wasn't here.

Out of her pack, Emily pulled a large cast-iron frying pan that Lauren recognized from her rare visits to their place. The pan usually had pride of place, hanging from a nail in their kitchen wall. It would fetch them a lot of goods and food, if they bartered carefully. And it would leave them without a frying pan.

The wind gusted from the east and Lauren turned her head, sniffing. There was something odd about Emily's scent, like ginger mixed with wild roses. Then she glimpsed the curve of Emily's belly as her coat strained against it.

Four kids? Damn it all.

Lauren turned away. She couldn't help them any more than she already was—she had herself and Rupe to look after.

But Emily's eggs traded well, especially when Stan sweetened the deal with a dope stick. Lauren watched covertly as women clustered around Emily's end of the table, vying to trade for her eggs. A few of the women pushed bags of baby clothes and cloth diapers into Emily's hands. Lauren shook her head in wonder. It never ceased to amaze her how quickly news made the rounds.

It was hard to hide her smile when Stan surreptitiously slipped the frying pan back into the backpack.

Lauren's pelts traded well, too—they always did when the cold weather swept in. Soon enough, all she had left was her marten pelt and that one she set aside in hopes that Jimmy had coffee. When Stan shooed Emily off to warm up at a barrel, Lauren went with her. After a while, they gave up their spot to wander through the market.

The river swept past the park, slowly narrowing as the ice crept in toward the middle. Wisps of ice fog rose above the water, as if the river breathed. The air smelled of wood smoke and cooking meat.

Lauren and Emily each accepted a cup of rosehip tea sweetened with fireweed honey that Jilly Amherst poured for them from a battered thermos.

"Thanks," said Lauren. "Bees did well this year?"

Jilly's cheeks were rosy with cold, but her blue eyes sparkled as much as ever. She had always been friendly with Lauren, if not close. No one was close to her. "Yep. Wanna trade?"

Lauren shook her head. "I still have lots left from this summer."

Emily laughed. "You have the best stocked larder in these

parts, Lauren Tom. Best trapline, best fishing spots... even your garden produces well." She grinned but there was envy in her eyes.

Lauren's heart sank a little but she smiled as if Emily had meant it kindly. She was used to the reaction. And it wasn't just Emily. Lauren hated that some folks resented her abilities. She was a good trapper and fisher. Her mother had taught her how to bait a trap for marten, wolverine and lynx, and how to build a weir to keep her and Rupe in salmon. But it was Lauren's instinct for animals—their habits, their preferences, their reactions—that kept her meat cache full. She knew animals the way Emily knew babies.

The green thumb, that she got from her dad. Her garden had suffered these past few summers because of her long absences, but she always managed to get a good root crop.

Jilly stepped into the awkward silence. "When's the last time you saw Mary?" she asked Lauren.

Lauren's heart skipped a beat. Jilly lived close to Charlie and Mary, in what used to be downtown Whitehorse. "What's wrong?"

"She hardly goes outside anymore. I've been by to visit her, and she always looks happy to see me, but I can tell she's in pain."

This was what Charlie was keeping from her—the arthritis was spreading. She tried to think through the implications. Finally she shook her head.

"I'm done here. I'll go see her."

"Good." Jilly nodded her approval.

They headed back toward their table and Emily glanced back to smile at Jilly. Then the smile changed to surprise.

"Holy cow—it's Cade McAllister."

Lauren started in surprise but kept walking on legs suddenly gone rubbery. Her heart thumped painfully against her rib cage. So. Cade was back. He must be the mysterious owner of the ATV.

Did Charlie know? The old man had chased Cade McAllister out of Whitehorse five years ago at the end of his rifle when Cade's courtship of Lauren became too... insistent. At the time, Lauren had bitterly resented Charlie's interference. The incident had prompted her decision to move out of Charlie and Mary's home. But after a while, she forgave Charlie—even realized that she was grateful that he had chased Cade off before she could sleep with him. Cade was twenty years older than she was—too old for the sixteen-year-old she had been.

And now he was back.

"He's coming over." A hint of malice tinged Emily's smile. "I'd better go see if Stan needs me."

Oh no, you don't, thought Lauren, her body filling with frantic butterflies. "I'm coming, too."

"Lauren."

She stopped, paralyzed by the familiar voice.

Cade's voice started about a foot below his feet and rumbled all the way out. The butterflies inside Lauren clumped together and formed a knot in her stomach.

She turned to face him.

"Hey, Cade." To her relief, she sounded coolly polite.

Cade was bigger than most men, in the same way a mountain was bigger than a hill. Everything about him was proportional. Seen from a distance, he looked average. Then he moved closer and perspective shifted. At six feet three, Cade loomed over her five feet four inches. She used to love it that he was so tall. Now she had to control an urge to step back as he approached.

He wore no hat, no scarf, and his wolf fur coat was open. Five years hadn't aged him. If anything, he looked better than ever. He still kept his blond hair short, emphasizing the strong bones of his face. His gray eyes always reminded her of a wolf's eyes—or maybe it was the intensity of his gaze that was wolf like.

He stopped too close to her, his nostrils flaring, and she knew he was sniffing her. His gaze took in all one hundred and twenty pounds of her, from the tip of her moose-hide moccasins, to her doeskin pants and oversize dog-hair sweater. He looked at the red, work-hardened hands, the work-lean body, the chapped lips... She lifted a hand to touch her black, wavy hair. It was much shorter than when he had last run his fingers through it.

Had she changed? Her eyes were still green, her cheekbones still high, her chin still firm. Some might consider her an attractive woman. But Cade was the only man to ever want her. In the five years he'd been gone, no other man had even approached her, let alone wanted to bed her.

And then the wind shifted and she caught the musky scent of his desire. She let out a shaky breath.

Whatever else had changed, he still wanted her.

He leaned down to her, his gaze holding hers, and for a moment she thought he was going to kiss her. Then he closed his eyes and inhaled deeply of her scent. When he opened his eyes again, his gray eyes looked darker.

Full of promise.

"You look like your mother," he said.

Lauren jerked back in shock. The tentative smile that had trembled on her lips slipped away. Her mother?

Cade had known her mother?

Whatever she had expected, it wasn't that.

If Cade noticed her confusion, he gave no sign. One big hand reached up to cup her cheek. Five years ago, she would have turned her head into the caress and kissed his palm. Now she just looked at him.

"I hoped to find you here," he continued. His thumb stroked her cheek, and without consciously deciding to, she stepped out of his reach.

Cade's eyebrow rose in surprise and something moved behind his eyes, but she couldn't tell if it was hurt or anger. Maybe both.

"What brings you back, Cade?" As if her ears had been blocked, she suddenly heard the noises of the market again—the rushing water, the rasp of steel on stone, the neighing of a horse in the parking lot. Somewhere a man laughed and a woman called out to a friend.

He smiled at her and shook his head, looking puzzled. "You, of course," he said gently. "I came back for you."

Five years ago, those words would have thrilled her. Now they just made her wary. Why had it taken him so long to come back? She'd spent a lot of time alone since he left, done a lot of thinking. She might not know what she was looking for, but she knew it wasn't him.

"Cade—"

"No, let me speak," he urged. Before she could move away again, he captured her arms in his hands, forcing her to stay where she was. Her breath caught in her throat and she pulled against his hold, hating the feeling of being trapped.

"Lauren," he said sharply. "Listen to me!"

"Let go, Cade." She tried to pull away but he only tightened his hold. Her heart raced in alarm. Was she going to have to hurt him?

"I've waited long enough, Lauren."

A sharp bark brought Lauren's head up. Rupe stood growling on top of the berm separating park from parking lot, lips peeled back from his teeth. Next to him, a grim-faced Charlie stood with his shotgun held casually in the crook of his arm. Both were looking at Cade.

Rupe's bark had attracted attention. Folks from nearby tables turned to stare at them. To Lauren's surprise, a few men stepped forward, obviously ready to intervene.

Cade's face hardened with hatred as he stared up at Charlie. The old man held his gaze calmly and finally Cade turned back to Lauren. She looked pointedly at his hands on her arms and he released her. His mouth twisted in a bitter smile.

"We'll talk later." Without a backward look, he shouldered past two men and headed out of the park.

Immediately, Emily Pounder came up to Lauren and slipped an arm around her waist. "Are you all right?" Gone was the malice, replaced by concern.

Lauren nodded, not yet trusting her voice.

"What was that all about?" asked Emily, staring after Cade.

Lauren shook her head.

She had no idea.

❧ TWO ❧

L AUREN stopped at Jimmy's on the way home. The price of gas had gone up again and she handed over the marten pelt to pay her outstanding bill without asking about the coffee.

The sun cast long tree shadows across the road. She usually tried to make it home while there was still enough light to unload the truck, but her visit with Mary had taken longer than expected.

Her foster mother had been happy to see her, but hadn't risen from her chair to welcome her in. After more than six decades of hard work, Mary's body was wearing out. The arthritis had moved into her hips and her shoulders. Willow bark tea barely helped anymore.

Meridy Tom had known all about plants and their medicinal values. She had kept an extensive library of reference books, but Lauren hadn't looked at them in years—she never got sick. She would look tonight. One of her mother's books might contain information that could help Mary. And, by extension, Charlie.

No wonder he looked tired. Charlie had to do most of the work around the house as well as find a way to earn a living.

They had taken Lauren in when she needed help. Now it was her turn to help them. It was time to move into town.

Her throat tightened and she swallowed hard. She had been welcomed into Mary and Charlie's home with warmth and love. They had encouraged her to make friends and she had tried. She had tagged along with the other kids on the rare days it was hot enough for a dip in Long Lake. She had taken her turn on bear duty, watching over berry pickers in the fall. She had helped build the new meeting hall and learned to dance on its rough wooden floor with Jeremy Simons.

She had tried. They had tried.

Every single person in her foster parents' circle of friends and acquaintances had treated her with kindness. But as she grew older, the distance between her and the town's folk grew. She just didn't fit.

It had to do with her need to be alone, to walk on the land and see nothing but trees and rabbits and rivers, while everyone else she knew seemed to need to gather together.

And now she would have to live among them again.

Rupe nudged her shoulder. His anxiety smelled sour.

She rubbed the top of his head but kept her gaze on the road. "Relax, pup. It'll be fine. You like Mary and Charlie."

Her presence would make the old couple's life easier. She glanced at the stack of goods on the floor of the truck. She'd gotten the wire, plus dried peas, flour, oatmeal and twenty pounds of potatoes. None of which she needed but it would help feed two extra mouths. Her cache was full of smoked and frozen salmon and she even had dried caribou left, enough to last until she and Rupe went hunting again. Charlie would have his own cache, too. They would be all right.

Best of all, a sturdy plastic sled waited in the back of the truck. It was old but still had its original hinges. It would replace the heavy wooden sled she'd been using for six years on the trapline.

Her trapline. She would have to abandon it and stake one closer to town. Which meant competing with every other trapper in town.

Damn. She and Charlie would have to discuss this. Maybe Charlie was ready to give up his trapline. He might have to anyway, to stay home and look after Mary. Lauren was the better trapper.

The sun was sinking behind the mountains by the time she pulled into the rutted track that served as her driveway. Her ancient headlights hadn't worked in years and she squinted as she entered the gloom of the black spruce forest, scanning the quarter-mile track to her cabin.

Long before the cabin came into sight, she stopped and sat in the idling truck, staring down the track. The small hairs on the back of her neck prickled and next to her, Rupe growled softly. She swept the woods and back with a quick glance, trying to see what was wrong. It was on the second sweep that she caught it. She had driven out that morning over fresh snow. There should be only one set of tire tracks.

Not two.

She shut the engine off, slid the Winchester along the seat toward her, and eased out of the cab. Rupe jumped out next to her and with a quick hand signal, she motioned him to heel.

She gently pushed the door closed, blessing the bear grease on its hinges, and cocked the Winchester. She was glad she had the shotgun, instead of the Remington rifle she used for hunting. The smell of burning oil caught at her nose and she moved away from the truck to examine the tracks. The wheelbase was too narrow for a truck, or even a car, but just about right for an ATV. And the tire tracks showed lots of tread.

Cade.

She stared at the dark track for long minutes, trying to get her breathing under control as uneasiness traced a thin, chilly line up her spine.

He'd said he had come back for her. And now he was at her home. Uninvited.

She didn't want him here.

She slipped into the trees, Rupe at her side. Cold stung her cheeks and the shotgun soon burned the flesh of her fingers as the metal froze, but she kept her finger on the trigger. She didn't think Cade would try to hurt her, but their encounter in the market had unnerved her.

She studied the ground carefully but in the cover of the trees there wasn't enough snow on the ground to show tracks.

A faint wisp of wood smoke trailed through the forest, left over from her fire this morning. She crept through the woods, circling the cabin to approach it from the rear.

Cade would expect her from the road.

Rupe followed, his growling so low that she felt it more than heard it. Uneasiness flowed up from the ground through her moccasins.

Rupe pressed his nose into her hand, whining softly. She patted his head. "Hush, boy," she whispered.

The dog stiffened just as a twig snapped behind her. Lauren whirled and aimed.

Cade stepped out of the dusk between the trees, less than twenty feet away. His smile gleamed briefly in the growing darkness.

Rupe barked a warning but stayed by her side. Cade didn't even look at the Lab.

"We need to talk, Lauren." His coat flipped open in the breeze.

The inevitability of the confrontation seeped into her like blood seeping into cloth. "Come back in the morning, Cade." She allowed the tip of the Winchester to drop toward the ground. She didn't want to hurt him. She just wanted him to go. Couldn't he understand that his presence was making her uncomfortable? For the first time since she'd moved back to her family's cabin, she felt vulnerable.

She suddenly remembered that he had compared her to her mother. How well had he known Meridy Tom?

Stillness seemed to surround Cade as he stared at her. She could barely make out the look of frustration on his face. Finally he sighed.

"I've missed you, Lauren." His hands lifted slightly, palms

open, pale as aspen bark in the gloom. "I hope you've missed me, too. I didn't want to leave, you know, but you weren't ready." He smiled. "Now you are, and I want you back."

As she listened to his words, Lauren wondered why they had so little effect on her. This man clearly wanted her, clearly desired her. And once, a long time ago, she had wanted him, too. Why wasn't that enough for her?

Because she didn't believe him. When she set aside her confusion and opened up her senses, she realized that everything about him contradicted his words. He tried for a relaxed stance but it was forced and awkward. His voice grated with a harsh undertone. And his sweat stank of stress.

Somewhere in his honeyed words was a lie. Did it have anything to do with her mother?

"Lauren, it's time," continued Cade, taking half a step toward her. "Come away with me."

Lauren's mouth fell open in astonishment.

"*Away?* Where?"

"Somewhere special," he said eagerly. "Ben-My-Chree. I have a cabin there. It's a beautiful area, a great place to start a family." His gray eyes pierced through the gloom. "We were always meant for each other. Come with me."

He kept talking, but the name Ben-My-Chree echoed in her mind, drowning out his words. Charlie had been there once, when he was a young man. Only a few hundred miles south of White-horse, at the tip of Taku Arm Lake, inaccessible by road. He said it was the most beautiful place on earth.

Cade's voice dropped even lower, so low that she strained to hear it over the sighing of the spruce trees. "There's no need to be alone anymore. Let me look after you." His hands rose again, open and beseeching. "No more empty cabin to come home to. No more weeks on end with no one to talk to but the dog. We would be so good for each other, Lauren."

Lauren's eyes closed as his words wove a web of longing around her. No more emptiness. No more waking up alone in the dead of night. No more wondering what was wrong with her that no one wanted her.

Cade was strong. He would be a good mate. Their children would be strong, too.

Rupe pressed himself against her leg, trembling. Even the trees seemed to be whispering at her to be careful. Her eyes slowly opened.

A moment ago, she couldn't wait to be rid of him. Now she was considering starting a family with him. Sweat suddenly drenched her, in spite of the cold. How had he done that?

The wind whipped strands of hair into her face and she took a deep breath. She forced herself to meet Cade's expectant gaze and for the first time, she realized she was afraid of him. She had always been afraid of him.

"I'm moving into town," she said. The words came out clipped and cold, a stark contrast to the way she felt.

Cade's hands dropped to his sides.

"Why?" He sounded genuinely surprised.

"It's none of your business."

He stared at her, frowning. Then understanding cleared the frown. "It's those two saps, isn't it?"

It was Lauren's turn to be surprised. "Saps?"

"The old man and his wife."

Except for the thudding of her heart and the rising wind, there was no sound. She took a deep breath, her hand tightening on the Winchester in anger. "Just go, Cade."

He took a step toward her.

She could still feel the roughness of his fingers on her face and the strength in his hands. Every cell in her body screamed at her to run. It took all her courage to hold her ground. Rupe whined, waiting for her order.

"Stop it, Cade." She raised the tip of the shotgun and aimed it at him.

An expression of rage swept over Cade's face and for the first time Lauren saw the true danger in the man. If she showed any weakness, one of them would die. Either she convinced him that she was serious or she would have to kill him. The thought was compelling. *Kill him now,* the trees seemed to urge.

She aimed at the sky and squeezed the trigger. The sound roared through the forest, startling ravens and magpies out of trees to squawk in alarm.

As if that was the signal he'd been waiting for, Rupe launched himself at Cade's throat, his lips drawn back in a snarl.

"Rupe!"

Cade raised a massive fist and in a movement that was so fast it became a blur, struck Rupe down in mid-air. The dog landed heavily five feet away and lay still.

All the air seemed to leave her lungs while she waited for Rupe to get up again. As the slow seconds ticked by and he didn't move, she deliberately brought the muzzle of the Winchester to bear on Cade's solid chest.

Before she could squeeze the trigger, Cade moved between her and Rupe. She couldn't shoot him without risking hitting Rupe in the shotgun blast.

Without thinking, Lauren stepped into Cade's reach and jabbed the end of the barrel as hard as she could into his gut. His eyes widened in surprise and, too late, a big hand swept the barrel away as he doubled over in pain. Lauren spun around to swing at his head, but he was already straightening, his arm up to block the blow. Only then did she see the knife in his hand. A quick glance at Rupe showed the blood glistening darkly on his shoulder.

Her emotions finally unlocked and rage exploded through her.

"You bastard!" She ignored the knife and threw herself on him, swinging the precious shotgun. Off balance, he took her momentum on one shoulder and fell, taking her with him. He landed hard and the knife went flying. The breath whooshed out of him as he ripped the Winchester out of her hands.

Without giving him a chance to recover, Lauren gouged at his eyes with her thumbs. He had wit enough to squeeze them shut before her assault. Then he grabbed her by the front of her sweater and with a massive heave, shoved her off of him. She landed on moss and rolled to her feet.

Cade was on his feet, too, laboring for breath. The shotgun was still in his hand and he threw it against the nearest aspen. His eyes were almost incandescent with fury. They stood panting at each other, separated by five feet and a universe of hatred.

Then an amused voice from the darkness beyond Cade said, "You should stop now before she really hurts you."

Cade's head whipped around and Lauren stepped back, startled. They both turned to face the newcomer. A small, slender man stepped out of the trees. He wore a dark coat and pants. Before she could get a clear view of his face, Cade spoke up.

"This woman is mine. I claim her."

Lauren reeled back as if she had been slapped. "Nobody gives a damn what you claim, you bastard."

The two men ignored her.

"Sounds to me like she doesn't want to go with you."

Lauren peered at the man. There was just enough light filtering through the trees to see short, black, straight hair and a long face. No one she knew—where did he come from? He was a few inches shorter than her. Nothing her Winchester couldn't take care of, if she could get to it.

"Willing or not, she's mine." Cade stood between her and the newcomer. Like a bear guarding a kill. She moved sideways, scanning the ground for her shotgun.

Cade had gone insane. Nothing else could explain why he suddenly wanted her so badly. And who was this other man?

Just then, her toe touched the barrel. "Go away, Cade," she said, and surprised herself by the weariness in her voice. She stooped to pick up the shotgun, keeping her gaze on the two men. "I don't want you."

"There you go," said the stranger. "Why don't you go before someone gets hurt?"

Lauren clutched the Winchester to her chest. Just because the man defied Cade didn't make him her friend. She would deal with him after she had gotten rid of Cade.

Cade turned his back deliberately on the other man and looked at Lauren. She caught her breath as fear thrilled through her. He wasn't afraid. He was going to try to take her anyway. Without a second thought, she raised the Winchester. Before she could squeeze the trigger, the stock moved in her hand, loose.

She kept her dismay from showing and kept the Winchester aimed at Cade. He didn't know the shotgun was damaged.

Then a second man walked out of the trees and stepped between Cade and Lauren. She moved back, startled for the second time in a few minutes.

"Enough," said the man, looking at Cade.

Cade appraised the newcomer for a long, silent moment. Then he looked past the man's shoulder straight at Lauren, his face expressionless. Without a word, he whirled and melted into the trees.

Lauren stared at the forest where he had disappeared, trying to understand what had just happened. Then her instincts kicked in and she stepped away from the two men.

Two men. The two strangers walking down the highway this morning. They had probably been at her cabin for hours.

The bigger of the two men turned toward her.

"What do you want?" she asked, covering them with the shotgun.

The big man stood very still. "We're not here to hurt you."

"What do you want?" she demanded again, putting all the frustration she felt into the question.

"We're here to help you."

She had worried about this for years. Women didn't live alone any more, not since the Troubles. But Rupe and her shotgun had always been enough of a deterrent.

Rupe.

Pain caught at her heart, tearing the breath out of her. Keeping the Winchester aimed at the two men, Lauren walked over to Rupe and squatted next to him. She put her hand on his shoulder and he whimpered. "Rupe," she whispered in relief. Then warm blood seeped through her fingers and she felt as if the blade had sliced into her.

Rupe.

Grief and fear swirled inside, making clear thought difficult. The hand holding the Winchester shook and she didn't even look up. "You'd better go now."

The first man spoke up then. "We can't. My grandfather sent us here to protect you."

❧ THREE ❦

PROTECT her?

Lauren stared at the smaller man.

"From what?"

He shrugged and waved a hand in the general direction Cade had taken.

"My guess is from the big bad wolf."

As if on cue, Lauren heard the sound of an engine start up and quickly fade as it moved away. A part of her relaxed as she realized that Cade really was gone. She glanced around the rapidly darkening woods. Rupe needed tending. She had to get rid of these two, broken shotgun or no. It was too dark to tell how deep the wound was, but Rupe twisted his head in an effort to lick her hand, heartening her. "And how did your grandfather know what Cade was going to do?"

There was a long pause. The big man looked down at his companion expectantly. Apparently he wanted to know the answer, too. Finally the smaller man sighed.

"Silas is psychic."

Silas being the psychic grandfather, of course. *Humor him,* she told herself. *You need to get them out of here.*

"And you are?"

"Dante Longman. This is my friend, Gautier Leblanc."

Deranged but polite. Lauren found she was shaking her head and stopped.

"And where is this Silas?"

Dante paused for a long, reluctant moment. Finally he sighed. "Montreal."

Lauren glanced at the big guy, Gautier, who glanced at her before looking back at his friend.

Dante shrugged helplessly. "It's a long story."

Lauren shook her head again. "Look—"

Gautier held up a hand. "Miss Tom. Lauren." So they knew her name. "We can work this out later. Right now your dog needs looking after."

Dante took a step toward her, his hand out as if to help, and Lauren stood up in surprise, her bloody hand up to stop him.

She could *feel* him. Like a humming in her belly.

Dante stopped and watched her warily.

"Back off," she said and used her shotgun to wave him back. He took a few steps back and the humming stopped. Her hands started shaking again.

"Are you all right?" asked Dante.

"No, I'm not all right!" She spat the words out, suddenly furious—at him, at Cade. At the world. "Just go!"

"But—"

"Dante," said the big man, Gautier.

Dante turned to his friend. "We can't leave her."

Gautier turned to Lauren. "Let us carry your dog to the cabin, then we'll go."

Lauren shook her head, not trusting herself to speak. He looked at her in silence before nodding. "All right, then."

"But—" said Dante.

"Come on," said Gautier, placing a hand on Dante's arm and leading him away.

Lauren watched them disappear into the bush. Dead branches

snapped as they walked away, almost as if they were making a lot of noise to reassure her they really were leaving. Putting them out of her mind, she turned back to Rupe.

* * *

She was trembling with exertion by the time she got Rupe inside the cabin and onto the kitchen table. With efficiency born of long practice, she lit the precious kerosene lamp and put a kettle of water to heat on the wood stove before rummaging through her dad's metal trunk for old bed sheets. While the water slowly heated, she used a strip of sheet to wipe away the worst of the blood and get her first good look at his wound. Cade's knife had plunged into the meaty part of Rupe's shoulder. While the wound was deep, the bleeding was already slowing down. She didn't know enough about dog anatomy to tell if any tendons had been severed, but she was reasonably sure that no organs were hurt.

"It's okay," she whispered. "We'll get you fixed up, and then you'll be all right." Rupe watched her every movement. She knew she had hurt him carrying him in, but every time he whimpered from the pain, he licked her face as if to apologize.

As she worked, she paused occasionally to wipe away her tears. If she'd listened to her instincts and shot that bastard Cade when she had the chance, Rupe wouldn't be lying on her table, maybe dying. A sob caught in her throat. It was just his shoulder. He wasn't going to die.

She couldn't smell him past the coppery tang of his blood.

The wound was too deep—she would have to sew it up. She found her mother's old sewing kit in the basket by the bookshelf and picked a big, sharp, sturdy needle and heated more water in a pan to disinfect it. Then she pulled out the lye soap and a couple of battered metal bowls. Rupe watched her preparations, his eyes glazed with pain.

When she was finally ready, she leaned her cheek against his. "This is going to hurt, old friend, but you have to stay still and trust me, all right?"

For an answer the black Lab licked her face.

She worked as quickly and as efficiently as she could, but it still felt like an eternity before she cut the final thread. Soaked in sweat, she looked down at her dog, her best friend. Sometime in the last few minutes, he had lost consciousness. He had trembled and twitched under her hand, but aside from an occasional whine, he hadn't made a noise.

She washed the last of the blood off his glossy fur and sat down, looking at him.

He had come to her half-wild, left to fend for himself as a puppy. As he grew to trust her, they became friends and partners. He was always there to protect her.

But she hadn't protected him.

She finished bandaging him and cleaned up the bloody mess. Then she found a blanket and covered Rupe, tucking in the edges so he wouldn't feel a draft. She built a fire in the wood stove, but didn't trust herself to pick him up and carry him to his bed by the stove. He would be all right on the table for now.

Finally, when she was sure he was resting as comfortably as possible, she took the kerosene lamp and headed outside to find the Winchester. Maybe it could be fixed.

The temperature was beginning to drop. As she retraced her steps toward the tree where she had left the shotgun, her fingers reached out to stroke Rupe's head only to stop short. Her hand curled into a fist.

Hatred for Cade surged through her, leaving a taste like bile in her mouth. She wished she had thought to pull her knife on the man. He had tried to kill Rupe. And he had felt no fear, even when Dante and Gautier showed up. For a minute, she'd thought he was just going to sweep her over his shoulder and stalk off into the woods.

She stopped walking. He had looked at Gautier the same way he had looked at Charlie, earlier that day. What was it he had said, just before Dante showed up?

"It's those two saps, isn't it? The old man and his wife." There had been so much contempt in his voice... so much hatred...

In sudden fear, Lauren whirled and ran for the truck, the lantern bobbing crazy shadows ahead of her.

* * *

Gautier wrapped his hands around the cup of hot, sweet Labrador tea, his back to the small campfire. He didn't want to lose his night vision by sitting with Dante next to the fire. It didn't bother Dante. His night vision was always acute. Their camp was far enough away that Lauren wouldn't overhear their low conversation and close enough to get to her quickly if she needed them.

Dante hadn't moved from the log since they built the fire. Gautier could hear him tearing away at a strip of deer jerky.

They had spent the hours before Lauren returned home checking out her place. Besides the cabin, there was an outhouse with a great view of the mountains, a lean-to that kept neatly stacked wood dry and another smaller one for skis and snowshoes, shovels and axes. Everything was clean, repaired, and put away.

Her cabin was sturdy, if small. There were wooden shutters on the inside to barricade the windows when necessary. Rungs ran up to the roof, starting outside her loft window. Gautier was willing to bet that there were ropes on the roof, strategically placed to allow for a quick descent.

A good cabin in which to survive the Troubles.

"We shouldn't have left her alone," said Dante.

Gautier watched the trees and remained silent.

Dante changed tacks. "She wouldn't have hurt us, you know. In any case, we could easily have taken the gun away from her."

It was a shotgun, Gautier thought. *Not a gun.* Winchester, thirty years old, at least. And besides, it was broken. He gulped the rapidly cooling tea. Its woodsy fragrance mixed with the wood smoke from their campfire.

"If I'd taken it away from her," continued Dante, "we'd be sleeping inside tonight."

Lauren Tom outweighed Dante by twenty pounds and she had a knife. By the way she had attacked that stranger, Gautier wasn't sure Dante could have taken anything away from her.

"Are you ever going to talk to me again?" asked Dante plaintively.

Gautier sighed and tossed the last few drops of tea into the night. "You told me she was ten years old."

There was a long silence from Dante. When he finally spoke, his voice sounded troubled. "I know. That's what Silas told me."

Gautier gritted his teeth. "This would be Silas, the now psychic grandfather?"

"I know it sounds strange—"

Forgetting his night vision, Gautier turned to look at Dante. "Strange? Now, why would any of this be strange?"

"Lay off," said Dante testily. "I'm just as surprised as you are. I expected a kid, too, not a grown woman. I need time to think."

Gautier stared at him. "What is there to think about?" he demanded. "Your grandfather made a mistake. She's not his granddaughter. And what the hell is this about him being psychic?"

But Dante was shaking his head. "She's my cousin," he said with grim certainty. "And she's in even more danger than I thought."

The sound of a twig breaking brought both their heads up sharply. They could see a glow moving rapidly through the trees, to the east. Gautier sensed more than heard Dante rise. Without thinking, he kicked the pot of tea over, dousing the small campfire.

The glow moved away from them, accompanied by the sound of breaking twigs.

Gautier said, "She's going for the truck!" just as Dante said, "It's her!"

They took off toward the track that led to the cabin, Dante leading the way because of his better night vision. Gautier kept his ears open for the big stranger, but he heard nothing. What was chasing her, then?

He heard the door of the truck open just as he burst out of

the trees and onto the track. The truck was only twenty feet away and he ran to join Dante, who stood watching Lauren through the driver's side window.

She was a dark figure behind the windshield, frantically searching for the key, her head and shoulders disappearing from sight as she bent to search the floor. Gautier fingered the well-worn key in his pocket, his lips pressed into a thin line.

Good thing he'd thought to take it out of the ignition.

Finally Lauren straightened and turned her head, looking directly at him. It was too dark in the cab to see the expression on her face, but he could imagine it.

The door opened and she leaped out.

"Give me the key!" she said, putting her hand out palm up.

Dante stepped closer and she abruptly backed away, as if she didn't want him close. Dante stopped.

"Lauren," he said, "I know this is hard to accept, but you really are in danger. You're safer staying here where we can keep an eye on you." His voice trailed away on the last word and Gautier looked at him. Then he looked at Lauren and understood his friend's uneasiness.

She was covered in blood.

Lauren's voice dropped an octave. "I don't have time to deal with this. Give me the key now."

Gautier's hand clenched around the key with its beaded leather fob as he controlled an impulse to give it to her. The force of her will was almost enough to make him obey her, in spite of Dante's very real fear for her.

"Lauren—" began Dante, his arms spreading wide in an apology.

Lauren turned away from Dante to look straight at Gautier. He felt her gaze more than saw it, as if her attention were a weight on his face.

"My foster parents are in danger," she said softly. "I think Cade is going to hurt them. Please. Give me the key."

It was one thing to make decisions for a ten-year-old. Gautier was damned if he was going to keep a grown woman prisoner, even if it was for her own good.

He looked down at her, hoping he wasn't going to regret his decision.

"You can have the key back," he said. "But we're going with you."

Next to him, Dante sighed softly and Gautier knew his friend wished he hadn't done it. But it was too late. He pulled the key out of his pocket and waited for her answer.

"Get in," she said, not even hesitating, which told Gautier all he had to know about the level of her anxiety. She took the key from him and turned back to the truck, leaving them to follow or not.

❧ FOUR ❧

G AUTIER hung on to the dashboard with one hand and to the dog with the other as his body levitated a few inches, then fell back to the ripped and torn seat with a jarring thud.

He glanced at Dante, who was hanging on to the door's armrest with one hand and the dog's hindquarters with the other. Dante kept his gaze firmly on the darkness outside the windshield, as if willpower alone would keep them from going off the road.

Beneath Gautier's hand, the dog trembled and growled. Gautier couldn't blame him. The animal was stretched out on both their laps, his eyes fixed on Lauren in the driver's seat.

Lauren accelerated and shifted into fourth, hitting Gautier's knee with the stick shift. She took a curve so fast that he fell into Dante and the dog yipped in alarm. Her hand briefly touched the dog's head then went back to the steering wheel.

"Lauren!" yelled Dante over the racket of the exhaust system. "You won't be any good to them dead!"

Lauren didn't even look at them but she did slow down a bit.

Gautier gritted his teeth and peered out the cracked and pitted windshield. The truck no longer had headlights—probably hadn't had any in decades.

He desperately wanted to take over the driving, but he couldn't see a damned thing. The road was nothing more than a memory snaking through the dark boreal forest. Either she drove from memory, or she could see a lot better than he could.

She swerved again, sending him crashing into her. Without taking her eyes off the road, she shrugged her shoulder to push him off.

In exasperation, he flung an arm over the backrest behind her shoulders and hooked his fingers on the corner of the seat, bracing himself as best he could. He held the dog close to him with his other hand, trying to minimize the jarring to the animal's shoulder wound.

He'd been surprised when she headed for the cabin, instead of backing the truck out onto the road, but it all became clear when she returned from the cabin, carefully carrying the dog, and laid him gently on their laps. She hadn't wanted to leave him behind.

Cold air whistled through the cab of the truck. He didn't even want to think about the state of the floorboards. He just hoped the truck would survive the trip into town.

The inside of the truck smelled like burning oil and wet dog. He stifled a sigh. If he'd been a bit faster, he might have been able to keep the animal from getting hurt.

Gautier examined the overlapping shades of black outside the truck's windows. In a place like this, a dog would be your best friend. He looked at the woman so close beside him, but couldn't tell what she was thinking.

For over an hour they traveled that way, the only sounds the loud rumbling of the engine and the wind whistling through the floorboards.

Then she slowed marginally before twisting the wheel to take a turn at a ninety-degree angle. Gautier reached out to wrestle the wheel from her before he realized that they were on a different road, and going downhill. He looked out and saw a few pinpricks of light in the valley below. Whitehorse.

The truck swerved again, but not fast enough. They hit a pothole that loosened his grip on the backrest and would have lost him his tongue if his teeth hadn't been clenched tight. The dog yelped in pain.

"Cut it out, Lauren!" cried Dante.

Ignoring him, Lauren leaned forward and drove even faster. When the road finally flattened out, Gautier realized that they were driving next to a river. Then Lauren slowed to turn again and they lost the river. They were in the town of Whitehorse.

The texture of the road beneath the truck changed and Gautier realized they were driving on frozen ground. To the right and left, he saw the hulk of homes looming out of the darkness. Only a few had lights in the window, some so faint that they had to be candlelight.

"What's that?" yelled Dante over the sound of the engine. Gautier turned to see the dark line of Dante's arm pointing and followed its direction. To the north, a yellow glow rose in the sky.

"Oh no," said Lauren, so low that Gautier could have imagined it.

"Is that where your foster parents live?" he asked, his belly tightening with dread.

Lauren didn't even seem to hear him. She slowed abruptly, her gaze scanning the road, being careful. Soon he saw why.

There were people on the road, dozens of them, all running toward the glow. Lauren made her way through and past them, the sound of her engine parting them. She turned up the dark side streets, heading always north.

As they turned a final corner, they saw it. The fire had taken hold in the roof and upper floor of the little wooden house. The flickering light revealed a scene of confusion. Fifty feet away from the house, a nervous horse snorted steam. It was harnessed to a cart on which stood a dozen large barrels.

On the cart, a man frantically poked with an axe handle at the layer of ice in a barrel. Another man stood next to another barrel, scooping buckets full of water and handing them over to the five or six people milling around the cart.

Each person then ran to the house and threw the bucketful against the fire.

Might as well spit on it, thought Gautier.

Then Lauren slammed on the brakes and the truck lurched to a stop, stalling. She pushed open the door and jumped out.

"Lauren!" Gautier scrambled out from under the dog and out of the truck through the driver's side, almost tripping over his feet, and caught up to her. He grabbed her arm and stopped her before she got within twenty feet of the house.

A smell like burning garbage came from the house. "You can't go in there!" he shouted, to make himself heard over the crackling of the flames. Already the heat pushed at him, flushing the surroundings with ruddy light. Her arm twisted under his hand but he tightened his grip.

More and more people streamed in from the side streets, heading for the fire, each person carrying a bucket.

"Harris!" shouted Lauren and Gautier looked back to see who she was talking to. An older man was running clumsily back from the house, an empty bucket in each hand. He stopped at the sound of his name and came toward her.

"Harris," said Lauren, her whole body leaning toward the older man, "Mary? And...?"

Harris looked frantic, his eyes flickering between the fire and the horse cart. "They're still in there!" he cried. "We have to put out the fire!" He ran back toward the cart to hand his buckets up to be filled.

A massive shudder ran through Lauren and she redoubled her efforts to free herself from Gautier's grip. He didn't let go.

"Let me go!" yelled Lauren. "I can get to them!"

Jesus. The whole upper half of the house was now engulfed in flames. If they were up there, they were dead. But the bottom half only had flames in the back part, probably where the fire had started.

If they were on the main floor, they could still be saved.

Dante caught up to them. "It started about half an hour ago, according to the neighbors," he shouted, nodding toward the house. "As far as anyone knows, the old folks are still inside."

"Mary!" shouted Lauren, her body straining away from Gautier. "Charlie!"

Suddenly she turned on Gautier and lashed out at him with her free hand. He saw the fist—a hard and callused fist—heading for his eye and jerked his head away. Her fist grazed his cheekbone.

It hurt like hell.

"Dante!" he yelled as she drew back for another blow. Her face was a mask of determination, her eyes glazed with firelight. Then Dante caught her arm and pushed it down. Caught between the two of them, Lauren struggled futilely.

"I'll get them!" Gautier shouted. She kept struggling, so he grabbed her chin and forced her to face him. "Lauren! I'll get them! Stay here!" To Dante he said, "Hold her and be careful, she's strong."

Dante nodded and grabbed the arm Gautier was holding. When he was sure Dante could hold her, Gautier released her and ran toward the water cart.

The first woman he saw had a scarf around her head.

"Excuse me," he said and whipped the scarf off the surprised woman. He grabbed a full bucket from her neighbor, then ran toward the front of the house.

There were fewer people on this side, since most of the flames were on the other side of the house. When he reached the door, he saw that the door had been boarded over some time ago.

But there was a big window next to it and a porch running under it.

Gautier set the full pail on the cement stair and dunked the scarf in it. When it was sopping wet, he wrapped it around his head and face. Then he poured the rest of the water over his head and coat. It was poor protection, but the best he could do right now.

Then he took the heavy wooden bucket and swung it at the window. The window cracked but didn't shatter. After a few blows, the plate glass broke into great jagged pieces. Gautier sprang away as some of the glass fell toward him. Heavy smoke rolled out the window, stinking of wet garbage and hot ash.

Sweeping the rest of the glass out of the casing with the bucket, he peered inside, eyes watering. The smoke obscured the dimensions of the room and he couldn't see if anyone was in there. At least there were no flames.

Without giving himself a chance to think about it, he tossed the bucket behind him, placed his hands on the windowsill, and vaulted inside.

The smoke was ten times worse inside and he immediately started coughing. Above him, the fire sounded like a windstorm and he heard ominous cracking in the ceiling. He didn't have much time.

Eyes streaming from the acrid smoke, he slowly felt his way around the room, trying not to breathe too deeply. He couldn't see past the smoke to the floor, but he got lucky. The toe of his ancient work boots hit something yielding and he immediately bent down to check it out.

His groping hands felt something woolen, then warm flesh. He grabbed the shoulders and hauled the body toward the window. It took some doing, but he managed to pull the dead weight up until the body was half out the window. Then he jumped out, missed the stoop, and fell five feet to the hard ground.

He lay there for a moment, sucking in deep breaths. Finally he forced himself up. The other person was still inside.

He got back up the stairs and pulled the body—a man, he saw—up over his shoulder. Then he carried him to the side of the house.

Someone saw him as he stumbled around the corner and suddenly there were hands reaching for the man on his shoulder.

"It's Charlie!" a woman cried.

They carried him well beyond the house to the street.

"Is he still alive?" asked a man's voice.

"I don't know," said the woman.

Someone ran past Gautier and water sloshed on him. There were people everywhere, some running back and forth with water buckets, many just standing in the street, staring at the fire.

Gautier suddenly became aware of heat. He looked back at the house just as something crashed inside. The top floor was starting to buckle.

Then a movement caught his eye and he saw Dante at the edge of the crowd, being held by two big men. He struggled against them, but they just held on, although they didn't seem bent on hurting him. Dante looked up and saw him.

"Gautier!" he yelled. "She went inside!"

Hell.

The scarf wasn't nearly wet enough anymore but there was no time to find another bucket. Gautier ran back to the picture window, took a deep breath of clean air, and climbed back inside the smoke-filled room.

"Lauren!" he shouted. The ceiling creaked a warning and suddenly a beam crashed through, opening a gaping, burning hole in the ceiling and sending burning debris crashing to the floor much too close to Gautier. He jumped back, tripped over something that could have been a footstool, and fell hard to the wooden floor.

As he was shaking his head, he realized that the air was relatively smoke free near the floor. He still had a clear route to the window, if he needed to leave quickly.

"Lauren!" he called again.

Breathing shallowly through the drying scarf, he crawled on the floor, listening for any sound that would tell him where Lauren was. All he heard was the roar of fire and the ominous creak of the ceiling as the rest threatened to crash down on him. He crawled along the edge of the wall, leaving the window farther and farther behind.

Suddenly the wall disappeared. It took him a moment to realize he had reached a doorway. He could barely make out the bottom of a bed, with blankets half off the mattress and pooling on the floor.

Past the roaring of the fire, and the drumming of his heart, he could hear his own gasps as he struggled for breath. It was no use. He could crawl right past Lauren in all this smoke and never see her.

All he would accomplish was to die with her.

He was about to turn around and retrace his steps when he remembered that the old man he had pulled out had been fully dressed. Maybe the old woman had been in bed when the fire started and the blankets tripped her up when she tried to get out of bed.

He crawled farther into the room, panting. "Hello?" he called. His voice sounded more like a croak and he tried again. "Hello? Is anyone here?"

There was no reply but he reached for the pile of blankets and pulled them toward him. He recoiled in shock when something heavy fell off the bed and landed on the floor.

It was a body. He didn't think it could be Lauren. She hadn't passed him to get to the front of the house and the entire back was in flames. If she had made it inside, somehow, she was dead.

He made himself reach for the body and encountered an arm. Feeling his way up, he found the face. It was the old woman. She hadn't even made if off the bed.

She was probably already dead of smoke inhalation. If he didn't get out soon, he'd die right here next to her. More of the ceiling crashed into the living room, sending a whoosh of flames toward the broken window. Most of the walls were now on fire and the fire was racing for the window.

Too late, Gautier saw that the broken window was letting more oxygen in to fuel the fire. He had to get out. Now.

He started crawling out of the bedroom, then stopped. He had promised Lauren he would get her foster parents out. If she survived this, she shouldn't have to dig through the ruins of a burned out home to find the remains of her family.

You're a fool, he told himself.

He pulled himself to his feet, went back inside the smoke-filled bedroom, and hauled the old woman over his shoulder. She weighed nothing.

As an afterthought, he grabbed the blankets and pulled them over on top of her. They might protect her from embers or burning ash.

His throat and lungs felt clogged with smoke as he stood in the bedroom doorway, trying to get his bearings. The roar of the fire filled his head and he had to fight down a surge of panic. His singed hair stank, and the skin around his eyes, the only flesh exposed to the fire besides his hands, felt tight, as if he had a sunburn.

He couldn't see the window, only smoke and flame as the fire raced down the walls toward him. In the bedroom, the ceiling cracked as the fire ate through the floorboards of the room above.

Then a second beam crashed through the ceiling of the living room, blocking off his access to the window.

Gautier stumbled back as cinders blew toward him and the old woman. A racking cough shook him.

He couldn't believe he had survived the Troubles only to die in a house fire saving a woman who was probably already dead.

"Mary!"

Gautier's head snapped up. "Lauren?"

"Where are you?" Her voice cut through the roaring of the flames and the crackling of the burning wood, but he couldn't tell where it was coming from.

"I don't know!" He drew in another lungful of smoke and coughed. He couldn't get enough oxygen. "In a bedroom."

"Do you have Mary?" she called, and finally he placed her as being no more than fifteen feet away, on the other side of the living room, on his side of the fire.

"I have her, but she's unconscious." No need to tell Lauren that the woman was probably dead.

"Stay there, I'm coming."

"No!" Gautier coughed and tried again. "It's too dangerous!"

But suddenly something bumped against his feet and Gautier was so startled he almost dropped the old woman. A hand grabbed his calf only to let go immediately.

Lauren hauled herself to her feet and finally he could make her out. Her head and face were also covered in a wet cloth. He wanted to yell at her that she was going to die for nothing, but he had no more breath to spare.

"Put her on the floor," ordered Lauren. "We'll pull her on the blanket."

Gautier knew he didn't have much longer. If she had a plan, he was willing to give it a chance. He placed the old woman on the bed, tossed the blanket on the floor, and while Lauren spread it out, he picked up the old woman again and placed her on it.

Lauren grabbed two corners and started pulling the old woman out of the bedroom. Gautier bent down and almost fell over. He caught himself and grabbed the two remaining corners.

Together they pulled the old woman along the only remaining wall that was free of fire. It was a load-bearing wall. As soon as the fire reached it, the whole house would cave in.

It was only fifteen feet across the room, but it was the longest fifteen feet in Gautier's life.

To his surprise, Lauren led him to a small room that was filled with smoke, but hadn't been touched by fire yet.

"Get down," she ordered, and although he couldn't see her, he got down on the floor. The air immediately felt cooler, even smelling damp and moldy.

"You go down first," she said, nothing more than a muffled voice above him. "I'll hand her to you, then I'll come down, too."

Only then did Gautier notice the square hole in the floor. It led into darkness.

A crash in the living room shook the house. The load-bearing wall had buckled.

"Hurry!"

Gautier turned around and slid his body over the opening, trusting that there would be stairs. His dangling feet struck something wooden and he immediately stepped down onto the rung of a ladder.

"Give her to me," he said, or tried to say. His throat was so raw that nothing intelligible came out. Still, whether she understood him or not, she slid the old woman toward him, holding on to her head and shoulders until she was sure Gautier had her.

Gautier pulled her back onto his shoulder and went down the rungs as fast as his burden would allow. The damp air of the cellar was the sweetest he'd ever inhaled.

"Come on!" he tried to shout as the house shook again from another crash.

But she was already on the rungs and he had to move fast to keep from getting his fingers stepped on. Then there was a thump as the trapdoor slammed shut, and the sound of the fire suddenly muted.

He stood there gasping for air, aware that they only had a few minutes. If the main floor didn't buckle under the weight of the fallen walls and roof, then fire would make sure it fell into the cellar space.

Then he noticed that he could make out dim shapes in the darkness, including a rafter less than six inches from his nose.

"What is this?" he asked.

"It's the crawlspace," said Lauren, standing next to him. She unwrapped the scarf as if it were choking her. "These houses were built in the 1950s. They all had crawlspaces under them for the oil tank and sewer and water pipes."

Pipes must have frozen every winter, thought Gautier, suddenly aware that he was cold. And crawlspace wasn't quite right, either. He couldn't straighten out his six-foot frame, but he could navigate if he hunched over.

"We can't stay here—" he started to say just as she tugged the old woman off his shoulder.

"The door's less than twenty feet away. I'll take her feet, you take her head—and be careful!"

A loud thump overhead galvanized him into action. He made sure the old woman was securely wrapped, then grabbed the excess blanket near her head.

"I'm ready," he said.

Without another word, Lauren moved away and he followed, shuffling his feet in the tamped earth of the crawlspace.

As his eyes adjusted to the dark, Gautier began to make out shelves against earth walls and barrels in the nearest corner. The crawl space also served as a cellar. The air grew colder and cleaner the farther away they got from the trapdoor.

Somewhere down here was a door leading outside.

Lauren began to climb and he realized that they were at a set of concrete steps leading up into the night.

Faint sounds of shouting reached them over the roaring of the fire.

"Watch your—"

Gautier's forehead slammed into a beam and he stumbled back at the shock of pain.

"—head," said Lauren. "Sorry!" she said. "The frame is low. We're almost out."

And they were. Gautier was careful to lift the old woman's head and shoulders high as Lauren climbed higher. Then they were outside and the air was full of shouts and the stink of fire.

"Don't stop!" called Gautier when Lauren slowed. "We're still too close!"

Together they carried the old woman around the corner of the burning house and into the crowd of neighbors, who surged toward them and took their burden away.

And then Gautier found himself standing alone on the street outside the milling crowd, coughing and watching the roof of the burning house cave in. A cloud of sparks and burning debris flew into the air like a volcano and the crowd backed away.

The fire brigade had given up on fighting the fire. People now concentrated on the roofs of the nearest houses, even though as near as he could tell, the homes were abandoned. It made sense. If a fire caught in nearby buildings, the whole town could go.

Gautier pulled the scarf away from his nose and mouth and dragged in his first clear breath in what felt like hours. His lungs felt seared and his throat raw. His eyes felt half-cooked.

He stared at the fire and breathed in and out, trying to clear his lungs of smoke and hoping he hadn't damaged them permanently.

That was, bar none, the stupidest thing he had ever done.

❧ FIVE ❧

L AUREN couldn't stop shaking. The hot water slopped over the rim of the bowl as she dipped the cloth in. She squeezed the excess water out and wiped more soot and grime away from Mary's face, listening for each labored breath, willing the old woman to keep breathing.

Mr. Chiang's bedroom was tiny but neat. An oil lamp on the bedside table lit the lovely Log Cabin quilt his wife had made a few years before she died. It now covered Mary's frail shape. Lauren hoped the soot would wash out.

Mr. Chiang had insisted they bring Mary and Charlie to his place, even though he wasn't their nearest neighbor. He had known her foster parents for longer than she'd been alive. She could hear him now, fussing in his kitchen with the wood stove and the kettle. The smell of eucalyptus wafted through the house as he infused hot water with the precious leaves.

A tingling in her belly warned her of Dante's approach and she looked up, tensing. On top of everything that had happened, she didn't need the added confusion of this physical reaction to his presence. He stopped just inside the bedroom door, as if unsure of his welcome.

They all reeked of smoke. Even now, Dante's arrival refreshed the stink and Lauren's nose wrinkled.

Mr. Chiang's low voice murmured soothingly in the background as he ministered to Charlie, who was awake and insisting that he could sit in a chair, for God's sake.

He would probably be all right. He hadn't been exposed to the smoke for very long and he'd been lying on the floor, where the smoke was lightest.

But Mary... Lauren glanced down at her foster mother's slack face. Mary had been in the smoke a long time.

She'd never seen the woman look so frail.

"How is she?" asked Dante.

Lauren looked up at him. He seemed genuinely concerned.

"I don't know," she said. Her throat hurt from the little bit of smoke she had inhaled. She could imagine in graphic detail what it had done to Mary's lungs. The old woman's skin looked gray in the lamplight.

"Are you crying?" asked Dante, his voice tinged with wonder.

Lauren glanced at him, then away. She wasn't sure how to answer that. She rarely cried, but he didn't know that. Why should anyone be surprised to find her crying at Mary's bedside?

Into the odd silence came Arnold Chiang's voice.

"No, I don't know where Cade lives."

Lauren's hands clenched on the wet cloth, squeezing water onto her pant leg. The drops rolled off before they could penetrate the deerskin.

Dante stepped away from the doorway as she stood up. She hesitated, torn between wanting to care for Mary and wanting to be part of the discussion in the kitchen.

Dante looked down at Mary, then back at Laura.

"I'll stay."

Without a word, she handed him the cloth. She would listen for Mary's breathing from the kitchen.

Mr. Chiang jumped up when Lauren walked into the kitchen.

"I've made tea," he said and poured her a mugful of rosehip

tea from a black teapot painted with white gold-edged flowers and women in long belted robes. Her mother once told her that Mr. Chiang's family had come from China, across the Pacific Ocean. Lauren had been eight years old when Mother pointed out China in the atlas. The teapot was the only one of his family's treasures to have survived the Troubles.

Her gaze automatically sought out Rupe, but he was still in his cozy nest of blankets next to the wood stove. He blinked up at her and his tail thumped twice against the floor. She squatted next to him and stroked his glossy ears. With a sigh, he leaned his head back down and closed his eyes.

She would have to check his bandage soon.

Charlie and Gautier sat at either end of a rough kitchen table that consisted of an old hollow brown door with the knob removed, set on four mismatched legs that were more or less the same height. Charlie cradled a chipped white mug in his big hands. He had tried to wash off the worst of the grime, but soot deepened his wrinkles and his nostrils were rimmed in black.

"How is she?" he asked. His voice was a whisper, as if he didn't want to irritate his vocal chords any more than they already were. His eyes were red.

Lauren shook her head. "Not good." She set the mug Mr. Chiang had given her on the table. She didn't think tea would make it past the lump in her throat.

The men met her statement with silence. Mr. Chiang cradled the teapot against his narrow chest and stared at the floor.

Lauren fixed her gaze on Gautier until he finally looked up from the table. His eyes were red-rimmed, too, and his singed brown hair stood on end, as if he'd been in a windstorm.

Charlie looked up. "It was him, Lauren. Cade. He knocked me out." His hands wrung each other until he noticed her watching them, then he stopped. "He did this to us."

There was weariness in every sloping angle of his body and Lauren's heart twisted in pity. In anger.

Cade had done this to them.

"Why do you want to know where Cade lives?" she asked Gautier.

His eyebrows rose. "You've got good hearing." Then he leaned back in his chair and rubbed his face with his hands before running them through his hair.

"We have to bring him back to stand trial," said Charlie, his voice firm despite the hoarseness.

A trial. There hadn't been a trial in Whitehorse—maybe in the whole Yukon—since the Troubles, when all those sick strangers came to the Yukon.

It seemed sometimes as if her entire childhood had been filled with fear of the plagues. Her mother had told her that the first Ebola epidemic devastated Uganda, Congo, and Gabon in 2025, when she was four.

The disease then moved into Egypt and Europe. Before the western world could stem the flood of deaths, there was an outbreak of Severe Acute Respiratory Syndrome in Berlin. SARS then spread to London, and from London to New York and Moscow. Within a year, cases of SARS were being reported all over the world.

Then an old enemy returned and the bubonic plague swept through China. The Chinese government, reluctant to admit it had a problem, kept the news of the disease secret while trying to contain it. Within a year, the plague had traveled to the Americas. According to her mother, several unusually warm years made things worse because fleas no longer became dormant in winter. The antibiotic-resistant disease devastated populations throughout the world.

By 2028, strangers were streaming into the Yukon, trying to escape the deadly germs and viruses. Instead, they brought death to ninety per cent of the population.

Including her dad. She'd been seven.

Some Yukoners had turned against the newcomers, venting their rage and grief in terrible acts of brutality. The courts and jails were full back then.

And now Cade needed to stand trial.

"I know where he lives," she said.

"Good," said Gautier, getting up. "Dante and I will go after him."

Lauren listened for Mary's breathing and found it. No change. "I'll come with you."

Gautier shook his head. "Your place is here, with your foster parents."

Lauren just stared at him. Next to her, Charlie bristled.

"You've got no call telling my girl where her place is," said the old man quietly. "She'll do what she thinks is best. Always has."

For the second time that night, tears came to Lauren's eyes. She knew that Charlie and Mary loved her, but the display of loyalty on this night of horrors was almost more than she could take.

Mr. Chiang cleared his throat. "Can't go at night anyway. And Cade is a big man—you'll want help. I'll go talk to the neighbors." He grabbed the coat hanging on the tarnished hook by the door and went outside without putting it on.

"Come on, Jasper," he said to the Samoyed waiting patiently outside the door. "We're going for a walk."

Jasper barked once and then Mr. Chiang closed the door.

Lauren gave Gautier a cool look and went back to check on Mary. To her surprise, Dante was sitting in the rocking chair next to the bed. He was holding Mary's hand. He looked up when she came in. Could he feel her approach the same way she could feel him?

As she was trying to interpret the expression on his face, she heard the rattle of liquid in Mary's chest. Her lungs were filling with fluid.

Anxiety and denial flooded through her. The look on Dante's face was clear now. It was pity. He let go of Mary's hand and stood up.

"It just started," he said softly. He looked for a moment as if he wanted to comfort her, but something in her expression must have warned him off. Without another word, he left.

Lauren sat heavily in the rocking chair he had vacated. She gathered up Mary's hand in hers and rubbed it to warm it. Her foster mother's face was almost peaceful now, but each exhalation ended on a faint burbling.

Oh, Mary.

Charlie limped into the room, bringing the stink of smoke and fear with him. He held on to the doorjamb with one hand and looked down at his wife. The rasping of his breathing mingled with the burbling in her chest, audible now, even to him.

He looked at Lauren and she saw the same knowledge in his eyes. Her free hand reached out for his. After a while, she got up and left him alone with his wife.

* * *

Mary died in the deepest part of the night when the soul is at low ebb. Lauren and Charlie undressed her and washed her, then dressed her back in her clothes. It bothered Lauren to put the stinking clothes back on her, but there was nothing else. Mr. Chiang had long ago given away his wife's clothing, and all that Mary and Charlie had owned was now in ashes.

Anger was becoming a familiar companion and she tamped it down as she worked, refusing to let this last duty be tainted by rage. She'd never had the chance to do this for her mother. And a daughter, even a foster daughter, should be loving and gentle in her last ministrations to her mother.

But every time she looked at Charlie, at his crumpled up face, his red-rimmed eyes, and his stooped shoulders, the anger spiked.

Cade had done this to them.

Finally, they were done and Mary lay like a queen on a bier, her hair neatly pulled back in its customary bun. Her face was soft, with the lines of pain smoothed out.

Mr. Chiang came into the bedroom when they were done, his eyes full of sadness. He placed a gentle hand on Charlie's shoulder.

"Come have some tea, old friend."

Charlie shook his head. "I want to sit with her." He looked around at Lauren. "You go. Eat something."

Mr. Chiang and Lauren exchanged looks. Clearly, Charlie wanted to be alone. Lauren gathered up the bowl and the cleaning cloths and followed Mr. Chiang to the living room.

From the kitchen came sounds of cutlery clanking against bowls and the yeasty smell of sourdough bread.

"Let me take that," said Mr. Chiang and she handed him the battered steel bowl.

In the kitchen, Gautier and Dante were preparing food. Gautier spooned a dollop of fat out of a clay pot and dropped it in a cast iron skillet where it danced around, coating the bottom, filling the house with the smell of bacon fat. Then he poured beaten eggs out of a bowl into the skillet. Meanwhile, Dante sliced bread and a moose roast.

Mr. Chiang came back inside from emptying the bowl and saw her standing there. He set the bowl to dry next to the small wood stove in the corner.

"Sit, Lauren," he said gently. "Have some tea." He nodded at the cups and the pot of tea sitting on the table.

"I need to change Rupe's dressing," she said dully.

Gautier glanced back from the cook stove. "Already done. There's no sign of infection and he's sleeping."

Lauren glanced at the corner where Rupe slept. The bandage looked startlingly white against his black coat.

"Eggs'll be ready in a minute," said Gautier. His gaze swept her from top to toe. "You need to eat."

Lauren shook her head. "I'm not hungry." She knew that people always turned to food when there was a death—she'd seen the ritual too many times—but the thought of food right now turned her stomach. Mary was dead.

Mr. Chiang put his hands on her shoulders and gently pushed her down on the chair. He pulled a cup toward her and poured fragrant tea into it. Then he added a generous spoonful of honey from the honey jar. "Drink," he ordered. "I'll bet you can't remember when you last ate. In a few hours, people will be coming by to pay their respects. You'll need your strength."

She drank. The tea was too sweet but it felt good going down. And when Gautier placed a plate of scrambled eggs, warmed up moose meat, and sourdough bread in front of her, she ate every bite.

She would need her strength to find Cade.

* * *

Morning came, and with it all of Whitehorse, it seemed. Gautier and Dante spent the morning splitting wood from Mr. Chiang's wood pile, staying out of the way while Charlie and Lauren accepted condolences and food from their neighbors and friends. By lunch time, they had two cords neatly stacked against the house.

Cade was out there—planning what, Gautier couldn't guess— and he chafed here, chopping wood.

The Samoyed had found a patch of sunshine on what looked like a garden bed in the frozen yard and now watched them with endless patience.

In spite of lungs still raw from last night's smoke, the exercise did Gautier good. Even Dante, who avoided physical labor whenever possible, put his back into it without complaining. The neighbors streamed past them, giving them solemn nods as they went inside and as they left. Two men, brothers by the cast of their faces and the identical receding hairline, gave Dante a hard look before going inside.

Gautier thought about asking Dante who they were, but he wasn't ready to talk to the man yet. Better to keep swinging the axe down to bite into the surprisingly soft wood. It was spruce, most of it pecker pole. Not like the hard maple and oak in Ontario.

A sense of unreality washed over him and he set the axe down to rest against his leg before he cut his foot off.

Two weeks ago, he'd been in Klineburg, Ontario, working on

his house, unaware that his old friend Dante was about to arrive and turn his world upside down.

Dante had called out, "Hello, the house!" and Gautier had looked up from the pail full of four-inch nails and squinted into the sun at the figure striding down the path. He'd dropped a handful of nails back into the pail and shaded his eyes.

"Dante!" He grinned like an idiot and dropped the hammer into the pail, too.

Dante met him halfway and they hugged fiercely. Then Gautier pushed Dante away and, holding him by the shoulders, examined him. They hadn't seen each other in nearly a year, since they parted ways, he for Klineburg, where he'd found work as a carpenter, and Dante for Montreal, where he fixed pre-Troubles gadgets.

The last rays of the setting sun turned his friend's dark complexion ruddy. Except for the serious expression on his face, Dante looked almost the same as the day they met, back in grade eight. Before the first plague hit Toronto.

"I thought you weren't coming 'til spring," said Gautier, finally releasing him. "Come on. Pull up a chair." Although a rudimentary postal system existed between Klineburg and Montreal, it was still hit and miss. Maybe he'd missed a letter from Dante.

"Sounds good," said Dante. His gaze went to the view of the shallow Klineburg valley, with its homes nestled like jewels in green velvet. Then he examined the second floor of the house with its partial roof and framed-up wall critically before nodding his approval. "How're you going to get the trusses up?"

Gautier glanced at the two trusses waiting on the east side of the house. They'd been easy enough to build, but hauling them up to the roof would be something else. He wasn't about to try alone.

He liked Klineburg. Liked it enough that he'd decided to settle here. Then it was just a question of finding a house—easy enough when nine out of ten houses were abandoned—and moving in. Of course most of the abandoned houses were falling apart, which explained why this little salt box gem had been unclaimed. A tree had fallen on the house, destroying part of the roof and the front wall.

Easy enough for a handy guy to fix.

He pointed Dante to a rough sawhorse and dragged another one closer. "I've made some friends here, and some of my clients have strong boys. I'll manage." He studied his friend. No backpack. "You going to be around long enough to help?"

Dante turned away from the view and looked at Gautier.

"That's why I'm here," he said quietly. "I need your help."

Gautier's smile faltered and disappeared.

"What's the problem?" He couldn't imagine any situation where Dante would need his help. Except maybe in a fight. At five foot four, Dante's only advantage was speed.

Dante took a deep breath.

"My cousin is in danger and I need your help to help her."

Gautier blinked slowly once. Twice. "You have a cousin?" In fifteen years of friendship, Dante had never mentioned any family.

His friend nodded. The setting sun cast long two-by-four shadows across the ground, bisecting him in darkness. "She's in the Yukon."

"In the Yukon." This just got better and better.

Dante nodded again.

Gautier had trouble getting mail from Montreal, and he was only a couple of hundred miles away. He was pretty sure Canada Post hadn't reestablished connections to the Yukon yet.

"What kind of trouble is she in?"

Dante shrugged and his shadow danced on the sawdust covered ground. "I'm not sure. Grandfather thinks someone is trying to hurt her."

Whoa. A cousin *and* a grandfather?

Then Gautier started to grin. "You son of a bitch," he said admiringly. "You almost had me."

Dante's expression didn't change. "I'm not joking, Gautier. I want you to come with me to Whitehorse."

Gautier stood up abruptly and walked over to the ridge overlooking the valley. He stared at the forest of maple and elm trees below him. Here and there, a burst of brilliant yellow announced the coming of fall. The forest smelled of mulch and freshly turned earth. By the end of the week he wanted to have the trusses up and the rest of the roof tiled. He wanted the house clad before the first snow.

"Gautier?"

Gautier turned around. "Fifteen years we've known each other. Not once did you mention family. Not once." Dante had never directly said so, but he had implied that his family was dead.

Dante met his eye. "No."

"Why the hell not?"

Dante stood up and came to stand next to him. "Have I been a good friend in those fifteen years?"

Gautier gritted his teeth. He wouldn't have survived the Troubles without Dante. "Yes," he said at last. "And I thought I'd been a good friend, too."

"You were," said Dante, sighing. "You are." He ran a hand over his face, suddenly looking tired. "It's not you, Gautier. It just wasn't something I could talk about." He looked at Gautier. "I still can't."

Well, hell.

Gautier looked over Dante's head at the house. There was a lake, hidden by the trees, less than a hundred yards away. This place felt good. It was a place he could call home. Come winter he'd be snug in his own house, with a wood stove keeping him warm. Next year, he'd work on a garden.

Finally, he sighed and looked down at Dante. "Tell me."

Dante nodded and returned to his sawhorse. "Her name is Lauren. She's ten and she lives in a small cabin about fifteen miles south of Whitehorse. That's all I know. That, and the fact that she's in some kind of danger."

"Your grandfather told you that?"

Dante nodded but didn't speak.

"He can't be more specific?"

Dante shook his head.

"Dammitall." The house wouldn't be clad until spring if he left now. And when he got back—if he survived the trip—he'd have to find a place to spend the winter, a place not his own. Gautier blew out his frustration on a gust of air. It wasn't as if he had a choice. If there was one thing he had learned in his twenty-eight years, it was that you never turned your back on a friend.

Finally, he shrugged. "When do we leave?"

Dante grinned his gratitude. "My chariot awaits."

"You have a *car*?"

Dante waved a hand deprecatingly. "Such as it is. I've been working on it for a while. It's a 2019 Audi Max. As long as we can find gas along the way, it'll keep going."

Gautier looked at his half-erected roof and his tools and supplies scattered nearby.

"I'll need a couple of hours," he decided. "I need to brace the walls and store my tools. I need to put a tarp over the roof. Then I have to pack my gear."

"I'll help you," said Dante, jumping off the sawhorse. "It'll go faster."

They had made good time in the old Audi until they got to Edmonton. Then the gas stations came at greater intervals. By the time they crossed into the Yukon, they were in trouble. With the gas tank and all four jerry cans empty, they hid the Audi in the bushes outside of Teslin and hiked the last hundred miles.

Only to find that Lauren was a grown woman who wanted nothing to do with them.

At least Dante had gotten the danger part right. What kind of a man would knife a dog, attack a woman holding a shotgun, and set a house on fire with people still in it?

A crazy one. And he was still out there.

Gautier glanced up at the sun. It was hard to tell this far north, but it was probably around noon. Weren't these people worried about this Cade running around loose?

Dante finished stacking an armful of wood and stood back to admire his work. His breath fogged in the below zero temperature. As if sensing Gautier's attention, he looked around and grinned tentatively.

"Not a bad morning's work, eh?"

Gautier just stared at him, examining him as if he'd never seen him before. He'd thought he knew everything there was to know about Dante Longman.

Dante's eyebrow rose. "Come on, Gautier, get it off your chest."

Gautier lifted the axe by the end of the handle and swung it down to thunk into the stump he'd been using as a chopping block. Then he turned to face his friend and crossed his arms over his chest.

"How did you know where she lives?"

Whatever Dante had been expecting, it obviously wasn't that. His lips pursed as he considered. Gautier recognized that look. It was the one Dante wore when he was trying to choose his words carefully.

It pissed Gautier off. That expression was for strangers, not him.

"Just tell me!" he ordered.

Dante's face lost all expression, as if a door had shut somewhere inside. "I told you," he said softly. "My grandfather learned about her..."

Gautier shook his head. "Don't bullshit me, Dante. I mean how did you know where to find her cabin? How did you know exactly? Did your 'psychic' grandfather beam the information directly into your mind?"

Dante's dark face flushed red with anger but before he could retort, the door opened and Mr. Chiang came out, followed by half a dozen young men, two of them the surly strangers who had glared at Dante.

Gautier recognized them now. They were the two men who had held Dante prisoner last night. They stayed on the top steps while the other four waited at the bottom.

Mr. Chiang joined them at the wood pile.

"These men are going after Cade," he said, his face grim. "This isn't your fight. You don't need to be involved any further."

Gautier didn't even need to look at Dante to know there'd be a mulish expression on his face. And even though he was mad at Dante, he agreed with him. This became their fight when Cade murdered an old woman because her daughter rejected him.

He needed to be sure Cade wouldn't harm Charlie and Lauren any more than he already had. Gautier hadn't rescued the old man just to abandon him to Cade. He studied the men's faces and their gazes slid away from his. Tough as these young bucks looked, none of them had stopped Cade before he did the harm.

"Nice of you to worry about us, Mr. Chiang," he said calmly, "but Dante and I are coming too."

"It's not your fight," said the bigger of the two brothers. His chin jutted out slightly, as if inviting Gautier to take a swing at him. "We take care of our own."

Gautier gave him a long, contemptuous once over, ending at his eyes. "He burned down a house and killed an old woman. Not what I call taking care of your own."

The others shifted uncomfortably but anger sparked in the man's eyes. He stepped off the cement stoop onto the frozen ground.

"You're a stranger here, mister." He stopped a foot away and stuck a forefinger in Gautier's chest. "You've got no say."

Dante's amused voice pierced through Gautier's rising anger. "I wouldn't do that if I were you."

The man's lip curled slightly in what could have been a smile. "Like. I. Said." His finger jabbed Gautier harder with every word. "You've got no say."

Without a word, Gautier stepped onto the man's left foot, pinning it under his, and shoved with all his strength. Arms flailing, the man lost his balance and fell over backward. He landed with a tail-jarring *thump*.

"Warned you," said Dante softly, and Gautier wasn't surprised to find his friend standing by his side.

The man's brother ran to help him and the others closed in on Gautier and Dante.

Mr. Chiang stepped between them, but before he could say anything, the door opened and Lauren walked out onto the small cement stoop. She took in the scene with a sweep of her green eyes. Her mouth tightened and she fixed a cold look on the older brother.

"Mary is dead, Dan. If you can't respect that, then leave."

He bristled under her gaze. "It's not us, Lauren. They've got no right to butt in—"

The muscles in her face were suddenly taut, as if a great force were exerting pressure from within and only her will kept the pressure contained. Her arm rose and she pointed at Gautier. He almost stumbled back, but she wasn't looking at him.

She was looking at each of the other men in turn.

"That man," she said softly, each word dropping like a stone in a deep pool, "went into a burning house to save two people he had never met. He risked his life for them. That gives him every right."

Her arm dropped to her side and she took a deep breath, her nostrils white with suppressed fury. "Now I'm driving over to Cade's place and they're coming with me. What the rest of you do is your own business."

She brushed past the six stunned men and Mr. Chiang and walked toward the Ford parked in front of the old man's house.

Gautier and Dante exchanged a glance then ran to catch up.

❧ SIX ❦

THE GLARE of sunlight off the cracked windshield forced Lauren to squint and gave her a headache but didn't slow her down.

Anger sat uncomfortably in her belly, burning hot, filling her mouth with the taste of ashes and her limbs with the need to lash out.

But she contained it, already ashamed of herself for losing control in front of Dan and the other men, most especially in front of Gautier and Dante.

The way to Cade's cabin was along the Old Alaska Highway, a dirt road that was old when her mother was young. It threaded a serpentine course alongside and crossing over the "new" highway. Because there was no pavement to disintegrate, the road remained passable, especially in winter when ruts filled up with snow and puddles froze over.

Lauren ignored the increasingly frantic rattling of the truck as she sped down the road. Cade's cabin had been only a few miles out of town. She didn't know when he had returned to Whitehorse, or where he was staying, but it made sense to check his cabin first.

Next to her, Gautier and Dante kept quiet and hung on.

She glanced in the rearview mirror and saw Bert's battered

gray pickup trailing far behind her. Good. She hoped some of the men had thought to bring their rifles.

An image of Cade lying still and dead in a pool of his own blood flashed in her mind before a wave of nausea washed it away.

This wasn't her way. Yes, she wanted to find Cade, but it was to stop him from hurting Charlie.

But that wasn't all she wanted. The ball of anger in her belly grew bigger whenever she thought of Mary laying so still, her nostrils black-rimmed and her breathing shallow, or of Rupe, recovering from sudden, brutal violence, or of Charlie, sitting by his dead wife's bedside, looking so lost.

Cade had done this to them.

Part of her wanted to destroy him. *Lusted* to destroy him.

"For Christ's sake, Lauren!" shouted Dante. "Slow down before we shake apart!"

Surprise shocked her into taking her foot off the gas. She glanced at Dante, sitting between her and Gautier. He sat stiffly, his jaw clenched. He turned to look at her and his eyes almost sparked with fury.

"I know you want to kill the bastard, but we have to get there in one piece first!"

He was shouting.

Lauren glanced at the road to make sure she was still on it, then at Gautier. He looked as surprised as she felt.

She didn't know Dante, but somehow, this outburst didn't feel right. He had been calm when they left Mr. Chiang's house.

Her driving wasn't *that* bad.

"How much farther?" asked Gautier, raising his voice to be heard above the roar of the exhaust. But not shouting.

She recognized the question as an attempt to defuse the tension and appreciated the effort. She turned her attention back on the road.

"I'm not sure," she said. "I was only here once, five years ago." Heat rose in her cheeks as she remembered the circumstances of that visit, how close she had been to sleeping with Cade. And she would have, too, if Charlie and his shotgun hadn't arrived. She peered out the windshield, trying to pierce through the glare of early afternoon sunlight. The wind whistled through the gaps in the floorboards, cooling her embarrassment. Her hands were cold on the hard plastic of the steering wheel.

She slowed down even more, searching for a break in the trees. With the all-terrain vehicle he wouldn't necessarily have taken the road, but he used to have a truck, and that meant a track leading to his cabin from the road.

Bert's pickup caught up and she slowed even more and moved to the far right of the road when it became obvious he wanted to pass. She didn't dare roll down her window to wave him on—it had fallen off its tracks a dozen times already and she didn't want to freeze if it happened again, or take the time to repair it now.

Bert passed her and she saw Dan and Rocky McGraw squeezed in the front seat with him. In the bed of the pickup sat a half-dozen more grim-faced men, spaced out around the wheel wells so they could hang on to the truck's sides. A few waved at her as they passed by.

Then Bert slowed and stopped. The men in the back jumped out, two of them carrying rifles.

"I don't see a driveway," said Gautier as she slowed to a stop behind Bert's gray Dodge.

"Me neither," said Lauren and got out of the truck.

Bert limped toward them. He'd gotten his foot caught in a trap six years ago and lost three toes and part of his foot. Winters were hard on him. He could never seem to keep the foot warm.

"His track is a quarter mile down," he said, hooking a thumb over his shoulder to show where. "If we cut through here," he pointed northwest, "we should get to his place from the back."

"Good thinking," said Gautier, nodding his approval.

But Lauren frowned and Bert looked away, studying the trees, the frozen ground, anything to avoid looking at her.

Because Lauren had remembered that Bert used to run with Cade. Used to make moonshine and sit drinking with the big man, used to swagger through the market, half-drunk and smelling half-dead.

Was he still Cade's friend? Was he leading them into a trap, or sending them in one direction while Cade escaped in another?

The sun warmed the top of her head, even as the wind chilled her ears and her bare hands. The McGraw brothers waited by the gray pickup, watching Lauren, while the other men milled around, stamping warmth back into their feet.

She was aware of Gautier's sharpening attention as the silence grew uncomfortable, but still she watched Bert. Dante stood behind her and although she could still feel him like a humming deep inside, she no longer sensed anger from the man.

Finally, Bert looked at her, his blue eyes direct. Although his color was high, his tone was calm when he spoke.

"That was a long time ago, Lauren. I was too stupid to see what he was until he tried to take Celie away." Celie was his wife now, but six years ago, he'd been courting her. Lauren nodded encouragement. She hadn't seen Cade for what he was either.

Bert took a deep breath. "I paid for crossing him with this." He waved at his maimed foot.

Gautier looked enquiringly at Lauren, but she was staring at Bert in growing horror. "Cade did that to you? I thought it was a trap...?"

Bert shrugged and his lips tightened. He looked in the direction of Cade's cabin. "I could never prove that he set that extra trap on my trapline. It was the same type of trap I always used. No one knew where I set my traps, except for him." He smiled slightly. "Celie said she'd marry me, but only if I didn't go after Cade."

It was Lauren's turn to look away, ashamed of herself for the second time that day. She should have known this about Bert. She was sure Mary and Charlie had known. But she was the outsider among their friends and neighbors—and maybe the fault was hers.

If she hadn't held herself apart, maybe she would have been accepted.

Gautier stepped into the awkward silence.

"Sounds like it was a good trade," he said, grinning. "You got a good woman in exchange."

Bert shrugged again, but this time his smile was pleased. "I've got no complaints." He looked directly at Lauren. "We okay?"

Lauren nodded. "We're okay."

Without a word, Bert limped back to his truck and reached inside to pull out a rifle. Lauren took a deep breath. It was time.

She went to the back of her own truck and climbed in, rummaging through the bags and supplies she had obtained at market—was it only yesterday?—until she found the coil of brightly colored, plastic-coated wire that she kept there. Charlie had salvaged the stuff from a telephone company shed next to an old microwave tower on Gray Mountain. It was stronger than rope.

She found her dad's old tool box and used the wire snippers to cut a twenty-foot length, which she then coiled around her fist. She tucked the wire snippers in the pocket of her jacket.

Gautier offered his hand to help her down, but she pretended she didn't see it and swung herself down with one hand on the side of the truck.

They followed Bert through the trees, walking on crunchy-frozen moss, avoiding all but the smallest of twigs. These men all made their living hunting, fishing and trapping. They knew how to move silently in the woods.

But to Lauren's ears, they sounded like a herd of bison tromping through the underbrush. Only Dante moved as silently as she did, his feet seeming to float over the frozen moss, fallen spruce needles, and aspen leaves of the forest floor.

He and Gautier remained on either side, far enough not to crowd her, but close enough to reach her before anyone else did.

She sniffed the air but there was no wood smoke, no smell of exhaust or gasoline. By the time they reached Cade's cabin, she wasn't surprised to find it empty.

The men fanned out, looking for sign, while Lauren and Bert entered the deserted cabin, followed by Gautier. Dante stayed outside, close to the cabin.

The door swung open with a protesting squeak. It led to a short, narrow, dark hallway that ran parallel with the wall. In the light from the open door, Lauren could see a series of empty wooden pegs set in the log wall for coats and hats—not that she had ever seen Cade wear one.

"No clothes here," said Bert, glancing at the rough wooden shelves beneath the pegs before pushing open the door to the kitchen. Light worked its way in from the dirty kitchen window. "He used to have half a dozen pairs of mukluks, one decorated with beads and lined with fur. Good for fifty below."

Lauren nodded, filing the information away. Assuming he still had the boots and the wolf fur parka he'd worn yesterday, he could be planning to be outside for a while.

Gautier followed Bert into the kitchen, his gaze taking in the empty kitchen and living room, then settling on the steep, narrow staircase that led up to the loft. Lauren's gaze followed his. Everything from the table top to the stair railing was covered in thick dust. Moccasined feet had scuffed through the dust on the rough spruce floor. Cade hadn't been back in Whitehorse long enough to clean the place up.

Lauren was surprised at how small the cabin was. She remembered it as larger, more luxurious. But the kitchen was barely ten feet by ten, although it flowed into the larger living room. Cade must have kept most of his tools in a shed out of sight of the cabin.

Most cabins in the area were built along the same simple plan. Living areas on the main floor, with an open space on a second level to take advantage of the rising heat for sleeping. Less of a footprint to heat.

Gautier walked through the living room and started up the staircase to the sleeping loft. Lauren could have told him that it was empty, too, but she didn't. She barely knew Gautier, but she understood him well enough to know he would need to check for himself. That's what she would do.

"Nothing much here," called Bert, examining the empty kitchen.

A small cook stove, carefully repaired and maintained, took pride of place in the kitchen. On the log wall beside it were not one, but three cast iron skillets, in varying sizes. It was a testament to how much the locals feared Cade that the skillets were still there five years after Cade's departure.

A bright yellow kettle, dinged and singed by heat and dulled with dirt, sat on the stove. It looked so out of place that Lauren stared at it, trying to imagine Cade using it. He hadn't taken his cooking utensils when he left five years ago.

Bert placed a hand on the black metal cook stove. "Cold," he said. He walked over to the big wood stove by the far wall of the living room and touched its surface. "This one, too. No fire in this one for at least two days."

Cade had been here but only briefly. She didn't know whether to feel relief or disappointment. Leaving Bert and Gautier to finish searching the cabin, she turned toward the door.

On a mottled brass hook on the back of the door hung a band of moose-hide, intricately beaded in a pink, blue, and white flower pattern. Lauren stared at it for a moment, her mind completely blank. Her mother had owned a hair band just like this. Meridy Tom used to wear it every day to keep her thick, shoulder-length hair back. Almost of its own volition, her hand reached out to stroke the soft leather, to feel between her fingers the rough elastic that joined both ends of the strip. The beads gleamed in the sunlight and the leather looked clean.

Then she saw the dark hairs twisted in the elastic and anguish swept through her, leaving her trembling. The hair band *had* belonged to her mother.

Lauren hadn't seen it in over ten years, had assumed her mother was wearing it when she disappeared.

And here it was, hanging from Cade's door.

"Loft's empty," said Gautier, peering down at them from the rail-less floor above.

Bert nodded and waved in the direction of the kitchen. "No food or supplies—" He stopped, suddenly noticing Lauren's face.

"What is it?" asked Gautier, making his way down the stairs.

But Lauren just shook her head and lifted the hair band off the hook. She had to leave Cade's cabin before she suffocated.

* * *

After the funeral, they picked at a supper of leftovers culled from the mountain of food Charlie's friends and neighbors had brought in. Afterward, Gautier and Dante helped Mr. Chiang store much of it away in the cellar beneath the house while Lauren and Charlie sat at the kitchen table, drinking tea.

Charlie reported that Rupe had taken a few pieces of moose meat from his hand a few hours earlier and managed to drink water sloppily from a shallow bowl. He even allowed Charlie to pick him up and carry him outside where he relieved himself. He licked Charlie's face when the old man brought him back in.

Night had fallen while they ate, and now the room felt cozy with the light from the candlestick on the coffee table and warm from the dying fire in the small kitchen cook stove. Two beeswax candles burned on the table next to Lauren and Charlie, cocooning them in a smaller circle of light. The smell of beeswax mingled with the lingering odor of the moose stew they had eaten.

Lauren's fingers fidgeted with the spoon she had used to add honey to the tea. The headache was still there—no stronger, but distracting. Beneath the table, her knee bounced up and down until she noticed and stopped.

Charlie placed a rough hand on hers, effectively stopping her from toying with the spoon.

"What is it, little girl?"

In spite of herself, Lauren smiled. Charlie always saw her as the ten-year-old who first came to live with him—probably because she always felt like a ten-year-old when she was around him.

"Is it those two fellas?" His voice was low, pitched for her ears only.

She looked up in surprise to see him nodding toward the back of the house, where Dante was handing food down to Gautier, partway down the cellar ladder. Gautier then turned around and handed it to Mr. Chiang, who was deep in the cellar.

Dante glanced up at her. He had heard.

She turned back to Charlie, saw the concern in his eyes, and wondered when she had decided to trust these two strangers.

Was it when they tried to keep her from going inside the burning house? Or when they followed her to Cade's, when they knew how dangerous he was?

Or was it when Gautier saved Charlie's life, and tried to save Mary's?

She shook her head. "No. It's not them."

Charlie nodded slowly. "Good. I think they're good men, but maybe you can tell me who they are."

This time, Lauren sat back in her chair and stared at her foster father in open surprise. She thought back to the last twenty-four hours and found that no, she hadn't once told him who they were or how she had met them.

In fact, she hadn't told anyone how she came to have them as two permanent shadows.

A bubble of laughter caught in her chest and she swallowed the budding hysteria. She rubbed her tired eyes and blew the hysteria out on a gusty sigh. She needed sleep. Sleep would take care of the headache, if nothing else.

"Cade was waiting for me when I got back home yesterday." She told him the whole story, watching his eyes widen when she got to the part about Cade attacking her.

When she told him about how Rupe was hurt, Charlie's eyes filled with anger and he held her hand for the rest of the story.

When she finished, he nodded once and released her hand.

"I never liked that man. There was something a little crazy about him." He cleared his throat and drank the last of his tea. "But we were all a little crazy after the Troubles." He remained silent for a moment, then swallowed hard. "If I'd known what he was going to do..." His fists clenched on the table, cording the muscles in his forearms.

It was Lauren's turn to place a hand on his. "Don't. If anyone's to blame, it's me—"

"No. The only one to blame is Cade himself," said Charlie grimly.

Lauren squeezed his hand then picked up her mug to drink. When she placed it back on the table, she'd made up her mind.

"At Cade's place..." She trailed off, then stopped to marshal her thoughts. Finally she pulled the hair band out of her pocket and placed it on the table in front of them. The candlelight picked out the flower pattern in the beads. "I found this hanging on his door."

Charlie stared at the hair band for a moment then looked at her blankly. He didn't recognize it.

"It was my mother's, Charlie."

Charlie shook his head, obviously baffled. "I'm sorry, Lauren. I don't pay much attention to hair frippery."

Anger spiked through Lauren and her headache threatened to take over her entire skull. She breathed deeply, controlling the anger, pushing back the pain. "She always wore it. My grandma made it for her—my father's mother. I remember Mom telling me about the primroses growing by Primrose Lake and how she loved it there, and that was why Grandma made it for her."

Grandma Tom had died when Lauren was seven, but she still remembered her laughter and the smell of cinnamon whenever she was around. Lauren suspected now that Mom had worn the hair band mostly to please Dad and because she had loved the old woman. That hair band was the only 'frippery' she owned.

"What was it doing on the back of Cade's door?" she asked.

Charlie's hands spread wide in ignorance. "He used to like

your mother. Maybe he took it?"

Lauren's head snapped back as if she had been slapped. So Cade *had* known her mother! Just how much had he *liked* her? A sour taste filled her mouth but she had to know.

"What do you mean, he liked her?"

Charlie looked uncertainly at her. "After your dad died, he came sniffing around her for a while. When she made it clear that she wasn't interested, he stopped pestering her."

For a moment, Lauren thought she was going to be sick. Cade had been interested first in her mother, then, ten years later, in her.

Charlie's mouth pursed. "That's why I couldn't stand having him sniffing you up. Wasn't natural."

Lauren couldn't help but agree. The niggling suspicion inside her heart grew to certainty. "He knows something about Mom's disappearance," she said softly, staring at the dregs of her tea. "He's involved, somehow."

Charlie straightened in alarm. "There's no proof—"

She cut him off. "That hair band is proof enough! She always wore it. And there was no dust on it—he left it there for me to find!"

"What are you—"

"Charlie—"

Dante walked into the room, Gautier right behind him.

"What are you saying?" demanded Dante.

Good hearing didn't give him the right to butt in. Lauren stood up. She didn't have to explain herself to them.

But you owe them something, her traitorous conscience reminded her. *For Charlie's life, if nothing else.*

"I'm saying that Cade knows something about my mother's disappearance," she said grudgingly. "He knew I'd go to the cabin looking for him. He left the hair band where I'd find it."

Charlie stood up, too, scraping his chair back on the wooden floor in his hurry.

"You are not going after him!" he ordered. "He's gone and good riddance. The man is insane." His eyes burned fiercely in the candlelight.

"He's right," said Dante, leaning in as if she were hard of hearing. "You need to come back to Montreal with us. My grandfather can keep you safe."

Charlie turned an outraged face to Dante and Lauren burst out laughing at the absurdity of the suggestion.

"I'm not going to Montreal," she said. "I'm going to Ben-My-Chree."

And despite the loud objections from Dante and Charlie, it was Gautier's calm gaze that caught and held hers, his stillness the only peace she could find in the storm that her life had become.

❧ SEVEN ❧

BEN-MY-CHREE.

The name settled in Gautier's imagination like a firefly—lighting up every time he was about to fall asleep and filling him with wonder. He shifted on the hard floor, rearranging his bunched up jacket under his head.

The kitchen door opened and closed softly as Dante went back out for another circuit of the house. It was his turn at watch. Without discussing it with the others, Gautier and Dante had decided to keep watch, just in case.

Gautier wasn't worried. Cade was gone—he could feel it in his bones. But he wasn't willing to bet anyone's life on his instincts.

Ben-My-Chree. It sounded like something in one of the fairy tales his mother used to read him when he was a boy. He'd asked Dante, but his friend had never heard of the place.

In the end, while Charlie and Dante tried to persuade Lauren to change her mind, Gautier stepped outside to sit with the old man, Mr. Chiang, on an upturned log. Jasper, the Samoyed, woofed a greeting.

Mr. Chiang had been to Ben-My-Chree as a young man. It had been a long trip from Whitehorse, a 150-mile trip that took him three days by power boat up the Yukon River, down the length of

Marsh Lake into Tagish Lake and from there, south to Taku Arm, at the very tip of which was Ben-My-Chree.

While they watched the stars come out, Mr. Chiang told him about Ben-My-Chree and the couple who had built a home there. The Englishman and his wife who had settled the spot were long dead by the time Mr. Chiang arrived. But in the 1920s and '30s, people came from as far away as England to visit their home and the formal gardens growing in the wilderness.

Mr. Chiang's voice grew soft as he described the remains of the large, sturdy cabin and the small, wooden boat slowly disintegrating on the beach. He talked about the wild roses, delphinium, lupine, yarrow, bluebells, and gentian that still grew around the lodge against the startling backdrop of white glacier and blue sky. He spoke of the perfume of the wild flowers and the buzzing of hundreds of bees floating from flower to flower.

A wonderful place, Mr. Chiang had said. But it was over a hundred miles away and winter was closing in. A sane person would be hunkering down for the season, not heading out into the wilderness after a murderer.

Gautier sighed and opened his eyes. Only the pale wash of starlight coming through the picture window lightened the darkness of the living room. He stared at the ceiling, noting darker patches where the roof had leaked.

His eyes still stung, and with each breath he felt the tightness in his chest. It would take a while for his lungs to recover from the smoke he had inhaled. The he gingerly felt his cheekbone, noting the tenderness where Lauren had hit him.

He was a wreck.

The house creaked as the cold slowly worked its way inward, barely held at bay by the damped down wood stove. He thought about putting another log on but decided to wait until it was time to relieve Dante.

Charlie was sleeping in the room where his wife had died. Gautier could understand that, almost. In a strange way, it probably comforted the man. Mr. Chiang and Lauren had the two up-stairs bedrooms—rooms that hadn't been used in years.

Gautier and Dante were making do with the floor and some spare blankets Mr. Chiang had borrowed from neighbors.

Charlie and Lauren had been in bed by the time Gautier and Mr. Chiang came back in. By the mulish look on Dante's face, the discussion hadn't ended well.

He wondered if Lauren was sleeping. He hoped so. She hadn't looked well—a little feverish maybe, her eyes definitely too bright. She didn't look like a woman who should be taking a long trip.

It was none of his business. She was a grown woman. If she wanted to throw her life away, let her. There was a life for him back in Klineburg. A few of the women had let him know that he looked like good husband material, and maybe he was just about ready for that. Maybe it was time to start a family and watch kids grow.

But it might already be too late to beat winter back to Kline-burg. He didn't like the thought of starting out on a long trip, on foot, just as the weather was turning. Maybe he'd have to spend the winter in Whitehorse. Find an abandoned cabin—not Cade's—and do some hunting. He'd seen quite a few places around that could use a good carpenter.

Then he'd set out in the spring and pick up where he'd left off.

Dante could do what he bloody well pleased.

A noise from upstairs brought him to sudden alertness. He sat up and shoved the blanket off his legs. He heard it again, and before his mind could register it as a female moan of distress, he was on his feet and running for the stairs.

* * *

There were voices in her head—thousands of voices, all clam-oring to be heard at the same time. They filled her to cracking, a dull roar that threatened to spill her over into chaos.

Then someone touched her and she reared out of sleep, claw-ing and hitting.

"Lauren!" The harsh whisper cut through the noise in her

head, and then hands caught her wrists and she finally opened her eyes.

Cade loomed over her threateningly. With a rush of fear, she surged out of bed, using his grip on her for leverage. Before she could raise her knee, however, he closed the space between them, clamping her hands behind her back and trapping her against him, and swung her off the bed so that her feet couldn't touch the floor.

Only then did she realize that he was talking to her.

"It's all right," he said softly. "You're safe—it's only me."

And then his scent reached her consciousness. Beyond the faint male musk that had panicked her were other smells: wood smoke and unwashed clothes, clean male sweat, a cross between sweet hay and rich, loamy soil—Gautier.

"Awake?" he asked softly, his warm breath fanning the top of her head and her cheek. She nodded and he released first one of her wrists, then the other, but kept his arms around her to support her as he lowered her to the floor. Her bare feet touched the cold linoleum floor of the spare bedroom and he stepped back, giving her room.

"You were dreaming," he said.

Lauren nodded, unable to speak.

Then someone cleared his throat in the doorway and Lauren and Gautier started in surprise.

"I heard something," explained Dante, staying in the doorway.

She hadn't felt him. Hadn't felt the humming in her belly she had come to associate with his presence. Now that her fear was abating, she began to feel the humming again.

Interesting.

"I had a nightmare," she said, reaching for her pants at the foot of the bed. To her amusement, both men looked away as she slipped them on. She wouldn't be getting any more sleep tonight. Oh well. Morning wasn't far off.

"What's going on?" came Mr. Chiang's voice from down the hall. Then his door opened and they heard him pad down the hallway in his bare feet as a faint light came closer.

"Lauren had a nightmare," said Dante, turning to block the doorway. Lauren quickly finished lacing up her pants and slipped her sweater over her thin shirt.

"Lauren?" called Mr. Chiang. Dante glanced over his shoulder to make sure she was dressed and stepped aside to let Mr. Chiang in.

The old man carried a candle on a small pottery plate with a handle. A smoky glass chimney protected the flame from air currents but threw weird shadows on the walls and ceiling.

"I'm fine, Mr. Chiang." She smiled at him and sat down on the bed to put on her wool socks. "Sorry I woke everybody."

Mr. Chiang shrugged, making the shadows waver. "I don't sleep so much anymore." He examined her state of dress. "Now that we're up, we might as well have tea."

Rupe looked up at them as they entered the kitchen, tail thumping on the floor in greeting.

Gautier and Dante patted the Lab's head on their way out to get wood and Lauren sank to her knees next to him and hugged him.

"How're you doing, old friend?" She rubbed his silky black ears and scratched his nose. For an answer, he licked her hands and tried to stand up. "No, stay," she warned, pushing him back with a firm hand on his shoulder.

Mr. Chiang busied himself preparing tea from the kettle that had remained on the stove all night, filling the dry air with moisture. Spoons rattled as he rummaged through his cutlery drawer.

Rupe's dressing didn't need changing, and when she peered underneath it, she saw that the cut was already starting to scab over. It smelled clean. Maybe tomorrow he could stand up for short periods of time.

Then she sat back as the realization hit her. Tomorrow, she would be gone. Rupe had to stay behind.

Her eyes prickled with tears as dismay flooded her. Rupe always came with her wherever she went. She stood up, looking down at her best friend. He looked up at her, his brown eyes trusting.

Before she could start to cry, Lauren went to the cupboard for the cups, which she set on the table.

"Charlie will never ask," said Mr. Chiang, not looking up from the tea ball he was filling, "but he wants you to stay."

Lauren's hands stilled on top of the tea mugs and she looked at the back of Mr. Chiang's head. She had never known him to give advice. This was more than Charlie not wanting her to go to Ben-My-Chree. This was about her staying with him.

"I know," she finally said, pushing the words out past the lump in her throat.

Mr. Chiang looked up at her then. "He's never asked for anything from you. He took you in—"

"That's enough, Arnold."

They turned to see Charlie standing in the doorway of the kitchen. His hair was mussed and his eyes were red-rimmed, but his voice sounded more normal. He frowned at Mr. Chiang.

Lauren looked away, fighting the wave of guilt that made her hands shake. How long he had been standing there?

Mr. Chiang abandoned the tea and crossed his arms over his skinny chest. His eyes glittered in the light from the kerosene lamp on the table.

"She has no respect for you," he said calmly.

That's not true, she wanted to protest, but guilt kept her quiet. Mr. Chiang was right. Her duty was to remain with Charlie and look after him. Protect him.

"Arnold. Leave it be," said Charlie. There was exhaustion in his voice, the bone weariness of a man who had seen and endured too much.

Mr. Chiang shrugged but she could see by the tightening in his jaw that he was upset. Without a word, he put on his coat and boots and went outside.

Lauren went to the tea pot and finished filling the tea ball.

"Lauren."

She didn't look up as her tears finally spilled over. Then Charlie was next to her and pulling her into his arms. She hung on to his bony frame for a long time, fighting the grief and guilt.

She knew down to her bones that the best way to protect Charlie was to find Cade and make sure he never hurt anyone again.

But she knew herself better than that. She wanted to protect Charlie, but more than anything she wanted to find Cade and demand answers from him about her mother's disappearance.

Finally, Charlie eased her away. "Time for that tea, eh?"

Lauren nodded and finished making the tea while Charlie sat down at the kitchen table.

He stared down at his hands cradling the empty cup and Lauren knew he was thinking of Mary. He looked better this morning than he had yesterday, but he still looked older than anyone should at fifty-six.

Finally, she turned to him. "Charlie, you know I have to go, don't you?"

He looked up at her, his face creasing in a gentle smile. "I know you feel you have to go, Lauren. I won't hold you back."

Oh God. This was worse than if he'd argued with her.

"You can move into my cabin," she said quickly. "The larder is full and you know my trapline as well as I do. Besides, it'll be nice having someone to come home to."

As she said the words, she felt like an ungrateful wretch. Mr. Chiang was right. She should be staying to look after him. But even as she thought it, she knew she wouldn't stay.

Charlie grinned, and for the first time since Gautier pulled him out of the burning house, he looked like himself. "I know you mean well, little girl, but—and I mean this in a kind and loving way—you're the most antisocial person I've ever met. And that's saying a lot. If I moved in with you, I'd never see you. You'd always be gone." He nodded at the outside door. "Arnold's invited me to stay, so I'll try living here for a while. At least until I decide what I want to do."

It took a moment for Lauren to realize he was giving her a way out. She brought the tea pot to the table and poured two cups full of fragrant rosehip tea.

Perversely, she found herself arguing with him.

"I'm not antisocial," she said stiffly. "I lived in town for five years before moving to the cabin."

Charlie's eyebrows rose. He added a liberal teaspoon of honey to the tea. Like most people, he drank the tea because it was full of vitamin C, but couldn't stomach its bitterness without some sweetening.

Lauren watched his lips purse as he stirred the tea. He raised the spoon a couple of times to check on the melting honey. She recognized that expression. It was the one he used when he was trying to find the right words to express something difficult.

Finally he licked the last of the honey off the spoon and set it down.

"When your mother was pregnant with you, Mary got real sick. We figure it was pneumonia. I was on the trapline. Your mum came and stayed with Mary, nursing her until she got better. She wasn't alone, of course. All the neighbors came and helped. They brought food and kept the house warm."

Lauren added two teaspoons of honey to her own tea and stirred, waiting patiently.

"By the time I got back," Charlie continued, "Merry couldn't wait to leave town. She couldn't take all those folks around her." He looked at Lauren with a wry smile. "You're a lot like her." He studied her for a moment. "In fact, the older you grow, the more like her you look. Except for your eyes, of course. Those you get from your dad's Irish side."

Lauren smiled too. She had no photographs of her parents but she remembered them clearly. She had inherited her mother's high cheekbones and wavy, glossy black hair—although she kept hers short—and her dad's green eyes. And though she was nowhere near as tall as her dad's six feet, she was taller than her mom's four feet eleven.

"Now," said Charlie firmly, his hand tapping the table to get her attention. "About Rupe." He frowned at her. "He'll have to stay with me, of course."

Lauren's heart tightened but she nodded. Of course he would. She didn't glance at her friend but knew his ears had pricked up at the sound of his name. "I may be gone a while."

"I know," nodded Charlie. "He'll be healed up by the time you get back. Don't you worry about him. Or me," he added seriously. He took her chin in his hand and forced her to look at him. "We'll look after each other just fine."

At that moment, the door opened and the three men returned, carrying wood and letting cold air in. They dropped their loads into the wood box with a clatter. Rupe barked a greeting and Jasper pushed his way past the men to sniff at the injured dog before settling down next to him.

"Food?" asked Dante hopefully.

"Food," agreed Mr. Chiang, not looking at Lauren or Charlie.

As darkness slowly lifted, Mr. Chiang and Dante served scrambled eggs with caribou sausage, sweet rosehip tea, and bread soaked in hot bacon grease. The aromas mingled with the smell of kerosene and beeswax and the friendly odor of wet dog.

It took all of Lauren's determination to finish the meal. She had no appetite, but knew she would need the sustenance.

When they finished, she helped Gautier wash and dry the dishes. Then, while Mr. Chiang fed the wood stove, she stood in the middle of the kitchen, looked at Dante and Gautier, and took a deep breath.

"I'm leaving now. If you want to get your stuff, you're welcome to ride back with me to my place."

"But—" Dante began.

"There's a condition," Lauren overrode him. Looking hard at Dante, she said, "You can ride with me only if you stop trying to change my mind. Otherwise you can walk."

"But—" said Dante and stopped abruptly.

Gautier turned to her and smiled.

"Thanks. We accept."

Only when she saw Charlie's grin and followed his gaze did she see Gautier's big foot over the top of Dante's.

* * *

They kept their word and the ride back was quiet, except for the full-throated roaring of the Ford's exhaust. Fumes leaked in through the floor boards but didn't mask Rupe's smell.

They left Whitehorse at dawn, but as they drove out of the valley and onto the Alaska Highway, the sun finally crested Golden Horn mountain to bathe the world in pink light.

Lauren's thoughts were too dark to fully appreciate the beauty of the morning. She had just buried Mary and now was abandoning the only family she had left, not to mention her best friend.

She should give up this fool's mission, stay behind and look after Charlie.

But the need to follow Cade to Ben-My-Chree was undeniable. Already she chafed at having to go to the cabin first to get her gear.

Next to her, Dante stared straight ahead, his mouth a straight line of disapproval. Lauren sighed. She couldn't understand why he cared so much. In fact, she had no idea why they were still hanging around.

Charlie was right. She didn't do well around people. But when she searched herself for the familiar irritation she always felt when she was around people too long, it wasn't there. Not that it mattered—she'd be free of them once they picked up their gear. If they were smart, they'd turn back right away before winter really settled in.

Gautier stared straight ahead, obviously lost in his own thoughts.

At the Cut-Off, she topped up the gas tank, giving Jimmy the beaver she had saved for Mary. All her jerry cans were already full, but until she pulled out the Southern Lakes map in her father's things, she wouldn't know the best route to reach Ben-My-Chree, so better fill up now in case she didn't come back this way.

She didn't tell Jimmy about the fire or Mary's death, but he already knew. As he filled up her truck, he eyed Dante and Gautier with suspicion. When she caught him giving his son behind the counter a surreptitious sign, she hurriedly assured him that she was fine and that Dante and Gautier were friends.

Still, it was only when she took him aside and told him how Gautier had saved Charlie and tried to save Mary that he finally gave the boy the sign to stand down.

Within an hour of leaving Mr. Chiang's house, she turned up the narrow dirt road that led to her cabin. In spite of everything, Lauren breathed a small sigh of relief to see the cabin still standing. She had half-expected Cade to burn it down, too.

She left the truck in first gear and turned the engine off, making sure to pocket the key before opening the door and jumping out.

She looked around, expecting Rupe to come bounding out of the trees in pleasure at seeing her. The stab of pain at his absence only redoubled her guilt.

"I'll build a fire," said Dante, sliding out through the driver's side door. "The cabin will be cold."

Lauren didn't look at him. "I'm not staying." She walked around to the back of the pickup and climbed into it. The hinges had long ago rusted the gate shut so that she had to clamber over the top. She pulled off the stained tarp and looked down at the contents strewn on the truck bed. The potatoes were probably no good—she had left them in the truck to freeze; they might be salvageable in a stew... she'd drop them off at Emily and Stan's place, if she could. The flour she could use, and the dried peas and the oatmeal. The wire was light and would easily fit into a backpack.

All right, then. First, the map. Then food and gear, including snowshoes. She didn't know how much snow she'd encounter. She jumped out of the truck and headed for the cabin.

She noted in passing that the two men had disappeared and

wondered if they'd say goodbye before leaving.

* * *

"We can't just leave her," said Dante, staring at Gautier as if he had grown a third eye. He held his ragged sleeping bag tucked under his arm, half stuffed into a too-small canvas bag.

"Sure we can," said Gautier. He had already packed his sleeping bag, and the plastic tarp was rolled tightly and strapped to the bottom of his backpack.

"Gautier..." began Dante.

"No." He didn't look up from the battered aluminum pot he held in one hand. They had left so quickly—was it yesterday? No, day before yesterday—that he'd only had time to knock the pot off the fire before running for Lauren's truck. The remnants of the tea had frozen unevenly in the bottom of the pot.

Finally, he looked up at Dante, who stood staring at him with that familiar stillness, the stillness that said he was prepared to wait forever if he had to.

"She's crazy, you know." Gautier took a deep breath and told himself he wasn't being disloyal—to Dante or to her. "You know damn well she should stay behind to look after her dad. Instead, she's haring off to the ass end of nowhere. And why? Because she thinks that the man who murdered her mother and burned down her parents' house is going to Ben-My-Chree. And she has a couple of questions for him." He shook his head and banged the pot against a spruce tree, trying to dislodge the ice but only gaining another dent.

"Jesus, Dante," he continued when his friend said nothing. "Think about it. It's almost winter. If we don't leave now, we'll be stuck here until spring. This isn't my home. It's not yours, either."

Dante nodded. "That's all true."

Gautier looked around at the dense forest of spindly black spruce and naked poplar trees. The ground was covered in thick moss grown crunchy with cold. It was a far cry from the hardwood forests of Ontario that would now be in full fall color.

If he left now, he might make it back before the first snow. In any case, he'd be closer to civilization by the time the snows came.

But the truth was, he didn't want to stay because he didn't know who Dante was anymore.

"Dante," he tried one last time, "why don't you tell me what's really going on?"

Dante sighed. "You're right," he said. "This isn't your problem. She's my cousin. I'll go with her."

The manipulative little bastard. It wasn't going to work. Gautier didn't owe the woman anything more. He'd already risked his life for her foster parents. And he sure didn't owe Dante anything, not when he wouldn't tell him the whole truth.

And going to Ben-My-Chree was dangerous. A trip like that, cross-country at the beginning of winter? It would cost someone's life.

And Dante knew it, too, but he still expected Gautier to risk his life. What rankled most was knowing that Dante wasn't telling him everything. The man he had thought was his friend was, in reality, a stranger.

A stranger who wanted him to risk his life for another stranger.

"Won't work, Dante." He gave up on the pot and threaded a piece of twine through the handle and tied it onto his backpack. "I'm going home. If you're smart, you'll come with me."

Dante finished stuffing the sleeping bag into its bag. "Okay, Gautier," he said softly. "Thanks for coming with me this far. Could you get a message to my grandfather in Montreal? Tell him what happened and where I'm going?"

Gautier gritted his teeth and nodded. *Be a fool,* he thought grimly. As if the world needed one more.

* * *

Lauren looked up from the map when the tingling warned her of Dante's approach. She peered through the kitchen's small window but didn't see him. She stood up from the kitchen table and carefully folded the laminated map into four. It was actually an ancient place mat featuring businesses and services in the Southern Lakes of the Yukon from when there used to be some. Her dad had picked it up at the Cut-Off Diner, almost fifteen years ago. Its laminate was yellow and peeling around the edges, but it had survived the years better than any of her father's other maps.

It was a simplified representation of the area. There were no elevations, only lighter splotches indicating mountains, and only the bigger lakes were identified—Tagish, Tushi, Bennett, Marsh, Atlin—but she always consulted it before going off on a walkabout. It was like getting her father's blessing.

According to the map, it was over sixty miles to Log Cabin, going past Carcross on the South Klondike Highway. From Log Cabin, she would have to take the Fantail Trail cross-country over forty miles to reach Ben-My-Chree.

She hadn't been past Carcross in about five years. The road to Carcross was barely passable—she had no idea if she'd be able to drive all the way to Log Cabin.

But she could walk if she had to.

The sun's rays hadn't reached her windows yet and the cabin was freezing. She rubbed her hands together and looked around. Her gear lay piled in the middle of the big room: two pairs of snowshoes, one narrow and long, one rounder; an extra pair of mukluks, lined with sheepskin; her heavy anorak with the wolverine fur ruff around the hood; a pair of sheepskin mitts; the beaver hat Mary had made her; an assortment of ropes, wire, extra hinges, and bolts for the sled; and a small tool kit wrapped in a narrow moose-hide apron. Resting against the pile was her father's ancient, stained, green backpack with the multiple pockets.

Still rubbing her hands together, she walked over to the ladder that led to the loft, where she kept the rest of her clothes. She'd need a change of clothes, an extra wool sweater, her second best deerskin pants, several pairs of wool socks, and the frayed silk-and-wool long johns Charlie had exchanged a pound of coffee for when she turned seventeen.

But when she got upstairs, she froze in shock.

Someone had pulled back the quilt cover of her bed to expose the pale blue, woolen blanket beneath it. And in the middle of the bed, where she couldn't miss it, lay a ring.

She walked stiffly over to the bed and picked up the plain gold band. Inscribed inside were the words: Merry and Zack, 2019.

Her hand clenched over the wedding ring so hard that its edges bit into her palm.

"All right, you bastard," she said to the room. "I'm coming."

* * *

Ten minutes later, she opened the outside door to find Dante waiting patiently ten feet away. He wore an old gray backpack, with multiple patches and a rope coiled and tied to the outside. A sleeping mat lay rolled up and clipped to the bottom.

He smiled as she stepped out.

"Need help?"

She shook her head and looked around for Gautier. "No, thanks. Are you off, then?" Her hands no longer trembled with rage, but she didn't want to have any long discussions. She headed for the cache behind the cabin. She had left the wedding ring on top of her mother's bookshelves, but the hairband she kept in her pant pocket.

Dante followed her. "As it happens, I've never been to Ben-My-Chree. Want some company?"

Lauren stopped and looked at him over her shoulder. Again she took in the surrounding trees, expecting Gautier to come striding toward them at any moment.

"I'll be fine, Dante," she said firmly. "You don't need to worry."

"Well, that's just it, isn't it?" He came closer and stopped within a few feet of her. "I can't just leave and tell my grandfather that yes, I did find you, but you had to go on this long trip and I have no idea what happened to you."

His dark gaze was piercing and brilliant. For a split second, she was reminded of her dream and the thousands of voices clam-oring for her attention. Despite the cold, tiny pinpricks of sweat suddenly appeared on her hairline and her armpits grew damp.

"Why—" Her voice came out as a croak and she cleared her throat. She turned to fully face him, her belly suddenly tight with dread. "Why do I matter to you, Dante? Why does your grandfather care? He doesn't even know me."

Of course, the grandfather could be a lie. Dante could have made the whole thing up. But she didn't think so. Nobody would make up such a far-fetched story.

Dante blinked slowly. The sun glinted on his straight black hair, hair so black it looked blue. He stood erect, as if the weight of the pack on his back were nothing.

"But he knew your mother," he said softly. "He's *your* grandfather, too, Lauren."

Relief loosened the knots in her belly and she laughed. "See? I told you there was some mistake. Both my grandfathers are dead. My father's father died in a car accident in Vancouver before I was born, and his mother died in the Troubles. My mother's parents died of the plague when I was three."

Dante nodded. "I'm sure that's what you were told. The truth is your mother and grandfather had a terrible fight and she left Montreal. He lost track of her—he didn't even know she was dead until..."

Lauren swallowed hard. "Until what?" she demanded. Maybe her first impression had been right and Dante was crazy. Or at least cruel.

But he looked so certain of himself.

"He found out when Cade tried to kill him."

Lauren's head filled with the murmur of voices and she shook her head to clear it. "Cade tried to kill him? Why?"

Dante shrugged. "It doesn't matter now. As soon as Grandfather realized that Aunt Merry was dead and that you existed, he sent me. He wants me to take you home to him." He raised his hands beseechingly. "Don't you want to meet him?"

Too much talking. His words just added to the buzzing in her head, confusing her.

"Why didn't you tell me this sooner?"

Dante's hands dropped to his sides and he shrugged. "Cade had just attacked you. He'd hurt your dog. I was this strange man who just showed up on your turf. You weren't inclined to listen to me, let alone believe such a weird story." He smiled tightly. "We've been through a bit since then. I figure you can handle it."

'A bit,' he said. She didn't know whether or not to believe him, but it didn't matter. She might eventually meet this grandfather, if he existed, but not right now. She had things to do.

She shook her head. "First Ben-My-Chree, then I'll deal with this supposed grandfather."

Dante sighed. "I figured as much. Then let me come with you." He put up a hand when she opened her mouth to object. "I am not going back there empty-handed, Lauren. You either come back with me or I go with you." He crossed his arms over his chest and frowned at her, as if daring her to refuse him.

Lauren stared at him for a minute, considering. If his story was true, that meant he was her cousin. Family. Finally she shrugged. Family or not, he'd made it here in one piece, so he obviously had some survival skills. He could probably pull his own weight. And he wasn't interested in her sexually. That much she could smell.

"What about Gautier?" she asked. "Is he coming, too?" Her belly tightened again, but this time the cause wasn't fear. Well, maybe a little fear.

But Dante shook his head. "No. He's going back to Ontario."

She heard the disappointment in his voice and it matched hers, though she couldn't think why it mattered. She barely knew the man.

"We'll need more food," she said and turned back to the cache.

* * *

Two hours later, their packs were stowed in the back of the pickup along with water jugs, food, the sled, and the rest of the gear. A snug tarp covered everything to keep the wind and ravens from plucking anything out.

"Ready?" asked Lauren, looking across the seat at where Dante sat in the passenger side.

He grinned at her. "Ready."

In spite of everything, Lauren grinned, too. The sun was high and finally warm, and the sky was the blue of adventure. She had plenty of food, good gear, and companionship. This was almost like going on a walkabout.

Then she remembered how Rupe would sit up in the seat, tongue lolling, panting in anticipation of the road, and her grin faded.

"Then let's go," she murmured, and turned the engine on. They rumbled down the track. At the last curve, just before her track reached the Carcross Road, known in earlier years as the South Klondike Highway, she slammed on the brakes.

The truck slid forward, finally stopping less than a foot from the tall man who stood in the middle of the road. Lauren and Dante watched in silence as he walked around the truck to drop his pack in the back. Then he walked to the passenger side door and opened it. Dante slid over wordlessly and the man climbed in.

"Oh shut up," said Gautier in irritation as he slammed the door shut.

❧ EIGHT ❧

MARSH LAKE, YUKON, CANADA
SEPTEMBER 2041

S ILAS sat on his solar-powered four-wheeler on the shore
of a vast lake. His breath plumed in front of him on
the crisp, morning air and his cheeks tingled with the
kiss of the breeze. Moisture from the lake covered the trees and
shrubs in frost, making them sparkle in the sunshine. Half a dozen
ribbons of white smoke rose in a ragged arc from homes hidden
around the northern rim of the lake. The fragrant wood smoke
brought him back to his early years when the only source of heat—
inefficient, but heart-warming—was wood. From wood to oil and
electricity and solar panels and solar cells—and now back to wood.

In his one hundred and fifty-six years, he had never been this
far north, but he knew from the ancestors that this was Marsh
Lake, which fed the Yukon River, and which in turn flowed through
the city of Whitehorse. If the city still existed.

After almost four thousand miles, he was finally close. *Oh,
Meridy,* he thought, his heart full of grief for the daughter he had
failed so miserably. His eyes closed as the memory washed over him
again, shaking him with its intensity.

Cade's attack in Montreal had dragged him at breakneck speed, frightened and disoriented, into an unfamiliar part of the underworld. The young obeah had sent creature after shrieking creature in to attack him. Wings had brushed against his face in the darkness, reeking with the stench of blood, and Silas had shouted as he flailed against the creatures, striking only air. Where were the ancestors? The forest? What was this place of horror?

The wind whistling past his ears had been icy cold but the thing dragging him down left a burning ring of pain around his left ankle. Although he had tried to peer into the void, there was nothing to see but blackness.

In growing panic, he had realized that the young obeah's strength was greater than his—he couldn't break away.

Something had screeched in his ear and he flinched, flinging up his hands to protect his head and shouting hoarsely.

Then a voice he hadn't heard in twenty years broke through his panic. His precipitous feet-first rush suddenly stopped, as if whatever pulled him wanted to hear, too. The voice came again.

"Dad."

"Merry?"

"They're not real, Dad."

Then something had struck him in the back and he'd stumbled to his knees onto a hard surface. At once the snapping creatures swarmed over him, covering his body, suffocating him. He couldn't breathe!

Through the roaring in his ears, he had heard Merry.

"They're not real, Dad! Don't give in!"

Only then did he understand what had killed the two obeahs. Fear. For the first time, he had wondered where the young obeah was. Why had the man sent creatures to attack him instead of attacking himself?

Because he wasn't strong enough, Silas suddenly realized. Despite his size and fierceness, the young obeah's true strength lay in turning Silas' fears against him.

The thought had calmed him. He would not die this way. Especially now that he had finally found his Merry again. He had searched for and found the slim thread connecting his underworld self to his real world body. It glowed in the darkness above his head like a ghostly anchor chain, and he reached for it with relief.

Reassured, he ignored the snapping jaws and the stench of hot, furry bodies pressing against his face and slowly stood up. He raised his arms and spread his fingers. From them came beams of light that quickly merged and spread until he stood in a pool of light. As the pool grew, the creatures had fallen away from him, scuttling back to remain outside the circle of light.

He had taken a deep breath and looked around. The light revealed nothing but a featureless white space—no floors, no walls, no ceiling.

"Merry?"

"Are you okay?" Her voice sounded far away but he could still make out the worry in it.

"I'm fine, honey. Where are you?"

There was a long silence. "I don't know," she said finally. "In some kind of prison. All white and deep, like a well."

Silas looked around but saw nothing. "Keep talking," he said, and began to walk, creating the floor beneath his feet. "I'll find you."

"There's no time, Dad," came his daughter's disembodied voice. "I think Lauren's in danger."

"Who's Lauren?" asked Silas, walking in the direction he thought her voice was coming from. "And who trapped you here?" The creatures fell behind until he could hear only the sound of his breathing and see his breath fogging before him.

"Oh, Dad." There was so much sadness in her voice that Silas stopped walking. For the first time, dread began to work its way into his heart.

"Merry?"

"I'm dead, Dad." Her voice filled with pity. "I died when Cade took me."

"Merry…" Silas fell silent. There, in that frightening, feature-less part of the underworld, his heart broke. For over twenty years he had searched for his darling girl, only to find her dead.

"Dad, please listen," urged Merry. "It's too late for me, but you can still help Lauren, my daughter. Your granddaughter." Her voice hardened with anger. "Cade will try for her next."

Her words hit Silas like a blow. A granddaughter. His baby had had a baby, and he hadn't known.

"Dad?"

"Yes, Merry?" he managed.

"She's only ten."

Silas closed his eyes. Ten. He had a ten-year-old granddaugh-ter. Finally he opened his eyes and straightened. Merry needed him.

"Cade is the obeah who attacked me?"

"Yes. You have to keep him from getting Lauren."

"What does he want with her?" *Or with any of us?*

"I don't know. But he's dangerous. Dad… she's just a little kid."

Silas swallowed an unfamiliar anger. This Cade was an obeah. His duty was to protect gaians, not hurt them.

"All right, Merry," he said. "We'll get you out, then we'll go find Lauren."

"Don't waste time looking for me. I'll still be here when you find Lauren. Please, Dad."

Silas' light had reached as far as his eye could see and still there was nothing but blank whiteness. Merry was right. He could search for days and not find her. Meanwhile, his helpless body was lying on the cobblestones, at the mercy of this rogue obeah.

He wouldn't be of any use to his granddaughter if he were dead, too, and stuck in the underworld.

"All right. Tell me where she is."

When Merry had finished giving him directions, he followed the connecting thread back to his body. The ancestors' voices had grown stronger the closer he came to his body, all of them warning him to beware.

At last he had opened his eyes to the rainy night. His head still rang from striking the cobblestones and he struggled groggily to sit up. The stranger stood, feet braced, head back. As Silas watched, the man's head came forward and he looked down at Silas.

He's going to kill me now, thought Silas, with a jolt of alarm. *He couldn't do it in the underworld, but here he is much stronger than I am.*

"Hey, mister, are you all right?"

Silas looked around, shocked that he hadn't been aware of an audience. A group of people, men and women, had spilled out of the library entrance, headed by the woman who had arrived late. *Bless you,* he thought.

Silas looked back at the stranger, but he was gone.

That had been almost three weeks ago. Silas had wanted to go north at once to find his granddaughter, but before he could leave, the ancestors warned him of a great danger stalking them. A creature roamed the underworld forests, they said, snatching gaians who were never seen again.

Silas had no doubt that Cade was responsible.

He couldn't go north—at least not right away. First he had to discover what the creature was and disable it. Then he had to track down those obeahs who might know what Cade was up to and enlist their help against the rogue.

Once again feeling he was failing his daughter, Silas sent the only other man he trusted fully—his grandson.

But within days of sending Dante after Lauren, Silas realized his mistake. Merry had told him that her daughter was ten and he had believed her, forgetting that time meant nothing in the underworld. Merry had disappeared from his life twenty years ago. Lauren was ten when Merry died—the child could be anywhere between ten and twenty years old.

And if she was older than fifteen, then Dante's arrival would trigger her transition.

Dante was no obeah and Gautier, though apparently a fine friend, was still only a sapiens. So Silas followed his grandson north, hoping to catch up to him.

He had been on the road for over two weeks, sleeping outside, pushing himself harder every day. Every night he searched the underworld for the beast haunting the forests and for his Meridy, but had yet to find either. His daughter was in prison and he couldn't help her. Cade was ravaging the underworld and he couldn't stop him, either.

What he could do, however, was save his grandchildren.

And even as he longed to see this granddaughter he hadn't known existed until weeks ago, even as he grieved for the loss of Meridy, and worse, the loss of what she would have grown to be, he felt the siren call of Ben-My-Chree pulling at him.

Had he been a man prone to bitterness, he would have dwelt on the irony of his daughter choosing to hide from him here, so close to the Tree of Life. He had searched many years for her, but Merry was a powerful obeah. It had never occurred to him that she would come here with that sapiens husband of hers.

And now she was dead. His beautiful daughter...

Grief caught him by the chest, squeezing his heart until he felt he could no longer breathe.

He had pushed himself too hard in following Dante and his friend. Especially since yesterday, when he found Dante's ancient Audi abandoned in the bush just past the tiny community of Teslin. He had wanted to catch up to them as quickly as possible.

Now his body was telling him he needed to rest.

His gaze followed the glacier-fed water south. If he followed this lake, he would reach another one, which would eventually bring him to Ben-My-Chree.

With a sharp shake of his head, he pressed the starter button on the four-wheeler and maneuvered it back onto the disintegrating road that used to be the Alaska Highway.

* * *

Lauren, Gautier, and Dante stood side by side, staring at the

Natasaheeni River Bridge. It was less than fifteen feet wide and its bed had once been composed of long, narrow boards. Now frost heaved the roadbed and warped wide gaps between the boards.

All of which she could have handled in the truck. She would just have gone slowly, avoided the worst of the frost heaves, and eased her way across the bridge.

Unfortunately, there was a big gap in the bridge, about two-thirds of the way across. It was roughly circular and ten feet across at its widest. Too wide for the truck to maneuver around.

Damn. She had hoped they could drive to Log Cabin—now they would have a sixty-mile hike to the start of the Fantail Trail, then another forty miles to Ben-My-Chree.

She looked back over her shoulder in the direction of Carcross, hidden behind the bend. The village had been abandoned for almost ten years, as the survivors of the Troubles moved into town. One or two old timers might have stayed behind, but she saw and smelled no smoke.

The sun glared off the fast-moving water twenty feet below and she squinted as pain stabbed into her eyes. The headache just wasn't going away. She'd never suffered from headaches, but had often treated Mary's with willow bark tea. Unfortunately, she didn't have time to break out the small cache of herbs and supplies she had packed away in her backpack.

Finally Gautier sighed.

"Dammitall," he muttered. Then he looked at Lauren. "Stay here. I'll check it out."

Lauren bristled at his tone, but he headed for the bridge without waiting to hear what she had to say. Lauren opened her mouth but Dante's hand on her arm silenced her.

He shook his head. "Let him go," he said softly. "He needs to work off his mad."

Lauren closed her mouth. If checking out the bridge would keep the waves of anger from rolling off Gautier as they had in the twenty-mile drive to Carcross, she was all for it.

She wondered who he was mad at—himself or Dante. She wouldn't have been surprised if he was mad at her. Aside from everything else, he had a purple bruise on his cheekbone where she had hit him.

Dante released her arm and they watched Gautier carefully cross the bridge. He stayed close to the rusted railing and examined the bed of the bridge as he walked.

There was an unconscious grace in the way his long legs moved, in the way his head swung from side to side as he examined the bed, in the way his arms swung with each step. She remembered the feel of those muscled arms under her hands.

Suddenly embarrassed by her thoughts, she glanced at Dante. He kept his gaze locked on Gautier, but his color was high.

Was he entertaining the same thoughts she was?

About Gautier?

Suddenly, Lauren didn't know what to think. Some of the books in her parent's library spoke of men who loved other men. Was Dante one of them? Was Gautier?

She wished she had more experience, but her only gropings and fumblings were with Cade—and she was trying to forget them.

"How does it look?" called Dante.

Gautier held up a finger to ask for patience and jogged back to them.

"Okay," he said, coming to a stop in front of them. His eyes were blue, Lauren noticed for the first time. Almost navy blue. "I think the bridge is still solid. We need to find something to put across the hole, something strong enough to take the weight of the truck." He looked directly at Lauren. "We passed a road just before the bridge. Where does it go?"

"To Carcross," she said. "The village is abandoned."

"How far?"

"Just around the bend," she said. "Maybe a quarter mile."

"Good." He nodded and headed back to the truck. "We'll probably find what we need there."

Lauren and Dante watched Gautier's purposeful stride without moving. When he got to the truck, he opened the door and looked back at them.

"Well? Are you coming?"

Dante glanced sideways at Lauren. "See?" he murmured. "I told you he'd get over his mad."

Lauren smiled and headed for the truck.

* * *

"Caribou," said Dante, pointing.

Lauren eased her foot off the gas pedal and followed Dante's pointing finger. Two caribou stood looking at them, their dun coats merging into the weather-beaten, sun-bleached siding of what had once been the RCMP building at the entrance to Carcross.

A long-submerged fact came floating up to her consciousness.

"Caribou Crossing," she said.

Dante and Gautier looked at her.

"This place used to be called Caribou Crossing," she explained. "It was shortened to Carcross."

The caribou edged back until they disappeared behind the building. The place dredged up other memories long buried. She and her parents used to come here when she was a child. On impulse, she turned right onto one of the side streets instead of continuing down the main road.

Many of the homes had broken windows and parts of their roofs missing. The tiny library still stood upright, though it seemed to be listing to the left. The school, a squat building that had never had more than thirty students at any one time, no longer had a front door. As she watched, a coyote trotted out of the shadowed entrance and stopped to stare at them.

Then they reached the last curve before the lake and Lauren stopped the truck and turned off the engine. Without a word, she got out and walked up the short sand dune, covered in scrub grass that acted as a windbreak.

Her gaze swept upward to the mountains that had awed her as

a child, then back down to the dunes that flattened out to a narrow strip of beach ending at the edge of Bennett Lake.

Frost covered the bushes and trees on the dunes, and swirls of snow chased each other on the damp beach. The wind whistled as it swept down the valley, carrying the dust of other valleys, other mountains. Lauren breathed deeply. The air always smelled fresher here, which was just plain silly. It was the same air as back home. But even as a child she'd loved knowing that beyond those mountains were other mountains, with nothing for hundreds of miles but more mountains, and trees, and lakes.

Her parents had brought her to the Carcross beach many times over the summers. There were always lots of other kids to play with and she had spent hours building castles and dikes with Susie Martinelli.

Susie had died in the first wave of SARS, along with her parents and her little brother. She'd been eight years old. Lauren blew out a breath on a soft sigh.

Bennett Lake was almost thirty miles long. If she had a boat, she could travel to the southern tip of the lake and reach Bennett, where the Gold Rush stampeders had built their boats in a frantic attempt to get to Dawson's gold fields. From Bennett, it was just a short hike to Log Cabin and from there, to the Fantail Trail.

The wind whipped snow and sand in her face and she blinked. The water had always been too cold to spend much time in, but she had loved coming here with her parents. She remembered a rubber dinghy with mini paddles. Her dad had tied a long rope to it and waded in as far as he could go without getting hypothermic, allowing her to paddle out even farther, farther than anyone swam in the cold water.

A warm hand settled on her shoulder. She turned to find Gautier looking down at her, his cheeks ruddy with cold. "Special place?"

She smiled. "I used to come here as a kid. That's Bennett Lake." She nodded in the direction of the water.

"Looks like no one's lived here in a while," said Dante behind them.

Lauren looked around. Small cabins and summer homes had circled this end of the lake when she was young. Now all of them had fallen to the prevailing south wind.

Gautier's hand was still on her shoulder and he squeezed in mute sympathy before releasing her.

"I saw a boardwalk near the entrance to the village," he said. "If we can find long enough pieces, we should be able to cross the bridge."

She nodded. "Right," she said and turned her back on the lake.

* * *

The boardwalk had once been painted with a preservative and so had survived the extremes of Yukon winters with better grace than the building in front of which it stood.

Gautier and Dante had collected half a dozen boards, two by sixes, all warped.

Lauren didn't see how this would work but they seemed happy to have something to do, and they didn't need her help. If it worked, it would save them days.

She studied the faded sign that, miraculously, still hung on the board-and-batten siding of the long, low building.

VISITOR RECEPTION CENTRE

The centre used to have a big boat in it. Not that she knew how to sail. Or where she'd find sails. Still, she left the sounds of the men grunting with effort and the wood protesting, and wandered in through the open doorway, her footsteps echoing hollowly in the cavernous room. The building had lots of windows, all of which had a thick coat of mountain dust. The counter where the guides used to work still stood in the middle of the room. A huge, faded map covered in yellowed plastic was tacked to the wall next to the counter. Lauren wandered into the next room, where the boat had hung from wires. The wires still hung from the ceiling, swaying in the wind, no boat connected to them.

Someone else had had the same idea. She hoped they had reached their destination safely.

She wandered back to the main room and stopped in front of the map. It was a topographical map of southern Yukon and northwestern British Columbia. She spent long minutes studying the contours of the Fantail Trail. Near as she could tell, it was all pothole lakes. The trip overland would be a lot easier if the lakes were frozen.

As if in response to the thought, a massive shiver shook her body and she headed back outside into the sunshine.

Dante and Gautier were wrenching at yet another board, and every screech of rusted nail against frozen wood was another stab of pain in her head. She breathed deeply and headed to the truck for her canteen. Maybe she was dehydrated.

As she drank, she examined the dilapidated buildings across the street. The one on the left used to be Matthew Watson's General Store.

After every beach outing, they would round out their visit with an ice cream cone from the General Store. She smiled at the memory. Her favorite flavor had been bubble gum.

"Okay," called Gautier. "I think we've got enough."

She took another swallow of cold water and screwed the cap back onto the metal canteen. Then she went to help them load the boards onto the truck. Fifteen minutes later they were back at the bridge.

"I think it's safe to drive right up to the gap," said Gautier.

"All right," nodded Lauren, behind the wheel. "But first, the two of you get out."

Dante looked at her blankly but Gautier frowned. He looked at her over the top of Dante's head.

"I'll drive," he said.

She almost gave in right then to stop the coming argument in its tracks. But headache or no headache, it was her decision.

"My truck," she said.

"My call," he replied.

She frowned. "How do you figure?"

"I'm the one who thinks the bridge is safe. Nobody else should have to pay if I'm wrong."

"I'm the one who wants to take the bridge in the first place," she pointed out.

"Oh, for the love of St. Bernards and little children!" Dante glared at each of them in turn. "We'll all go. Now drive!"

* * *

The bridge shuddered slightly as she eased onto it, but the boards held.

So far, so good.

Lauren stopped five feet from the gap and they all piled out of the truck.

"All we need to do," said Gautier, hauling on four boards at the same time, "is lay a few across the narrowest part of the gap."

The narrowest part of the gap turned out to be seven feet wide. The longest boards were barely eight feet long.

"Doesn't give us much leeway," murmured Dante, after they had finished.

Lauren studied the planks. They looked safe enough, but there was no way to secure them at either end, or to each other. The minute she tried to drive onto the two-inch high planks, they would likely shift forward. With only six inches of overlap at either end, she didn't have room for mistakes.

And even if she managed to get on the six-inch wide planks, they could easily part and her wheels would end up in the gap. The truck might not fall through, but it would be stuck there.

She didn't want to have to walk all the way to Log Cabin. And even if it was on its last legs, she didn't want to lose the use of her truck any sooner than she had to.

On the other side of the gap, Gautier had been studying the situation, too. He looked at her, then at the truck. To her shock, he stepped onto a board and began to walk across.

"Geez, Gautier," said Dante, his voice strangled.

But Gautier kept his head down and his focus on the planks. As he approached the middle, the plank began to sag and Lauren held her breath. The wind tousled his brown hair and Lauren shivered again. The temperature was dropping.

Then he reached the middle of the plank and it sagged a good four inches, leaving the two ends precariously perched on the edges of the gap. Lauren swallowed hard. Three feet left. He was almost safe.

Then he pushed off too hard and the plank shifted sideways.

The next movements were so fast that Lauren had to reconstruct them later from her memories. The plank Gautier had been using slid off the bridge bed just as he stepped lightly onto the next one. It was shorter than the first, and his weight immediately pulled the end off the edge of the bridge. But by then he was only two feet from the pavement and Dante caught him as he leaped to safety.

"You friggin' idiot!" yelled Dante, shaking his arm.

Lauren was too busy watching the two planks twirl through the opening and into the river twenty feet below to tell Gautier what she thought of his little stunt.

"I weigh a hundred and seventy pounds," said Gautier grimly. "If the planks won't hold me, they sure as hell aren't going to hold the truck."

"We need to set up cross planks," said Lauren slowly. She tore her gaze away from the river. "To spread the weight out."

Dante and Gautier glanced at each other, then at her.

"That just might work," said Gautier, hurrying to the back of the truck. "But we don't have enough planks left."

"Then we'll get more," said Lauren. She got back into the truck and waited for the two of them to get in.

It took another half-hour, but finally the missing planks had been replaced and a series of planks were placed crosswise on top. Gautier crossed with no sagging or shifting of the planks.

They emptied the back of the truck, placing their packs and supplies on the far side of the bridge. Just in case.

Then they stood side by side, looking across the bridge to the Tagish Road that would lead them to Log Cabin, if only they could cross.

The headache was now a dull throb in the back of her head. Lauren glanced at the sky. Barely two hours of daylight left. They had wasted too much time on this bridge. Once they stopped for the night, she'd pull out the willow bark and make herself some tea.

The wind whistled through the spruce trees and Lauren controlled a shiver. In the time they had been here, the wind had shifted from south to east. She sniffed the air. It smelled like snow.

"Time to get going," she said, and turned toward the truck.

Gautier's hand shot out and grabbed her arm. "Lauren, I'll do the driving."

She saw the concern in his eyes and knew that he wasn't trying to imply that she was incapable. He just didn't want to see her hurt. She twisted her neck, trying to ease the tension in it.

"I know the truck better than anybody," she said softly. "I know where the clutch's sweet spot is, and how much gas is too much gas." She gently pulled her arm free.

"That doesn't guarantee that you'll make it," he said grimly.

Dante remained silent, for which Lauren was grateful. Between the headache and arguing with Gautier, she had no energy to spare.

"I stand the best chance," she said simply. "We need the truck or we're walking the whole way."

She could tell by the way Dante's mouth tightened that he had hoped she would change her mind if they lost the truck. But that wasn't an option. Losing the truck would only mean more hardship, not a change in plans.

Gautier looked like a man fighting a battle. He clearly didn't want her taking the risk, but he also couldn't argue with her logic.

"All right," he finally said, grimly. "Dante and I will stand on the cross plank at the edge, to try to minimize any shifting. Drive with your door open and be ready to jump out if the truck starts to fall through."

Lauren nodded, though she wasn't convinced jumping out would be safer than staying inside. Then she looked at him and something in her leapt in answer to the fierceness in his eyes.

If she fell, he would come after her, no matter what.

"All right, then," said Dante testily. "Let's do this."

Lauren turned slowly away from Gautier, held by his blue gaze. Finally she got into the truck and, keeping the door open, started the engine.

Dante and Gautier carefully walked around the hole and stationed themselves at either end of the last cross plank, their weight acting as an anchor.

Lauren hoped it would be enough.

She pulled the gear stick into second and slowly released the clutch. The truck rolled forward gently. She played with the clutch and accelerator, keeping the speed low. Three feet. Two.

And then a soft bump as the truck's bald tires reached and climbed over the first layer of planks. Before she could even begin to worry, the tires found the cross planks and easily climbed them.

Her front tires were now on the wooden planks. She rolled forward slowly, easing onto the bridge. One foot. Two.

She risked a glance at Gautier. His face was a mask of concentration as if he would get her across by willpower alone.

A loud groan of protest announced the wood's reluctance and Lauren suddenly wondered if the planks would stay put only to crack under the weight of the truck.

Her armpits were suddenly clammy. Three feet. The groaning grew louder. Lauren refused to look at Gautier and kept her gaze fixed on the yawning distance between her and the other side of the gap.

Four feet. She was in the middle of the gap, with the weight of the engine bearing down on the front wheels and the back wheels still on the bed of the bridge.

A loud crack sounded like a rifle shot and the right side of the truck lurched as a plank beneath the cross planks suddenly gave way.

In the same split second, Lauren looked up to see Gautier's ashen face. He started toward her, yelling something but she couldn't hear him over the series of subsequent cracks that rent the air. The truck shuddered as more planks began to give way and instinctively, Lauren floored the gas pedal and shouted over the sound of the engine. "Get out of the way!"

In the cracked rearview mirror, she saw cross planks spewing out from under her back wheels. Dante jumped out of the way as her front wheels found the cracked pavement of the bridge.

"Did it!" she shouted with glee.

Then her right rear tire fell through a gap in the planking, jerking the wheel out of her hands. The truck lurched to the right and the driver's door slammed shut. She looked up to see Dante staring at her in horror but she couldn't see Gautier.

Her first terrifying thought was that she had somehow run him over. Then a movement in her rearview mirror caught her eye and she looked up to see Gautier at the back of the truck. He caught her eye and nodded before putting his shoulder against the corner and pushing.

Lauren's heart squeezed in dread. The planks were giving way. He would fall through.

Then Dante was next to her and opening the door. "Come on!" he shouted. "Go!" And he braced himself against the frame of the truck and pushed.

Gritting her teeth, Lauren eased off the clutch and applied pressure on the gas pedal. The engine revved but the truck didn't move.

"Straighten your wheel," yelled Dante.

She turned the wheel until it was straight but still the truck didn't move.

"I'll have to rock it!" she said. Dante repeated it to Gautier and he nodded in the rearview mirror.

She put the truck in first gear, then as gently as she could, she eased off the clutch and pressed on the accelerator. The truck strained forward. She pushed in the clutch and it rolled back amid ominous cracking.

Back and forth she rocked, with Dante and Gautier pushing with each forward movement.

"Almost had it that time!" Dante yelled as she rolled back. "Give it more gas."

Lauren nodded, not taking the energy to answer. Her head was going to explode. It was dangerous to try to go too fast, but it was even more dangerous to stay on the planking. So when the truck reached the end of its backward movement, she slipped it into second gear and pressed on the accelerator, giving it more gas.

The truck engine strained loudly as the bald rear tire scrabbled for purchase on the planks. She kept her foot on the accelerator, fighting with the steering wheel, and then the back wheel popped out of its hole and the truck surged forward.

Dante jumped out of the way and she saw movement in the rearview mirror as planks spewed away from her spinning wheels. Then the back tires were on the pavement and the truck off the planking. Ten feet beyond the gap, she stopped the truck and jumped out.

Dante was just picking himself up off the bridge beyond the gap, but Gautier was still on the planking, gingerly making his way toward safety.

Lauren held her breath as he picked his way over gaps in the cross planks. She couldn't tell how many of the original planks were left beneath the cross planks. And of those, how many the weight of the truck had damaged past safety.

Almost there. Another three feet and he'd be safe.

Gautier looked up at her and grinned.

Then the cross plank he stood on broke in two and he plunged twenty feet to the frigid waters of the Natasaheeni River.

❧ NINE ✦

G AUTIER!" shouted Dante. He raced to the railing and looked down.

"He's alive!" He ran for the other side of the bridge, heading for the riverbank.

Lauren was already at the truck. She wasted precious seconds scrabbling around the back of the truck before she finally found the yellow nylon rope.

She jumped off the back and ran as fast as she could down the slope to the riverbank while trying to find Gautier in the water.

There! His dark head bobbed up to the surface and his arms struck out as he began to swim for shore. Already his movements were growing sluggish.

As she ran, she untied the rope and worked to fashion a noose. The ground was slick with moisture and ice and she had to work while watching her steps.

How long had he been in the water? Thirty seconds? The fall alone could have killed him. If they could get him out in the next few minutes, he might stand a chance.

The river was short, barely long enough to separate Nares Lake from Bennett Lake, and the current wasn't very fast. They might be able to get far enough ahead of him to throw him the rope.

She glanced at the man in the river and her heart sank. Even if he caught the rope, his hands would be too cold to hang on to it.

Dante was already a hundred feet ahead of her. He was trying to intercept Gautier's path. She glanced up the river and saw nothing—no branch, no spit of land, not even a log they could use to reach him.

If Dante jumped into the water to rescue Gautier, then she'd have two hypothermic men to deal with. If they didn't drown first.

"Dante!" she screamed. The water flowed by almost silently, full of death. "Wait!" He didn't even glance back at her.

She ran as fast as she could, leaping over deadfalls and rocks, avoiding obvious ice patches. The edges of the river were already icing over. As she ran, she kept an eye on Gautier, who struggled against the current to reach shore. He was still fifty feet away. He wouldn't last much longer.

"I have a rope!" she cried to Dante as she finally caught up to him. He nodded and grabbed the end with the noose.

"I'll go in," insisted Lauren, tugging on the rope. "You're stronger, you can pull me back in!" And as a woman, she had more body fat, more insulation against the killing cold.

Dante ignored her and yanked the rope out of her hands. He slipped the noose open and shrugged it over his head and onto his waist. Gautier was rapidly approaching.

Dante tossed her the other end of the rope. "Tie it around a tree and get ready to haul," he said.

Then he stepped into the river, cracking through the thin ice at the edge and slipping on wet, icy rocks. Cursing his stubbornness, Lauren scrambled to find a big enough tree to wrap the rope around. She found one and barely had time to wrap the rope twice around it before it suddenly grew taut as the current caught Dante and pulled him in. Lauren almost felt him gasp as the cold bit into him.

She tied off the rope and followed it back at a run to the water's edge. Dante floated, tethered to the rope, forty feet from shore. His hands were outstretched, as if reaching for something, but Lauren couldn't see anything in the fast flowing waters.

Gautier had disappeared.

Then Dante dove and almost immediately resurfaced holding Gautier by the collar.

Lauren grabbed the yellow rope and hauled.

It took forever, but with Dante kicking and half-swimming, she managed to pull them in close to shore. She dropped the rope and grabbed Gautier by his sodden coat and hauled him out of the water. As Dante crawled out of the river, she dropped to her knees next to Gautier and felt for a pulse in his neck.

"B-b-b-breathing?" chattered Dante.

She nodded then pulled Gautier completely out of the water. Dante stood on tottering legs, fumbling with the rope around his waist. His hands were shaking so much that Lauren batted them away and pulled the noose loose.

Then she looked at his face and saw that she didn't have much time. He already looked confused.

"Dante!" She shook him by the shoulders. "Help me get Gautier to the truck."

He nodded as if he understood and walked stiffly to where Gautier lay unconscious on the cold ground.

In the end, she carried Gautier by the head and shoulders while Dante carried his legs. Her choice was justified when Dante dropped Gautier's legs twice on the way up the slope to the truck. She dragged Gautier the last fifty feet when Dante dropped to his knees and then curled up on the ground.

The wind had picked up, chilling the exposed flesh of her hands and face, leaching the life from Gautier and Dante.

Hurryhurryhurryhurryhurry.

She got Gautier to the truck and left him on the ground while she found his backpack and hauled things out of it until she found a change of clothes. Then she spent ten minutes getting him out of his wet clothes and into dry ones. She didn't find another pair of boots, but there were two pairs of woolen socks in the bottom of the pack. She put them both on him. Then she opened the truck's passenger door and spent five minutes pushing and pulling his dead weight inside. Finally he lay on the truck's seat and she wrapped a woolen blanket around him, covering his head, and topped it all off with the dirty tarp she kept in the back.

Then she ran back down the slope to get Dante.

* * *

C-c-c-cold...

Gautier slowly became aware that he was shivering, his teeth chattering, his body shaking with the effort to generate heat.

He had dim memories of being forced to drink something warm and sweet, of falling, of water.

So cold...

A weight lifted from his groin, only to be replaced by another, this one blissfully warm. Then someone moved his arm and something scraped on wood. When his arm was shifted back, he found something warm in his armpit.

He slept again.

* * *

When he woke up, his first thought was that his bladder was full. He was still shivering, but not like before. Somewhere nearby, a fire was crackling lustily, releasing faint odors of wood smoke, wet wool, and burning resin.

He opened his eyes to flickering firelight and spent a few moments adjusting. A log ceiling glowed ruddy above him and he seemed to be in a big room with oversized furniture—a leather couch that mice had dined on, a big wooden rocking chair, two love seats with tufts of stuffing poking out of huge rips in the fabric. Everything else was lost to shadows.

His perspective seemed all wrong and it took him a minute to realize he was lying on a table, next to a wood stove with the door open.

He had never been so cold in his life. He felt as if he had swallowed half the river and it had turned to ice inside him.

He tried to shift himself up to one elbow, but his hands seemed to belong to someone else.

Something scraped on the wood floor beside him and he started. Then a hand grabbed his shoulder and pushed him back down.

"Gently," said Lauren.

Gautier looked up to find her smiling down at him. Her dark hair was tousled and knotted, her cheekbones jutted prominently, and her eyes looked like two piss holes in the snow.

"Jesus, Lauren," he said. "You look like hell."

Her eyebrows rose and the smile grew lopsided. "The pot calling the kettle black." She turned and Gautier realized there was another rocking chair next to the table, with a small side table next to it. From the small table she took a chipped cup and brought it to him.

"You need to drink some more," she said. "I'll help you sit up."

Lauren pulled the blankets off him and only then did Gautier notice the weights at his armpits and on his chest and belly.

"Hot rocks, wrapped in rags," explained Lauren as she set them to one side. "You've got one on your crotch, too."

Gautier reached down. Sure enough, something hard and heavy rested on his groin. He pushed it off and it fell with a muted *thunk* onto the table. He noticed with relief that his hand sensed the residual warmth in the cloth-wrapped rock.

He felt colder for the absence of the blankets and the rocks but refused to let Lauren help him up. It took a while, but he finally pushed himself into a sitting position on the table, keeping one hand on the table as a brace. His heart beat sluggishly and he thought of cold blood pumping through a half-frozen heart.

To give himself time to recover, he sniffed the contents of the cup she handed him—water sweetened with honey—and had a sudden memory of being spoon fed the liquid.

How long had he been out? And then the memories finally kicked in and he looked around the room, twisting his head to look over his shoulder.

"Where's Dante?" he asked sharply. The fool had jumped in after him. Of all the stupid—

"Getting more wood," said Lauren calmly.

Relief washed over him, warmer than the fire, sweeter than the honey.

"You have to drink some more," said Lauren. "Your body needs the calories."

But Gautier's bladder warned him off and he shook his head.

"First things first," he said, and swung his legs off the table. Only he couldn't catch himself in time, and if Lauren hadn't grabbed the back of his shirt, he would have fallen right off the table. He sat on the edge, feet dangling in midair, and waited for the world to stop spinning.

Lauren set the cup down and carefully edged around the table, keeping a grip on Gautier's shirt. "Need to pee?"

Gautier nodded, then wished he hadn't. "Like a horse."

Lauren nodded. "So did Dante. I've been feeding you both sweet water for hours." She looked around the room. "I can bring you a container."

Gautier shifted the blankets around until they covered his shoulders and he could hold them closed in front. His hands felt stiff, clumsy, and clammy.

He needed to examine himself for frostbite and see what damage the river had done, but first...

"I am going to do it standing up outside, Lauren, like my father before me and his father before him."

Lauren laughed and Gautier looked more closely at her. He'd never heard her laugh before, and there was a hysterical edge to the laugh that made him uneasy.

She helped him slide off the table and kept an arm around his waist while he found his balance. His feet were slabs of meat that belonged to someone else.

He remembered her running alongside the river, her face a mask of determination.

"I don't remember how I got out of the river," he said, as they shuffled away from the light and warmth of the wood stove. His feet were beginning to tingle. He hoped that meant circulation was being restored and not that frostbite had damaged them. He had to look down to know that he was wearing socks. They headed for the kitchen and a door that presumably led outside. Two fat candles squatted on a debris-covered counter. In the middle of the kitchen floor lay their backpacks, all of them open and leaning against one another.

"Dante jumped in after you," she said, holding him tightly. Her small body was compact and lean, and she was much stronger than she had a right to be.

"I remember that part. How did we get out?"

At that moment, the door opened and the candles flickered in the sudden draft. Dante came in, his arms full of split wood, and closed the door with his foot. When he turned around he saw Gautier and Lauren.

"What are you doing up?" he said sharply.

"Going to pee," said Gautier, trying to suppress his shivers.

"You can pee in a bucket." Dante frowned and looked at Lauren. Gautier shrugged and let go of Lauren's shoulders.

"Did you?"

Dante looked away and Lauren laughed, again with that edge. At the sound, Dante looked at her. Gautier couldn't read his expression.

"Let me drop this wood off and I'll help you."

Gautier sighed. "Look, you two. I've been peeing on my own for almost thirty years. Now I'm going to walk out that door and do it before my bladder explodes. When I come back, you can fill me in."

He could feel their gazes on him as he carefully shuffled to the door. He fumbled with the handle but finally got the door open. Cold air drove all other thoughts out of his head. He gathered the blanket more tightly around himself and closed the door.

Under a sliver of a moon and a wash of stars, he saw that he stood on a porch that ran the length of the cabin. It had been well built, and as far as he could tell, didn't sag anywhere. Beyond the porch, trees reached for the sky with dark, rattling, skeletal fingers. He looked up at the roof to see smoke from the chimney flattening out against the sky. An easterly wind, stronger than in the afternoon.

Somewhere behind the cabin, close, the river rushed by. The sound made him even colder.

He headed for the railing at the far corner, braced himself against a sturdy post holding up the porch roof, and pissed for what seemed like an eternity. Somewhere nearby an owl hooted. Farther away, coyotes yipped.

Finally he finished and turned away from the ghostly night. Before he could reach the door, it opened and Dante helped him back inside.

While Lauren prepared food for them, Dante filled him in. Dante had saved his life by jumping into the river—stupid, stupid, stupid—but Lauren had saved both their lives by getting them into dry clothes and to shelter.

"You recovered fast," said Gautier, staring at his friend.

Dante nodded. "I wasn't in the water as long as you were."

Gautier glanced at Lauren, who had her back to them at the wood stove, stirring something that smelled a lot like stew. Even though he knew he needed the nutrition, he didn't think his stomach could handle food right now.

"How did you know about this place?" he asked her.

"I didn't," said Lauren. She glanced at him over her shoulder, her eyes dark sockets, her cheeks drawn. But her voice was normal enough when she spoke. "I drove 'til I found a side road and followed it until the first driveway. This was cottage country for people from Whitehorse."

Gautier yawned suddenly and the yawn stole the last of his energy. All he wanted to do was crawl into the wood stove and sleep. As though guessing how close he was to passing out, Lauren immediately poured something from the pot into a metal cup and handed it to him.

"It's broth," she explained. "It'll give you calories and help warm you up inside. Drink it, then get some more sleep."

Gautier obediently sipped at the broth while Lauren dished out the more substantial stew for herself and Dante. It tasted wonderful and he guessed it was a caribou broth.

In the end, Dante gently took the half-empty cup from his fingers and led him back to the table next to the wood stove. Lauren wrapped woolen blankets around him, covering his head but keeping a breathing hole free. With the broth warming him inside, and the fire warming him outside, Gautier dropped into sleep like a stone in a river.

* * *

The voices came flying at her out of the darkness like black-winged birds. Lauren flinched in her sleep as voice after voice cried out for her attention. Then the voices turned to snatches of memories, other lives lived, some recognizably modern, in big cities, others primitive and alien. The voices and memories filled her brain until there was no room left for her, the Lauren who was born and raised in the Yukon, who lived in a cabin, who was searching for her mother.

Lauren reached for and clung to the concept of mother, suddenly sure that she was no longer dreaming but in a fight for survival. Her hands flailed at the air, trying to push the images and voices away.

"Lauren!" Another voice, different from the others. "Lauren, wake up!"

Oh, God. She *was* awake. The images faded but the voices continued to clamor for her attention—a babble that filled her head to cracking.

Suddenly she was hauled up and a small part of her identified that she had been sleeping on the floor and was now sitting in a chair. She opened her eyes. Dante was leaning over her, his eyes fathomless and dark in the pale moonlight filtering through the filthy windows.

Someone was moaning—*she* was moaning.

"Gautier," said Dante, and even in her distress she heard the urgency in his voice. "Let's get her outside."

She closed her eyes again, and someone pulled her hands away from her hair. Then she was outside. She gasped at the shock of the below zero temperature and emerged from the nightmare just enough to realize the voices were receding. She gulped the cold air greedily. Her cheeks felt wet with tears.

Someone wrapped a blanket around her and she found herself seated on the stairs of the porch, staring at the waving branches of the trees and the millions of stars in the cloudless sky.

When she finally looked down, Gautier was standing in front of her on the ground, his big hands hanging by his sides as if he couldn't figure out what to do with them.

"Better?" asked Dante, and she realized he was crouching by her side on the stairs.

She drew a shuddering breath. The voices were still there. Only the cold on her hands and bare feet kept them at bay.

"Listen to me, Lauren," said Dante. He took her hand and squeezed it to draw her attention.

"Voices," she said thinly. Her own voice sounded far away.

"I know," he said.

"What's she talking about?" demanded Gautier. He sounded angry. Another angry voice.

"Shh," said Dante. "I'm trying to help her."

"Make them stop!" Her voice rose on the last word, a quavering weak thing that she didn't even recognize as hers.

"Listen!" He pinched her arm, hard.

"Don't!" she protested and tried to pull her arm away. But the voices receded.

"What the hell—?" That was Gautier.

Distraction helped. If she focused on something else, the voices grew more muted.

"That's it," said Dante encouragingly. "You have to learn to keep them behind the door, or they'll drive you crazy."

He knew. He knew *exactly* what she was going through.

"What are they?" she whispered. Her hands clutched his as if he would keep her from drowning.

"They're your ancestors," he said. "Their memories, their essence. You're connected to them."

Lauren shivered massively. She wanted to drop his hands but they were the only things keeping her from sinking into terror.

As if guessing her thoughts, Dante squeezed her hands even harder.

"Look at me," he ordered.

She looked at him. The voices rose louder and she groaned, squeezing her eyes shut once again.

"Lauren!"

His sharp tone brought her eyes open once more.

"Think of one word and keep repeating it."

What? What did he want? She blinked, trying to make sense of the whirl of her senses. Too much. Too—

A sharp slap across her cheek brought her back. In the moment of lucidity, she saw Gautier looming threateningly over Dante, holding the smaller man's arm as if to keep him from hitting her again.

"I know you're trying to help her," said Gautier softly, "but if you hit her again, so help me, I'm going to deck you."

"There's no time for this!" Dante sounded exasperated. "If you want to help her, stay out of my way!" He pulled his arm out of Gautier's grip and dropped to his knees in front of Lauren.

"Have you ever meditated?" he asked, looking into her eyes. His face was less than six inches away, as if he wanted her to focus on him.

Lauren shook her head. Another massive shudder shook her and she realized that her feet were blocks of ice. Her teeth began to chatter.

She could almost feel Gautier chafing to pick her up and take her back inside, but he stood back.

"You need to focus on one thing. Visualize an object and keep your mind focused on it. Or a word and keep repeating it."

What? What did he want?

Dante grabbed her by the shoulders and shook her. "You have *got* to try! Lauren!"

Maybe if she tried he'd stop harassing her. An object. Her gaze flitted around the dark yard. Trees. Stars. A rusted wheelbarrow hulking in the shadows. Her truck.

The truck reminded her of Cade, and thinking of Cade made her think of her mother's hair band. She closed her eyes and saw it again, the moose-hide smooth and dark from years of use, the primroses etched in green and pink, the blue beads edging both sides of the band. She could almost feel the cool beads between her fingers, the soft tanned leather warm and worn.

"That's it," whispered Dante.

The voices receded behind the image and for the first time since she woke up, Lauren could think clearly. Whatever was happening to her was connected to Dante somehow. She desperately wanted to demand answers, but didn't dare open her eyes or speak in case she lost her focus.

Oh, God. What if the voices never went away?

"Shh," whispered Dante. He rubbed her freezing hands with his.

She didn't know how long she had been outside, but the temperature was well below zero and she had nothing on but her long johns and a long-sleeved shirt under the blanket.

Gautier was obviously thinking along the same lines.

"We have to get her inside," he said. "She's freezing."

But Lauren wanted answers more than she wanted warmth. If they went back inside, the voices might come back and she'd have to work harder at keeping them at bay.

"Not yet," she said, shivering. She opened her eyes, keeping the hair band to the forefront of her mind. The voices surged and she struggled not to panic. She breathed deeply, aware of each cold breath as it entered her lungs, warmed to her body temperature, and left. If she remained calm, the voices were easier to control.

After a moment, she became aware that Gautier was crouched by her side and putting something on her feet—her mukluks. She hadn't seen him leave.

Then he draped another blanket around her and she closed her eyes in bliss as warmth began to seep back into her frozen body.

In that unguarded moment, the voices rose up again and she spent a few grim minutes focusing on the hair band before she could trust herself to open her eyes.

Finally she looked at Dante, still crouched next to her.

"Explain," she said shortly. In the starlight, his hair looked inky and his eyes were pools of blackness. For a moment his face looked strange, and she remembered that forty-eight hours earlier, she hadn't even known of his existence. She knew nothing about him, or about Gautier.

Yet Gautier stood next to her, his presence a comfort, where Dante's filled her with anxiety.

Dante rocked back on his heels and she had a sudden image of hundreds of Dantes through the ages rocking back in just that way, in front of a campfire. She shook her head and refocused, keeping her mother's hair band firmly in mind as she waited for him to speak.

"What did you mean," said Gautier slowly, "when you said her ancestors were responsible?" He took a quick breath and she flashed to the sound of Mary's breathing, so shallow and slow. Again she shook her head. Focus.

"You said they were her memories," prompted Gautier when Dante hesitated. "What the hell is going on, Dante?"

His voice sounded strange, even to her, and she realized that he was as upset as she was.

Dante blew out a sigh and stood up, apparently deciding that she could handle herself for now. He descended the last two steps, walked a few feet, then turned around and walked back to them.

"Not *her* memories," he said. Then he stopped and looked down at the frozen ground.

Out of the corner of her eye, Lauren caught a movement and flinched but it was only a poplar tree bending in the wind. The bulk of the house protected them from the worst of the wind, but she shivered again as cold fingers found the gap between the blanket and the back of her neck.

"I know they're not my memories," she finally said. She stared at Dante. "Just tell me." She balled her hands on her lap. "Tell me what's going on. Tell me how *you* know what's going on."

Dante glanced up at Gautier standing next to her, and Lauren felt Gautier's flinch. Only then did she understand Dante's reluctance.

He doesn't want to talk in front of Gautier.

Gautier made a small noise, as if he was going to say something, but before he could, Lauren spoke up.

"It's too late for secrets," she told Dante grimly. "You'll have to tell him, too."

After a moment, Dante nodded, as if he had known it all along.

"All right," he said softly. He looked straight at Gautier, as if he wanted to say something else, then he sighed again and looked back down at Lauren.

"I know what you're going through because I went through it myself, at puberty."

Gautier's hand squeezed her shoulder gently and he moved away. She immediately felt colder for his absence. But he walked behind Dante to sit down next to her on the step. His shoulder and thigh touched hers, warming her.

"What, exactly, did you go through?" he asked.

Dante took a deep breath and looked down at his bare hands.

"It's called the Transition," he said softly. "It's the time when the body reaches physical maturity—puberty—and the mind is ready to open. You begin to dream of the past, of lives you haven't lived. You hear voices—faintly at first, but then more loudly the deeper into puberty you go. But you've had training all your life in meditation, in focusing, and you know what to do. It's not frightening. It's a time of great celebration."

Lauren and Gautier stared at him. The voices in her head murmured like the wind through pine trees and she relaxed her focus enough to speak.

"Dante, I'm almost 21. I reached menarche at 13."

He nodded, unsurprised. "Most of our girls reach menarche at around 15 or 16," he said. "But you're not a full-blooded gaian. Your father was a sapiens."

She had no idea what to say to something like that. Neither did Gautier, apparently. They both stared at Dante for long seconds.

"Okay, I'll bite," said Gautier finally, his voice grim. "What's a sapiens?"

Dante hesitated.

This is it, thought Lauren in curious anticipation. *This is the part he doesn't want to share with Gautier.*

"Homo sapiens," said Dante at last. He looked directly at his friend. "Like you."

Gautier's head jerked back as if he'd been hit. His breathing grew shallower. Lauren's mouth opened as if to pant.

Homo sapiens.

Saps?

Cade had called Mary and Charlie saps. As if they were something other than he was.

"If my father was a... a sapiens," she said, working hard at staying calm, "then what was my mother?"

"She was Homo gaians," said Dante. "Like me."

Gautier shook his head as if to clear it. He leaned toward Dante, his hands on his knees. "You mean like worshipers of Gaia? The ancient goddess?" He sounded baffled, and Lauren couldn't blame him.

Dante was crazy. Somewhere in one of her mother's books, she might even find a name for his kind of crazy. Why had she thought this stranger could help her?

"No, Gautier," said Dante firmly. "This isn't a religion. At least, not the way you think it is."

"Are you trying to tell me that you're an alien, then?"

She could tell by Gautier's voice that he really wanted to believe Dante was joking.

Dante's tone was gentle. "No more than you are. We're just another species. Cousins. We have the same ancestors—near as I can figure out, somewhere around Homo erectus our paths branched off."

Lauren stared at Dante in disbelief. For a moment, the voices were pushed back as she focused on his words.

"Different species."

Dante nodded.

"You look pretty human to me."

Dante sighed. "I am human, Lauren. Gaians are just a different branch of humanity, that's all."

Lauren glanced sideways at Gautier. He frowned at his friend, as if trying to guess what game he was playing. But Lauren could hear voices murmuring in the back of her mind. And Cade—Cade had called Mary and Charlie saps.

"The voices," she prodded. "How can they be other people's memories?"

Dante began to pace in front of them, as if he could no longer stay still. Or maybe he couldn't stand to look at the suspicion in Gautier's face any more.

"Your direct line of ancestors," he said. "Every gaians is connected in this way. Our parents, their parents, their parents' parents..." He waved a hand loosely at the sky. "Not frame for frame, of course. More like emotional memory. For as far back as we go. We call this pool of memory the underworld." He stopped and looked directly at her. "It's our greatest strength, Lauren. It's how we learn, how we stay hidden among the sapiens."

Gautier's sharp intake of breath told her that this hit hard. He was no doubt wondering if his friend was insane or—and she couldn't decide if this was worse—telling the truth.

Either way, it was going to affect their friendship.

"Usually," continued Dante, "a gaians' special ability manifests at this time, too."

Special abilities. Different branches of humanity. Underworlds. The words swirled in her mind, making no sense at all.

"It must be so hard for you," he said softly. "I can't understand why your mother didn't tell you any of this."

"Because it's all a crock of shit?" asked Gautier angrily. He stood up, towering over Dante and Lauren. "This is a pretty sick game, Dante." A breeze ruffled his singed hair.

A few hours ago she had feared for his life. He was still in no shape to be out in the cold. She stood up too. "We can talk about this in the morning." She glanced at the night sky. A good four hours before it was light enough to drive. "I'm going inside."

* * *

Gautier listened to Lauren tossing and turning on her pallet. Dante was rolled up in his blanket at the far end of the room, his back to the wood stove, and to Gautier.

Gautier couldn't sleep. Dante's fantastic story kept playing through his mind and he kept trying to fit facts into the fantasy, to poke holes in it.

After an hour, he realized he wouldn't be sleeping any more tonight and rose from his spot on the other side of the wood stove from Lauren.

She murmured in her sleep, as if she was talking to someone, and the small hairs on the back of his neck stood up.

He dressed warmly and let himself out into the night.

❧ TEN ❧

THE SUN had yet to rise over the mountains when Silas finally reached Whitehorse. He stopped the four-wheeler at the top of a road that descended into the valley. Tendrils of smoke rose like gray wraiths from still-invisible chimneys.

The road was obviously well-tended. Potholes had been filled with small stones. Broken asphalt had been pushed to one side and a detour cleared to avoid a disintegrated section of the road. From the tracks he guessed that the road got more four-legged than four-wheeled traffic.

The breeze carried wood smoke to him from the valley. There was even the faint odor of bacon frying. Someone was up.

A coyote trotted out of the trees bordering the highway and stood blinking at him in surprise. A raven cawed loudly in the silence and was answered from far below.

Before the compulsion to turn around and follow the road south to Ben-My-Chree could take him over, he pushed the starter button and headed into the valley. The solar-powered battery ran the engine silently.

This was the likely place to learn about his granddaughter's fate. Meridy had been clear about the friends who would have taken Lauren in. Mary and Charlie Sproule.

The four-wheeler, though silent, vibrated beneath him and already his hands felt numb. At least the vibrations kept him warm. Artificial shivering.

The Yukon River cut through the valley. The closer he got to the valley floor, the louder the sound of the river became. About halfway down, he spotted the bleached blue remnants of a massive building. A faded pink and white sign that read "Yukon Energy" hung askew from the siding.

The power company building had hidden a dam, which the river had breached many years ago. Now the river raged through a narrow canyon, frothing and foaming until the canyon widened and the river calmed itself.

Clay cliffs, some of which had crumbled and taken homes with them, surrounded Whitehorse. The road ended suddenly in a T and he stopped again to look around. To his right, the T dead-ended at the river. A bridge had once connected both sides of the river, but had probably been taken out when the dam broke. On the other side of the river, a large building with broken windows and a sagging roof emerged from the gloom. It looked like a school.

Silas turned left and followed the disintegrating road past what had once been the long, low territorial government building—according to a carved and split wooden sign—with its attached library. A small part of him longed to enter the building, just to see if any books still survived.

As he drove, he looked for signs of life, sniffing for the scent of his grandson. He took side streets whenever he could, looking for a house that was inhabited.

The sun finally crested the mountains, bathing the valley in soft shadows and a pink glow. It almost tricked him into thinking that it was suddenly warmer, but the tingling in his cheeks told him otherwise.

The streets he followed were—or had been—residential. Many of the homes had fallen in on themselves. Some had burned down long ago. By the lingering stink, one had burned down recently.

Amid the wrecks, the few inhabited homes stood out like the living among the dead. Still, all the houses he passed, inhabited or not, remained dark. In spite of the aroma of bacon, which, now that he was in the town proper, seemed to have disappeared, the good citizens of Whitehorse apparently saw no reason to rise early.

Finally he caught a movement out of the corner of his eye and turned to see someone walking in the growing light. It was a woman, wearing worn jeans and a ragged wool sweater.

She walked quickly, head down, from a dark house to an outhouse perhaps thirty feet away. Her arms were crossed in front of her to conserve heat.

Silas stopped the four-wheeler and turned the engine off. He got off and waited politely for her to finish. When she emerged, he cleared his throat gently.

The woman jumped and whirled, her expression startled but not fearful. That alone told Silas that this place had recovered well from the Troubles.

"I'm sorry to startle you, Ma'am," he said. He smiled the easy smile of an inoffensive old man. "I'm looking for someone who is supposed to live in Whitehorse."

The woman approached tentatively. It occurred to Silas that there wouldn't be many strangers this far north.

"Who you lookin' for?" Her voice was deeper than he had expected. Nor was she as young as he'd first thought. At least forty, maybe older.

"Her name is Lauren Tom," he said and the woman nodded in recognition.

At that moment, a man emerged from the back of the house, still buttoning his pants. It was obvious from the ruffled hair and the pillow creases still stamped on his face that their voices had awakened him and he'd come outside to check.

"Everything okay, Sherry?" his voice was rough with contained concern and Silas immediately warmed to him.

"He's lookin' for the Tom girl," said the woman. They both

turned to look at him, their faces frank with curiosity.

Silas bided his time. In spite of his impatience to get going, he understood their curiosity.

"I think she's gone," said the man. He ran a hand through his hair, smoothing it. Silas noticed for the first time that he was barefoot and his respect for the man increased. He hadn't even taken the time to slip on his shoes before checking that his woman was safe.

"Gone where?" he asked.

The man shook his head. "Don't know for sure. You'd best talk to Charlie. He'll know more."

Silas obtained directions to Charlie's place and left the couple staring after him, an odd expression on their faces. In less than a minute, he was in front of the house they had described, a two-story affair with gables and a wrap-around porch. Even dilapidated and in need of repair, it stood out among its abandoned and smaller neighbors.

There was a light on in the front window, so Silas walked up to the door and knocked. An old man of Oriental extraction answered and Silas asked to see Charlie.

The old man stared at him for a moment, then politely stepped aside to let him in.

Silas nodded his thanks and stepped into a warm kitchen. A town where women weren't frightened of strange men and people opened their homes to strangers. Lauren could have done worse than grow up here.

The smell of dog filled the kitchen. A Samoyed, big for the breed, came to stand next to the man, who placed a hand on the dog's head. Silas turned at a sound by the wood stove and saw a black lab, smaller than the Samoyed, lying on the floor by the stove. As the dog struggled to stand, Silas noticed that he had a bandage wrapped around his chest.

"Rupe, down," said another man as he came into the kitchen. He frowned at the lab until the dog lay his head back down with a resigned sigh.

The newcomer looked older than Meridy's memory of him, but he was unmistakably Charlie Sproule. An odor of ash and grief clung to him and there was pain in his eyes. Silas' heart squeezed in fear. Did the pain involve Lauren?

"Mr. Sproule." Silas held his hand out and Charlie automatically shook it. It that brief touch, Silas sensed an unutterable weariness.

"I don't know you," said Charlie, retrieving his hand. "How do you know me?" The questions were direct, but not aggressive, and the look Charlie gave him was curious. And worried.

"It's a long story," said Silas. The other man had disappeared into a back room, taking the Samoyed with him, but Silas could almost feel him straining to hear their conversation.

He hesitated for a moment and finally decided to tell Sproule as much of the truth as he could. "My name is Silas MacGregor. I'm Meridy's father."

Charlie Sproule's face went from surprise and curiosity to anger, fear, and suspicion. He studied Silas in silence for a few minutes and Silas stood in the warm kitchen, enduring the inspection. This man and his wife had looked after Meridy when she was alive, and likely Lauren after Meridy died. At the very least, he owed him the courtesy of waiting while he made up his mind.

"What are you doing here?" Sproule finally asked.

Silas hesitated for just a moment. "I've come for Lauren," he said. "I believe she's in danger."

Sproule suddenly looked older, as if all the wrinkles in his face had grown deeper.

"That I already knew," he told Silas grimly. "You'd better sit down."

An hour later, Silas and Charlie stood outside Arnold Chiang's house. Silas had some of Chiang's caribou jerky and half a loaf of heavy bread wrapped in cloth and stored in the containers strapped to the four-wheeler. He was full of sweet tea and sadness. He had never met Mary Sproule, but she had been a friend, whether or not she knew it. Charlie Sproule had lost home, wife, and foster daughter in one twenty-four hour period.

All because of a rogue obeah.

"You'll bring her back safely?" asked Sproule.

Silas climbed onto the four-wheeler and looked at Sproule.

"I can't promise that," he said. "I can promise that I will do everything I can to make sure she's safe. Whatever she decides to do, I'll get word to you about her."

Sproule stared at him for a long time, then nodded, satisfied. He was too old and had seen too much to believe in empty promises.

* * *

Every time she closed her eyes and tried to sleep, the voices swelled, filling her awareness, making her head ache. Lauren tossed and turned on her hard bed, aware that Gautier and Dante were tip-toeing in and out of the cabin. It only added to her irritation.

She didn't want all these people inside her head! She wanted to be herself again—alone and private. She'd always been self-sufficient. Now it seemed she would never be able to make a decision again without the input of every single one of her ancestors.

No, that wasn't quite right. It wasn't opinions she was getting. It was more like emotional echoes. Mostly the voices were a cacophony of noise, a roar of emotions, with an occasional spike of emotion or even a snatch of visuals, like a waking dream or being in a noisy crowd and catching a snippet of someone's conversation.

This must be a little bit what it was like to grow up in a big family. All those people around all the time, butting in, and being unable to shut them out. Some of her friends had come from big families—up to five kids.

As frustrating as those big families had been to her friends, they had also been a comfort. It occurred to her that always having someone to turn to for advice might be nice, if she could learn to shut it off when she didn't want it.

And surely among all those ancestors there were a few who would like her and be rooting for her.

As her attitude softened, she realized that the voices had calmed down. She had stopped resisting them, and they had stopped forcing themselves on her.

A wave of approval swept over her, warm and welcoming.

She sat up abruptly, her eyes wide, barely noticing the morning light bathing the room.

The approval had been in response to her thoughts. She was sure of it. How could that be? These... ancestors... they were dead—how could they be reacting to her?

The door opened and she looked up to see Dante framed by the doorway.

"They're alive, aren't they? The ancestors?" she asked.

But Dante shook his head. He came into the kitchen and closed the door behind him. "Not in the sense that you're alive, no. But their essence, the parts of them that defined who they were— their experiences and emotions—those survive in the underworld."

Nothing in her parents' books had given her a basis for understanding Dante, but she groped for a comparison. "Do you mean hell?"

"No." Dante shook his head again and walked over to where she sat on the floor by the wood stove. "Not hell, unless it's one of your own making." He sighed at the look on her face and tried again. "I'm going by what Grandfather's told me. He knows more about the underworld than most other gaians." His gaze flickered away from hers and she knew there was something he wasn't telling her. "In the underworld, as in this world, you gravitate toward like-minded souls. If you loved laughing and sunlight in life, then those are the ancestors you will seek and who will seek you out in the underworld."

"What if you were a bad person?" asked Lauren.

"Like Cade?" asked Dante softly. "Then you'll end up with other bad souls."

"Cade?" asked Lauren, startled. "Cade is... gaians?" The word stuck on her tongue.

It was Dante's turn to look surprised. He nodded. "Yes, he's half-gaians, just like you."

Lauren disentangled herself from her blankets and got up, more unsettled than she wanted to show. As she folded her blankets into a bedroll, she considered everything she had learned.

"Do you feel me?" she asked abruptly. She turned in time to catch the surprise on his face.

"Excuse me?"

"Every time you come near me," she explained, tying the bedroll tight, "I feel you like a humming in my belly."

Dante stared at her for a long moment, then he nodded. "Certain gifts run in some gaians families, like an affinity for healing, or a strong sense of weather. In ours, we're sensitive to other gaians. Some gaians, like Grandfather, are even sensitive to sapiens." He held his hand up to forestall her questions. "Usually it's only members of our family that we feel. I feel you, too," he said, "but the gift is very strong in me. I feel the emotions of nearby gaians, whether they're family or not."

The voices remained blessedly muted, allowing her to concentrate on what Dante was saying. She dropped the bedroll onto the table that still stood in front of the woodstove, and leaned against the edge.

"Something's been bothering me," she started, then smiled wryly at the look on his face. "Okay, something *else* has been bothering me. Why now?" He looked confused, so she tried to put into words the muddle of questions that had twined around the voices since last night's middle-of-the-night revelation.

"This... Transition," she began. She scrubbed her face with her hands, trying to force herself to think more clearly. "This puberty thing... why now? Why did it happen now? Why not when I started menarche?"

Dante walked over to the kitchen and crouched next to his

pack in the middle of the kitchen floor. He pulled out an old water bottle with a faded blue cap and swallowed some water before tightening the cap and dropping the bottle on top of his pack. He straightened up and finally looked at her.

"It's because of me," he said.

Lauren took a deep breath. She knew this, not only because it was logical—she started hearing voices only after he and Gautier entered her life—but because the voices knew, and that meant she did, too. A sense of wonder threatened to derail her, wonder that she had access to knowledge from so many generations.

But the knowledge didn't seem to be specific. "What does that mean? What did you do to trigger it?" And could he undo it?

Dante shook his head. "All I had to do was show up," he said. "Transition is triggered by pheromones—and only pheromones from your own family. Otherwise, proximity to Cade would have triggered your Transition a long time ago."

He looked at her with eyes full of regret. "We thought you were ten," he said softly. "It never occurred to me or to Grandfather that my presence might trigger your Transition."

"Why didn't you warn me when we met?" she asked. It was hard to be resentful when he was so clearly sorry. Still, some warning would have been nice.

He sighed. "There was a chance it wouldn't happen to you, because you're only half-gaians." He put up a hand once again. "I know, I know. I could have told you yesterday morning after you started having the dreams, but I thought I had more time—the Transition takes about a month. And it's usually much more gradual than what you're experiencing. I was trying to figure out a way to warn you and protect my friendship with Gautier."

Lauren stayed quiet, digesting the information. Gautier must feel betrayed and confused, but she could understand why Dante had kept the truth a secret. Life might be difficult if people knew the truth.

As if in answer to the thought, a flood of images filled her mind. Images of brutality, burnings, shunnings, betrayals—in its long history, Homo sapiens had never reacted well to the discovery of gaians living among them. She shivered and mentally turned away. It was hard to think that people she had known all her life might now turn against her.

Would Charlie turn against her?

She closed her eyes. What a way to live—hiding in plain sight. Among the enemy.

She shied away from that thought, refusing to believe that Homo sapiens were her enemy. That Charlie was her enemy. Or Gautier.

When she opened her eyes, she found Dante watching her, his expression weary and sad, and she felt a sudden rush of sympathy for him. She couldn't even begin to imagine what it would be like to be constantly buffeted by other people's emotions.

"You poor man," she murmured. "It must be terrible."

Dante looked startled. Then he shrugged. "I've learned to adapt. Mostly by living with sapiens, and not gaians." He grinned.

"You don't feel the sapiens?" How easily the word came to her now. He shook his head, and that's when the full import of his words hit her.

He could feel her emotions.

He had been standing next to her yesterday as she watched Gautier walking on the bridge...

Heat rose in her cheeks as she realized that she would never have any secrets from this cousin of hers.

Dante watched her in sympathy but didn't turn away. "Yes," he said softly, "that's usually the reaction I get."

Lauren struggled past the embarrassment. There was nothing wrong with admiring a good-looking man. And then she remembered wondering if Dante admired Gautier, too, and seeing the high color in Dante's cheeks.

Dante didn't want Gautier. He had looked flushed because he was reacting to her attraction to his friend.

Too funny. She grinned and Dante smiled uncertainly.

"What's so funny?" he asked.

Lauren shook her head, but a giggle burbled out in spite of herself.

"Now *that's* a reaction I never get," said Dante, obviously at a loss.

Lauren swallowed the laughter and decided not to share that particular thought with her cousin. He had enough to deal with. Still, she couldn't wipe the smile from her face as she picked up her bedroll and walked over to the packs in the middle of the kitchen floor. Dante eyed her with suspicion.

"We should get going," she said.

"Are you sure you're up to it?"

"I feel fine," said Lauren. And she did. She felt strong and relaxed for the first time in days. The voices were still there, but they weren't as overwhelming as they had been at first.

"Really?" said Dante and something in his voice made her pay attention.

"Why?"

"Because it's only been two days." He looked at her with concern.

"I must be lucky." She shrugged. "Where's Gautier?" She bent over to tie her bedroll to her pack and promptly toppled over as her ability to balance suddenly abandoned her. She fell into the heap of packs before Dante could catch her. As she twisted to right herself, she closed her eyes to control a dizzy spell.

Then she realized that the voices were gone. That, more than her sudden loss of balance, made cold sweat break out on her forehead.

* * *

"What's wrong?" asked Gautier. He'd gone down to the river to fetch the yellow nylon rope that had remained tied to the tree. Now it hung from one hand, coiled and neatly tied off.

In the early morning sunlight, Lauren sat on the same step as last night, hugging her knees as if she were cold. She looked pale, with red blotches on her cheeks.

Like she's got a fever, he thought. He automatically reached for her forehead but stopped when she flinched away from him.

Dante came out of the house with his water bottle. He glanced at Gautier before sitting down next to Lauren and handing her the canteen.

"Drink," he ordered. Lauren took the canteen and drank, spilling some water on her sweater. When she handed it back, she looked a little better, but her eyes were still glassy.

"Are you sick?" asked Gautier. If she was, they would have to turn around, even though he didn't want to cross that bridge again so soon. The river still ran cold and deadly inside him.

Lauren glanced at Dante and Gautier couldn't help feeling apart. She seemed to be leaning on Dante more and more, seemed to trust Dante more than she trusted him.

This isn't a competition, he warned himself. *Dante's her cousin—apparently—and she's got no other family. Of course she'll turn to him.*

But it didn't make him feel any better.

"Whatever it was," she said calmly, "I'm better now." She stood up, keeping one hand casually on the railing, as if she didn't really need the support. She looked up at the sky, which was the pale blue of cold fall mornings. The sun was already well on its way to high noon—at least as high as it got at this latitude.

"We could stay an extra day," he offered without any real hope. "Start early tomorrow morning..."

She shook her head before he could finish. "I figured out something," she said calmly, her eyes still glittering strangely. She looked at Dante. "I can't hear my mother."

Gautier caught his breath in fear. She was sicker than he'd thought. But Dante stared back at her silently, attentively, and she continued.

"If I can't hear her, she must not be dead. Cade must have her at Ben-My-Chree."

Now Dante looked doubtful, though not nearly as doubtful as he should.

"That's quite a leap, Lauren," he said carefully. He was looking at her strangely.

Gautier lost patience with the two of them.

"A leap?" he said. "No kidding. She went from wanting to get to Ben-My-Chree to ask Cade some questions, to wanting to rescue her long-dead mother. A *leap*?"

Lauren raised her chin and narrowed those green, glittering eyes. As worried and angry as he was, he couldn't help but appreciate how beautiful she was.

"I'm right here," she said. "Don't refer to me in the third person."

Gautier's childhood and its rules of politeness came rushing back, making him flush with embarrassment and anger. She was upset because he had been rude?

"I know you don't understand," she said more gently. "I'm not sure I do, either. The last couple of days have been the strangest of my life. But I'm not crazy." She turned to Dante. "Tell him," she ordered. "Tell him what it means that I can't hear my mother."

Dante studied Lauren's face uncertainly. "Lauren, Grandfather could explain it. I can't."

She turned away from him in frustration. "It's the voices," she told Gautier. "I hear all of them, these thousands of ancestors. Their voices, their dreams. And they're all dead!" she announced triumphantly. "I don't hear Dante. Or this grandfather of mine. They're alive." She came down one step. "Gautier, she's alive. That's why I don't hear her voice."

Gautier reached out without thinking and pulled her closer to him. Still holding on to her arm, he placed his free hand on her forehead and cheeks before she could get over her surprise.

Cool.

"I feel fine," she said, pulling out of his grip. "And I'm going on." *With or without you,* said her eyes.

Gautier shrugged. "Then I guess we'd better get going." He took the steps two at a time and went inside to get the packs. When he came out, Dante gave him a look full of misgivings and went inside to help.

❧ ELEVEN ❧

LAUREN felt better the moment they started moving. Gautier didn't even ask but slid behind the wheel, leaving her and Dante to sort themselves out as passengers. Dante nodded her into the middle and she climbed in without argument.

In spite of the quickly warming day, she felt chilled and her eyes ached. The color of the sky was a blue so vivid it threatened to swallow her so she turned away, concentrating instead on the inside of the truck.

It didn't help. Gautier started the engine and she clapped her hands over her ears. Both men turned to her in surprise and worry. With an effort, she smiled and took her hands away.

The cab stank of cured deer hide, unwashed bodies, and stale sweat. Without a word, Dante opened the window, letting in blessedly fresh air.

Lauren sniffed discretely. Rupe's scent was still there, but fading. The smell triggered a longing for her friend and she clenched her hands into fists, trying to control emotions that were too close to the surface.

Gautier backed the truck over the fallen branches and debris littering the cottage's driveway, then straightened to follow the road back to the Klondike Highway, the highway that would take her to Ben-My-Chree.

The rumble of the engine merged with the drone in her head and it was with a sense of wonder that she realized she must be sick.

She had never been sick. When all her friends had come down with chicken pox, she was allowed to play with them in the hopes that she would catch it as a child and not later when it would be so much harder on her.

But she hadn't caught it. Nor had she caught any of the colds and flus, measles or mumps that had come around. She and Mother had remained healthy during the Troubles when all around them people got sick and, more often than not, died.

They had buried Dad. They had buried neighbors and friends. But neither one got sick.

This is important, she told herself. *Pay attention.*

But the thought floated away on the smell of a family of rabbits in their warren.

* * *

She woke up with a start. Gautier was still driving and her head was leaning on Dante's shoulder. He seemed to be sleeping, too.

She had dreamed of mountains taller and craggier than the ones outside the window, snow-capped but still green at their feet. She had seen fields of wild flowers growing among the wild grasses—yarrow and bluebells, gentian and lupine, columbine and fireweed—growing right up to the cold waters of a secluded lake. And across the lake, she had seen a mountain with a giant, shadowy tree growing out of its flank, a tree unlike any she'd ever seen, with its roots deep in the belly of the world and its branches disappearing into the sky.

She felt rested, and much better than before. Whatever fever had taken hold of her seemed to be gone. The ancestors were still there, but now their voices murmured quietly, like the waters of

Kookatsoon Lake on a summer day.

With a muffled groan, she straightened from her slouch and rubbed the sleep out of her eyes. Gautier glanced at her with a smile.

"Feel better?"

He really does have a nice smile, she thought, and hoped she hadn't been drooling. A discreet rub of her mouth reassured her and she smiled back. "I do. Want to switch?"

Gautier shook his head. "Doin' fine. No idea where we are, though."

Next to her Dante stirred and straightened. He blinked bleary-eyed at the scenery then turned to the other two.

"How long was I asleep?"

Gautier shrugged. "About two hours. You and Lauren both."

Unlike her, the nap hadn't helped Dante. His mouth stayed tight and his eyes were full of pain.

"Dante?" she asked softly.

The look he gave her was so weary that she reached for his hand. He let her hold it, but closed his eyes again, effectively shutting her out.

Gautier glanced at his friend, obviously worried, but he was busy negotiating the potholes and sinkholes. He couldn't deal with Dante right now.

She squeezed Dante's hand. "What is it?"

"Someone's coming," he said grimly.

Startled, Lauren looked out the windows of the truck but saw only trees, rocks and mountains, and a road that was a few years shy of being reclaimed by the forests. There wasn't even a lake to see.

"Where?" she asked just as Gautier said, "Who?"

Dante's hand squeezed Lauren's but his eyes remained closed.

"Obeah. With a lot of gaians. There." He pointed due west. "About two miles away."

"Who's Obeah?" asked Gautier, scanning the surroundings

again. His foot eased off the gas pedal and they slowed to a crawl. The roar of the exhaust subsided to a dull growl.

Lauren opened her mouth to ask Dante the same thing, then she closed it again as a flood of information filled her brain with knowledge.

A shudder coursed through her, shaking her like a dog shakes a toy. She hated this! She now knew everything the ancestors knew about obeahs, just by wondering about the word. It was like being possessed by thousands of ghosts. She was beginning to lose her boundaries. Soon she wouldn't know where she ended and they began.

Dante looked at her with something close to pity, but Gautier was less patient.

"Well?" he demanded.

Dante retrieved his hand and wrapped his arms around himself, then leaned his head against the rattling door.

You tell him, he seemed to be saying.

Lauren clasped her hands together on her lap to hide their shaking.

"An obeah," she began haltingly, trying to put words around the concept that was fully formed in her head, "is a gaians with powers."

Gautier drove in silence for a few hundred rattling feet, then turned to look at her.

"What kind of powers?"

There was wariness in his voice and Lauren couldn't blame him. Most of what she now knew of obeahs was reassuring, but not all.

She thought about what to tell him, then realized that she had to go farther back, and start from the beginning.

"Apparently, certain gifts run in gaians families."

She could tell he wanted to stop the truck. Or maybe she sensed the minute slowing of the truck as he began to ease his foot off the pedal again. She didn't want him to stop or waste time.

"Keep driving," she said. "I'll try to explain as best I understand it."

He nodded curtly and settled back. She told him everything Dante had told her that morning, about being gaian, about her Transition being triggered by his arrival, about Dante's deep, far-ranging gift of sensing gaians emotions.

She stopped to take a breath and to gauge his reaction. He was silent for a long time, then said, "Poor guy."

"Pardon?"

"It must be hell to feel everything everyone around you is feeling."

It was Lauren's turn to nod. From the pool of knowledge that now resided in her, she knew that very few with Dante's abilities or sensitivities ever survived past puberty with their sanity intact. It spoke well of Gautier that he could recognize the gift as the curse it could be.

"He's strong," she said, as much in acknowledgment as in reassurance.

"So..." said Gautier slowly, "what's Dante's range?"

It hadn't occurred to her to wonder about that. She glanced at Dante but his eyes remained closed, as if he were shutting them out.

The ancestors were no help. Apparently the gift varied widely in its strength.

"I don't know," she admitted. "But he said obeah, not gaian. Maybe obeahs send out stronger vibrations."

It wasn't like that, really, but she couldn't explain it clearly to him.

"He also said "gaians," plural," reminded Gautier. "I need to know what kind of powers this obeah has and if they're going to bite us on the ass."

Lauren studied his craggy profile, noting again the bristly stubble, the slight curve to his nose—a curve interrupted by the bump of a healed break—and the determination in the set of his chin. For the first time, she realized that Gautier saw himself as the protector of their small group. Her protector.

Her champion.

She should have seen it earlier. The way he had tried to persuade her to go to Montreal instead of to Ben-My-Chree. The way he couldn't stay away when she and Dante decided to go ahead. The way he stood by her last night, on the porch, protecting her from Dante. It wasn't Dante who held him here.

It was her.

The engine vibrated through the floorboard and through the soles of her moccasins as she tried to understand how she felt about her new-found insight. As if drawn by her study of him, Gautier turned to look at her and she felt suddenly exposed under that blue gaze. Then he turned away and she could breathe again.

Beware, whispered the voices in her mind.

"Is this obeah a danger to us?" asked Gautier.

"I don't know," admitted Lauren. "Obeahs are considered the wisest among the gaians," she began. "But they're not all good." She sifted through the mass of information to find the kernels that would help them in the here and now. "Obeahs can talk to all the ancestors, not just those in their direct line." Another pause. "Some smell the truth, in gaians or sapiens." Another kernel. "They never get sick, but can identify disease in gaians. Some can even cure it."

Gautier waited as she explored the maelstrom of thoughts and emotions of her ancestors. There. The knowledge that weakened her legs and made her stomach clench in fear. "Some can kill with their minds."

Gautier greeted this information with silence, as if it didn't surprise him. But it surprised her. She couldn't imagine any need for such a power. How would something like that have evolved?

"Other gaians only?" asked Gautier finally. "Or... sapiens, too?"

Before Lauren could answer, Dante spoke up. "Those with the power to kill can kill everyone," he said. Lauren and Gautier turned to him in surprise. She had thought him asleep, but his eyes stared back at her unblinkingly, shining with something more than fever, less than sanity.

Then the truck slammed into something soft and stalled. Gautier's arm shot out to brace Lauren and Dante and keep them from hitting the dashboard.

They hadn't been going very fast into the turn and weren't hurt by the sudden stop. As it was, the three of them sat in mute wonder, staring at the mud slide that had stopped them.

It reached across the road, at least six feet deep with compacted soil and rocks. Willow bushes and dead fireweed grew out of the soil, poking past two inches of snow. It was an old slide.

Gautier eyed the mountain of dirt and rock. "We're not getting past that."

He was right. Digging a path wide enough for the truck was out of the question.

"All right," she said. "We walk."

A massive shiver shook her and Gautier turned to look at her with a frown. "What?"

"Nothing," she hastily told him. "Let's get going." She didn't want to tell him that she was starting to feel feverish again.

Gautier glanced at the sky. "We don't have much daylight left. Let's camp here and wait for morning."

Lauren shook her head. "We have to take advantage of every minute we can." Gautier looked at Dante, who still had his arms wrapped around himself but was now watching them with more awareness.

"There's an old train station at Log Cabin," she said. "It's only two more miles, maybe less. The trail head is there—if we spend the night at the station, we'll be ready to take the trail first thing in the morning."

Gautier eyed the sky, then looked at Dante and Lauren, his gaze assessing. She could almost smell the worry on him and did her best to look fit.

"I want to go on," said Dante and he sounded almost like himself again. He relaxed his grip and rested his hands on his lap. Lauren wondered if they were shaking.

"The gaians?" she asked.

"Gone for now. Two groups, not traveling together, but heading south east."

"To Ben-My-Chree," she breathed. Dante nodded and they looked at each other. She saw in him the same compulsion she had to get to Ben-My-Chree, a compulsion that all but disappeared as long as she was moving toward her goal. She wanted to find her mother. What was driving Dante?

It didn't matter.

"All right, then," she said. "Let's go."

Without giving Gautier a chance to object, Dante slid out the passenger side door and Lauren followed him.

The wind caught her short hair, whipping it into knots. She breathed deeply. The scents were intoxicating. The north wind carried the sharp resinous scent of pine trees, the musky smell of a nearby fox, the sharp, pale scent of lake water freezing. When she closed her eyes, she became aware of the wind sighing through pine needles; the distant, harsh cawing of a raven chasing a thermal; the growl of a black bear scavenging for old berries.

So much life. She had never noticed before how full the winter landscape was.

It took them half an hour to load the sled and rearrange their packs. Then Gautier tied the strap around his waist, shifted his backpack to a more comfortable position, and started out over the slide.

There was barely enough snow to make the sled useable and they had to lift and shove it over sections of the road. Even if the slide hadn't stopped them, it soon became clear that the truck wouldn't have been able to go much further. The road had disintegrated to a rough track, with huge chunks of asphalt pushed up by permafrost, and sinkholes that would have swallowed her poor pickup.

As they walked, her fever grew, and with it, her perceptions of the world. The same north wind that brought roses to her cheeks also carried the faint sweetness of willow sap retreating deep to the core of trees, the sound of voles scurrying through underbrush, the smell of snow carried down mountains. Her gaze traveled up the flanks of a nearby mountain and she found a group of five mountain goats staring down at them.

She tucked her hands under her armpits as she walked because they suddenly felt heavy and were dragging her down toward the ground. Next to her, Dante's concern smelled like warm bread. It gave her strength. *Not far,* she kept telling herself. *Then you can sleep.*

They hadn't gone half a mile, with Lauren and Dante leading and Gautier pulling behind, when Dante's head suddenly snapped up. He whirled to face the way they had come and stared intently at the track they had left in the snow.

Gautier quickly undid the strap around his waist and turned to scan the road behind them. Lauren peered, but saw nothing.

"What?" asked Gautier, still watching the road.

"It's Grandfather," said Dante in a strangled voice. Without giving either one of them the chance to react, he took off at a run back the way they had come.

❧ TWELVE ❧

"DANTE!" Gautier took off after his friend, but stopped abruptly after ten steps and turned to look at Lauren. She was sick again, her cheeks flushed with fever, her eyes glittering with that uncanny light. She looked like she might start muttering an incantation at any moment.

"Go after him," she ordered. Her voice was deeper than normal and a shiver ran up his scalp. *Don't be an ass,* he told himself. *She's not possessed—just sick.*

Still he hesitated. Dante had said there were strangers around. In this state, Lauren wouldn't be able to defend herself.

"Go!" she said roughly. "I'll yell if I need you." She sat down heavily on the sled, mindful of the food, and that convinced him she was aware enough to call him if she needed help.

Without a word, he turned and ran. Dante could run faster than him, but he'd left a trail in the thin snow that Gautier followed like a map.

Dante had left the road almost immediately, dipping down the embankment toward the lake hidden by the trees. Gautier scrambled down, breaking his descent by catching at trees and bushes. The whip-thin branches left welts on his unprotected face and scratches on his hands. At the bottom, he wasted precious time finding Dante's trail again, but once he did, he ran as fast as he could.

Before long, he smelled something so unexpected and familiar that he almost stopped in surprise. Oil. Then he burst through the trees to find a frozen, snow-covered lake. At the edge of the lake, Dante crouched over a still figure lying in a heap next to an over-turned four-wheeler. Oil slowly leaked from the exposed engine.

Dante looked up at Gautier's appearance. His face was ashen. "He's hurt," he said. "Help me with him."

* * *

Night seeped into day from the ground up, giving the fresh snow between the trees a blue tint. Already the familiar looked strange, and Lauren couldn't tell how far they had gone or how much further the station was.

The only sounds were the thick rasp of her breathing and the crunching of her moccasins and Dante's boots as they poked through the icy crust over the snow. Five miles they had gone al-ready—well past her estimated two miles. Normally five miles would have been nothing. But five miles when she was sick and carrying a sixty-pound pack and had to move as fast as she could to save an old man's life...

She glanced over her shoulder, ignoring Dante's questioning look. She didn't know how far the damned station was. She only knew they had to keep going. Gautier and the sled were back there somewhere, out of sight. They had all taken turns pulling and it was his turn to haul the heavy sled through the trees.

She met Dante's eye and shrugged. She wanted to get the old man to warmth as badly as he did.

Dante and Gautier had hauled Silas up from the shore and back to the sled where they rearranged the sled's contents to make room for the old man. Lauren had examined him only to look up and find Dante's gaze on her. She knew exactly what he was think-ing. They could both smell the muskiness on the old man's clothes. Something wild had jumped him, maybe a lynx. Still, his only injury was a small lump on the back of his head, as if he had hit it when he fell. She couldn't see what was keeping him unconscious.

And why would an animal attack him and then not finish him?

Her legs trembled from exhaustion and her breath fogged in front of her face, freezing her nose and cheeks. The fever still dogged her, keeping her warm but weak.

At least the sensitivity to sounds and smells had died down. And the ancestors were very quiet. Maybe the fever affected them, too.

As the shadows lengthened, she took to scanning the trees for signs of movement. Stupid. Wolves had better things to do than attack humans, and bears were getting ready for winter. Nothing else out here to hurt them, except maybe whatever had jumped the old man.

A branch cracked to her right and her head whipped around. She held her breath, peering into shadows, waiting for the noise to repeat.

"What is it?" asked Dante.

She shook her head and blew her irritation out in a gust of breath. "Nothing. It's getting colder. Trees are cracking."

They had to get out of these woods before night set in. The old man wouldn't survive a night outdoors in these temperatures. And if he died, so did a lot of her answers.

A sudden stab of guilt made her feel ashamed of herself. She knew that Dante cared about him, but she didn't know this man. She couldn't drum up any false sentiment when all she wanted to do was get to the cabin and from there, to Ben-My-Chree.

But when she turned back to the trail, she couldn't find it. Her breathing grew increasingly shallow as she examined each tree in turn, ignoring the darkness pressing in on her. When she saw the gleam of eyes staring back at her from the darkness, she froze. Man height. A big man's height. She blinked, and they were gone.

Then an owl hooted and she jumped.

Bloody hell.

At that moment, she saw the lightness beyond the wall of trees. Relief spurred her on and she put on a burst of speed, over-riding the protest in her legs and back. It must be the road. She had found the South Klondike Highway again. Log Cabin station couldn't be far now.

Dante kept up but now she could hear his ragged breathing, too.

A moment later, she emerged into a break. Not the road but the ancient railroad. And there, just off the tracks, was the small log station identified on all the maps as Log Cabin, as if it were a settlement instead of a pit stop for the trains that ran from Skag-way to Bennett. She stopped at the sight, breathing hard and weak with relief.

Dante stopped beside her. He glanced at her, a world of worry in his eyes.

"There'll be a wood stove in there," she said, pointing out the chimney. Warmth. Food. She headed for the cabin, Dante right be-hind her, and stopped a few feet from the door to shrug out of her backpack. It landed with a muted thud in three inches of snow and a wave of dizziness almost sent her down next to it. Dante steadied her with a hand on her arm and she nodded mutely. There was much more snow up here than back home, but still not enough to break out her snowshoes.

"Lots of dead wood," she said, glancing around. Wind storms and time had taken care of that. She turned toward the trees. "Light a fire—we'll all need the warmth tonight."

Dante just looked at her. "Where are you going?"

"I'm going back for them."

He shook his head and stepped in front of her. His pack was off, too. "You're sick. If you can start the fire without burning down the place, do it. I'll go help Gautier."

Not giving her a chance to argue, he turned and ran back into the forest, following the trail they had just made. Lauren watched him until the trees swallowed him, then turned back to the cabin.

She would never have admitted it, but she was glad to stay behind. She wasn't sure how much longer her legs would support her. And for the first time in her life, the forest frightened her.

The cabin was small, barely twenty feet by fifteen. It had been designed as a storage space and had later been adapted to a small station. Lauren remembered the building from the summer she turned nine. She and her parents had hiked the Chilkoot Trail all the way to Bennett, where they had taken the train back to Log Cabin. By then, the cabin was a rest stop and meeting place for hikers dropping off a second vehicle before driving into Skagway and the head of the Trail. There had been a skinny woman presiding over the cabin, offering cold drinks and snacks and allowing people to store their belongings in the cabin until they returned, days later, at the end of their hike.

The only window was long gone, broken by flying branches and cold weather, no doubt. But there were shutters that still worked. Lauren tried to push open the door, applying her shoulder when it didn't move easily. Finally the door gave way and she stumbled inside.

* * *

Gautier kept his gaze on the faint track, afraid that if he looked up, he'd never find it again. He knew Dante and Lauren were somewhere up ahead, but the forest around him was silent and hushed.

His legs moved steadily and his breath was still regular, although the weight of the sled was starting to wear on him. He could go on for another five miles if he needed to, but darkness would erase the track long before that. At least the exercise kept him warm.

He didn't know what to think of the old man he pulled in the sled. Dante's love for his grandfather was clear and it pointed out once more how little Gautier knew of his friend. How could Dante not have mentioned *once* in their fifteen-year friendship that he had a grandfather?

Then Gautier snorted in amusement. This was what bothered

him most? In the last two days he'd learned that his friend was of a different species, a 'gaians' species hidden for thousands of years among 'sapiens,' and that he had special powers.

But of all the secrets Dante had kept, the secret of his grand-father's existence was the one that hurt most.

It would have been nice to have a grandfather, even a surro-gate one of a different species.

Gautier shook his head at his foolishness and picked up his pace. There wouldn't be a grandfather at all if they didn't get him to warmth and figure out what was wrong with him.

Above the sound of the sled scraping on twigs and the sound of his breathing, Gautier gradually became aware of another sound, a soft swishing, like fur brushing against a tree. He didn't change his pace or look around, but all his senses came to immediate attention. For the first time, he realized that the silence wasn't a natural one. Even in the dead of winter there would be sounds of small animals foraging for food or birds startled out of trees at his passage. He'd seen gray jays and ravens, and even magpies as they drove earlier that day. But now that he was in the woods, nothing.

He didn't bother checking the knife in his belt. It was always there, ready. He hadn't survived the Troubles by being stupid. But he did risk a glance behind him at the sled. The old man was still bundled in the nylon envelope, strapped tightly to the plastic shell of the sled. The sled was stable, the old man secure. If he had to run, he wouldn't worry about the sled flipping over.

But when he turned back, the trail was gone.

Dammit.

He stopped. The silence of the woods felt all wrong, as if some-thing was holding its breath.

He scanned the forest floor, looking for the damned trail. He just couldn't see it. It was a trick of the failing light, he knew that, but a shiver still ran up his scalp. The sled and the long rod con-necting it to his waist strap hadn't moved, and so he still had to be pointed in the right direction. But the tracks that had guided him so far seemed to have disappeared.

Then he heard the swishing again. Someone was out there, in the woods. He pulled off his gloves and unbuckled the waist strap before sliding the knife out of its sheath. As quietly as he could, he lay the connecting rod of the sled down on the ground and moved away from the sled.

A branch snapped behind him and he whirled, both arms up and the knife hand leading but there was nothing to see except black shadows between black trees. Moving slowly, he circled the sled, examining the forest.

Then something growled softly.

The shout burst out of him before he could stop himself. "Get out of here!" he yelled with as much force as he could. "Hai!" He kept up the shouts, waving his arms and generally making himself sound as big and aggressive as he could. Whenever he stepped on a stone or a branch, he quickly picked it up and flung it at the trees, accompanying the missiles with guttural shouts.

He finally stopped next to the sled, breathing hard and trying to see all around him at the same time. He couldn't tell if whatever had been out there was still there, but if it hadn't attacked by now, it probably wouldn't.

He checked on the old man before strapping on the waist strap again, but all he could tell in the darkness was that he was still alive.

He still had no idea where the damned trail was, but he wasn't staying here waiting to be something's next meal. He would keep walking and hope that he'd find the trail again.

Then a familiar voice came floating out of the darkness.

"You sure are a noisy bugger."

Dante.

Relief pasted a silly grin on Gautier's face and he didn't have the heart to wipe it off. A dark figure detached itself from deeper shadows and came closer.

"What were you shouting about?" asked Dante.

His voice sounded so distant and distracted that Gautier's heart sank. It wasn't over. Whatever was affecting Dante was still there.

"There was something following us," he said. "Probably a wolf. Just letting it know we weren't easy prey."

Dante was now close enough for Gautier to see the gleam of his pale face.

"The cabin's not far," said Dante. "Want me to take over?"

Gautier immediately sheathed his knife and unbuckled the waist strap. He wasn't convinced he had chased off their stalker. He would feel better guarding their rear than trapped inside a harness.

"Where's Lauren?" he asked while Dante tightened the strap around his waist.

"At the cabin, hopefully lighting a fire."

"How is she?"

Dante stood still for a moment, then turned to look at him. "Not good, Gautier. If this is what I think it is, it's going to get a lot worse before it gets better."

Gautier's chest suddenly felt tight as he tried to force air past a ball of fear.

"What do you mean?" he asked. "What's wrong with her?"

"I think she's becoming an obeah," said Dante, and there was no mistaking the concern in his voice.

Obeahs again. Gaians with special powers. "What does that mean?" he asked roughly. "Why is that going to make things worse?"

Dante stood silent for a long time, tethered to his grandfather, his back to his friend. Finally he turned to look at Gautier.

"Because most gaians don't survive the transition to obeah. Of those who do, many go insane."

Without another word, he started toward the cabin and Lauren.

* * *

They smelled the wood smoke long before they reached the cabin. Gautier's spirits lifted. Lauren had been strong enough to find wood and light a fire. All good.

When he and Dante broke out of the trees they were met by the glow of light through shutters. It was now full dark and that light was the most welcome thing Gautier had ever seen. The cabin wasn't big, but it was shelter.

The door opened as they were unlacing the ties on the sled. Gautier looked up to find Lauren leaning against the door jamb, looking at the woods.

"Everything all right?" she asked. Her voice still sounded deep, but she had her back to the light and he couldn't make out her expression.

"Gautier encountered some wildlife," said Dante, as he pulled the nylon bag away from his grandfather. The two men carried the old man inside and put him down on a trestle table in the middle of the room. A moment later, Lauren followed with the sled and parked it at the far end of the one-room cabin.

Dante didn't waste any time looking around. He was busy pulling clothes away and examining his grandfather for injuries. Finally he rearranged the unconscious man's clothes and stepped back.

"Nothing," he said. "There's no mark or injury on him, except for that bump on his head."

"It's not his body," said Lauren. "It's his spirit. It's trapped."

Gautier turned to look at her. She was sitting on a bench by the wall, leaning forward with her elbows on her knees and her hands clasped together, hanging loosely between her knees. Her head was bent as if she was studying the floor.

"Lauren?" he said, taking a step toward her.

Then Dante's head jerked up and he turned toward the door.

Jesus, thought Gautier. *Not again.*

"More gaians," said Dante, his voice unnaturally tight. "Three, maybe four. Not together."

"How close?"

"Maybe a mile. Maybe more."

Gautier relaxed a little. A mile might as well be ten. He turned back to Lauren, but she had straightened from her slump and now was staring back at him, her eyes glittering with fever, her face flushed.

Before he could reach her, she toppled off the bench to land in a heap on the cold wood floor.

᚛ THIRTEEN ᚜

L AUREN opened her eyes to a sky blue with diffused light. A warm breeze caressed her face, leaving behind a scent of wild roses and something else, something sweet. She was lying on damp earth, her fingers clutching grass, with twigs poking into her thighs.

"Lauren?"

She turned her head to see a pair of legs covered by a cotton dress moving quickly toward her.

She let go of the grass and reached for her throbbing head. Good grief. She felt as if she'd fallen down the embankment instead of her grandfather.

At the thought, she sat up in alarm only to clutch her head again when it threatened to fall off her shoulders in protest. Through squinting eyes, she saw a forest of tall, unfamiliar trees. They were all in leaf, but so widely spaced that she had no trouble seeing the sky. The underbrush was unfamiliar, too, with none of the willow and aspen bushes she had grown up with. This underbrush was lush with fronds and ferns, plants she had only ever seen in her mother's books. She began to tremble, starting deep in her core. There were wildflowers, but the only familiar ones were bluebells. She scanned the trees in increasing panic, but saw not a single black spruce. Her hands slipped from her head to cover her mouth. Although she couldn't see them, birds called to each other in the high branches. She didn't recognize any of their calls.

Where was she?

"Lauren." The woman belonging to the pair of legs stopped a few feet away and held a hand out. Lauren examined her cautiously but didn't recognize her. She didn't recognize anything. The trembling travelled outward to her limbs.

"Who are you?" she asked. "Where am I?"

The woman was tiny, barely coming up to Lauren's shoulder, and wore a cotton dress in a small cornflower print. The older First Nations women had worn dresses like that when she was a girl, and brightly patterned scarves over their hair. Mary had owned several scarves like that, faded and threadbare, only worn on special occasions. But this woman's hair, although up in a bun, was uncovered. It was completely black, even though the lines in her face told Lauren she was old, even older than Mary had been when she died.

"My name is Morag. Don't stay on the ground, dear. It's damp." Though small, her outstretched hand was brown and callused, as if the woman had done a lot of manual labor.

After a moment, Lauren accepted her help and stood up shakily. Her clothes were damp where she had been lying down and the plants she had crushed now released a scent that was half pungent, half sweet.

The woman was built wide and strong. Something about the way she stood, with her legs braced and her back straight, told Lauren that she would be hard to knock off her feet.

"Well," said the woman with a frown, "no one has tried in a very long time."

Lauren fixed the woman with a stare. "Where am I?" Her voice throbbed inside her skull and she controlled an urge to grab her head and groan, but she couldn't keep from squinting at the pain.

"I know," murmured the woman sympathetically. "The Transition hurts."

Lauren scowled. She didn't want sympathy—she wanted answers. In spite of the headache, she finally recognized the sweet smell. It was sap—sap rising in the trees. She swept the forest with her gaze—green everywhere, with spots of color where flowers peeked through.

She had been in Log Cabin, at the beginning of winter. Her gaze returned to the woman's face and her heart began to race as recognition finally dawned.

The woman had the same dark complexion and deep brown eyes as Dante. As her mother. Except for the fact that she looked thirty years too old, she could have been Meridy Tom. She looked at Lauren with a mix of pride and concern—a motherly look, Lauren thought. Even the smile was the same.

"Mom?" asked Lauren uncertainly. Hopefully.

An infinite sadness filled the woman's face and even before she shook her head, Lauren knew she wasn't her mother. Of course she wasn't her mother. The headache was making her stupid.

"Not your mother, Lauren. Your great-grandmother, Morag."

Lauren took a deep breath, trying to think past the disappointment and the pain in her head. Her great-grandmother. All the elements finally fell into place.

"This is the underworld," she said, wonder struggling with dismay in her. How had she gotten here?

And better yet, *how could she get out?*

Dante hadn't said anything about her going to the underworld during this Transition.

"That's because you shouldn't be here," said her great-grandmother gently, "even if you're transitioning into an obeah."

Before Lauren could bristle at the fact that her great-grandmother was reading her mind—would she never have privacy again?—knowledge filled her up, making her poor head feel like it was about to burst. With dawning horror she riffled through the details to learn that if she was indeed transitioning into an obeah she was likely to die or go insane. The only consolation she could find was the realization that every generation of her family had consistently produced strong, sane obeahs.

Of course, she was the only half-breed in her family and there was no telling how that would affect the Transition.

Lauren closed her eyes, longing for her own cabin, for Rupe and Mary and Charlie, for the solitude of the winter woods and her trapline.

And to her surprise, she longed for Gautier's calm presence. Her last memory of him was the look of concern on his face as the floor rushed up to smack her.

A cool breeze suddenly shook leaves and Lauren shivered. The forest rustled, as if hidden people moved stealthily from tree to tree. Then she thought she heard her name as a faint cry on the wind but though she strained to listen, she didn't hear it again.

Morag glanced around, her mouth tightening. Her voice when she spoke again was lower. "You have no business here, child. You're not an obeah. Not yet." There was something in her voice that made Lauren shiver again.

"This is..." *Too weird,* she had been about to say, but the words seemed inadequate. The underworld. Where her ancestors were. Not heaven, not hell, Dante had said. Just... other.

Aside from Morag and the nagging feeling that she was being watched, Lauren saw no one else in the forest. And then she looked sharply at her great-grandmother as another thought occurred to her.

"Is my mother here?" she demanded. "Is Meridy Tom here, in the underworld?"

Once more Morag shook her head and Lauren didn't know if she should feel relieved or disappointed.

"No, child," said Morag. "And neither should you be."

Lauren frowned. "I didn't exactly plan this. The last thing I remember is being at Log Cabin. And Silas..."

Again that cold wind blew through the forest, stirring fallen leaves on the forest floor and lifting her great-grandmother's dress.

And again, Lauren strained to hear what it said. Her name. That was her name on the wind.

"Someone's calling me," she said slowly.

"Not you," said Morag grimly. "All of us."

Lauren glanced around the deserted forest. "Who is *us?* Where are the rest of my ancestors?"

"In hiding." Morag studied her for a moment, then seemed to come to a decision. "Silas is calling to the obeahs," said her great-grandmother. "He is in danger."

"What kind of danger?" asked Lauren, putting her hand on her great-grandmother's bare arm. The old woman's skin was warm and wrinkly, with strong muscles underneath it. It was covered in goose bumps, surprising Lauren. She didn't know what she had expected but surely a dead ancestor shouldn't feel so... alive.

Morag gently pulled her arm out of Lauren's grip. "There is nothing you can do for him, child." She patted Lauren's cheek. "There is nothing I can do, either."

"Why not?" asked Lauren. She didn't know Silas except as a name, really, but Morag was his mother—she should want to help. Shouldn't she?

Morag smiled bitterly. "I am the only obeah left of my—our—family line," she said. "All the others are gone. My responsibility is here, to protect the ones left behind."

"Gone *where?*" asked Lauren. "For the love of Pete! Just tell me what's going on!"

Morag sighed. Without a word, she grasped Lauren by the hand and lifted. The old woman rose in the air and before Lauren could do more than gasp, she was off the ground, too, being towed through the air like a fish through water.

It's not real, she told herself frantically. *Not real.* But the cold wind rushed through her hair and brought tears to her eyes, and below them the trees grew smaller and smaller. Lauren clutched Morag's small hard hand and tried to make herself lighter.

When she finally looked past her great-grandmother's billowing skirts, she caught her breath in wonder.

The forest spread out below her, looking deceptively soft, for as far as she could see.

A gentle squeeze on her hand brought her attention back to Morag, who pointed at the horizon. Lauren squinted in the glare of the sky, finally putting her free hand up to shade her eyes. In the distance was a line of darkness smudging the horizon. Just before it, the forest abruptly switched from park-like to a dense tangle of close trees and thick underbrush.

"What is that?" she shouted above the wind.

"It's where Silas is being held."

Lauren's mouth went dry. "What do you mean, 'being held'?"

Morag shook her head. "We don't know what goes on there. It's opaque to us."

"Can't you go there and see?"

"Only obeah can leave these woods," said her great-grand-mother. "And of those who have traveled there, none have come back. It's the same with the other families."

Lauren was only half-paying attention. She was looking all around, seeing for the first time that the forest was actually a se-ries of forests separated by long swaths of grasslands dotted by wildflowers and saplings bowing in the wind. Her eyesight seemed miraculously sharp because she could see for miles—around the world, it seemed to her.

Then Morag's words sank in and she dragged her gaze back to her great-grandmother. "What happened to them?"

"One by one they went to the dark place," she said, "and never came back."

"Why did they go?"

"They were trying to stop that," said Morag and she pointed at a dot in the distance.

Lauren strained to see, but it was only when the speck grew bigger that she saw it was a human figure.

"Who is it?" she whispered. She doubted the figure could hear her—it was miles away—but just in case...

"Not who," said her grand-grandmother grimly. "What."

The speck drew closer and birds flew up in its passage to whirl around the treetops, calling in alarm. Lauren controlled an urge to pull on her great-grandmother's hand. She wanted to duck back into the forest. They would be safe there.

"No," said Morag. "We are not safe in the forest." Her voice tightened and Lauren looked up at her great-grandmother to see her face hard with anger, her eyes fierce and hot. "We're hunted like animals by something that came out of another obeah's mind."

Lauren swallowed hard. "What does it do when it catches someone?"

Her great-grandmother turned a bleak face to her. "We've only ever found blood and bits of bone. We think it eats them."

A wave of horror rolled over Lauren and she almost let go. "*Eats them?* But... if this is the underworld and everyone here is already dead..."

There was a grimness to the old woman's voice when she spoke again. "We don't know what happens to gaians who die again. It had never happened before."

Lauren looked at the far away figure. Nobody should have to die twice.

Then the figure turned toward them and seemed to pause. When it resumed its flight, it was coming straight toward them.

Lauren's heart slammed against her ribs as fear spiked through her. Although the creature was still miles away, her preternaturally sharp eyesight picked out its glossy blond coat, its coal-red eyes and, worse, its fangs and claws. There was something grimly familiar about the beast.

"Morag..."

"I know," said the old woman calmly. "We'll hide." And with that she yanked on Lauren's hand and they began to sink back down to the ground.

Lauren landed softly and looked up at the sky, feeling terribly exposed.

"Come," said Morag and she led Lauren to a tree that was easily the circumference of her cabin. There was a wide slit in the bole where the tree curled in on itself. Morag pushed Lauren through the opening and followed her in.

The inside was hardly hollow, but there was room enough to accommodate both of them.

"When we lived above, we hid from the sapiens who would harm us," said Morag. "Now, we hide again, this time from an obeah's nightmare."

"Not heaven, then," murmured Lauren, shifting in the tight quarters. The smell of sap was strong here, as was the smell of mulch and growth. Not unpleasant.

"It *was* heaven," said Morag. She leaned back against the damp interior of the tree. "It was wonderful. Until the wendigo came."

"That's what it is?"

Morag shrugged. "It seems to be what the obeah called out of his mind. Obviously it's part of his personal mythology."

"Whose?" whispered Lauren. She couldn't hear anything beyond the tree, but she could feel the hushing of the forest. The wendigo was getting closer. Before Morag could answer, the truth dawned on Lauren. That blond pelt. The familiar cast to the creature's features... "It's Cade, isn't it?"

Morag's anger was clear in her voice. "Yes. He's behind all this."

Then the ground vibrated beneath Lauren's feet as something heavy landed just beyond the tree. Before she could stop the old woman, Morag slipped outside. Lauren reached for her great-grandmother but only caught her arm.

Then Morag was pulled out of Lauren's grasp and with a cry Lauren lost her balance and tumbled out of the tree into blinding daylight. She had a glimpse of feral eyes and glistening fangs before landing on the forest floor on all fours, her head spinning and the world turning black all around her.

She scrambled back inside the tree just as the underworld began to fade into darkness. The last thing she smelled as blackness engulfed her was the stench of rotting meat.

❧ FOURTEEN ❧

Gautier picked Lauren up and sat down on the bench, cradling her in his arms. Her head fell back and he readjusted his arm to support her neck.

"Lauren?" he said softly. Her bottom nestled in his lap but her legs threatened to slide off. With his free hand, he gathered her closer. "Lauren?"

She was burning hot. Expressions chased each other on her face so quickly he barely had time to identify one before another replaced it: *pain, confusion, wonder.*

For the first time since he was a young man, he felt completely helpless. The last person he had held like this had been his mother. He had returned home from London with Dante only to find that the plagues had reached Toronto. His father was already dead and he arrived just in time to hold his mother as she died.

He drew Lauren even closer. He wasn't going to let that happen to her.

"She's burning up," he said roughly. He turned to see Dante standing a few feet from the table where his grandfather rested. Dante's face was taut with control; his fists balled at his sides, his dark eyes glittering in the candlelight.

Jesus, thought Gautier. "What?"

"They're under attack."

Gautier half-rose, hampered by Lauren's dead weight. He automatically glanced at the door but it remained closed.

"In the underworld."

Gautier sank back to the bench. The underworld. Gaians, obeahs, and now the underworld.

He had an injured old man, a sick woman, and Dante didn't look so good, either. For a split second, Gautier wanted nothing more than to walk away from the cabin and everyone in it, walk away, and keep on walking until he got to Ontario and the house he was fixing up for himself.

He understood how to use a hammer and a plumb bob, how to build a bearing wall and lay down a pine floor so that it wouldn't warp or separate. In that world, he could keep a woman safe.

He didn't understand about different species or underworlds. Or how to protect Lauren there.

He looked down at her troubled face. It would be so simple to put her down on the bench and walk away. But his arms refused to let go and as his heart squeezed with pain, he finally understood that it was too late for him.

It had been too late the first time he saw her determined, alarmed face as she drove past him and Dante. Four days ago. A lifetime ago.

Her breast pressed against his ribs and he could feel her heart beating against him.

"How can we help them?" he asked.

"We can't," said Dante flatly. "Only obeahs can go to the underworld while they live, and I'm no obeah. And you're not even gaians."

Frustration filled Gautier's chest and he had to control an urge to curse. "What kind of attack?" he asked instead.

Dante shook his head helplessly. "I don't know," he said. "Whatever it is, it's scaring her."

Gautier clamped his mouth shut. Lauren was afraid, and all

he could do was sit here like a fool and do nothing.

"What about the old man?" He glanced at the figure on the table, but Silas hadn't moved. "Is he afraid, too?"

Dante nodded. "But I think he's afraid for Lauren."

Oh, Jesus.

Then Lauren jackknifed in his arms and her head collided with his chin. The blow caught Gautier by surprise, snapping his teeth together and his head back.

"Morag!" she screamed, and struggled to free herself from his restraining arms.

"Lauren!" cried Dante as she finally slipped out of Gautier's arms to tumble on the floor.

Before Gautier could reach for her, Lauren scrambled to her feet and stood tensely in the middle of the room, her eyes darting wildly. Gautier and Dante both reached her at the same time and Gautier took her wrist to keep her from bolting again.

He almost let her go as soon as he touched her—her flesh was searing hot. His heart jumped in fear. His mother's fever had been high like this right before she died.

"Lauren?" he asked softly.

She didn't pay any attention to him, but her gaze fixed on the old man on the table. "He's in trouble," she said urgently, her whole body straining toward the unconscious man. "So is Morag."

Who the hell was Morag?

"What kind of trouble?" Gautier looked over her head to his friend. Dante's face was drawn with worry but Gautier couldn't tell if it was for Lauren, his grandfather, or this Morag. Maybe all three.

Dante shook his head. "The only Morag in our direct line was my great-grandmother. Maybe Lauren spoke to her in the under-world." His voice dropped to barely a whisper as he stared at his grandfather. "He's fighting something," he said.

This was completely out of Gautier's experience. He glanced at Lauren, who was still straining to free herself from his grasp. He resisted the urge to take her in his arms and soothe her fretfulness away. He had to do something—nobody could survive that high a fever for long.

"I'll try to calm her down," he said. "Melt some snow—we have to get her fever down."

Already she was trembling and her eyes looked glazed in the candlelight. Dante moved jerkily to where he had left his pack and started rummaging through it.

"She's not supposed to be able to go to the underworld until after her Transition," he said.

"So...?" invited Gautier, wrapping an arm around Lauren's trembling back. She didn't once glance away from Silas.

Dante shrugged. He pulled out a piece of rag he had been using as a face cloth and a battered aluminum pot. "I don't know. This has never happened before that I know of."

Well, if Dante didn't know, Gautier sure as hell couldn't guess. "She seems obsessed with his safety," he said. Lauren pulled fitfully against his hold and he gave in, walking her to where Silas rested on the rough table. "Would he still be in danger if he woke up?"

Dante shook his head. "That's just it. Something is keeping him there—otherwise he would just wake up."

Lauren stopped by the old man's side and stood teetering, staring down at him. Gautier and Dante arraigned themselves on either side of her, supporting her with an arm around her. Gautier could feel the heat from her body through his sleeve and he couldn't understand what kept her standing.

"What is it?" he asked her softly. "What's going on there?"

Lauren turned her green eyes, now bloodshot, on him.

She doesn't see me, he realized with a start. Was it the fever? Or was she half here, with them in the station, and half... there?

Then her body stiffened and Gautier barely had time to tighten his hold on her before she slumped into unconsciousness again.

* * *

Lauren came to, her body jammed uncomfortably inside the

tree. The stench of rotting meat still fouled the air, only now it was accompanied by the rich coppery tang of blood.

Morag.

Her first impulse was to rush outside, but her survival instincts kicked in and she waited quietly inside the tree, straining to hear.

It was quiet out there, so still she couldn't even hear the birds.

Finally, she eased herself up from her crouch. Her cheek scraped against damp bark, dislodging little bits of wood that fell into her shirt. A bird called somewhere nearby and some of the tension left her shoulders.

She had a vague memory of standing over Silas' unconscious body, of Gautier and Dante speaking, of seeing and hearing through a shimmer of heat, but that world seemed far away now, unreal.

Certainly not as real as this one with its smell of blood.

A breeze found its way inside the tree and she sniffed. The stench was receding.

Cade's wendigo was gone.

She slipped out of the tree and searched the sky. Nothing. Next she scanned the soil, looking for the source of the copper smell, but didn't find any telltale wet spots.

Although the birds had begun calling to each other again, they remained hidden in the lower branches of the trees. Every other creature stayed hidden, too—no squirrels scampering from branch to branch, no voles skittering through the underbrush. She sniffed again. The only smell now was that of fear.

Lauren stood on the loamy ground of the underworld and hugged herself tightly.

Morag was gone.

Curious how Silas receded in importance now that she was in the underworld, as if he weren't as real as Morag.

The tree that had seemed so improbably big when Morag was there now seemed puny, much too small to keep her from the wendigo's sight. Involuntarily, she looked up again but there was only blue sky and a few white clouds.

The wendigo had taken Morag back with it. Or maybe it had already killed the old woman.

Lauren shuddered away from that thought. Morag was an obeah and very wise. If anyone could survive the wendigo, she could.

The brave thought dissipated under the memory of the wendigo and its feral eyes and claws, its matted blond coat, its grin of anticipation.

She thought of those sharp canines tearing into her great-grandmother's flesh, and her entire body tensed with the need for action. She had to do something, anything, to help the old woman.

Maybe the wendigo hadn't killed her yet.

"Hang on, Morag," she whispered to the wind. Then, because she suddenly thought of the old man on a table in the wilderness, she added, "You, too, Silas. I'm coming."

* * *

The dark smudge Morag had pointed out was to the east, so that's where she headed. There was no sun by which to take her bearings but she always knew her directions, even at night. Part of her mother's gaians heritage, she supposed.

As she struck out toward the east, she wondered about the rest of her ancestors—Morag had said they were hiding, but hadn't said where. She kept an eye on the sky as she walked and tried to extend her awareness beyond her immediate surroundings, but she sensed nothing. Wherever they were, they remained well hidden.

She walked in the unnatural stillness for hours, watching for any sign of attack or signs of gaians presence. In spite of the unfamiliarity of the forest, a sense of contentment gradually filled her. She was used to spending long days traveling her trapline, hunting, and fishing. She liked the feel of moss and soil beneath her moccasins, the sound of wind through the spruce trees, the sweet smell of green willow. Although the smells were different here, they were close enough for her to feel at home.

The only thing missing was Rupe padding by her side, his

quick eye watching for the telltale flicker of a grouse pretending to be invisible or a rabbit bolting for cover.

Lauren sighed. No matter how strong and healthy she felt here, back at the station she was very sick. But that world seemed unreal now. Her presence there was like a shadow seen through a sheer curtain. She knew that Gautier was fussing over her, that her fever was dangerously high, that Dante was buffeted by her fears and Silas'.

But as she walked through the fragrant woods, surrounded by huge, unfamiliar trees and wildflowers more brazen and abundant than what she was used to back home, it occurred to her that she liked it here.

After a while, she shrugged out of her heavy wool sweater and tied the sleeves around her waist. Her feet were roasting in the moccasins, but there wasn't much she could do about it. There were too many twigs and sharp stones to go barefoot.

As she walked, she considered the brief glimpse she'd gotten of the dark zone, the place where so many gaians had disappeared. It was hard to tell, but she estimated that it was at least a two-day walk—probably three. She would have to cross at least four stands of forest, which were separated by narrow strips of grassland, like a winding border.

Morag had said that ordinary gaians could not leave their home forests, that only obeahs could. Lauren was only half-gaians even though she was apparently transitioning into an obeah. There was no guarantee she would be able to cross these grasslands. And there was nothing she could do about it until she reached the first border strip.

The long walk gave her time to examine her motives in ruthless detail. She had thought she wanted to save the old woman because she was her great-grandmother—and maybe that was partly true—but the harsher truth was that Morag seemed to know about Meridy, and Lauren wanted to know everything the old woman could tell her about her mother.

And then there was Silas, who meant so much to Dante. She didn't know what she could do for the old man, but she would try to help him, if she found him. If only for Dante's sake.

After hours of traveling through the damp woods, the diffuse daylight seemed to dim, as if someone, somewhere, was turning down a wick.

Still, there was enough daylight left for her to notice that the forest was thinning. She was nearing the end of the trees. At least, this stand of trees.

She stopped, suddenly unsure of herself. Maybe she should wait until night before crossing the open grasslands, where she would be much more exposed. But she hated the thought of wasting all that time. She felt strong enough to walk all night—she didn't seem to get tired here—but couldn't help a twinge of discouragement. This was only her family's forest. She still had four more forests to cross before reaching the dark smudge that she was coming to think of as Hell. This was taking too long.

Morag might not have days. She might already be dead. At the thought, Lauren's heart tightened with dread. She liked the old woman more than she had thought.

"You would go faster if you flew."

Lauren whirled around, her hands out in a defensive posture, but there was no one there.

"Up here," came the voice, and she looked up to see a young girl, no more than ten years old, perched on a low branch.

Lauren's first reaction was amusement that this kid could have snuck up on her without her noticing. Her second reaction was dismay that this kid could have snuck up on her without her noticing.

She was dressed in blue denim pants and a short jacket in a different blue, with fancy sports shoes that used violet and pink laces. Her hair was black and her eyes the same deep brown as Dante's and Morag's, her chin the same pointed tilt.

She was family.

"What's your name?" asked Lauren.

"Rebecca," said the child promptly. "And you're Lauren." She grinned.

Lauren grinned, too. "Since you're so smart, Rebecca, how about telling me how to fly?"

Rebecca stared at her with solemn eyes. "I don't know," she said. "Only obeahs can fly."

Lauren sighed. "Well, that would be a problem, then."

The girl swung her legs while studying Lauren thoughtfully. "I saw you talking with Grandmother," she said finally. "I thought you were an obeah, too."

Lauren shrugged. "Maybe one day. Right now, I think I'm still Transitioning."

The little girl's eyes suddenly seemed to focus in on Lauren. "So it's true? You're not dead?"

"Nope," Lauren shook her head. *At least I hope not...*

Rebecca stopped swinging her legs and pushed herself off the branch, dropping the six feet to the ground to land gracefully on her feet. She straightened and looked Lauren up and down as if she hadn't been studying her intently for the last five minutes.

"How come you're Transitioning now?" she asked. "You're a grown-up."

Lauren shrugged again. She seemed to do a lot of shrugging around the girl. "I think it's because I'm only half-gaian."

A strange look crossed the girl's face, half fascination, half revulsion.

Surprised at the girl's reaction, Lauren tapped into the well of knowledge at her disposal. For the first time, she realized that these unions were considered unwise. There was a whiff of disapproval, a taint of inappropriateness to her very existence. Her ancestors didn't approve of her mother marrying a sapiens and then having the bad taste to have a child with one.

Well, hell.

A slow burn of resentment heated her as efficiently as the fever had. Her father had been a wonderful man, smart, capable, and loving. Nobody had the right to think less of him because he was sapiens.

Rebecca's expression changed suddenly to one of dismay. She reached hesitantly for Lauren's arm but stopped short of touching her. "I'm sorry," she said. "It's just that you're the only one in our family—I didn't even know it was possible until you told me."

Lauren nodded stiffly. She knew what the girl meant. She had access to all the ancestors' knowledge and experience, but only when she thought about a particular subject would that information become available.

Rebecca had obviously not spent much time thinking about inter-species unions.

Abruptly, the resentment left Lauren. It wasn't the kid's fault. It was disappointing that even a species as old and apparently wise as her mother's was capable of racism. Specieism.

"It doesn't matter," she said. She tried a smile and thought it came out well, even if Rebecca looked at her a little doubtfully. "The point is I can't fly."

Rebecca nodded, accepting the truce. They looked at each other for a moment and then the girl said, "Have you tried?"

Lauren opened her mouth, then closed it. Of course, she hadn't tried. She *knew* she couldn't fly. What was she supposed to do—launch herself from a branch and hope for the best? Flap her arms all the way to a painful landing?

She looked around at the trees and mossy ground, at the tall grasses just beyond the border of trees, at the twilight sky.

She hadn't thought it was possible for her to be here, either.

"Why are you here?" she asked the child, because the question finally occurred to her. "Why aren't you in hiding with the others?"

Rebecca stared at her, her mouth set in a mutinous line. "It's boring there. I like it here better."

Lauren tried not to smile. Obviously curiosity had lured her out of hiding.

But "here" was deserted and dangerous, in spite of the apparent calm of the day. Lauren hadn't forgotten the wendigo. What chance did a childlike Rebecca have when an obeah like Morag couldn't fend off the monster?

Which meant that Rebecca had to leave and leave quickly, before the wendigo came back. Lauren couldn't understand why the elders had allowed the child to come, alone and unprotected.

Then she remembered that Rebecca had referred to Morag as "Grandmother," which made her Meridy's sister or cousin. Lauren's aunt, maybe. Another relative she had known nothing about.

The child had died before reaching puberty.

And if she stayed here, the girl might die again.

"Any idea how this flying thing works?" she finally asked.

Rebecca shook her head, but there was a canniness to her expression that made Lauren doubt her. She shrugged elaborately.

"Then I guess I'll have to do it the hard way," she said. "I think Morag's in trouble, so I don't want to waste time finding her." She smiled at Rebecca. "It was nice meeting you."

The girl's mouth pressed shut in a familiar line, then relaxed into a grin that admitted good-natured defeat.

"I have noticed that Grandmother often closes her eyes and bends her knees a little before she takes off."

Lauren stared at the girl. It couldn't be that easy, could it? With a shrug, she closed her eyes, flexed her knees and concentrated on flying. Something in the pit of her stomach fluttered and she opened her eyes, already half-convinced she would be airborne, despite the very solid connection of her feet to the ground.

Rebecca stared back at her, disappointed.

"I guess there's more to it than I thought."

"I guess so," agreed Lauren glumly. She felt more than a little silly.

But there had been that fluttering in her belly.

"Well," she said with determination. "Looks like I walk from here."

Rebecca stared past the thinning trees, doubt written all over her face. "I hope you can," she said. "I can't leave the forest." She shrugged. "Not that I want to."

"Only one way to find out," said Lauren. She looked down at Rebecca and suddenly wanted very badly to know what had killed the child before she got a chance to grow up. Her mother had never mentioned a sister.

But she kept quiet. Hundreds of generations of ancestors whispered in her ear that it was bad form to ask. If the girl volunteered, that was different. But Rebecca didn't volunteer and Lauren set off through the trees with a wave. She walked ten feet into the high grasses before turning back with a grin. She had intended to say, "Go hide!"

But Rebecca was already gone.

* * *

After a few hours of nothing but trees, Lauren stopped walking. This was ridiculous. At this rate, it would be days before she reached her destination. Obeah or not, her feet were starting to ache and anxiety sapped her energy.

Flying was the answer. It had to be. She sank to the ground and leaned against a big tree with spreading branches that afforded some cover from the sky. *Think!* she ordered herself. How had Morag done it?

Lauren closed her eyes and concentrated on rising in the air the way Morag had. Once more, something fluttered in her stomach, but she didn't rise one inch into the air.

She spent an hour that way before rising frustration finally snapped her patience. She wanted to fly, damn it!

At once, the fluttering in her belly fused into a ball of fire and to her astonishment, she suddenly rose ten feet in the air before a branch caught her shoulder. She yelped at the pain and dropped just as suddenly to the forest floor.

She landed feet first, then fell onto her backside before flopping over onto her back. Although the ground was forgiving, it took a few minutes for her to catch her breath and sit up. When she finally did, she was grinning.

She could fly!

* * *

An hour later, she could rise at will and from there, it was only a matter of minutes before she figured out how to propel herself forward instead of up.

At last she rose above the tree level and automatically scanned the sky for signs of the wendigo. There was the dark smudge—still far away, but so much more reachable now. In spite of her tiredness, she exulted in her newfound ability. She could fly! All it had taken was a good old burst of sapiens anger.

Something to keep in mind.

* * *

Hell was a place of shadows.

After waiting out a brief night on the ground, Lauren finally stood twenty feet from the wall of darkness and looked up. In the light of a new day, shadows merged and separated, seeming to lunge at her, stopped short by an invisible barrier, like a pane of glass. The wall looked thick, as if shadows pressed on shadows. Occasionally she could make out a distorted face, dark holes for eyes, and mouth open in a scream.

Lauren shivered in fear but forced herself to stay where she was.

They're shades, she thought in horror, *straight out of Dante's Hell.* The thought brought her to Dante. He would be half-mad with worry for his grandfather, and for her. Silas' voice was louder here but still muffled, as if it were having trouble penetrating the shifting shadows.

Then she looked more sharply at the shadows in the wall. Could one of those shades be Silas? Or Morag?

She craned her head back and peered from side to side, but the wall went on as far and as high as she could see.

A wall of shades. She swallowed hard. She had to know if

Silas and Morag where on the other side of that wall. Taking a deep breath to try and control her trembling, she rose in the air and followed the wall up. It had to end somewhere.

Just below Silas' muffled voice was another sound, a sound so low it reminded her of wind soughing through spruce trees in winter. After a while, she realized what the sounds were.

Moans. Hundreds of voices, moaning.

All those shades—they were in pain. The realization filled her with dismay. All those people, all suffering... Why was Cade doing this?

Lauren stopped flying and hovered. There seemed to be no end to the rising wall.

As if in reaction to her thought, Silas' voice suddenly rose above the drone, a new urgency in his tone, but she still couldn't make out more than her name.

Even if she found a way in, she might end up like one of those shades, trapped and in pain, and then she would never find out what had happened to her mother, would never learn if Cade had taken her to Ben-My-Chree.

Would never have a chance to kill Cade for stealing her mother.

She never knew what made her look around. One moment she hovered before the wall, wondering if she dared go higher. The next moment she spun around, staring in horror at the sight of the wendigo bearing down on her from the pink sky, its lips spread wide to display its fangs, its eyes gleaming in the rosy glow of a sunless dawn.

Fear choking her, Lauren turned and flew as fast as she could away from the creature. Even as the wind whipped her hair away from her face, she knew it wasn't fast enough. A glance over her shoulder tore a cry of fear from her. Too close!

Without thinking, she launched herself at the wall.

There was no crash, as she half-expected. It was like being smothered by hundreds of Mary's down pillows. Her forward momentum suddenly slowed as shadowy arms pulled her farther and farther inside and up the wall. She instinctively fought the shades, trying to catch her breath, but it was like trying to push smoke. Every time she pushed one of the shades off, three slipped into its place.

She couldn't breathe!

"Lauren."

The quiet male voice came from just ahead. Lauren stopped fighting to listen.

"Lauren."

The shades immediately surrounding her pulled away slightly and she took a shaky breath.

"Silas?"

"Listen to me, granddaughter. There isn't much time. The ancestors are trying to protect you—stop fighting them."

Lauren obeyed. It wasn't that she trusted Silas, but she had nothing else to go on. She worked at controlling herself but it was hard. The shades pressed in against her, covering her entire body, barely an inch away from her skin. Her heart thudded with anxiety and finally she closed her eyes. Better not to look.

"Where are you?" she whispered.

"Hold your hand out," came the calm voice.

Against her instincts, she slowly pulled her right hand away from her body and pushed it through the shades. It was like pushing her hand through a pool of warm water, resistant but not unpleasant. As her hand eased through the shades, she caught wisps of emotions: confusion, fear, anger, but most of all, sadness.

Then a warm hand grasped hers and she bit off a yelp.

Using her hand as an anchor, Silas towed himself to her. At first there was nothing but variations on darkness, then the darkness eased and Silas was by her side, still grasping her hand, both of them cocooned by shades.

It was too dark to see his face, but his grasp on her was real, as was the strong, gnarled hand that held hers. And she recognized his smell—tanned leather, old man sweat, and pipe tobacco.

"They won't be able to keep the wendigo out," said Silas, leaning his dark head closer to hers. His breath smelled yeasty and sweet. "Are you ready?"

"Ready for what?" asked Lauren, her trepidation rising as she tried to see all around her.

The shades surrounding them all seemed to exhale at the same time, then pressed in closer, like bison herding their young into the safe center.

"To go back!" cried Silas just as fear spiked among the shades. Then Cade's wendigo tore through the nearest shades, shredding them in its fury to reach Lauren and Silas, and before she could tell her grandfather that she didn't know how to go back, she opened her eyes to find Gautier staring down at her, his blue eyes bloodshot and worried.

At the same time, Dante cried out, "Grandfather's coming around!"

Then Lauren closed her eyes and fell into a sleep of utter exhaustion.

❧ FIFTEEN ❧

SHE NEEDS to sleep," said Gautier stubbornly. He shook out his blanket, and the wind sent twigs and dust swirling into the cold morning.

Silas shook his head. "She needs to get to Ben-my-Chree as soon as possible."

The old man sat on a log, his hands resting on his knees, as if he was about to stand up. He'd been in that same position for the last few minutes, his face raised to the October sun, his eyes half-closed. He looked like Death warmed over.

Unmoved, Gautier finished rolling up his blanket. "When she wakes up. Not before."

It was mid-morning, after a long night. Lauren had phased in and out of awareness for hours until the fever finally broke in the early hours of the morning. She had been sleeping peacefully since then.

Silas had revived long enough to look around the station with relief, and then he, too, had fallen into a deep sleep from which he had emerged less than fifteen minutes ago. He'd eaten so ravenously that Gautier was a little worried for their supplies. He might have to do some hunting.

The day promised to be cool but sunny, with the wind picking up. High above, a couple of ravens played in the updrafts, their raucous calls harsh to his southern ears.

Dante emerged from the woods, where he had gone to relieve himself, and headed toward them. Although he had bags under his eyes from lack of sleep, he still looked better than he had in days.

"How are you feeling?" he asked his grandfather.

"Alive," said Silas, smiling. "Thanks for the food."

Dante's eyebrows rose and he laughed. "Glad you enjoyed it—I hope you still remember how to hunt!"

"I can hold my own," said Silas with a trace of smugness.

Dante laughed again and squeezed his grandfather's shoulder. The casual gesture of affection jarred Gautier and he looked away, turning his attention to his pack.

He fought the recurring feeling of betrayal. He could understand why Dante hadn't confided in him. Really, he could. Especially during the Troubles, when everything was crazy and people were suspicious of anyone who looked or behaved differently for fear they were carrying a disease.

But they had been friends for a long time. Somewhere in all those years, Dante should have confided in him about Silas. About being gaians.

Gautier could hear them murmuring to each other in the background but he tuned them out, concentrating instead on repacking his backpack. He didn't know what Lauren would want to do once she woke up, but they weren't staying here. Whether they went to Ben-My-Chree or back to Whitehorse, they would have to move fast. Already he could smell snow on the air. He wasn't familiar with the seasons this far north, but winter would come earlier and stay longer.

One way or the other, he wasn't staying here for the winter, to survive on hunting and trapping. He had a life waiting for him back in Ontario.

But the thought didn't have the same appeal it once had.

"What happened, Grandfather?"

The serious tone in Dante's voice caught his ear and he turned his attention back to the two gaians, looking expectantly at the old man.

Silas breathed deeply for a few moments, as if storing oxygen, and his hands shook.

"Grandfather?"

"It was Cade," said Silas after a long moment. He glanced from man to man, his eyes black as Dante's. "He's very strong."

Dante crouched next to his grandfather, his hand on the old man's knee. "How...?"

"A lynx," said Silas. He sounded bemused and a little offended. "He sent a lynx to attack me."

"Lynx?" said Gautier involuntarily. Lynx didn't attack people. They were shy creatures that went after rabbits and hares. They rarely attacked dogs, for Pete's sake.

"I know," said Silas, nodding as if Gautier had spoken out loud. "I knew the lynx was there, of course, but I didn't expect it to jump me. Cade attacked while I was dealing with the cat."

Gautier tensed up. Cade was this close? Maybe that's what he'd sensed in the woods last night. But Dante had caught his slight movement and shook his head.

"Not here," he said grimly. "He pulled Grandfather into the underworld." He turned back to the old man. "How did he keep you there?"

The old man looked down at the ground. His shoulders hunched as he leaned his forearms on his knees.

"He's created a kind of prison." His voice was so low that Gautier abandoned his pack to walk closer to the old man. He adopted Dante's crouch as the old man continued.

"It's a bad place," continued Silas, his gaze on the frozen ground. "He's got obeahs trapped there, and other gaians. Hundreds of them. Thousands. I think he's even killed some." He looked at his grandson. "There are other things in there, too," he added. "Bad things. In Montreal I thought I was stronger than him, but

I was wrong. I fought him off thanks to Meridy's help, but I can't stop him by myself."

Before he could continue, Gautier put up a hand palm out. "Meridy?"

Dante answered. "Lauren's mom. My aunt. Grandfather's daughter."

Now Gautier was completely confused. "I thought she was dead."

"She is," said Silas sadly.

Seeing the look on Gautier's face, Dante tried to explain how Meridy had been able to help her father, even though she was dead and imprisoned. After a while he stopped and Gautier just shook his head.

Too weird.

Silas shook his head, too. "All you need to understand, boy, is that we have to get to Ben-My-Chree." His voice had an edge.

"Why?" asked Gautier. "What's so special about Ben-My-Chree?" He tried to keep the frustration out of his voice but he didn't really care if it showed. Getting to Ben-My-Chree might get them all killed. He sure as hell wanted to know why he should risk his life—and Lauren's—to get there.

Grandfather and grandson turned to look at him, both so similar it was eerie.

Purebreds, thought Gautier suddenly. *Purebred gaians.* Lauren looked like them too, but also different. Half gaian, half human.

He wondered what the old man thought of that.

"Ben-My-Chree is a place of power," said Silas, "where the Tree of Life joins the underworld to the overworld through this world." He stamped his booted foot on the ground. "Something is drawing all the gaians to Ben-My-Chree, even Cade."

"But why?" demanded Gautier. "And why now?"

Now Dante turned to look at his grandfather, as if he wanted to hear the answer, too.

"I don't know. Not exactly. All I know is that I am being called to Ben-My-Chree. I felt the call as soon as I started this trip."

"Well, who the hell is calling?"

Dante fought to keep a smile off his face, but Silas looked completely serious. "I think the call is coming from the overworld."

The smile disappeared from Dante's face. "The overworld?"

At his grandfather's nod, Dante looked bemused. He glanced at Gautier, saw the expression on his face, and explained.

"The overworld is... unknown to us." He shrugged. "All gaians know this world, of course," he waved at the trees and sky, "and the obeahs know the underworld, but no one's ever gone to the overworld."

Even as he asked the question, Gautier couldn't escape a feeling of unreality.

"Then how do you know it exists?"

The gaians remained silent for a moment. With a glance at his grandfather, Dante finally answered.

"We can sense it," he said. "We know there's more than the *here* we see and the underworld."

Gautier straightened slowly. "Are you saying you have faith that it exists? Like some people—sapiens—believe that Heaven exists?"

He tried to keep his skepticism from showing, and knew he'd failed when Silas bristled.

"It's more than blind faith, young man." Those white brows met in a frown, lending Silas a fierceness he didn't normally have. "For centuries obeahs have sensed another plane of existence, a... gathering of thought and wisdom, just out of our reach. We've tried to access it but we were never successful. Now, however, it seems the overworld is reaching out for us."

Gautier crossed his arms across his chest, refusing to ask.

"We don't know why," said Dante, attuned to his skepticism. "I didn't even know what the call was until just now. I've been feeling it, too, only worse. I've been feeling the compulsion driving every gaians I've sensed on this trip. Lauren feels it, too."

Right. Time to give up on this line of questioning. He turned back to the old man.

"You said you only felt the call once you were on the road. What made you come in the first place?"

Silas looked blank for a moment, as if the question caught him by surprise. Then his expression shifted and he sighed.

"It was only after Dante left that I realized my mistake," he said. "I tried to catch up before you reached her but you both moved fast."

Once again, Dante translated. "Lauren's age," he said.

Gautier frowned, trying to remember what Dante had said about Lauren's age earlier. Something about puberty...

Silas took pity on him. "I learned of Lauren's existence only to find out she was in danger from Cade," he said. "When I sent Dante to fetch her, I forgot that time means nothing in the underworld. To Meridy, Lauren was still the ten-year-old she last saw."

Dante nodded as if he understood, but Gautier still struggled. "So Lauren was actually older than her mother remembered?"

"Yes. Old enough for Dante's arrival to trigger her Transition. I knew she'd be in danger." Silas sighed and rubbed his cheeks, still smooth. Gautier reflexively scratched his short beard, wishing he could shave it, or at least wash the damned thing.

It made sense now, or at least, as much sense as any of this did. Part of him felt relieved that the old man was here. He was an obeah—he'd be able to help Lauren. But something still bothered him, although he couldn't pin it down.

"She's going through hell," he said finally. "This Transition thing is killing her." He took a deep breath and looked the old man in the eye. "I think I should take her back home. You and Dante go to Ben-My-Chree if you need to."

Silas looked at him consideringly, as if weighing which words to choose. Finally he shook his head. "She's a part of whatever is happening there. She needs to be there."

"Jesus," said Gautier. "Do you think you could be more specific?"

Once more, the old man shrugged. "No."

This was his granddaughter he was talking about. He was being pretty damned cavalier about her safety!

Suddenly Gautier's eyes narrowed as an unpleasant possibility occurred to him.

"How did Lauren get into the underworld?" he asked. "I thought she could only... go there if she survived her Transition." He didn't want to think about the possibility of her failing.

An expression flitted over the old man's face, so quickly that it was gone by the time Dante turned to look at him. But Gautier saw.

It was shame.

"I called her," said Silas. His chin lifted slightly, as if daring Gautier to criticize him. "I was trapped and I needed help."

Gautier caught Dante's dumbfounded expression out of the corner of his eye, but he couldn't tear his gaze away from Silas.

The man had risked his granddaughter's life to save his own.

Gautier's hands tensed and he fought an urgent need to shake the old man until his squat little body broke in two.

* * *

In his mind, Silas could see the shimmering Tree of Life, each leaf shining with power, each branch limned in unearthly light as it reached for the overworld. Every cell in his body yearned to be in its presence. He glanced at his grandson, knowing that Dante felt the compulsion even if he couldn't see the Tree.

Yet the boy said nothing about leaving, seemingly content to wait until his cousin was awake.

In these few days, she had managed to command their loyalty. He didn't know what to think of this granddaughter of his. The chances were that she wouldn't survive her Transition. Few did. But she was strong. Even as a half-breed she had been able to cross into the underworld and return. So strong that she had been able to pull him back with her to the real world.

He hoped she would live.

And so he reined in his impatience and kept silent as the hours dragged by. The ache in his body gradually left as the sun warmed him and he began to move around. He rearranged the supplies in his own backpack, helped Dante carry the sled outside—quietly, so as not to wake his granddaughter—and re-arranged the supplies in it. He built a small fire outside and made tea.

Dante disappeared for a few hours and returned with a grouse and a rabbit, which Gautier skinned and cooked. Silas suspected that Gautier hadn't wanted to leave him alone with Lauren. He had seen the look in the boy's eyes when he told them that he was responsible for calling Lauren to the underworld before she was ready. Even Dante had looked shocked.

Silas didn't explain that his call had been the unconscious, instinctive response of an obeah in danger, a call to other obeahs for help. It hadn't been meant for her. A transitioning obeah shouldn't have been able to hear him from the real world.

He didn't explain because the truth was, he was willing to sacrifice them all, even his newly-found half-breed granddaughter, if that's what it took. They were all going to die unless he found a way to stop Cade.

They were enjoying the rabbit in the afternoon sunshine when Dante suddenly looked up at the door with a smile.

"The last rose of springtime," he announced.

Silas turned around and caught his breath. Lauren stood in the doorway of the small station, one hand holding onto the frame, a gray wool blanket wrapped around her shoulders. She had lines pressed into her cheek from where the blanket had been folded beneath her. Her hair was short and rumpled and her eyes were big and green—the same green as her father's—above high cheekbones. Her chin came to a point.

Except for those green eyes, she looked just like Meridy. His baby had had a baby and she'd been too angry to tell him. He wondered if she ever would have.

"Morag is still trapped," said Lauren, looking straight at him.

Her voice was her own, neither like her mother's nor her father's, deep, with a musicality that was foreign to gaians. She was taller than Meridy had been.

"I know," he said.

She frowned and then he saw it, a strangeness in those green eyes, a sense that she was not fully here. The child was still in danger—she was still connected to the underworld. If Cade figured that out, he could attack her here.

"We have to help her," said Lauren.

For a moment, he didn't know what she was talking about. Then he shook his head. "No," he said. He suddenly felt old. He couldn't help Morag, not until he got to Ben-My-Chree. Perhaps when he had been younger he could have but now... now Cade was too strong.

"She's your grandmother!" said Lauren, her face pale.

Gautier rose to his feet, drawing Silas' attention. He saw finally that the boy was in love with his granddaughter. His heart sank. He was always slow to see these things in sapiens. Another complication.

"Lauren, you need to eat," said Gautier.

She ignored him. Silas wasn't even sure she'd heard him. He sighed silently.

"Did you try to go back?" he asked softly.

She nodded, the movement more like a jerk than an assent.

"And you couldn't?"

She paused, still staring at him out of those strange eyes, then slowly shook her head.

"But I did it before," she said.

She had no idea how she had done it, or how to do it again. Thank goodness.

"You were able to get there because you followed my call," he said grimly, not looking at either of the two men. "Cade had me trapped. You saved my life."

Lauren finally released the door frame and came toward the

fire. Gautier took her elbow and guided her to the sun-warmed rock he had just vacated. He pushed her down then filled a tin plate with a rabbit haunch and a chunk of bannock he pulled out of his own pack.

"Eat," he told her, pushing the plate into her hands. Without a word, she sniffed the steaming meat. As if the act itself triggered her appetite, she was soon tearing enthusiastically at the meal.

Silas and the two men watched her eat in silence. Silas' thoughts kept returning to Cade. He had never met an obeah whose skill and power were greater than his, until his confrontation with Cade in Montreal. Whatever else awaited them in Ben-My-Chree, he would have to confront Cade again. He was ready to die, if his time had come, but the thought of leaving Cade behind to wreak havoc filled him with fear.

As if reading his mind, Lauren suddenly looked straight at him. "What does he want?"

"Cade?" At her nod, he nodded too. "He wants all the sapiens dead," he said baldly.

Gautier looked at him but Silas kept his attention on Lauren, studying her as she reacted to his words.

"He's always hated them, I think," he continued. "He blames sapiens for everything that's gone wrong with the world." He shrugged. "I only caught a glimpse of his thoughts when he attacked me in Montreal, but it's clear that he believes the world would be better off with gaians in charge."

"But he's half-sapiens," said Lauren.

"I didn't say it was logical. The man's insane."

Lauren nodded. "He killed Mary. He hurt Rupe." Her face took on a closed expression that made Silas' heart squeeze with pain. Meridy had hidden her feelings from him in exactly that way.

Not again. He wouldn't lose this child of his child because he couldn't hear what she was saying. He leaned forward and placed a hand on Lauren's knee. "Tell me," he offered.

She looked startled but then her face softened. He saw the look of surprise on Gautier's face but he couldn't see Dante.

"It was the day I met Gautier and Dante," she said. At first her voice was halting, as if she wasn't used to talking, but then the words began to tumble out and before long, she had told him about Cade's attempt to abduct her, the wounding of her dog, the burning of her foster parents' house, and her foster mother's death. He knew most of it already, from talking with Charlie Sproule, but he let her talk. Finally she slowed down.

"Then he left Mom's hair band and wedding ring and I knew the bastard had taken her. I think he's keeping her prisoner at Ben-My-Chree."

Shock sluiced through Silas like ice water. She thought Meridy was still alive. Gautier looked at Lauren as if she were made of crystal and would break at any moment. Then he turned to look at Silas.

"Tell her," he said roughly.

Silas couldn't speak. All these years... had she always thought her mother was alive?

"Tell me what?" asked Lauren, looking from face to face.

"Lauren..." began Silas, then fell silent. He had just found her. He couldn't destroy her like this.

Gautier turned his back on Silas, showing his contempt, but when he spoke to Lauren, his voice was gentle.

"She's dead, Lauren." Her face reflected her confusion, but Gautier kept going, doing the hard thing that Silas couldn't. In that moment, he felt the first stirring of respect for the young man. "That's how your grandfather found out about you—your mother told him about you in the underworld."

Lauren shook her head, obviously baffled. "But she's not there," she began. "Morag was there, and others, hidden, but not Mom—"

"Lauren," interrupted Silas, silencing her. "You couldn't sense her because Cade has her trapped in a pocket of the underworld. Morag didn't know either," he added. "It was only by accident that

I found her, because Cade was trying to trap me there, too."

His words were harsh, as was his tone, but he couldn't help it. It hurt enough that Meridy had been dead ten years before he found out—he couldn't take Lauren's insistence that her mother was still alive.

He forced himself to look at her as hope died in her face. Shock turned to grief and her skin paled to the color of ashes. She remained seated, hands grasping the rim of the plate on her lap as if it would save her from drowning. Gautier moved closer to her but didn't try to touch her. Dante finally moved from behind Silas and went to stand on Lauren's other side, offering his own silent support.

Finally Lauren rose and scraped the rabbit bones into the embers of the fire. When she straightened, her expression was unreadable.

"It's time to go," she said.

❧ SIXTEEN ❧

L AUREN found the Fantail Trail without a problem after clambering across the icy chunks of asphalt that were all that was left of the Klondike Highway. Winters were hard in the Pass. The snow cover was crisscrossed by patterns of tiny feet: voles, coyotes, even ravens.

She ranged far ahead of the others, wishing she could leave them behind forever. But no matter how fast she walked, every time she turned around, Gautier was within sight.

She didn't mind his presence so much. It was the other two, especially the old man, that she didn't want around right now. Although she couldn't see them, she knew Dante and Silas were still behind her on the trail. She could feel them.

She had been eight years old the first time she came to Log Cabin after hiking the four-day Chilkoot Trail with her parents. They had taken the small train from Bennett to Log Cabin at the end of their hike, and once they clambered out of the train, her father had pointed out the head of the Fantail Trail. He had shown her on the map how the trail led past Fantail Lake to Taku Arm. Ben-My-Chree was at the tip of Taku Arm, where the Swanson River met the lake.

He had told her the story of the man and woman who had settled there and the wonderful gardens they had grown. Even then she had longed to see those gardens.

But it was at least thirty miles of tough going. Even if she avoided the mountains and followed the dozens of river valleys, many of those rivers wouldn't have frozen over yet, despite the cold and the snow. Same with the pothole lakes. It would be at least three days of cold, wet traveling, at a time of year when only a fool traveled.

The sun shone cool, already on its way down. She avoided looking at it. Every time she did, it turned into Cade's big, white-blond head, his mouth split open as he laughed at her.

Cade.

Her stomach roiled unpleasantly, the mixture of hate and grief spoiling the rabbit. But she swallowed and ignored her stomach's distress. She would need all her strength to get to Ben-My-Chree.

To get to Cade.

A thousand times Lauren told herself to stop, turn around, go back home to Whitehorse while there was still time. But her feet kept walking and her nose kept pointing toward Ben-My-Chree.

Even knowing her mother was dead, she still kept walking, her long strides trying to put distance between herself and the three men behind her. Trying to eat up the distance between herself and Ben-My-Chree.

The temperature dropped along with the sun, tightening her cheeks with cold and sending steam ribboning out of her mouth with every breath. She saw at least a dozen rabbits watching her warily, barely twitching in their need to remain unnoticed, their coats already winter white. She could smell their fear. As she walked she grew aware of a familiar sound, one just below the call of the ravens and the stealthy padding of the wolves that kept a curious eye on her.

Her attention focused on the sound and as it did, her surroundings faded. She blinked and stopped walking. Everything around her turned filmy—the trees, the snow, the sky—and just beyond the film was another scene, a familiar one. She stared at it for a minute, trying to understand what she was seeing, then the scene snapped into focus and she was standing in front of the wall of shades again, their low moaning filling her ears and her heart with fear and pity.

Then she blinked and she was back on the trail, the wind cold on her cheeks and bare hands, the cawing of the ravens filling her with sudden trepidation.

* * *

Gautier caught up with her two hours later. The sun was down and the temperature had dropped well past the freezing mark.

"Lauren," he called. She glanced over her shoulder at him. "It's time to stop for the night."

Lauren turned back to the trail. There was still light. She could go at least another mile before it got too dark to see.

"Lauren." Gautier's hand on her arm stopped her and she looked at him in surprise that he had moved so fast. "It's time to stop," he repeated firmly. He nodded at the trail. "We can cross it tomorrow."

Lauren followed his gaze and saw a river only ten feet away. She had been about to plunge straight into it. The realization brought her back to herself and she nodded jerkily. In the morning she could find a better place to ford, one that might keep her feet dry.

"All right," she said. She turned her back on him and set about making camp.

Again his hand on her arm stopped her. She turned back to him.

"What?"

His head jerked back slightly as if he was surprised at her reaction. "It's too exposed here," he said. "We have to find shelter."

She glanced around and for the first time in a while, really saw her surroundings. The river cut through gray rock, heading steadily downhill and gathering speed as it did. The rock on either side was covered with a few inches of snow on top of lichen—treacherous walking, even in her mukluks. Mountains rose far and near, gray in the failing light with stripped poplar bushes and stunted black spruce. Wild grasses grew in crannies, their stalks bobbing stiffly in the wind.

She looked to the south. As far as she could see were mountains and gullies, gray with winter and growing darkness.

Gautier stepped close and peered intently down at her. "This is insane," he said urgently. "Even if we make it to Ben-My-Chree, what then? We'll be trapped there by winter." His hands found her shoulders and she could feel the intensity vibrating through him.

"Come back with me," he urged. His blue eyes seemed almost black in the fading light. "We can come back in the spring if you still want to."

A small part of her noticed the "we" and filed it away. At the same time as her heart warmed to his concern, she was shaking her head.

"It's too late," she said. Her voice sounded strange, as if it were coming from far away. She heard again the low moaning of the shades trapped in Cade's prison. Then Gautier's hands tightened on her shoulders and she focused on him. "I need to get to Ben-My-Chree."

Gautier's hands fell away and she thought she heard him sigh, but the wind snatched the sound away before she could be sure.

* * *

By their third morning on the Fantail Trail, Gautier was almost out of his mind with worry. There was something seriously wrong with Lauren.

She stalked like a mad woman out of one of the fairy tales from his childhood. She ranged as far ahead of him as she could and sometimes, it took all he had just to keep her in sight. Once, after she had relieved herself, she left her backpack behind and he had to carry the extra weight until he could catch up with her and strap it back on her.

She just looked at him blankly and set out again without a word. At least the weight of the backpack slowed her down some.

He followed her through frozen marshes, up and down gullies, across small frozen lakes, and sometimes, across shallow rivers. While he took the time to find a good place to ford or at least take his boots and socks off, she simply forged through in a straight line as if oblivious to the cold and the wet.

Every night he had a fire going by the time Dante and the old man caught up to them, with the sled in tow. No one spoke while he pulled off Lauren's mukluks and socks and dried them as best he could. Every night he rubbed her feet and examined them carefully for signs of frostbite, but either she was very lucky or her half-gaians body generated enough heat to keep her toes safe.

Every night, she rolled herself into her blanket and fell into a deep sleep while Gautier watched her like a hawk.

The third day dawned overcast. They rose and ate in silence and as Gautier settled the backpack onto his back, he looked back at the distance they had come. They had spent the night on a point overlooking yet another anonymous river and it caught him off guard to see how far they had descended while following the river valleys. When he turned toward the south, he saw no color. Even when the sun crested the mountains, the world would remain black and white.

"Smells like snow," said Silas, fitting on the sled's waist strap.

Gautier surreptitiously sniffed the air. It smelled clean and fresh and maybe a bit denser. He glanced sideways at the other man. You didn't have to be gaians to figure out from the slate-gray sky that it would snow at some point today.

Dante's mouth tightened and Gautier stared at him suspiciously. Was he trying to hide a smile?

Then Lauren set off and there was no more talking.

Gautier settled into the familiar rhythm of walking just fast enough to keep Lauren in sight. As he walked, his gaze scanned the terrain to either side and ahead of him. He had never worried about wild animals attacking him—wild animals were notoriously shy—but that was before the lynx jumped Silas.

Now that obeahs roamed the woods, setting off wild cats, he wasn't taking any chances.

Dante had been remarkably calm for the past few days. Every night when they warmed themselves around the campfire, drinking tea and eating the first warm meal of the day, Dante shook his head at Gautier's mute question. He sensed no one nearby.

At first Gautier thought that was a good sign, until he caught sight of Silas' worried face. For whatever reason, it didn't reassure the old man that there were no obeahs or gaians around.

Gautier wondered why, but didn't ask. He had enough to mull over in the few minutes before exhaustion caught him up and sent him into oblivion.

They were getting close. They had crossed the tree line yesterday afternoon. The further south they had walked, the bigger the trees were. Gautier figured they would make Ben-My-Chree by mid-morning tomorrow. In spite of not knowing what to expect, he looked forward to the end of this damned trek, if only for Lauren's sake.

The underbrush was thicker here and they'd had to stick close to the river. He didn't know its name but it was too big to cross.

Lauren had seemed disoriented. She had paused often, looking around as if to get her bearings. Gautier was able to shorten the distance between them and keep it short. Her pace slowed so much that Dante and Silas were able to catch up, though they too seemed withdrawn and uncommunicative.

Gautier finally stopped the group at midday and forced Lauren to eat some jerky and drink from her canteen. She refused to sit down but took long pulls from the canteen and tore at the jerky as if she hadn't eaten in days.

While Dante and his grandfather examined the bottom of the sled for damage from the rocky terrain, Lauren climbed a rock spur and Gautier followed her. They stood silently, watching the valley unroll below them.

For as far as he could see, the world was forest. Pothole lakes glittered through the trees, and bare patches gleamed bald with snow. Mountains rose along either side of the river valley and faded into smudged paleness in the distance.

The cold sun had broken through the overcast to shine wanly on Lauren's head, revealing snarls in hair that hadn't been combed in days. Although they all smelled ripe after days in the bush, there was something off about her smell, something sickly sweet that didn't fit. Her brow felt normal but her eyes looked sunken and feverish again.

His touch seemed to soothe her and she closed her eyes. When he cupped her cheek, she turned her face into his caress with a soft sigh. When she opened her eyes, she looked almost normal.

"How're you doing, kiddo?" he asked gently. He had stopped harassing her about turning back. There was no point. Tomorrow they would be at Ben-My-Chree. He'd deal with whatever they found there and hope he could get her out before winter set in.

She smiled crookedly and his heart squeezed when he noticed hollows in her cheeks that hadn't been there before.

"I'm fine," she said, looking away from him. Then something in her face slid away and he was looking at a frightened woman. He instinctively moved closer to her.

"What is it?"

"The voices," she said, still not looking at him, her voice low with anguish. "I hear them all the time now..."

"What do they say?" His hands moved and suddenly he was holding her carefully by the shoulders. "Are they threatening you?"

She shook her head and now the tears came. She seemed unaware of them as they traced clean paths on her wind-burned and dusty face.

"Begging," she whispered. "They're begging me for help..."

He pulled her into his arms, unable to give her anything but the comfort of his strong body to lean on and warm arms to hold her.

He wanted to whisper stupid little endearments to her, promise her that everything was going to be all right, that she would be fine.

But the words couldn't get past the rage caught in his throat.

At that moment, standing on a rocky outcrop halfway between heaven and hell, Gautier hated everything to do with gaians.

Everything except Lauren.

She held on to him as if he were the last stable thing in her world and he held her just as tightly, trying to press some of his strength into her body.

Finally she moved and he reluctantly relaxed his hold. She looked up at him, her green eyes red-rimmed, her face dirty, and he caught his breath as the realization hit him.

He loved her.

She smiled at him with a hint of her old self-confidence.

"Better now. Thanks, Gautier." Then she released him and he had to let her go. A noise from down below caught his attention and he looked down to find Dante staring up at him.

Gautier turned away from the pity in his eyes.

* * *

The rest of the day was a misery. Lauren pushed herself way too hard and Dante and the old man were no better. They were like thirsty horses smelling water—the only thing on their mind was getting to Ben-My-Chree.

At last Gautier called a halt, over all their objections. It was getting too dark to travel safely. At least for him. And he wasn't letting them go on without him, especially not Lauren. He couldn't trust them to make rational decisions.

Cade would be waiting for them and Gautier definitely wanted them rational. Or at least rested.

The spot he picked was in the trees, protected from the wind, near enough to the river that they could easily get water.

The three gaians stumbled around, getting in each other's way until Gautier lost patience.

"Dante, you get the wood. Silas, we'll need water. Lauren, you can start supper."

They all nodded numbly at him and went off to their assigned chores. Gautier watched the two men go and then turned to watch Lauren pull packets of jerky and nuts out of the sled.

She stayed apart, kept her distance from the others. If anyone came too close, she moved away. He didn't think she was doing it on purpose.

None of them had objected to him taking over, not even the old man. They reminded him of the bad days of the Troubles, when people who had lost everything—friends and family, jobs and homes—wandered around the streets of London, looking for a reason to live.

What stayed with him of those times was how so many of them shied away from kindness and help. More often than not, they wandered until they dropped of exhaustion, only to die where they fell.

Gautier shook the bad memory away. These people weren't sick. They were exhausted, yes, and maybe they were vulnerable to the weird pull of this Ben-My-Chree, but they weren't dying.

Silas returned, having filled all their gourds with water from the river. He had washed his face, which reassured Gautier.

Then Dante returned with an armful of twigs and branches and Gautier set to building the fire, using some of the precious matches Lauren had found at Log Cabin. Within minutes, fire kept the shadows at bay and water boiled in the pot.

The sight of the fire seemed to cheer them all up and Dante cut up the last of the rabbit, adding a few dried onions and dried parsley. As the rich odor wafted through the trees, Gautier pulled out the various sleeping pallets and set them out around the fire.

Finally Lauren pulled out some of the travel bread that Silas had brought with him and joined them at the fire. Gautier caught her eye and she smiled slightly. The wave of relief flooding through him was completely out of proportion to the smile.

They sat on their bedrolls to eat, balancing their hot bowls on their knees. After a few minutes of companionable silence, Dante belched with satisfaction. "That is the best stew I've ever eaten."

"Even if you do say so yourself," added Gautier, and he belched, too. Dante laughed.

"For Pete's sake!" Lauren sounded annoyed, but there was a thread of amusement in her voice. Gautier almost belched again, just for the joy of hearing her sound so normal.

Silas saved him the trouble by letting rip with the loudest, most sustained belch Gautier had ever heard. The three of them stared at the old man in various stages of admiration and outrage.

"Years of practice," said Silas smugly before taking a big bite out of his bread.

⤗ SEVENTEEN ⤖

SILAS woke knowing that something was wrong. He quietly pulled the blanket from his face to sniff the air, and flinched when something cold landed gently on his cheek and melted.

Snow. He opened his eyes to ghostly darkness and stretched his awareness out over the night.

Half a mile away, an owl hooted, its call echoing eerily against the mountains. Closer, a young wolf—male by its scent—curled into a lonely ball, cast out of his pack. Silas sent the young animal thoughts of quiet and peace, then turned his attention closer to camp.

Melted snow ran off his face into his ears and hair, and still Silas listened and sniffed.

Finally he realized that it was an absence that had woken him up. Something he had grown accustomed to was missing.

Next to him, Dante stirred as, even in his sleep, he sensed Silas' alarm.

Lauren.

Just as Silas sat up, a firebrand flared, swirling through the air. The hackles rose on the back of his neck even as he registered that Gautier's hand held the burning branch.

"What is it?" said Dante, rising quickly.

Silas rose more slowly, cursing the arthritis in his knees.

"Lauren!" called Gautier.

He turned when Silas and Dante came up behind him. He immediately pulled back the branch before the burning tip could hurt anyone.

"She's gone."

Silas stood still, staring up unseeingly at the young man.

"Grandfather?" asked Dante, moving closer. "What's happening?"

The sky was growing lighter—it would be morning soon. A massive shiver shook Silas and he automatically rubbed his arms.

All along he had served the child poorly, and now his lack of foresight might kill her.

"Silas!" said Gautier sharply. "If you know something, for God's sake, spit it out!"

Then Dante took a step back as Silas' dismay reached him. "Oh no..." he said. "The Passage?"

Silas nodded, unable to control the sick feeling in his stomach. It made sense. Her irritability, her strange scent, and especially her growing need to be apart from others. He hadn't helped an obeah through Passage in over fifty years, but he should have remembered the signs.

If she had followed the normal gaians pattern, the first signs of her Passage into obeah would have come a few years after her Transition. But all her patterns were skewed from being half sapiens.

Gautier dropped the firebrand into the fire, where it caught and spat sparks, and began putting on his boots.

"Where are you going?" asked Dante in alarm.

"I'm going after her, of course."

"No!" said Silas and Dante at the same time.

Gautier paused and looked up. Silas could tell by the squinting of his eyes that the younger man was having difficulty making out their expressions.

"Why the hell not?"

"This is the most crucial part of her Transition," said Silas. "Before a gaians can become an obeah, he or she must follow a... a sort of spirit quest."

Gautier stood up and picked up several burning branches from the revived fire. "I don't have time for this," he said grimly. "She's out there right now and I'm going after her."

"If you do," said Dante quietly, "you risk killing her."

Gautier remained silent, but in that silence Silas heard all the fears whispering in the boy's heart. Gautier didn't know whether to believe them or follow his own instincts.

But interrupting Lauren's Passage—an already dangerous quest —might destroy her. His granddaughter had been stumbling along the edge of insanity for days. She had to be allowed the time she needed to regain her sanity, her self.

Or lose it entirely.

"She needs to be alone right now," said Silas, trying to impart calm to this young man the way he had the wolf. "This is a time where her powers will be tested, here and in the underworld." Best not to think of what might await her in the underworld. Best not to think of Meridy and how he had failed her yet again.

"What powers?" asked Gautier, and even in the darkness before true dawn, Silas could see the whites of his knuckles as he gripped the burning branches. The boy's sweat smelled of anxiety.

"They are different with each obeah," said Silas gently. Warmth descended over him and he jumped, startled. Dante tucked the blanket tighter around him. "Thank you," said Silas, patting his grandson on the shoulder and grasping the edges of the blanket to keep it closed. He turned back to Gautier.

"She may learn to see through flesh and bone to the illnesses within them. Or she may learn to understand the calls of animals. She may be able to far-travel outside her body. We won't know until she returns. But she needs to find her own way through the maze of the underworld and discover what kind of obeah she wants to be."

He paused to take a deep breath and study Gautier's face. He didn't want to tell him of the trials Lauren would face, the dark places she would visit before she could find her way back to the real world. This was hard enough on the young man.

He saw suspicion on Gautier's face and realized that the young man still thought Silas had willingly risked Lauren's life to save his own when he was trapped in the underworld. He should have said something at the time, dispelled the misapprehension, but he'd been too tired—and too stubborn—to explain himself to a sapiens boy.

And now it might be too late.

"Gautier," said Dante into the silence. "Obeahs can die at any stage of their Transition, or go insane. And the Passage is the most dangerous part of the whole Transition. But this is the one part they have to do alone."

Alone, yes, but not unprepared. As an older obeah, he should have trained his granddaughter to understand what she would endure in the underworld. He should have warned her about the dangers of the spirit quest and taught her that fear could be her ally, if she allowed it.

Instead he had ignored all the signs in his obsession with Ben-My-Chree and allowed her to slip away into the night, obeying instincts she wouldn't even understand, to undergo an ordeal with no preparation.

"Bullshit," said Gautier with quiet intensity. "She's only half-gaians." He addressed Dante, ignoring Silas. "You said it yourself, Dante. You don't know how the Transition will affect her. I'm not leaving her out there alone."

Then he turned and headed further into the woods, carrying his makeshift torches. Silas wondered how the sapiens could possibly know which direction she had taken. Maybe he was right, after all. Maybe Lauren needed her grandfather more than she needed to be alone. He was about to call out to the young man when Dante's hand grasped his arm in an urgent warning.

"There's someone out there," he whispered. "Gaians and one obeah."

Alarm spiked through Silas. He had allowed himself to be distracted, again.

"Gautier!" Dante called a warning to his friend and to Silas' shock, the boy had a hunting knife in his hands.

A knife. For the first time, Silas understood that the danger they faced was perhaps more physical than metaphysical. In spite of the lynx attack, he hadn't worried about physical attacks. It wasn't the gaians way.

But it was Cade's way. Obviously Dante understood that more clearly than his grandfather.

Silas looked around, feeling suddenly deaf and blind. There was no noise anywhere in the woods—no scratching of voles just below the ground, no shifting of the wolf in his sleep, nothing. Unlike Dante, he had to stretch his perception out to feel them, just there in the woods.

Then something moved in his peripheral vision and he turned as swiftly as his knees would allow to see a shadow slipping between two fir trees.

"There," he whispered, nodding in the direction of the movement, but Dante didn't move.

"They're all around us," he said grimly.

In Montreal, the ancestors had breathed a warning to him, but that was before Cade imprisoned or destroyed so many of them. Now Silas felt disconnected and alone, in spite of Dante's presence.

Dante had said one obeah with the gaians, but Silas couldn't feel the obeah the way he had felt Cade, back in Montreal. It was as if the obeah wasn't connected to the underworld. And yet, he could smell menace on the dawn air. These gaians had elevated levels of adrenaline in their blood.

Then a half a dozen silent shadows surged from the trees and he focused his attention on the strangers.

As soon as he did, he felt a familiar wrenching sensation as something ripped his awareness out of the real world. He dimly sensed his body crumpling to the frozen ground and suddenly found himself rushing downward through the darkness of the underworld, his feet trapped in a hard grip.

A cold wind whistled past his ears, freezing his cheeks and nose, and the blanket whipped above his head like a cape.

This time he knew exactly where he was. This was the place Cade's dark psyche had created in the grim recesses of the underworld. This was the place the mad obeahs had found and couldn't leave. This was the place Cade had turned into a prison for gaians who did not want to follow him.

Silas could find himself trapped, like Meridy and so many others. And then Cade would have free access to Lauren.

Claws snatched at his blanket and he released it. A muffled cry rewarded him as the blanket wrapped around his would-be attacker.

He might be old, but he was still a powerful obeah, perhaps too powerful for Cade to take easily. Otherwise he'd be dead now. Ignoring the brutal hold on his ankles, Silas concentrated on creating light. It was time to see where the mad obeah was taking him.

He filled himself with light—sunlight, moonlight and starlight—and allowed it to spread from him in a glow that had him at the center.

At once he was released to float in mid-air. He looked down but the obeah had retreated to the darkness beyond the reach of his light.

Then, warned by a whisper of sound, he looked up.

Swift as a cougar and just as deadly, Cade swooped down on Silas, his fingers turned to claws, his teeth fangs.

It was all false, of course, but the effect was the same as if Cade had jumped on Silas in the real world.

Silas leaped to one side, wheeling to face his attacker. But

Cade wasn't there and neither was the obeah who had brought him here.

Instead, Silas found himself... nowhere. He squinted against a glare but could see nothing but white. He turned slowly, but saw no edges or borders, nothing to indicate if he was in a room or a hall or even outside.

He lifted a hand to his eyes and was reassured when he could see it. So it wasn't that he couldn't see—there was simply nothing to see.

He remained where he was, allowing his senses to passively absorb what they could, but there was nothing to hear, smell, or feel. He couldn't even tell if his feet were on the ground.

He looked up. Above his head was a small black dot. He stared at it for a long time, trying to make out what it could be.

Then he remembered Meridy and his perspective shifted.

He wasn't in a room. He was in a well like the one keeping Meridy prisoner. That pinprick above his head was an opening.

Now that he knew, he could distinguish the rounded walls of his prison and feel the cold emanating from them. His feet felt the ice through his boots and he shivered, missing the warmth of the blanket.

He had to get out. Dante was still in the real world, alone against a half a dozen gaians and an insane obeah who was working with Cade.

Although he had never needed to before, Silas knew how to create his own set of tools. He concentrated on his hands, thinking of his need. As he watched, his gnarled fingers melded together, fusing and hardening into white bone hooks.

He immediately began to climb.

* * *

Gautier turned back long before Dante called his name.

The unnatural silence of the woods warned him that something was wrong. He stopped not fifty feet from camp, straining to hear, to see. Lauren needed him. He could feel her danger, her need, in the marrow of his bones, and still he hesitated.

Something was wrong. Every instinct warned him to go back, that there was an even more immediate danger nearby. And the makeshift torches he was carrying were like a big neon sign pointing straight at him.

He tossed the flaming branches into the woods and was turning back toward the camp when a rustling in the underbrush froze him in position.

There was someone in the woods with him.

At once he was back in the woods near Log Cabin, pulling Silas in the sled, listening for whatever was stalking him.

Then Dante called his name in warning. Gautier shrugged out of his pack, pulled his hunting knife from its belt sheath, and ran.

Either he had been gone longer than he thought or his eyes had finally adjusted, but he could see just enough to make out five or six figures struggling among the trees. They were all about the same size and most of them seemed to be trying to reach the one figure in the center.

"Gautier!" cried Dante again.

At once Gautier realized that Dante was the focus of the attack. Where was the old man?

"Gautier!" Dante's voice sounded desperate. He couldn't hold them off much longer. It was too much like the Troubles, when gangs would attack loners for their meager possessions, or sometimes, just for the pleasure of killing.

The fear, frustration and anger of the past few days coalesced into one white-hot ball of rage inside Gautier's chest. With a roar of fury, he ran straight at the melee, his knife slashing at the strangers, kicking at unprotected knee caps, and slamming his fist into windpipes.

He could barely make out faces in the poor light, but they were all smaller than him, more like Dante's size. Still, he could see clearly enough to make out the flicker of a knife hand and the grimace of hate behind it.

The old habits came rushing back and he effortlessly blocked an awkward lunge with a knife, moving in quickly to knee the hapless attacker in the groin. Then he elbowed another man in the midriff and had the satisfaction of hearing the whoosh of escaping air. He was almost at Dante.

"Hang on, Dante!" he exulted. The blood sang in his veins and he felt invincible.

"Watch your back!" warned Dante. Gautier stepped sideways and swept his leg out, tripping his attacker, who landed with a thud. Dante kicked out and the man stayed still.

Then they were back to back, like in the old days. "How many?' asked Gautier over his shoulder.

"Two down, I think," said Dante. There was a funny catch in his voice. "Four more out there."

Before Gautier could turn to look at his friend, the remaining men attacked. He avoided one thrust and wrung the knife out of the attacker's hand. Behind him, he heard the soft sucking sound of a knife plunging into flesh and out again and his heart almost stopped beating. But then a body hit the ground and Dante still stood at his back, so Gautier turned his focus back to the fight.

The forest filled with the stench of blood and released sphincters and Gautier gritted his teeth against gagging.

The smell seemed to overwhelm the attackers. The two facing Gautier retched and gagged and Gautier saw his opportunity.

But just as he stepped forward to press his advantage, something hard hit him on the back of the head and he fell unconscious onto the blood-slick, frozen forest floor.

* * *

The ground heaved under Lauren's feet with every step so that she had to put her arms out for balance. In the pre-dawn darkness, the wind whistled green and branches creaked blazing red. Once, she leaned on a fir tree and the bark screamed at her until she stumbled away.

Her hands no longer belonged to her. They hovered before her like tiny birds, leading the way. As she walked, her clothes melted off her burning body and she left puddles in her footprints.

I am going crazy, she thought, and continued walking, her bare feet not touching the ground.

Strange animals appeared and spoke to her. A bat flew yellow, its human face that of Mary. It said something to her but there was too much pine sap in her ears and she couldn't make it out. She found herself sitting on a frail branch on an aspen tree, talking with an owl that kept blinking code at her. Although she tried to decipher the code, it was too musical for her and she floated down to the ground to resume her walk.

A bear followed her once, but she ignored it and it went away. Then a fox tried to engage her in conversation but she shooed it away. The wolf that came after the fox refused to leave, baring its fangs in annoyance.

She had never been this close to a wolf and this one had her curious. She stopped to talk to it, but its growls and yips made no sense, so she turned away only to whirl back when she sensed its rush toward her.

The wolf landed on her half-turned torso, its snapping jaws just missing her throat. She threw an arm up to protect herself and howled with pain as the powerful jaws snapped the bones. Then she was on the ground, twigs digging into her naked back, fighting for her life.

The wolf's growls sounded like hers as she gouged at the animal's eyes. Its claws took long ribbons of flesh off her breasts, her abdomen, her thighs. Screaming with pain and rage, she finally leaned in and bit the animal's muzzle with all her might.

With a yelp of pain, the wolf released her broken arm. She staggered to her feet, bathed in her own blood, and they stood staring at each other, both breathing hard.

She was dying. She knew that with complete and utter clarity. But she would not make it easy for the wolf to take her life. So when it leaped at her for the final snap of its jaws, she leaped to meet it. As its jaws opened wide to fasten on her throat, she shoved her good fist as far down the animal's gullet as it would go.

Her fist lodged in the wolf's throat and the animal fell to the ground on all fours. Suddenly its mouth was impossibly wide, so wide that she followed her fist and climbed inside the belly of the beast.

And when she turned around, she realized she *was* the wolf.

She padded away from the smell of blood, her paws soundless on the forest floor, sniffing air now redolent with hundreds of interesting smells, her sharp eyesight catching every flicker of a lemming tail, every ruffle of grouse feathers. She reveled in the grace and strength of her new body.

Then the scary ones came, the ones with fangs and red eyes, the ones that walked like men but smelled like the wendigo. They paced her, two at first, then ten, then a hundred. Their stench reached out to her in coils of illness, an illness that made them mad. She padded faster and faster and they kept closing in on her. When their hot breath fanned her furred back, she... shifted... and then she was no longer in the forest but in the other place, the place with the sad souls.

And suddenly she was herself again, with her hands her own, her feet planted on solid soil, her bare flesh human again. She looked for the wolf, already missing its presence, but though it was dark, she knew the wolf was gone.

She also knew that she wasn't at the wall with the shades, where so many gaians souls were imprisoned. Here their cries were only a faint echo below the wailing of a cold wind in a vast darkness. She stopped walking, aware that she teetered on the edge of a terrible abyss.

"Morag?" she whispered. But her great-grandmother wasn't there. No one was there. She was alone, as she had always been, and even Gautier couldn't follow her here.

At last she understood why she had always felt apart, why she had never fit. How could she? She belonged to neither one species, nor the other.

Like Cade. Mad Cade, who swallowed life and sunlight with every breath and spewed out death. Cade, who had stolen her mother.

If loneliness was her fate, at least hatred helped fill the void.

And suddenly the abyss was inside of her, was her, and she fell into it, plunged at a dizzying, frightening speed, turning faster and faster until she spun apart, her cry of fear lost in a kaleidoscope of bright colors and loud explosions.

Then she was no longer in the underworld, or in the abyss. She floated above the Earth among the cold stars, her awareness free at last of the constraints of her body. What had been her body was now tiny lights, powdered stars blown on a cosmic wind. She watched in rapture as every atom that had been Lauren Tom dispersed through the universe.

She was finally free.

* * *

After an eon, Lauren grew aware of a whisper among the stars. Curious, she gathered up those parts of herself needed for listening and turned her attention outward. The whisper grew louder. It was so lovely, and so hauntingly familiar, that she opened herself up to receiving it.

Only when the voice entered her did she make out the words.

"Lauren, Lauren, Lauren…"

She stopped her slow, endless spinning and focused on the voice. More of her atoms coalesced into eyes and she saw that the sound came from the star she had left so long ago.

"Lauren… daughter…"

Mother? Her voice box formed and her newly shaped heart beat faster.

"Mother?"

"Lauren!"

The voice was stronger now and Lauren kept her gaze fixed on its point of origin—at the bottom tip of a system of lakes shaped like a cross—while she purposefully reassembled herself. Her legs and feet were the last to reform and the moment they did, they began to transform, her legs melding together, elongating, becoming hard, with bark replacing her skin. Her feet spread out, her toes becoming roots that reached for the rich valley floor, her arms and fingers branches that stretched high into the universe, gathering starlight for energy.

Suddenly the transformation sped up, completely out of her control, and she was falling like a spear, her roots reaching thirstily for the warm waters of the valley, her trunk improbably thick and tall, her branches covering the entire world.

The stars began to speak to her and she realized with joy that this was the moment she had been striving toward all her life. She trembled on the verge of understanding, her entire being open to the transformation.

Then static electricity crackled through her in a sensation at once familiar and strange. She glanced down at her roots and saw a ball of fire surging up her roots, leaving a trail of smoke and burning bark. Then the pain reached her and she screamed soundlessly as the ball trailed up her mid-section. Only then did she recognize the flavor of the sensation.

Cade.

With a massive shiver, she whipped her branches down and reached for the ball, intending to crush it, but the movement was unnatural and she only managed to flick the ball of fire that was Cade into the ether.

Her relief was short-lived. Three more trails of fire began at her roots and she wailed with pain and fear. They were burning her roots! She would become disconnected again.

They were going to tear her loose when she was so close to her goal. Hate filled her, fueled by a hot rage, and this time, when she reached down, her aim was precise and deadly.

She grasped each of the balls of fire with her many branches and carefully, delicately crushed the life out of them.

As the last spark died out, she laughed.

Then the real pain began, growing until she writhed in agony as fire consumed her from the inside out.

⁂ EIGHTEEN ⁂

SOMEONE was tugging on Gautier's hair. It hurt. It hurt worse when something poked the swollen, tender lump on the back of his head. The pain triggered a body memory and before he was even fully conscious, his hand whipped out to knock the offending arm away. Then he was on his feet, looking around wildly, his hand scrabbling for his missing knife.

"It's over," said a familiar voice, and Gautier looked down to see Silas staring back at him dully.

It's morning, was Gautier's first thought. His nose wrinkled as a foul smell registered—a cross between an outhouse and slaughtering day on a farm.

And his back was wet. From the top of his shoulders to the back of his calves, his clothes stuck uncomfortably to his flesh. A gust of wind promised to keep him cold and shivering for most of the day. Then another thought made it past the thudding in his head. "Where's Dante?"

Silas' eyes filled with such misery that Gautier took a step back. Then he looked around more carefully.

The thin snow cover had been churned up. Chunks of moss and dirt mixed with blood combined to camouflage what he was seeing until his eye finally recognized a booted foot for what it was.

His gaze followed the foot up the leg and to the face frozen in open-eyed, painful death.

Not Dante. One of their attackers. Then he saw another, his hands clamped over his spilled guts, his body stiff with death.

Gautier counted three bodies before he finally saw his friend.

"Dante..."

Dante lay stretched out on the churned up ground, his arms and legs straightened as if he had just laid himself down for a rest. But in the gray light of morning, the terrible gash on the side of his neck and the pallor of his skin told Gautier everything he needed to know before he even saw the open, unseeing eyes.

Still, he stumbled over to his friend's side, slipping on the bloody slush, and dropped to his knees.

"Dante?" he whispered.

He looked so peaceful. So pale. Gautier reached for Dante's throat only to jerk away at the stickiness of the blood. He stared at his bloody fingertips for a long time before looking up.

A few snowflakes drifted down onto Dante's face.

Silas had come to stand across from him. He looked down at his grandson's body, his shoulders sagging.

"I'm sorry," said Gautier, and the words caught in his throat. *I wasn't watching his back...*

Silas looked down at him, his black eyes unfathomable. Finally he shook his head.

"Don't do that, boy. There's enough pain to go around today. Don't add guilt to your burden." He sank to his haunches next to Dante, as if his legs could no longer support his weight, and tried to wipe the blood off his grandson's face with a bit of snow. He finally stopped when all he accomplished was to smear the blood around. He stayed on his haunches, his hands dangling uselessly over his knees and looked over Gautier's head while he spoke.

"It was a curse more than it was ever a gift." His mouth thinned into a slash punctured by deep wrinkles. In the early morning light, he looked older than Death.

"He could never live with other gaians." Only his lips moved. Even his eyes looked dead. "He couldn't shut it out, none of it. He was always at the mercy of every gaians who happened to be near him." He blew a breath out in a silent sigh. "I sometimes feared he would take his own life, just to be free of it."

Gautier stared at the old man, trying to make sense of what he was saying. The Dante he was describing wasn't the man Gautier knew. Had known.

"You were his salvation, I think," continued Silas. He finally brought his gaze to bear on Gautier. "Once he met you, he started moving away from the gaians way and toward the sapiens way."

Gautier couldn't speak. He hadn't known his friend at all. Fifteen years of friendship had been based on lies. And yet, the Dante he had known had brimmed with laughter, even through the grimmest of the Troubles. Dante had loved life and had never turned away from hardship or from a soul in need. He was the only man Gautier ever trusted his life to.

And now Gautier had failed him. Like he had failed Lauren...
Jesus.

"Lauren!" he cried, surging to his feet. The old man stumbled back in surprise but even as Gautier looked around wildly he remembered that she was gone and that he had been going after her when the camp was attacked.

"How long?" he demanded. At Silas' confused look, he repeated, "How long was I out?"

Silas shook his head. "I don't know... Cade trapped me in the underworld. When I came to I found you and..." His gaze returned to Dante.

Dante. Oh, dear sweet Jesus, he couldn't just leave him there.

Gautier glanced up at the sky. It was the pale blue of early morning, but the sun had yet to crest the mountains. The attack had come just as dawn was giving way to morning—so, maybe an hour, no more than two.

"We have to bury Dante," said Silas, guessing his intentions.

He looked sick, Gautier suddenly realized. His usually brown face looked gray and the skin sagged as if it had melted a little. But it was the old man's eyes that made Gautier rethink his answer.

He had been about to tell the old man that it was more important to find the living right now than tend to the dead. But Silas' eyes looked haunted.

He's just lost his grandson, thought Gautier. But it was more than that.

"What is it?" he asked.

Silas blinked slowly. His lips pressed together tightly and Gautier suddenly remembered Dante being amazed at the sight of tears in Lauren's eyes. *They can't cry, these gaians.*

"I can't find him," said Silas. His voice was rough with emotion, but his eyes were dry. "If he's in the underworld, I can't find him."

Gautier shook his head at the feeling of unreality that settled over him. Death wasn't really death for gaians. He couldn't wrap his mind around the concept. For him, death was permanent, irreversible. No visiting the dearly departed in any underworld for him.

He'd lost Dante. There was nothing he could do about it.

"Stay here," he told Silas. "I'll find Lauren."

Silas nodded but he looked smaller, suddenly, as if he had lost something of himself in the last few hours.

Gautier didn't have time to deal with it. He wasted a few more minutes looking for his missing knife and found it underneath one of the attackers. They all looked alike, short and dark, with wiry builds.

Just like Dante.

Gautier wiped the knife clean on the man's buckskin pants and straightened. He'd been heading east when the attackers came. Now he couldn't remember why he'd been so sure that east was the right direction. He looked toward the rising sun, trying to make out Lauren's tracks amid the churned up snow.

Silas pointed northeast. "That way," he said.

Gautier looked the old man in the eye. Silas didn't say another word, but the look in his eyes spoke for him.

Gautier nodded. He would bring her back. Without another word, he turned toward the northeast and began to run.

Within minutes, he found her trail. He recognized the imprint of her small foot through the mukluks she wore. Her pace was sure and as straight as trees would allow. She knew exactly where she was going.

Then he found where the attackers' trail had crossed hers and he swore under his breath. Three men had peeled away from the main group to follow her. Then another one had joined them later.

Damn. Four men.

He ran as fast as the frozen willow bushes and fallen branches would allow. He blessed the sturdy soles of his ancient work boots more than once as he landed on a rock or knobby branch.

Lauren's pace never faltered. She hadn't been aware of her pursuers. Gautier's anxiety level rose another notch. What state was she in that she wouldn't be aware of four men following her?

His head pounded with every step and he gingerly felt the lump at the base of his neck. He'd survived worse. His breath plumed out in front of him as he ran but the run helped warm him up. He had left his pack behind when he ran to help Dante and he realized now that he should have brought it with him. At least the water. Stupid.

The sun rose high enough to spill down over the mountains and cast long tree shadows in the forest and Gautier squinted into the glare. He tried not to think about what four men could do to her.

He had been running for over half an hour when the smell first reached him. He didn't stop running but his knees grew weak. It was the smell of fire. Not campfire or wood stove. No, this was the back-of-the-throat stink of a forest fire. And overlaying it all was the crispy stench of burnt flesh.

Soon he saw the first dead bird—a gray jay, maybe, though it was too charred to tell for sure. Then a raven, its beak all but burned away. Then squirrels. After a while, he stopped counting.

When he reached the edge of the burned woods he stopped. The trees here—black spruce, balsam poplar, lodgepole pine—were nothing but standing charcoal, still smoking. There was nothing left of the bushes but cinders. He dug the toe of his boot through the ashes and cinders, then bent down to gauge how much heat was left. Warm, not hot. The stink of death rose from the disturbed ground, choking him.

Behind him, the forest was asleep for the winter. Before him: death.

He couldn't understand what would have started a forest fire in this season. Or why the fire damage stopped so evenly, as if a bowl had been placed over the area and the fire had burned whatever was inside the bowl, leaving everything outside safe.

He swallowed hard. Lauren was somewhere in that devastation. Maybe in danger. He glanced at the trees around him and swallowed again. Anything caught in this would be dead.

But he had to know.

So he stepped across the threshold onto the burned ground and kept walking, his feet kicking up ashes, cinders, and heat. He found more corpses—a deer, rabbits, what might have been a porcupine.

Then he found the first man's corpse. At least, he was pretty sure it was a man. He looked away from the cracked, charred mess of a face and saw another corpse further on. Breathing through his mouth, his heart slamming against his chest, he searched the area and found a last corpse. None of them was Lauren. He was almost sure of that.

Three in all. Where was the missing man? And where was Lauren?

Then he reached the epicenter of the devastation. There, in a small circle of snow and brush no wider than her outstretched arms, was Lauren. Everywhere he looked he saw death by fire. How had she escaped?

She lay on her side, her arms wrapped around her updrawn

legs, head tucked into her knees, snowflakes drifting gently onto her black hair.

Not her, too...

Then he became aware of a sound in the tomb-like stillness of the artificial clearing.

Weeping.

He looked closer and realized that Lauren's shoulders were shaking with the force of her tears.

Without another thought, he crossed the hot cinders and bent over her.

"Lauren?" he asked gently. He reached for her shoulder, hesitating when she didn't respond. Then he touched her and she started violently, her head jerking up to reveal her face. Then she recognized him and her expression metamorphosed from anguish to... fear?

"Lauren, what the hell happened?" His voice was harsh. He couldn't even begin to imagine what could have caused this destruction.

"Gautier." Her voice was ragged from crying.

He held his hand out and she stared at it for a long time before finally putting hers in his. After that initial glance at him, she refused to meet his eye.

The smell of death was making him sick. It was time to get out of here. He pulled her up and found her trembling. But when he tried to pull her into his arms, she resisted, and he had to be satisfied with just holding her hand.

Without a word, he led her out of the small circle that had sheltered her. Once or twice, she tried to pull out of his grasp but he just tightened his grip and kept walking.

Her trembling was contagious. As he led the way past the small and bigger corpses, he found himself shaking, too.

Cade had done this. Somehow, that maniac had found a cache of pre-Troubles weapons. Flame-throwers. Nothing else could account for the destruction he was witnessing.

But he knew, even as he tried to find other explanations, that Cade hadn't done this, nor any of his people.

If they had, Lauren would be dead, instead of being smack in the protected center. His nausea increased and he concentrated hard on keeping the contents of his stomach inside.

Was this the power she had gained from her Passage? What kind of people were these gaians?

Finally, they reached the end of the dead zone. Gautier kept walking until they were out of reach of the smell. When he finally stopped, Lauren immediately pulled her hand out of his.

He turned to look at her. Tears still ran down her face, tracing clean paths in the sooty residue. She looked like she had been crying for a long time. Like she would cry forever.

"What?" he asked. This time he didn't reach for her, but didn't step back, either. Then he asked the one question he wasn't sure he wanted answered. "Who did this?"

She wiped at her face with hands that shook badly. Then she took a deep breath and tried to control herself. Finally she looked at him.

"I did." Her face crumpled and for a moment he thought she was going to fall, but she waved away his assistance and regained control of herself.

He crossed his arms over his chest, then uncrossed them. He rubbed his hands over his singed hair, then over his face and swallowed a lump.

Finally he took a shaky breath and expelled it in a blast of frustration.

"What the hell does that mean?"

His anger seemed to brace her and her eyes flashed with an echoing anger, only to dull again with pain.

"It means that I made the fire come and I killed them."

"Jesus," whispered Gautier as his fear became reality. "Why?"

Her tears began to leak out again. "I didn't mean to," she said, her voice catching. "Cade attacked with three balls of fire. I didn't know where I was. I thought I was a wolf."

Gautier shook his head in confusion. He looked around and spotted a fallen log. He nodded to it. "Sit."

She obediently walked over to it and sat down.

"Now tell me," he said.

And she did.

❧ NINETEEN ❧

FOR MILLENNIA, gaians had left their dead in high places for the wild animals and the elements to dispose of. They knew that the death of their bodies was inevitable—even welcome since it meant they would join their loved ones in the underworld. They returned their flesh to the elements when they died as an homage to the world that had sustained them in life.

But as Silas stood looking down at his grandson's body, he suddenly longed for a shovel and a strong back to help him dig a hole. Dante had adopted sapiens ways, and now Silas wanted to honor his choice.

Silas piled the five gaians together, far from where Dante rested, and left them as they lay, refusing to so much as straighten their limbs.

Over the centuries the death ceremonies had become more formalized. Dante deserved to be honored, to have his body cleansed by his closest relative while the entire clan crooned the funeral chant like a lullaby to lead him into the underworld.

In the old days, the obeah for the clan would build a small fire next to the bier and sprinkle the sacred herbs to send purifying smoke wafting over the boy and into the obeah's lungs.

Then the obeah would accompany the boy into the underworld

where he would be welcomed by his ancestors. The death of a ga-ians was not so much a time of grief as a time of celebration.

But now...

Silas risked another trip to the underworld, to the part of the underworld that Dante would have found, but he found no one there. Not Morag, not Dante. Not a single ancestor. Silas even risked an overhead flight, his gaze darting between sky and earth, but there was no one left.

Anguish filled him. Had Cade killed them all? Were there none of his line left?

As he stood looking down at his grandson, whom he had thought was the last of his line, he wished he had the sapiens gift of tears.

Finally he began to gather stones and pile them on top of the boy's body. He removed his coat to carry the stones in it and ranged far, piling the stones higher and higher over Dante. Finally he sat on his haunches, keeping vigil and singing the funeral chant low and deep.

And throughout it all, he felt the pull of Ben-My-Chree. He was so close... he could just get up and walk until he arrived at last...

He lost track of time, only looking up when he heard someone coming. He stood up stiffly.

The reek of death preceded them and when he saw Lauren stumbling behind Gautier, he caught his breath in mixed relief and horror.

She had survived the Passage but he didn't need to see the tracks of tears—*tears!*—on her face and Gautier's grim expression to realize something was wrong.

Then he looked closely at his granddaughter, his only surviv-ing relative, and dismay flooded through him.

She hadn't survived the Passage—she was still trapped in it. Her eyes looked huge and he knew that she stood on the brink of losing herself.

"Tell me," he said.

Gautier looked at him, looking much older than he had a few days ago. Then Lauren caught sight of the pile of rocks and her face changed.

"Dante?" She took a step toward the grave, then another.

By the stricken look on Gautier's face, Silas realized that the young man hadn't told her. Silas felt even more uneasy. What had pushed Dante's death out of Gautier's mind?

Lauren stopped by the grave and slowly lowered herself to her knees. "Dante?"

The snow, which had ended sometime earlier, now started up again and Silas watched fat snowflakes settle gently on her dark hair, melting as soon as they landed. She looked bedraggled and lost.

Then she spotted the bodies he had stacked away from Dante and her face hardened. She turned accusing eyes to Gautier.

"Why didn't you protect him?" She turned on Silas. "And you? Were you so busy protecting yourself that you couldn't help him?" The tears flashed as she turned back to the grave.

"He did this." For a moment, Silas thought she meant Dante, but then she continued. "And he tried to kill me, too."

She stood up and walked over to Gautier. Even from this distance Silas could tell she was shaking with anger. "And you feel sorry for them, don't you?" The words landed sharply on Silas' ears as he glanced from one face to another.

Gautier kept his face closed and expressionless.

"Sorry?" he said softly. "No. But no one deserves to die the way they did."

Silas' stomach lurched. He wasn't referring to the dead gaians next to them.

"Tell me," he ordered again. Lauren turned to glare at him and he almost stepped back from that fierce anger, but didn't dare show her any fear. In her state, she was closer to the animal instinct than to the human one. She needed help to find her way back.

Gautier finally told him. His words were terse and clipped, as if he were angry, too, but Silas saw the watchfulness in his eyes. The boy knew there was something wrong with her.

"I don't know how she did it, exactly," he said. "All I know is that three men are dead and all she can tell me is that she crushed fireballs."

"They were trying to kill me!" Lauren's face filled with hatred and Silas felt himself grow colder, as if the snow were slowly turning him to ice. Hatred. No gaians felt hatred.

Not until Cade...

"Cade wanted to kill me! He was the first fireball—"

"Cade is dead?" asked Silas, startled.

"No." Lauren shook her head, a gesture of frustration that threatened to go on too long. "I was a tree, a huge tree that reached into space and my roots were in the underworld."

Silas controlled a start, but his mouth parted in wonder. Her Passage had involved the Tree of Life! He had never heard of such a thing. He couldn't even begin to think what it meant.

Lauren continued, oblivious to his surprise. "Cade wanted to burn me. I used my branches but missed. I just flicked him away like a bug."

"And then?" he prodded.

She shrugged. "Then the other three came after me. And I killed them."

She said it with such coolness that Silas stole a glance at Gautier. The boy was looking at Lauren as if she had just shed a skin to reveal a completely different creature underneath. Before Silas could warn him with a look, Gautier spoke.

"Lauren, you killed every living thing within a quarter mile of you! How can you stand there and act like that was nothing?"

The smile left her face, and she suddenly sat down on the ground, hard.

"I thought I was dead, too," she whispered. "I burned from the inside out. I didn't know I was alive until Gautier found me."

They stared at her for a long time. Silas didn't know what to say. Or do. He didn't know what she was describing.

There were ancestral memories, in his line and those of other clans, in which a Passage went awry, but he'd never heard of one in which the obeah-to-be had metamorphosed into the Tree. There were even older stories of a time when an obeah would be able to access the Tree and find out what lay in the Overworld, but these were only legends, left over from a race memory so old that no one clan could claim it.

"Lauren..." Gautier helped her up and put his hands on her shoulders. "You can't keep going like this." He looked at Silas in a silent appeal for help. "Nine men are dead. Dead, Lauren. Including Dante." His voice cracked on the name.

Silas had only just found his granddaughter and now she faced a danger she couldn't understand. If she was somehow connected to the Tree, that would make her something new in gaians history. Homo gaians couldn't afford to lose her, not now that Cade was on the loose. Neither could Homo sapiens.

"Lauren, he's right," said Silas. "I should have seen that this was a mistake, a trap of Cade's. We need to go back."

Lauren laughed bitterly.

"Do you think I wanted this?" The passion seemed to have evaporated. She shrugged out of Gautier's hold and stepped away from him.

With a trembling hand she indicated the dead bodies and Dante's grave. "I didn't do this. You did." Her voice rose. "I didn't ask for any of this!" She turned to look at Silas and he held his breath. There was real anger in her eyes. Sapiens anger in an out-of-control obeah.

That was how she had killed those men. And everything around her.

"I was doing fine until you meddled in my life," she said. Her voice rose. "None of this should have happened! Dante should still be alive doing whatever the hell it is he did." She closed her eyes and tears squeezed out.

"But you *did* meddle and I *am* here. And now I'm going to finish it." She put up a hand when Gautier opened his mouth and her lip curled away from her teeth. Silas held his breath.

"Don't, Gautier." She stared at Gautier, her head tucked down like a wolf's. "Stay away." For a moment, Silas saw a wolf's yellow eyes staring back at him.

Then she whirled and ran off in the direction of Ben-my-Chree.

"Damn it all, Lauren!" called Gautier and took off at a run after her.

Silas closed his eyes briefly, searching for help from the ancestors, but they were silent.

He was all alone.

* * *

Gautier was so damned tired of chasing after this woman.

If he weren't sure that she was going to get herself killed, he'd leave her to run herself into exhaustion.

And then what? he asked himself. *Throw her over your shoulder and take her back to safety?* There didn't seem to be any safe place for her.

A gust of wind blew flurries against his cheeks and he looked up at the sky. The snow clouds were clearing off. It was already afternoon.

He burst out of the trees and the wind caught him full face from the east, sweeping down the mountains, cold and biting. Lauren was already down by the lake's shore, heading for the narrow ribbon of short scrub brush and rock that made for better travel.

He didn't even know the name of the lake. Back home, he knew every path, every river, every pothole lake.

He opened his mouth to shout at her, then swore under his breath. He had seen her eyes. She wouldn't stop. And if any of Cade's men were around, he didn't want to alert them to Lauren's presence.

Dante would have been able to tell him right away if there were any gaians around.

Dammitall. He choked his tears back. There was no time to grieve. *Later,* he promised his friend. Later he would do it right.

His long legs kept her from outdistancing him, but she was running fast, faster than was wise on the broken terrain. His boots protected him from the worst of the stones and gave his ankles support, but all she had were those mukluks.

But she ran like a dog, sure-footed and fearless, and all he could do was follow and try to catch up.

Sometime in the past few hours his clothes had dried, but now they were getting damp with his sweat. He settled into the familiar lope that would eventually catch up to her and divided his attention between the ground, his surroundings, and Lauren.

He ignored the pounding in his head, knowing from experience that he probably had a mild concussion. Not much he could do about it now.

The mountains rose all around, snow-capped and imposing. Fir and spruce trees swept down their slopes all the way to the lake in spots, obscuring the bends.

He was breathing hard but Lauren showed no sign of slowing. Every time she disappeared around a bend, fear spiked through him until he caught sight of her again. He had no idea if Silas followed them or not.

Where the hell was she going in such a hurry?

The farther he ran, the less snow was on the ground. There were even leaves still on the trees—bright yellow aspen leaves trembling in the wind. He noted fireweed turned bright red but still standing, as if there hadn't been any frosts in this area. Yet he had just run through a section slick with snow and ice, with all the vegetation dead with winter cold.

There must be an underground warm spring nearby, to delay winter here.

Lauren disappeared around a bend again and he pushed himself into a burst of speed to keep her in sight. How long had they been running like this? Ten minutes? Fifteen?

He hoped the old man was all right. But he was an obeah and he could take care of himself in the underworld and the real world, which was more than Gautier could say about Lauren. *But Silas' ability was also a vulnerability,* thought Gautier. *As long as he was in the underworld, he couldn't protect himself in the real world.*

In a species that didn't experience violence, this wasn't a problem. There was always someone to watch out for your defenseless, unconscious body. But when someone like Cade came along, someone who wasn't afraid of violence, who seemed to thrive on it…

The hard, rocky shore was taking a toll on his legs—his shins protested each time his feet slammed into the ground. He didn't like to think what shape Lauren's feet would be in.

Then he emerged from the barrier of trees at a bend and staggered to a stop, breathing hard.

Less than a hundred feet ahead of him, Lauren had stopped, too, and stood with her back to him.

Down below, the lake ended in a bay surrounded by bright poplars and aspens. Farther west, a river fed into the bay, threading its way through wild flowers, though only the hardier ones survived this late in the year. He recognized asters and fireweed and something that looked like yarrow, but it was too far to be sure.

As his eye grew accustomed to the sudden color, he found patterns in the wilderness, straight lines when he hadn't seen any since leaving the railway.

The biggest pattern resolved itself into a good-size log cabin, half buried in tall grasses. It stood on a rise less than twenty feet from the lake, about six hundred feet from where he stood. There were windows, but the glass was long gone. The building looked tired, but the roof had survived time and the elements intact. Then Gautier realized that the roof was made of sod, which had dried up long ago, though some grasses still clung precariously to the edges of the roof.

Wild grasses grew right up to the walls, interspersed by fireweed and even a few purple columbines. Fireweed grew between the logs, giving the sun-bleached log building a festive look. In front of the door was crushed grass, as if many feet had trampled there. Smoke from the chimney caught in the breeze and wafted away from them.

Through the wilderness of wildflowers and bushes, he spotted more straight lines—foundations only. No walls remained of the smaller outbuildings.

This was Ben-My-Chree.

Gautier tried to remember what Mr. Chiang had told him about the place, but all he could remember was that an old couple had lived here for years in the last century. He hoped they'd had a boat.

Nice enough view, he supposed, with the mountains as backdrop and the bay in the foreground, but he didn't see why it had been so all-fired important to get here.

A movement caught his eye and he looked east. Beyond the main house, in a cleared area, a few figures moved around half a dozen small campfires. They were too far away to see clearly, but Gautier knew with a sinking feeling that these were Cade's people—probably the same ones Dante had been sensing for the past few days.

He counted twenty of them and there could be more out of his view.

Inside the main house, for instance.

All this he caught in the first ten seconds. Then a figure below caught sight of them and shouted a warning. In a moment, all the figures turned toward them.

Gautier glanced at Lauren but she didn't move. He looked back the way they had come but saw no sign of the old man.

What the hell was he supposed to do now?

He began to move toward Lauren just as the door to the cabin below opened to spill a few small figures and one much larger one.

Even from that distance, Gautier recognized Cade.

As if that was the signal she'd been waiting for, Lauren screamed a high-pitched, animal cry that lifted the hair on the back of Gautier's neck. Then she launched herself down the slope, screeching her banshee scream and running straight for the cabin.

"Lauren!" he shouted, but he was already running after her, glad at least that there was no snow or ice to send him hurtling into the water.

What the hell was she thinking? She was going to get herself killed—and him, too, he realized grimly.

She ran in a straight line, like an arrow directed at Cade, clambering over fallen trees and leaping over rifts in the rock surrounding the bay, her feet barely touching the ground.

Gautier split his attention between Lauren and the ground and the still figure that was Cade.

Cade watched Lauren's approach for a few moments, then he said something and a dozen men took off a run, heading for them.

Gautier put on a burst of speed, but before he could catch up to Lauren half the group angled off toward him, blocking his way.

"Lauren!" he yelled. "Stop!"

Then it was too late and six men blocked his way. They were all short and dark and could easily have been related to Silas and Dante.

He reached for his knife and found only an empty sheath strapped to his belt. Somewhere during the long run, he had lost his knife.

Dammitall to hell.

In growing desperation, he looked over the heads of the oncoming gaians and saw the group of men blocking Lauren's way. She staggered to a stop, looking from one man to another, as though she hadn't noticed them before.

The wind shifted south, bringing with it the smell of wood smoke, and he finally understood their hesitation. They knew what she had done to the three obeahs that morning. They were afraid of her.

They were plain gaians and not obeahs. He could handle gaians. He wasn't sure he could handle half-a-dozen obeahs.

Only then did Gautier notice the strangeness in the air around

Lauren. Color shimmered all around her, a rainbow aura, first yellow, then green and blue, then red and purple. She seemed to phase in and out of solidity.

A chill ran down Gautier's spine but he didn't have long to worry. Before he could go to her, the six men blocking his way attacked.

* * *

The pull of Ben-My-Chree was so strong now that Silas felt it like a singing in his blood. It gave him new energy, made him forget the painful creaking of his knees with each step, the sharp pain in his ribs with each gasping breath. He hadn't run like that in years—he was too old for this.

Then he emerged from the trees to see the Tree rising from the slope of the mountain at the foot of the bay. It was as thick as an old-time apartment building and rose so high that its branches disappeared into the glare of the blue sky. Its bark shifted with colors and in spite of its bulk, it seemed to be swaying with the wind.

Silas caught his breath in wonder. The Tree lived in the collective memory of every gaian, but no one had seen it in thousands of years.

The Tree cycled through colors light to dark and when it cycled black and stayed there, Silas stepped back.

Something was wrong. The tree should never be black.

He looked down at the valley and immediately movement attracted his attention.

No more than fifty yards downhill, six gaians surrounded Gautier, circling him as if they were looking for an opening. All of them moved cautiously, and Silas caught the glint of metal—some of them had knifes.

Inside the circle, Gautier moved from side to side, constantly twisting to keep from presenting his back to anyone for more than a split second. He had no weapons.

And beyond Gautier he finally saw Lauren. She faced her own barrier of gaians, six men arrayed in a semi-circle between her and the cabin by the shore of the bay.

A single figure hurried up the slope toward the small group. The sun glinted off hair so blond it seemed white. With a thrill of awareness, Silas recognized Cade.

The smell of fear carried on the wind and Silas glanced at Lauren again, to see why the gaians were so frightened. Her back was to him, but the air around her seemed to shimmer like that of the Tree. The aura surrounding her was the same color as the Tree's and it cycled through the same colors.

He glanced from Lauren to the Tree and back again, trying to gain meaning. No obeah had ever experienced this before, this direct connection to the Tree.

Then he realized that the changes were not simultaneous. The Tree shifted colors a beat after Lauren.

The Tree was tied to Lauren, not the other way around.

Then Gautier's grunt of pain reached him and he whirled to see that all six gaians had attacked the young man at the same time.

It was all happening too fast. Cade was running toward them, two of the gaians attacking Gautier had knives, and something was happening to Lauren.

First things first—he had to help Gautier before he was seriously injured.

Silas turned his attention back to the scuffle—for that's what it was. He saw at once that Gautier was the more able fighter, in spite of their superior numbers. These gaians clearly had never committed violence. They didn't know how to physically harm another, which was the only reason Gautier was still alive.

What could Cade have promised them to make them go against their nature?

A gaian, surely too old to fall under Cade's sway, lunged at Gautier and Silas saw a line of red appear under the young man's arm as the knife sliced through his leather jacket.

Hurry, he told himself.

Silas lay down on the hard stone above the lake, his aching bones soaking in what little heat the early winter sun had imparted. He closed his eyes to the brilliant blue sky, his senses to the smell of soil, wood smoke and his own sweat, and sank his awareness into the underworld.

He aimed for that place in which Cade had tried to imprison him that morning, the well of white. It had taken all his strength to escape it and he was a strong obeah. If he could create one of these traps for each of the gains, they would not escape. They were not obeah.

Then a familiar presence permeated his senses, one he had known for too few years, one he still missed and would always miss.

"Meridy?"

"Father."

He couldn't see her but felt her presence. "Where are you, daughter?"

"Still trapped," her voice trailed off like a breath of memory. "I can sense you."

Silas longed to search for her, but he had to help the living first.

"I'll be back for you, Meridy," he promised. "Right now, Lauren needs me."

"Look after my baby. I'll be here. Waiting." He thought he heard a familiar sardonic tone in her voice and his heart almost broke. She would be there, waiting, as she had been for over ten years. Time meant nothing in the underworld. To his trapped daughter, ten years might as well be ten centuries.

If I survive this, he promised himself grimly, *I'll make Cade pay for what he's done to her.*

Then fear swept over him as he glimpsed the trap. This was how Cade had subverted those gaians—by making their personal desires more important than the needs of the many. By teaching them passion.

He lusted for vengeance, wanted to kill Cade for what he had done to Meridy, to Dante, and was trying to do to Lauren, but to give in to that lust was to put himself above the needs of his species. Obeahs who did that became... Cades.

And Lauren, with her botched Transition, her incomplete Passage—Lauren would surely fall into that trap. Her half-sapiens heritage left her vulnerable. She had killed, and the deaths of those gaians in the forest, and worse, of the animals she had accidentally killed, preyed on her even if she had done it out of self-defense.

It would be so easy for her to go down the same path, this time out of fury rather than instinct.

And if she did, Silas would never get her back. The strain would push her too far off balance. She would never recover.

He finished building the wells and rose back through the underworld, noting again as he passed the terrible silence. All these struggles... what if it was too late?

He shook off the worries. There was only one course of action left and he was taking it.

He opened his eyes moments after he had closed them and sat up. Gautier had managed to disarm one of the knife-wielders and another gaians was down. But even as he watched, one man— quicker and younger than the others—circled around Gautier and lunged while he was distracted.

Silas started with that one, sinking quickly into the underworld and reaching, reaching for the other gaian's awareness. He found it quickly, for it smelled of fear and excitement. And hate.

Without giving the gaians time to realize what was happening, Silas swooped down on him and plucked his awareness out of his body. At once he dropped the gaian's screaming awareness into the first pen.

Thus had Cade first attacked him. Thus did Silas learn from his enemy. Thus did he become his enemy.

Not giving himself a chance to doubt his decision, Silas returned for a second, and third gaian, the men falling unconscious before the surprised Gautier, until finally all the attackers were safely penned.

When he returned, the first thing he saw was Lauren. Her aura was black and the Tree's matched. As he watched, dumbfounded, a ghostly, dark double of the Tree imposed itself between Lauren and the real Tree. Out of the dark trunk of the ghost Tree, a whip-like branch reached for her.

"Lauren!" he cried out a warning.

"No!" shouted a familiar voice and Silas whipped around to see Cade running toward Lauren, Gautier right behind him. Silas stood rooted to the spot in horror. Gautier wouldn't make it in time.

The tendril grew fast, its forked tip adder-like, and for the first time, Silas questioned his belief that the Tree of Life was intrinsically good.

Then the tendril reached Lauren and everything seemed to stop.

Lauren threw her head back and laughed, a rich, triumphant sound that sent chills of horror chasing each other down Silas' arms.

It was too late. The tendril pierced through Lauren's back and out her chest, through her heart. She remained standing, her head back, as blood gushed from the wound and cascaded down her chest and legs.

Then the tendril began to grow, and Lauren grew with it.

Silas watched in awe and fear as his granddaughter transformed into another level of being before his eyes. As he watched, one question thrummed through him, threaded through with horror.

What had she done?

❧ TWENTY ❧

Power rippled through Lauren, a stream of sparks that came from the Tree, pulsed through her, and fed back into the Tree. Her blood was the Tree's sap, her feet its roots. She was the rocky shore of the lake and the roots digging into the stone and soil and the wind blowing through Ben-My-Chree.

She was the beating heart of the Tree.

Strength filled her and she felt herself growing tall, taller than the surrounding trees, taller than the clouds. Taller than Cade.

Cade.

She turned her attention downward and found him. His face turned up to her, the same way she had looked up as the wendigo with its wolf-yellow eyes flew above the underworld forest, looking for its next victim.

Cade wasn't so big, after all. In fact, he was ever so squishable. She reached down but before she could touch him, he burst into flame, singeing her.

Her hand shot back in pain and she howled her displeasure. She glared lightning at him, hate filling her like acid until it brimmed over and fell in great, burning sheets, setting trees on fire and reaching the waters of the lake with a great hissing sound.

She laughed then, exulting in her strength, her power, her hatred.

"I've got you now, Cade," she whispered. Her voice rolled off the mountains like low thunder. Far below, ant-like figures ran from her but she ignored them. It was Cade she wanted.

But he had disappeared.

"Come out, come out, wherever you are," she sing-songed, and laughed again.

"Right here," said Cade.

She spun in surprise to find he had slipped behind her and now hovered, his body a mass of flames that didn't seem to burn him, between her and the Tree. And he had grown, too. He now stood nearly as tall as she did.

"Right here, Lauren," he repeated calmly. 'Right where I've always been."

And he sent her a wave of... awareness. Suddenly she was seeing herself through his eyes. She was a child still grieving her mother's loss and trying to fit in with people who didn't understand her—couldn't understand her. They were saps. She saw herself growing into young womanhood with young men approaching her but always veering off as they sensed the otherness in her. She saw herself finally alone, in her small cabin, with no lover, no friend.

The loneliness of her life dropped over her like a shroud, separating her, marking her forever as different.

She didn't belong with the saps.

Then she saw Cade as he threaded his way in and out of sap lives, a big, strong presence who didn't care that he didn't belong because he was stronger than any sap, more powerful than any obeah.

He was a hybrid. Just like her. He would fill up the empty spaces in her life.

His burning eyes devoured her with desire. He had wanted her for ten years, wanted her as a partner, as a lover, as a friend.

He had come looking for her, had drawn her to Ben-My-Chree

to free her from the bonds of false affection the saps had woven around her.

His hands reached out for her and now the flames seared with pleasure, not pain. She reached for him with a hunger born of longing.

But as she reached for him, a stray memory rose to the surface of her mind: Rupe, nosing between her arm and her side to lay his head on her lap and whine in sympathy, looking up at her with his great chocolate brown eyes. Rupe loved her.

But Rupe was hurt.

She looked at Cade. He had hurt Rupe.

Cade's flames seemed to burn a little brighter. "What does it matter?" he asked. "You don't need him."

It was true. She didn't. Rupe was just a dog, after all, and Cade had had to do it.

A tendril of uncertainty wound its way around her heart. But Rupe was her friend.

And there was Mary and Charlie, too.

The heat from Cade's hands encircling her waist grew stronger.

"Look at us," he demanded, drawing her gaze back to him. As if she stood outside of herself, she saw them, she dark and powerful, and he big and burning with passion, growing brighter by the moment.

"Now look at them," he ordered. She obediently looked down at the ground. She saw figures below, most running away, but two standing still and looking up, so small...

"That's right," he said. "They're insignificant."

That's what he had said about Mary and Charlie, and now Mary was dead.

She looked at Cade again. Saw his gray eyes through the flames.

He had hurt Rupe, and killed Mary.

His flames were growing stronger and for the first time she

noticed that as his hands clutched her waist, she was growing weaker.

She peered through the obscuring flames and saw the dark tendril growing through her heart and out her chest. While he distracted her with enticements, he had positioned himself in the path of the tendril, which now penetrated his chest, too. And through the tendril, he was stealing her strength.

This was why he had lured her here, not out of loneliness or desire, but to steal her power. Whatever it was he wanted to do, he couldn't do it alone or he would have. He needed her.

A rage as big as the world filled her. Yet again, Cade was taking from her. He had taken Rupe, and Mary, and Charlie's home. He had taken her life in Whitehorse, her peace. Her innocence.

He had taken Dante. And her mother.

"What did you do with my mother?"

Connected as they were, he was helpless to stem the flood of memories. She had been through this before, when Dante triggered her Transition and she gained access to her ancestors' memories. Now, even though she and Cade weren't related, the tendril acted as a conduit and she quickly found the memories she was looking for.

Cade had been studying Silas and his family for a long time. He knew how powerfully the obeah strain ran in the family. He knew when Meridy left her father's home over the man she loved, the sapiens who became Lauren's father. He followed Meridy to the Yukon. He bided his time and when Lauren's father died, Cade tried to persuade Meridy to come with him to Ben-My-Chree. But Meridy Tom wanted nothing to do with Cade. She recognized him as a powerful obeah, but she was powerful too, and knew her place in the world. He couldn't force her.

So one day he sent a wolf to attack her on the trap line. While she was fighting the animal off, he attacked from the underworld and trapped her there. Then he took her unconscious body, planning to bring her to Ben-My-Chree where he would tap into her power to access the Tree of Life.

But there was an accident with his all-terrain vehicle and the trailer in which he carried Meridy. A slippery mountain trail gave way and he barely managed to jump to safety. The all-terrain vehicle, with Meridy strapped inside the trailer, tumbled off the mountain and into the cold mountain lake below.

Cade scrambled down as fast as he could and dove in to rescue her, but the fall had broken her neck long before she could drown.

He left her there, alone in that watery grave.

A wail burst out of Lauren at the confirmation of what she had always known.

Her mother was dead.

Grief punched through her, as fresh as if she had just lost her mother.

He had left her there, to slowly settle on the bottom of the frigid lake, to be eventually eaten by fish, her bones slowly turning to phosphate and calcium.

How frightened had her mother been to suddenly find herself in the underworld, no longer able to return to the world of the living? She would have tried to contact her ancestors, even her father, only to find that she was trapped and unable to communicate with anyone.

The ultimate loneliness...

Ten years...

Cade's memories continued to unreel, even though she wanted nothing more to do with them.

He had returned to Whitehorse to wait for her to grow up.

Grow up she did, but she couldn't go through Transition without a member of her family to trigger it. So Cade tracked down her grandfather and attacked him, making sure he came close enough to Meridy's underworld prison to learn about his granddaughter's existence.

Then Cade waited. When Dante showed up and triggered her Transition, Cade moved in.

Her whole life. The bastard had manipulated, taken, lied, killed...

Grief cycled back to rage. Everything she had ever loved, he had taken from her.

And now he was taking *her*.

Just as suddenly, the rage turned into fear. What was so important that he needed years of planning to accomplish it? That he needed to lie and kidnap, even kill—

She caught her breath as the world began to spin around her. Through the flames, she saw the hatred in Cade's eyes and she suddenly realized her danger. Wrapping her hands around the tendril between them, she yanked it from Cade's chest.

Suddenly the flames surrounding Cade died. His form blurred and shifted, and then like smoke in the wind, he disappeared.

Abruptly, she was herself again, flesh and blood, her arms and legs back to their normal size. She reached for her chest but it was intact, with no tendril growing out of her, no blood gushing from the wound. Her entire body trembled and she drew in great, ragged gulps of air as her hands explored her body, making sure she was back.

Then her stomach heaved and she dropped to her knees, retching the foulness out of her system.

After a while, she felt a warm hand on her head, holding back her hair. She wiped her mouth and rose unsteadily to her feet. Her hand slipped into her pant pocket and found her mother's hair band, the beads cool and smooth against her fingers. Her thumb stroked the beaded pattern and the motion helped calm her. Finally she turned her face up to the sunlight and to Gautier, who was staring down at her in concern. Her grandfather stood next to him, barely coming up to Gautier's shoulder.

"What was that all about?" asked Gautier roughly.

Lauren closed her teeth on a gust of hysterical laughter. Her mouth tasted awful "I was a tree," she mumbled, unable to look him in the eye. She didn't deserve his concern. She had been ready to destroy them all, him included.

Her entire body trembled with fatigue. What had Cade done to her?

Silas held out a water bottle.

"Drink," he said softly, his dark eyes filled with compassion. Without a word, she accepted the bottle and poured some water into her hand to wash her face. Then she poured a little into her mouth to rinse it out. Finally, she drank.

When she finished, she handed the bottle back to Silas.

"Are you back?" he asked carefully.

She nodded. She hoped she was herself again. She never again wanted to feel that overwhelming urge to destroy. She could still smell the stench of Cade's madness, feel him connected to her, draining her... Nausea rose again and she took deep breaths to keep her stomach under control.

"There was something growing out of your chest," said Gautier suddenly.

She opened her eyes. He stood a little apart from her, facing her and Silas.

"You were huge and you were black." He sounded accusing and Lauren kept silent. She hadn't thought he'd be able to see what had just happened. She had thought it was all happening in her mind, or in the underworld.

"And you were connected to Cade," added Gautier grimly.

She shuddered with shame and looked away. She hated herself for it, but a part of her wondered what Cade would have done if she had allowed herself to be seduced.

When she didn't answer, Gautier crossed his arms. "What was he doing to you?"

Lauren looked away, unable to face him. Down by the cabin, Cade's men, all except for six who lay sleeping on the stony ground, had regrouped around the structure, apparently waiting for orders.

"He was robbing her," said Silas. His shoulder brushed hers and she felt absurdly grateful for his support.

And finally she was able to cut through the fuzzy thinking and the nausea to wonder why. Why had Cade tried to steal her strength from her? Her power?

Gautier, bless him, was preoccupied by more immediate concerns.

"Where did he go?" he asked. He glanced around them, then down to the cabin.

"There," said Silas suddenly, his arm pointing at the cabin. Gautier put a hand above his eyes to cut the glare.

"Where?"

Lauren caught the movement and pointed, too. "There," she said. "Past the cabin. He's heading for the Tree!"

She stared at the Tree, suddenly confused. Silas turned to look at her.

"What tree?" asked Gautier. He scanned the slopes behind the cabin.

"That's why he needed you," murmured Silas, still staring at the Tree. "Somehow, you made the Tree appear."

"Which tree?" repeated Gautier more forcefully.

Cade was a small figure running toward the Tree. Although she could see the mountains through its massive trunk, the Tree shimmered with life, its branches lost to the glare of the sky. How could she have thought *she* was the Tree? No one gaians could ever contain the Tree. It contained them. An ache awoke deep inside her. Her whole body yearned toward the Tree.

"And now he can use what he took from me to connect with the Tree by himself." She knew suddenly and clearly that she couldn't allow Cade access to the Tree. He wasn't destined to talk to the Tree. She was. Now Cade would reach the Tree and usurp its powers to his own ends.

"We have to go after him," she said urgently, forcing her legs to move. She spoke over her shoulder. "We can't let him get to the Tree."

Silas nodded and placed an arm around her, supporting her.

"Come on, boy," he said to Gautier. "We have to stop him."

Gautier looked from one to the other, obviously baffled. "What are you talking about?" he demanded. "What tree?"

Lauren glanced at her grandfather. Gautier couldn't even see the real Tree. She and Silas were on their own.

ᴥ TWENTY-ONE ᴥ

I'M GOING TO HAVE TO KILL CADE.

The realization drenched Gautier in cold sweat even as his body heated up from the running.

He glanced up from the ground to check on Cade's progress. The man was close to a quarter mile away, steadily running up the slope of the mountain behind the cabin. Cade's white doeskin coat flashed among the trembling aspen that covered the bottom of the slope. The trees thinned out among the firs and black spruce further up. Aspen leaves fluttered gold and yellow and bronze, reminding him again of winter's late arrival here. About halfway up, the trees gradually gave way to scrub brush. The very top of the mountain was rock bare, with only moss covering the gray and a thin dusting of snow over the top.

His breathing was ragged with exhaustion, but he stretched his legs and pushed himself to go faster. Far behind, Silas followed with Lauren, half-running, half-walking.

There was no way he was going to catch up to Cade. Gautier might be able to outrun the man eventually—he was as tall as Cade, and not as beefy—but he wouldn't catch up to him before he reached whatever tree it was Lauren and Silas were talking about. Gautier would run out of trees before he ran out of mountain. And

Cade didn't run like a man who'd been running for a few hours on not enough water.

The wind chilled his back, reminding him that his buckskin coat hadn't fully dried from its early morning soaking. The snow clouds had cleared off, leaving behind a sky so blue it hurt to look at it. Except for the mountaintop, there was no snow on the ground. In fact, the moss was still green and fireweed was rusty with fall coloring. He passed yarrow still blooming and even a few blue asters.

Cade was running toward the north, which placed the sun to Gautier's left. As he left the bay's rocky shore to angle toward the cabin, the ground grew springy with soil and moss. He caught wisps of wood smoke, reminding him that Cade's men were still around, somewhere.

He had lost track of them while he tried to talk Lauren and Silas out of following Cade. The men had melted into the trees, leaving no trace.

Dante had had that ability, too. He could disappear into a forest, and Gautier could walk within inches of him without spotting him. He put aside that particular ache for later—if there was going to be a later. For now, he kept peering around himself, fully expecting an ambush.

Cade's lone figure slowed as the mountain slope grew steeper but he never looked back.

Where the hell was the man going? Silas and Lauren had talked about a tree, but the slope was full of trees. Which one did they mean? And why would Cade care about one tree more than any other?

"Gautier!" cried Silas.

Gautier stopped, breathing hard, and looked behind him. Silas and Lauren had kept up, but were no closer. They had stopped, too.

"Watch out," called Silas. "They're in the woods."

Gautier nodded. He didn't need Dante's gift to know that. He had no choice but to keep going. If he didn't catch Cade, Silas and Lauren would try to, and he wouldn't allow that.

He wasn't sure she'd survive another encounter with that bastard.

Besides, he never again wanted to see Lauren and Cade joined by that obscene black thing, or the look on Lauren's face as she looked down at him from the height of a mountain. For a minute, as he looked up at her, he had thought she was going to crush him.

Maybe the gaians had seen the same thing and decided to take off.

Bad enough that image would feed his nightmares. He didn't want to see it again. He didn't know what Cade had done to her, but she was clearly vulnerable to him.

Whatever it took, he was going to reach Cade first, and kill him.

He half expected gaians to come spilling out of the cabin as he ran by, but it remained dark and mute, its windows gaping holes in the wall. The door had once been beautiful, built out of what looked like oak—imported, since no hardwood trees grew in this area. Now the door was too warped to shut tightly and it swung back and forth in the wind. The cabin was built out of hand-smoothed spruce logs that still fit tightly together. The spine of the roof, always the problem spot in an old house, held its straight line.

It probably wouldn't take much to make the place livable again.

Then he was past the cabin and it was out of his mind as he turned his focus to the woods that sprang up almost at the cabin's back wall. In spite of himself, he slowed down a little. He'd lost track of how many men had been milling around in the clearing next to the cabin—somewhere around twenty, he thought. He and Silas had stopped six of them, but that still left at least fourteen men. Out there. Somewhere.

Hell.

He fingered the two knifes he had plucked from the fallen men and pulled the biggest one out of his belt. One man and two knives

against maybe fourteen men. Not great odds, but none of the gaians he'd fought had been worth crap as a fighter. Now that he
thought about it, even Dante had lacked the aggressive edge a man
needed to be a good brawler.

The cabin cut off the wind, and once Gautier entered the
woods, all he could hear was his labored breathing and the sound
of his feet hitting the ground. He lost sight of Cade in the shifting
maze of the trees. The ground immediately started to slope upward
and Gautier leaned forward, ignored his aching legs and pushed
himself on.

A flash of white drew his eye upward. Cade was still running,
but the trees at that elevation had thinned out and he was easier
to see. He glanced behind him every few feet.

Cade was nervous. Maybe not all his men had followed him
into the woods. Maybe none of them had.

A soft rustle was all the warning he got as he passed beneath
a tall aspen with branches so thick the leaves looked like a solid
mass. He leapt aside just as a gaians dropped soundlessly from
the tree. The man landed lightly on hands and feet and sprang up
immediately.

He'd been watching for an ambush and still this man had tak-
en him by surprise. He hadn't expected them to drop from trees,
from such a height that the drop would kill a man. Would kill a
sapiens.

Then two more gaians appeared on either side of him. One moment there was nothing but skinny aspen and black spruce, the
next minute two grim-faced men stared at him, less than ten feet
away.

Not good.

Gautier glanced behind him, hoping he could at least back up
a little to give himself space to maneuver, but three more gaians
were behind him, moving cautiously closer.

How could they move so silently?

They were all smaller than him, but he saw the glint of metal in their hands. They were learning to even the odds.

All he had was brute force and determination. He launched himself at the man who had dropped from the tree, the one standing between him and access to Cade.

Pent-up grief, anger, and fear fused into one great ball of fuel that propelled him past the two surprised gaians on either side of him. One reached out with his knife hand but it was half-hearted, a heartbeat behind Gautier's passage, as if he didn't know what to do with the sharp instrument.

Then Gautier reached the young man who had dropped from the tree. Although startled, he held his ground, raising his knife just as Gautier bowled into him, knocking him flat on his back.

Gautier stomped on the man's knife arm with all his strength and twisted his heel viciously. The man cried out in pain and Gautier kept running, barreling up the slope and roaring a challenge.

Only once did he risk a glance over his shoulder, but there were too many trees in the way and he couldn't tell where his pursuers were, or if they even followed him.

He ignored pain in his ribs and his harsh breathing, ignored his heavy legs and the black dots that floated in his vision.

He had left the calm, reasonable Gautier somewhere in the forest by the bay, somewhere before Dante died and Lauren became a monster.

All that was left now was drive. Drive to climb, to find, and to kill.

* * *

Lauren lost sight of Gautier in the trees behind the cabin. Although she hadn't seen them, she could sense the gaians hiding in the forest behind the dark boughs of the black spruce and the bright medallions of the aspen leaves.

Be careful, she whispered to herself.

Silas glanced at her and she wondered if she'd actually spoken out loud. Her grandfather looked pale and drawn.

He shouldn't be running like this, she thought. *He's too old.*

And he was holding her back. At this rate, Cade would reach the Tree long before she did and would have time to… to what? She didn't know exactly what he had in mind. All she knew was that the Tree was a place of Power, and if Cade could tap into that Power…

She couldn't allow him access to the Tree's power.

Could she?

She almost stumbled at the traitorous thought. Silas' hand tightened on hers and she shook her head to indicate she was fine.

But the thought had taken root inside her heart, a dark thought like the tendril that had connected her to Cade.

Each footfall landed soundlessly on the loamy ground and she automatically jumped over deadfalls and ran around bigger obstructions. Sometime in the past few minutes, Silas' pace had faltered, and although he tried to keep up with her, he finally let go of her hand.

"You go," he gasped when she turned around. He stood with his hands on his knees, trying to catch his breath. "I'm slowing you down."

Lauren glanced around the woods. They had reached the deserted cabin and the Tree loomed over her head, so close.

"Stay in the cabin," she ordered. "I'll come back for you when…"

Silas nodded grimly, not needing her to finish the sentence. A gust of wind ruffled his short gray hair, like a fond hand tousling.

"Don't forget who you are," he said softly.

Not taking the time to answer, she turned and ran to the back of the cabin, toward the Tree. She didn't know how safe he'd be there. He was a powerful obeah, but so was Cade, especially if he accessed the power of the Tree.

Already she could feel its power humming all around her like static electricity on her skin. It was so close that it hurt to crane her head back far enough to take it all in.

The smell of the forest enveloped her, a smell of dying leaves, humus, and wood smoke from the nearby camp's extinguished fires. She could tell where they had kept their outhouse, where they had prepared their food, where they had bedded down.

They had been here for a while. Dante had felt them trickling in for days, answering Cade's call. Whatever he was preparing, he needed them for it.

She sensed the gaians' attack at the same time as she heard Gautier's roar of anger. For a moment she stood stock still, the sound chasing chills up her scalp as an ancestral memory of being attacked by small men painted blue shouting just such cries flooded through her.

Then she shook herself free of the memory and began to run toward the sounds of pursuit.

Before she could make it ten feet, she stopped, sensing their presence. One by one, ten silent gaians slipped from behind trees or rose from the ground to surround her.

She stood there, looking for an escape, as they tightened the circle. Their movements were cautious, their expressions half-fearful, half-determined. They needn't have worried. She had no strength left to fight them. Cade had taken too much.

They stopped five feet from her and one stepped forward. He looked so much like Dante that Lauren's heart filled with joy before her eyes caught the differences—the chin pointier, the brow wider, the hair long and tied back. His face was set in faint lines of cruelty, an expression she had never seen on Dante. And there was an aura around him, a gray fuzziness that repelled her. He was an obeah.

"Come," he said abruptly.

Lauren glanced around the faces she could see. None of the others had auras. Most stared back at her stolidly, but a few couldn't meet her eye.

So. Ordinary gaians, either called here by Cade or otherwise persuaded to come. And by the look of some of them, they were having second thoughts.

She turned back to the obeah. "This isn't our way," she said softly.

The obeah's dark eyes narrowed. "Our way?" he repeated contemptuously. "What would you know of our way, half-breed?"

Lauren's head jerked back as if she'd been slapped. The hatred in the man made his aura pulse darker and for the first time, she clearly saw in him a desire to hurt her. He hated her.

She couldn't defend herself here, not against so many. She knew at a visceral level that she would stand a better chance in the underworld. Maybe she could imprison him the way Silas had imprisoned the gaians who had attacked Gautier.

But she was too inexperienced and still reeled from her encounter with Cade. Before she could even begin to think about shifting into the underworld, the obeah reached for her arm, hauled her closer, and stared her in the eye. The mental blow was like a clip on the chin.

She dropped into unconsciousness without a word.

❧ TWENTY-TWO ❧

THE SMELL of crushed spruce needles, black earth, and men's unwashed bodies filled her nostrils while something hard pushed steadily against her belly, keeping her from breathing properly. She groaned a protest then realized she was moving. She opened her eyes to see the ground only a few feet below her, a pair of legs clad in homespun canvas moving rhythmically in front of her nose, and her arms dangling down. It took a long moment for her confused blood-engorged brain to tally the clues and reach a conclusion.

A man was carrying her over his shoulder, like a sack of potatoes.

Or a carcass.

With the thought, her memory flooded back.

"Let me up!" she protested. The only answer she got was a tightening of the arm clamped around the back of her legs.

With a spurt of anger, she reached a dangling hand between the moving legs and yanked on her captor's scrotum.

With a noise somewhere between a strangled yelp and a whimper, the man dropped to his knees.

Lauren's heels hit the ground first, then the man's arm released her and she sprawled backward, banging her head against the mossy ground. Before she could scramble up, she was hauled to her feet by two men on either side. They held her up while the world whirled around her.

The blood rushed from her head and she sagged within the gaians' grasp. When she could finally open her eyes without dizziness, she found the obeah standing less than a foot from her. The rest of the gaians were arrayed behind him, some perched in trees.

When he saw he had her attention, he drew his hand back and slapped her hard across the cheek.

Tears of pain sprang to Lauren's eyes and a collective gasp went up among the gaians. She tasted blood. The obeah nodded as if her tears confirmed something.

"You see now that Cade spoke the truth." He raised his voice to be heard clearly. "She is tainted with sap blood and not worthy of the Tree!"

A few heads nodded, but Lauren caught some expressions that looked doubtful.

"In case you hadn't noticed," she said. "Cade is 'tainted' with sap blood, too."

She half-expected the obeah to smack her again but he merely smiled.

"That's right. Just as was foretold. He's the one chosen by the Tree," he said.

Oh great. A fanatic.

"Foretold?" she asked carefully.

The obeah looked at her with pity and contempt. "If you were a true gaians, you would know this," he said. "When the time comes, the Tree will call on the chosen one to lead gaians to their true destiny."

Not exactly specific, thought Lauren. *You could fit just about any goal into a prophecy like that. If it were real and not something Cade invented for his own purposes. Silas never mentioned anything about a prophecy.*

A breeze brought a whiff of male sweat tainted by fear and

uncertainty, and she glanced around the faces surrounding her. A few gazes slid away from hers.

Not everybody liked the obeah's methods, apparently.

A memory struggled to surface through the overwhelming awareness of the Tree's nearness but she couldn't quite capture it.

"If Cade is the 'chosen one'," she said, "why does he need me?"

The obeah shrugged. "Whatever his reasons are, they're good ones."

I'll bet they are. Out of the corner of her eye, she tried to count the number of gaians in the trees. Too many. She couldn't fight them all and she couldn't outrun them.

Proximity to the Tree made her thinking fuzzy. All she could focus on was the tingle in her body, the need in her to touch it. If she could only remember how she had gotten to the underworld... she could find Morag and ask for her help—

A sharp slap jerked her head back and she cut off a cry of pain. When she turned back to look at the obeah, she noticed for the first time how short he was. How short they all were.

"I will knock you out again if I have to," promised the obeah, his fist raised in warning.

Lauren felt the inside of her mouth with her tongue and found it scraped and cut. The men's fingers dug into her arms warningly.

"Big man," she said softly. *Next time I'll be ready for you.*

Without a word, the obeah turned and led the way up the mountain. She thought vengeful thoughts as her captors dragged her up the mountain but she knew herself too well to be fooled. The anger only masked the fear.

After a while, the trees grew smaller and farther apart. The wind freshened as they got closer to the top of the mountain and she could smell snow and something else, like cinnamon mixed with ginger. The Tree. She stopped resisting and allowed herself to be carried along with the wave of gaians swarming up the mountain. This was where she wanted to go.

As they ran the gaians often glanced up. The Tree was so close that it loomed over them, a shimmering trunk through which she could see clouds and blue sky. Elation displaced the fear and the anger until she strained against the hands holding her back.

The Tree.

And then they were above the tree line and into scrub brush. The obeah stopped abruptly and Lauren looked past him to see that they had arrived at the base of the Tree. It rose above the willow bushes and stunted black spruce like a giant ghost, so tall she couldn't see the top, its multicolored bark cycling through all the shades of the rainbow in a hypnotic pattern that captured the gaze.

She stumbled to a stop, dimly aware that the other gaians had stopped, too, mesmerized by the sight. She felt the Tree's presence like electricity humming through her body.

Then a movement drew her eye down and she tracked the movement until her brain could make sense of what she was seeing.

By one of the Tree's huge roots, Cade had Gautier locked in a choke hold and even as she watched, horrified, Gautier sagged against Cade's arm, limp as a mink in a trap.

"No!" Lauren burst past the obeah so fast that her two keepers caught air when they reached for her.

"Gautier!" she cried. But before she could reach him, Cade shook him like a dog shaking a rabbit and dropped him.

Gautier fell heavily, loose-jointed and ungainly, and his head struck the root of the Tree before she could reach him. She dropped to her knees by his side and touched his face. "Gautier?" she whispered.

His face had the same slackness she had seen too many times during the Troubles. Her heart compressed under the weight of too much grief and she fought for breath as the world shifted in and out of her awareness.

"Gautier..." She ran her hands over his face, his chest, his hands, shaking him. "Gautier!"

This couldn't be happening. Not Gautier, too. In spite of everything, he had stood by her, by Dante and Silas. He had protected her against Cade, had kept her safe while she went through Transition, had been her one anchor throughout this whole nightmare.

He had loved her. She saw it clearly, now that it was too late. Gautier had loved her.

"He was nothing but a sap," said Cade, still breathing hard. He stared down at Gautier's still form with such contempt that some barrier in Lauren shifted and fell away. Without a word, she launched herself at Cade, her shoulder aimed directly at his solar plexus.

He was ready for her. He twisted and caught her as she lurched past him, off balance. With a cry full of hate, she twisted in his arms and raked his cheek with her ragged nails.

He snarled and snapped at her hand like a dog but she was too fast for him. Her left arm was trapped beneath his but with her free hand she clawed at his face and gouged at his eyes. Even as she tore chunks of hair from his scalp, he refused to let go of her and finally, she saw why.

Long black shadowy tendrils snaked out of Cade, almost invisible in the bright sunlight. They seemed to emerge from his spine and flowed around Cade to encircle Lauren. Then she gasped at the first sharp pain, like a bite from tiny sharp teeth, and she knew that the first tendril had penetrated her back. A scream tore from her as she felt the tendril burrowing through her heart.

She struggled frantically to free herself from Cade, dimly aware that she was screaming in mingled pain and rage. *Too much, too much, too much!*

Cade abruptly loosened his hold and Lauren looked down at the sudden gap between their bodies in time to see the bloody tendril emerge from her chest, quickly followed by six more.

Not again. She closed her eyes, found the ball of rage that threatened to consume her, and used its energy to burn away the tendrils poisoning her.

She'd had enough of this man. She was going to kill him.

The rage cooled to icy determination as she forced the last of the tendrils, the one penetrating her heart, into Cade's chest to draw the life force from him. As his energy poured into her, she felt herself growing.

His head snapped back and he groaned.

Lauren smiled. Then she shrugged and his bruising hands fell away. A look of uncertainty crossed his face, then he realized what was happening and looked down in horror at the last tendril joining them. His big hands wrapped around it and he yanked on it, trying to pull it out of his chest. The familiar flames suddenly engulfed him as he struggled against her.

Lauren laughed and the sound filled the world. "How does it feel, Cade?" She felt his energy surge into her, dark and primeval—powerful. "Do you feel helpless?" Her skin hardened, growing into bark. She was now much taller than him, her strength much greater.

Suddenly the flames surrounding Cade died. His form blurred and shifted, and then he was the wendigo, yellow-eyed, fur as white blond as his hair, fangs bared, claws tipped in blood.

Imaginary blood, she realized. Make-believe blood, like everything about him. She recognized those eyes. She had seen them recently.

She smiled, showing all her teeth. "I beat the wolf you sent after me," she said slowly. Her fingers curling into the fur of his chest. "Do you know how I did it?" she whispered, drawing him up toward her face. He struggled in her grip but couldn't escape. In desperation, he burst into flames again. Her smile grew. "I crawled into his belly, Cade. Just like this."

With wood fingers she pried wide his screaming mouth, then wider still until his mouth filled the world. Then she slipped her fingers inside, then a shoulder and finally her body until she filled him up, until her cells absorbed his and she became him.

His strength married with hers and power surged through her. This was why he had lured her here. He had wanted this power for himself. With this power, she could do anything. Triumph made her giddy and she searched until she found Cade hiding in the deepest recess of her being. He was curled into the fetal position, hands covering his head, gibbering.

She considered the many ways she could kill him, exulting in her power. But first, she had a question.

"Why?" she asked, her voice like thunder. She stared at the pathetic little man who had stolen every bit of happiness she had and wondered why she had ever feared him. "Why did you need my power?"

Then she shuddered as the force of Cade's hatred surged through her.

"To kill them!"

"Who?" But she knew.

"Sapiens!" He rose to his feet, the strength of his hatred overcoming his fear of her. "They don't deserve to live!" He stalked toward her only to shy back as if seeing her for the first time. "They've taken everything and spoiled it!" He sent her images of smokestacks polluting the air, factories discharging into rivers, pavement covering up farm land. Through his eyes she saw blood soaking into the ground as warrior after warrior fell in war. She saw torture and forests burned to make way for farmland. She saw wild animals forced into smaller and smaller wildlife preserves. She saw species disappearing unnoticed every day.

She saw Cade working in a laboratory, injecting rats with the bubonic plague and releasing them in a Chinese marketplace; concocting a mutated version of SARS that he released in a toy store in Berlin; and spraying the Ebola virus over magazines in an airport bookstore in Johannesburg.

"You?" she whispered, reeling. "You caused the Troubles...?"

"They overrun us like rats," said Cade. His eyes glittered with madness. "They carry destruction with them like a pestilence. It's only a matter of time before they find us and destroy us!"

The plagues had run their course, had found every corner of

the world, and for ten years, had devastated sapiens. At last the diseases died out, finding no more hosts, until all who survived were those with antibodies.

"It didn't work," she said. She jerked him closer. How could she ever have feared this man? "What were you planning here?"

As he glared at her she peered into his soul and saw herself striding through city after city, her great roots ripping up buildings, grinding bricks and steel into powder, pulverizing saps into fertilizer for the ferns and trees that would spring up in her wake. She saw rivers flowing clean, trees growing through pavement. She heard nothing but the roar of water sweeping away the filth of sapiens, the call of birds come to reclaim the woods, the wind sighing through trees.

He wanted her to finish what he had started. He wanted her to destroy Homo sapiens.

"But..." she stared at him. "You're half-sapiens."

But he had retreated into himself, muttering. He seemed to shrink as she stared at him, huddling like a sulking child. She swept him into her huge hand, wrapping her shaking fingers around his tiny body. She began to squeeze. He gasped in pain and tried to squirm out of her grasp, but she'd had enough of Cade and his killing ways.

Cade was responsible for killing her father, then. He had taken *everything* from her. If she allowed it, he would keep on trying until he destroyed every sapiens.

The thoughts and emotions whirled through her, faster and faster, merging into one big ball of horror. They were all responsible, every one of those who came with Cade. He perverted everything he touched. She stared down at him, determination rising slowly within her like a tide.

He had to die.

There was no other way.

"So you'll kill him," said a calm voice in her ear. "Then what?"

Frowning, she searched for the source of the voice, but the

miasma of Cade's soul obscured her sight and filled her nose and mouth with the stink of burning bodies. She fought her way through the film of insanity that clung to her like a membrane and found Silas floating before her in the fresh air.

She took great gulps of air. She hadn't realized how close and hot she had been, how Cade's madness had suffocated her.

"What do you want, old man?" she finally asked.

"Tell me what you're planning," said Silas. He was looking at her intently.

I'm going to kill Cade. She had wanted to from the moment she learned that he was connected to her mother's disappearance.

And now that she knew he was guilty of killing both her parents, Mary, Dante... of murdering millions of sapiens all over the world...

Of killing Gautier, whose body had desired hers and whose heart was true...

"I have to kill him." Her blood surged hotter with every beat of her heart. "He has to die."

To her annoyance, she found herself looking to Silas for approval. It didn't matter what the old man thought. He had forfeited that right when he called her to the underworld, putting her at risk to save his own life.

The decision was hers. It went with her power.

"Perhaps," said Silas. There was no fear in him, only compassion. "But after you murder him, what then?"

Murder? No. It was an execution. He couldn't be allowed to live. He was too dangerous. She glanced at the ground so far below where dozens of figures still ran, dozens of gaians—one of them an obeah who had betrayed the welfare of his people. All of them had followed Cade, had believed what he believed, that her father deserved to die. How many of them had helped kill sapiens?

She would have to execute them, too.

"And then what?" pressed Silas. "After you've killed your enemies, what will you do?"

Lauren stared at him. She didn't know what he meant. Once she killed Cade and his followers, she would be free.

"Do you think that's what the Tree wants from you?"

The question confused her. The Tree had no wishes. It just was.

Wasn't it?

She looked about her. She was so tall that she could see past the mountains to the coast of the Pacific Ocean, where the sun glinted on its way to setting.

She still felt strong, her trunk body immovable, her branches... She looked up suddenly, aware for the first time that something was wrong.

She had been a tree once before. She had reached into space and felt the heat of distant stars on her fingers. Her molecules had merged with those of the universe.

But now her branches stopped well within the Earth's atmosphere. She stretched, but her branches remained trapped.

She wasn't the Tree at all. She was something else.

She looked down at herself. Her body was hard with black bark, and over it ran something wet and glistening.

"It's blood," said Silas softly. "The blood of the three men you killed. The blood of all those animals who died when you attacked the men. All the trees, all the bushes, all the insects. Their blood."

A wave of horror swept over Lauren. Her branches reached down, trying to scrape the blood away. She still held the struggling Cade. Her hand opened of its own volition, freeing him. So much death—she was no different than Cade! She had taken innocent lives, even if she hadn't known it at the time.

Lauren.

She stopped, her breath catching raggedly. "Mom?"

You're off balance, sweetheart.

I'm off balance, thought Lauren. *Off balance, off balance.*

She looked down again and this time she could discern faces looking up in awe. She turned away, ashamed for the second time in one day.

This wasn't who she was. She didn't destroy.

As if that were the signal, she began to shrink back to her normal size, her arms and legs returning to normal, her skin resuming its fleshy state. Then the Tree drew her in.

❧ TWENTY-THREE ❧

GAUTIER slowly regained consciousness to the sound of the wind sighing through the trees and the awareness that his head was trying to kill him. As he emerged from the fog of confusion, he realized that it wasn't the wind he could hear, but the sound of men murmuring and whispering.

He strained to hear what they were saying, then groaned as the effort increased the pounding in his head.

He opened his eyes to see bark and earth. He was lying on the ground, his cheek pressing against something prickly. He raised his head and bit down hard on his lip as the movement propelled his headache into overdrive.

After a moment, he tried again and managed to raise his head high enough to look around.

He was at the foot of a stunted spruce tree, on a bed of dry needles, surrounded by low willow bushes. Gritting his teeth, he pushed himself into a sitting position.

Only then did he see the gaians.

They were gathered in a loose circle around two figures on the ground. Using the spruce tree for support, Gautier slowly pulled himself up, noticing for the first time the pain in his throat. He swallowed a few times, trying to figure it out, then fingered his neck.

As his fingers probed his flesh, the memory of Cade's arm around his neck choking the life out of him came flooding back.

Accompanied by the memory, just as he was passing out, of seeing Lauren running just ahead of a band of gaians.

Hell.

Suddenly, one of the figures on the ground stirred as the circle of gaians shifted back, and Gautier saw that it was Cade. The big man slowly got to his feet, his blond hair stirring in the wind. Total silence enveloped the top of the mountain as Cade stood looking down at the ground. Gautier followed his gaze to see Lauren, unconscious on the ground at Cade's feet.

Suddenly Cade's head went back and he screamed his rage at the sky, his neck bulged with muscle and taut tendons. It was a sound so full of frustration and insanity that Gautier was already running, headache forgotten, before Cade turned to the nearest gaians and whipped the knife out of the man's belt.

Gautier reached the first gaians as Cade bent over Lauren's still form, shoved past the startled man and barreled into Cade just as the man's knife arm arced down toward Lauren's heart.

Gautier's tackle had enough momentum to topple the bigger man. As Cade fell heavily onto the moss-covered ground, the knife went flying into the bushes.

"Stop him!" cried one of the men, and at once two gaians grabbed Gautier's arms. But they were smaller than him and he used his greater leverage to fling first one, then the other to the ground. Before he could take advantage of his freedom, five more gaians swarmed him, their combined weight bringing him down.

Gautier's head thumped against the hard ground and he saw stars. Then someone landed on his stomach, knocking the wind out of him, before scrambling up again.

"That's enough," said a familiar voice.

Struggling to drag air into his lungs, Gautier peered past the bodies pinning down his arms and legs.

Silas stood downslope, leaning on a flimsy aspen branch that acted as a walking stick. As air begin to seep into Gautier's starving lungs, he closed his eyes in dismay. Now he had two people to save.

Three, counting himself.

"You're Silas, the Montreal obeah," said the man who had ordered the gaians to stop Gautier. His eyes glittered in the afternoon light and his thick black hair waved stiffly in the breeze. He stared at Silas, a strange expression on his face.

Silas' expression didn't change. "And you are?"

The other man flushed. He glanced furtively at the expectant faces of the men around him, and Gautier suddenly understood that Silas' failure to recognize him was an insult.

He finally had enough air in his lungs to speak. "Silas!" he called and had to stop to drag in another breath. "Watch Cade! He—"

The gaians who had spoken casually drew back his foot and kicked Gautier in the ribs.

Gautier cursed him and kept shouting at Silas. "Protect Lauren!" He couldn't see what Cade was doing.

The thought drove him to a frenzy and he redoubled his efforts to free himself. Out of the corner of his eye, he caught the movement of the man's foot swinging back for another kick, but the foot never connected. With his foot back and his arms out for balance, the man's expression suddenly went blank. His eyes rolled up into the back of his head and he toppled over like a felled tree.

The men holding Gautier froze in shock, and grabbing his chance, he heaved and kicked the two men off his legs. The two pinning his arms relaxed their hold in momentary surprise and he managed to slip his right arm out of a slackening grip. It was enough. In a moment, he had shrugged the other man off and clambered to his feet.

Only then did he notice that the gaians were no longer paying attention to him. The man who had confronted Silas was unconscious on the ground, as was Silas—a fact Gautier was getting used to—but the remaining gaians, fourteen of them, were splitting their attention between Cade and a point above the ground.

Cade had evidently given up on finding the knife and now knelt on the ground by Lauren's side. His huge hands slowly reached for her and wrapped lovingly around her neck. On his face was an expression halfway between reverence and revulsion.

Time seemed to stop. All the figures staring at Cade stood still as his fingers closed in slow motion around Lauren's slim, tanned neck. Gautier had time to glance around the top of the mountain to fix everyone's position in his mind, gather his strength into his legs and cold air into his abused lungs, and propel himself toward Cade.

As he exploded into action, time snapped back into place. Heads turned toward him and hands lifted to stop him. Some of the hands, he noted, were reaching for Cade. To stop him?

Then he shouted Cade's name and the man looked up. He saw Gautier running toward him and his face split into a great, wide grin of happiness. Turning back to Lauren, he continued to slowly squeeze the life out of her.

With all the pent-up anger and fear of the last few days fueling his momentum, Gautier's feet left the ground and slammed into Cade's head.

There was an audible snap and Cade toppled over just as Gautier landed heavily on the ground next to Lauren.

* * *

The Tree pulled. Startled, Lauren put a hand out to brace herself against the trunk, but her hand sank through the trunk and she kept going past her elbow. As the Tree absorbed her momentum, she suddenly found herself hanging half inside the Tree, her toes scrabbling for purchase on the ground.

Panicking, she barely heard the gasps and cries of the gaians as she twisted and pulled. She put her free hand against the trunk to push herself away. Instead, the Tree swiftly drew her the rest of the way in. She opened her mouth to scream, but before she could utter a sound she was inside, pulled in by what felt like hundreds of tiny, gentle hands.

She couldn't breathe! She struggled against the Tree's hold, struggled to raise her arms, to breathe... until she realized that she *could* breathe, that she was moving fast and that soft air flowed over her face and hands. The wind of her passage brought the scent of wildflowers, baking bread, rotting vegetables, old blood, frying meat...

She opened her eyes and gasped.

Against all logic, she had expected something like the tree in which she and Morag had hidden. Instead, she was in a vast space where everything—including her—twisted, pulsed, and sparkled. There were swirling shapes in muted pinks and purples and bright white lights that coalesced then burst apart in a shower of sparks.

And sounds —

A violin played a heartbreaking solo over a background of rocks tumbling down an incline. Children shrieked with laughter. A ribald drinking song roared loudly as she moved past, only to be replaced by the baying of a hunting hound and the crash and thunder of a rain storm. A woman sobbed inconsolably, the sound fading as Lauren moved past.

She tasted tears and mud, felt parched and sated.

And underneath it all was the steady booming of a large drum, like a heart beating through the world.

Her own heart began to race with fear and awe. She felt overwhelmed by sensations, unable to stop moving or to understand what was happening to her.

This was the Tree. She shouldn't be here—Silas should be here. He would know what to do. He had implied that the Tree wanted her but that was wrong. The Tree didn't want her. It just *was*.

And even if it did want her, she didn't care. All she wanted was to stop moving and find her way back to Gautier, to protect him in case the obeah attacked while he was unconscious...

The tears came as she struggled to shut out her last view of Gautier, lying so still, his chest not moving...

He was dead.

Abruptly, the weight of the last week came crashing down on her. She was no obeah. She was Lauren Tom, of Whitehorse. A trapper, a fisher, a hunter. She knew nothing of this Tree and wanted nothing to do with it.

What she wanted, she realized suddenly, was a chance. A chance to live her life in contentment, if not happiness. Maybe, since she was dreaming, she could even love a man and have a family, like a normal woman. Maybe even love a man like Gautier. Her heart squeezed with pain and her movement stopped abruptly. She hung poised amid wonders, her heart breaking, halfway between heaven and hell.

She didn't want a man *like* Gautier. She wanted *Gautier.*

The cry that ripped out of her came from the depth of her loneliness and need. It spread among the stars like a ripple in still water, scattering the shapes and smells and tastes in all directions until finally she was in the center of a still island of silence and darkness.

Alone.

Her body sagged as despair sapped her strength, and she closed her eyes against the darkness.

Not for her a life like Emily Pounder's, who worried about feeding a third child but still basked in the love of husband and children.

"That's because you're not an ordinary woman," said a familiar voice.

Lauren slowly opened her eyes, hardly daring to breathe.

It was no longer dark. In fact, light permeated everything so that she had to squint to see the figure in front of her. When her eyes finally adjusted, she took a deep breath and released it slowly.

"Mom?"

Meridy came closer, and Lauren stepped back, confused. The woman looked like her mother, but was too old. Meridy had been a young woman just past thirty when she disappeared. When she died. But this woman's hair was mostly gray and her face was covered in wrinkles.

She looked like Morag.

Meridy smiled, deepening the wrinkles. "Well, Morag is my ancestor, after all."

The woman wore a tunic-like, long-sleeved, green top with the sleeves pushed up to her elbows, revealing still-strong forearms. Her loose pants were green, with small blue squares, and flowed down to sandal-clad feet. And her hair... Lauren had never seen Meridy with short hair, let alone hair that was so well cut. Lauren smiled. She couldn't help it. She felt better just being in this woman's presence, even if she wasn't her mother.

The older woman took Lauren's hand. "I'm glad to see you, too, Lauren." Her eyebrows rose. "We all are."

Lauren blinked at the sudden blurriness in her vision. But it wasn't blurriness. Where a moment ago there had been only the older version of Meridy, now she saw dozens of Meridys. Hundreds. Her gaze swept over face after familiar face, each at a different stage of aging, each with her own map of experience stamped on her features. Thousands of Meridys. Each dressed differently. Some holding children by the hand. A few with babies in their arms.

Each looking at her hopefully.

The hand holding hers squeezed reassuringly.

"It's all right, dear," murmured Meridy.

All right? Lauren glanced over her shoulder. She was surrounded by a sea of Meridys.

"What is this?" she whispered. "Who are they?" She turned to the older Meridy. "Who are you?"

Meridy smiled. "We're the future—or possible futures."

Lauren frowned, not in the mood for riddles, and Meridy sighed. "You were always too serious."

She sounded so much like her Meridy—like her mother—that for a moment Lauren forgot everything—where she was, what had happened, the strange, familiar women surrounding her—and smiled.

Meridy smiled, too, and so did all the ghostly Meridys in an eerie visual echo that wiped the smile from Lauren's face.

Meridy sighed again and all the women disappeared, leaving her alone with the older woman. Then the white room shifted and they were by a lake, with a hardwood forest at their backs and wildflowers perfuming the air.

Meridy led Lauren to the water's edge. The water mirrored the clear blue sky and the mountains rising like watchful fathers in the background.

Lauren looked at Meridy expectantly.

Meridy didn't look at her. "What's inside the lake, Lauren?"

Lauren shrugged. "Fish, I guess. Rocks. Mud. Snails, frogs... I don't know." She gave Meridy a sidelong glance. "Mermaids."

Meridy smiled but kept her gaze on the water. "That's just it, isn't it? You won't know until you actually are in the lake."

Okay. There had to be a point in there somewhere.

Meridy glanced at her in disapproval. "You never used to be so sarcastic."

"And you never used to read my mind," Lauren pointed out. Still, she felt herself blushing.

"There is a point, Lauren Tom," said Meridy. "Look." She pointed at the water and Lauren's gaze followed the pointing finger.

But the lake no longer reflected mountains and sky. Instead, in a series of images that reminded Lauren of the television of her youth, she saw the future. Or futures.

She saw coyotes trotting down the empty streets of Whitehorse and the boreal forest slowly reclaiming the city. The picture shifted and she saw a beautiful city with paved streets and sapiens driving small vehicles or riding bicycles. Then she looked closer and saw that it wasn't sapiens riding bicycles but gaians and that the gaians were poorly dressed and stayed out of the way of the sapiens.

She saw gaians living in the woods in small tribes, starting at every sound, hiding whenever a group of sapiens approached.

She saw gaians hunting sapiens for sport.

She saw cities with sapiens ghettos; others where gaians were slaves. She saw wars, with gaians supplying weapons. She saw sapiens bodies, ravaged by disease, lying in the streets.

Finally, she saw small cities surrounded by forests and interspersed with parks, with gaians and sapiens living side by side, intermarrying, and growing together.

That final picture lingered in Lauren's mind long after the lake only reflected mountains and sky again. At last, she looked at Meridy.

"Those were possible futures?"

Meridy nodded, her eyes grave.

Lauren looked at the lake again. Sapiens and gaians, together. Was it possible?

"That's up to you," said Meridy softly.

Lauren shook her head even before Meridy finished speaking. "No." How ridiculous. One person couldn't affect the outcome of two species.

"You're not alone," said Meridy, drawing her attention. "All over the world, obeahs like you have been called to the Tree of Possibilities. They've all been shown their possible futures. All must choose the future they wish to pursue."

Lauren stopped shaking her head and stared at the other woman as her words sank in.

"You're not Meridy at all," she whispered. Meridy was dead. She had no future.

The other woman looked at her with sympathy and shook her head. Only then did the truth hit Lauren.

"You're me," she whispered, as chills chased each other up her back.

The other woman nodded. "Yes. I'm what you will be if you choose this future." She waved and once more the lake reflected the beautiful city with its blended population of sapiens and gaians.

"And the others?" asked Lauren. She had trouble grasping the enormity of what she was learning.

"They represent other possibilities," replied the older Lauren calmly. As if this sort of thing was normal.

Lauren shook her head, trying to decide if she had hit her head when Cade attacked her. "Why are you the one to speak to me?" she asked.

The older Lauren shrugged and Lauren had a moment of complete unreality. *Which one of them had really shrugged?* "Because of all the futures, this is the one we all want."

A small, hysterical laugh escaped Lauren. "How do you expect me to make all that happen?" she demanded.

"You won't be alone," promised the older Lauren. "You will find many—sapiens and gaians—who believe in the same future. Look for them. Work with them." She squeezed Lauren's hand. "All over the world, other obeahs will be working toward the same thing."

Lauren felt like she was sinking. This was a terrible mistake. She wasn't strong enough... "Wait—all of us were drawn to the Tree. Why pick me? Why not one of them? Why not Cade?"

The older Lauren shook her head. "Cade..." She sighed and looked down at the ground. "In all possible futures, Cade dies. In some he engineers a virus that is lethal to all life, including gaians. In one, he dies in the same fall that killed Mom." She shrugged again. "Cade wasn't the one and he knew it. That's why he wanted me. You." She smiled. "The Tree is about life," she added. "Not destruction. It always seeks balance."

Balance. For a moment, Lauren felt the thread connecting her to Morag, Meridy, and this older version of herself thrum with energy. Her hands tingled with it and something inside her shifted to make room.

Maybe she wasn't meant for husband and children, but she could still have a meaningful life. She glanced at the lake. A future like that—it was worth working toward. Worth giving up her quiet life in Whitehorse, giving up the trapline and the cabin.

"I don't know if I can do it," she murmured, more to herself than to the older Lauren.

"You'd be surprised what you can do," said the older Lauren, but as Lauren watched, woman and forest, lake and mountains faded into darkness. Then the stars appeared, great swaths of them that shone like beacons, bathing her in starlight. The drum beat slowly returned, and her heartbeat slowed to match it. She breathed deeply, her arms out as if to expand her lungs' abilities, and rational thought became harder and harder as her soul expanded, rippling through and out of her, reaching...

And there, bathed in starlight, heart beating to the rhythm of the universe, she felt them, others like her, reaching out for her in hope and determination.

She wasn't alone. She would never be alone again.

* * *

It was night by the time they brought Cade down the mountain and buried him.

Silas stood at the foot of the grave, his thoughts on the man buried there. Cade had been powerful and imaginative, a natural leader. If not for his insane hatred of sapiens—of himself, essentially—he might have led gaians into a new future in which they no longer had to hide from their sapiens cousins.

But Cade had twisted his abilities toward destruction and the Tree had rejected him.

Silas glanced up, his eye drawn by the large campfire by the shore of the lake. Taku Arm, he suddenly remembered, the name of the lake popping into his mind. Not his memory, he realized with great comfort, but one he accessed from an ancestor who knew the area. He sighed with contentment. It was good to feel whole again.

He had been in the eerily quiet underworld, fighting Cade's lieutenant, when he felt the wall Cade had erected come crumbling down.

A cry of relief and joy spread through the underworld as gaians, released from Cade's prison, returned to their homes. Which meant that Cade was dead, or that somehow, Lauren had connected with the Tree. Overwhelmed by the sudden avalanche of memories and emotions, Silas had faltered.

Cade's lieutenant chose that moment to attack, and Silas would have fallen if not for Meridy's sudden arrival.

"Hi, Dad." She grinned. Silas' heart turned over with love and he grinned back.

"Hi, baby."

Meridy blinked the long, slow blink that always hid so much of what she was thinking. "I brought someone with me," she said. And suddenly Dante was beside her, grinning at his grandfather.

"Dante!" Was it possible for a heart to stop from joy?

"Let's get rid of this bum, okay?" said Dante, and the three of them turned to deal with Cade's lieutenant. When it was over and the obeah was safely ensconced in a prison next to the other four Silas had previously imprisoned, he turned to Meridy and Dante.

"Merry... Dante..." He couldn't find the words. How did a man apologize for failing his family so miserably?

Dante shook his head and looked his grandfather in the eye. "It's over, Grandfather," he said firmly. "I made my choices, just as you did." He stepped closer and pulled Silas into his arms for a fierce hug. "Tell Gautier not to blame himself, okay?" He stepped back and smiled. "I'll see you around." With a wink for Meridy, he left.

Merry placed a hand on Silas' arm. "He's right, Dad. It's over. I've had a lot of time to think about things. I was as much to blame as you." She shook her head. "I loved Zack, but I think in part I used him to get to you." She looked down at her feet. "It's not something I'm proud of."

They were standing in their ancestral woods, surrounded by the familiar scents of maple and pine and wild rose. Somewhere, a campfire wafted smoke through the branches.

His heart was so full of love and regret that it hurt. Still unable to speak or even to think, he took his beautiful daughter in his arms and held her tightly. Meridy held him just as tightly, but after a while, she stepped back. Her hands slid down his arms to capture his hands.

"You have to go back now and help Lauren."

He nodded, wishing again that he had the sapiens ability to cry. This seemed like a fine moment for tears.

"I think she's going to be fine," continued Merry, her brown eyes thoughtful, "but she's still a little off balance."

Silas finally found his voice. "I'll look out for her," he promised.

Merry smiled and placed a hand on his cheek. "I know, Dad. She'll be busy looking out for everyone else."

And so he left his daughter in the underworld, still sad but comforted by the knowledge that he could see her as often as he wished.

"Dad!" she called, just before he returned to the real world. He glanced back at her. "When Lauren's ready, tell her I'll be waiting for her at home."

Silas nodded and opened his eyes to the real world, just in time to see Lauren emerge from the Tree.

Now standing at the foot of Cade's grave and watching the campfire, he longed to sit down.

Lauren was down by the shore, talking to the gaians arrayed on stumps or perched in trees. Her arms spread wide to encompass them all, then her hands swept together, clasped to her heart. He couldn't hear what she was saying, but he knew she was telling them what she had seen and what it meant. Or could mean. How would Dante have reacted to all that gaians emotion?

His granddaughter had been changed by her time inside the Tree. There was a quiet confidence about her now, an acceptance.

In spite of his pride in her, Silas grieved for what she had given up. Just outside the circle of gaians, he could see Gautier standing still, next to a tree. He was just a darker shadow in the trees, but he hadn't moved since Lauren started talking.

He hadn't gone anywhere near her since she returned from the Tree.

* * *

Gautier finished tying his bedroll to his backpack and straightened up. It was a beautiful morning, with blue skies as far as the eye could see. The snow on the mountaintop was so bright it hurt to look at it. He glanced away, still unnerved by what he had seen.

All the time Silas and Lauren had referred to a tree, he had thought they meant a *tree*. Then he killed Cade, and a moment later, all the gaians gasped and stepped back. He had thought it was because of what he had done. Then he looked up and there was a tree, so big it blocked out the mountain, shimmering with colors.

And then Lauren emerged from the trunk, as easily as if she were stepping through a doorway. The moment both her feet were on the ground, the tree disappeared, leaving only mountain and brush.

And Lauren.

She was changed. As she walked toward the gaians gathered in a knot of awe, he watched power settle around her like a mantle. In his heart, he said goodbye.

He had listened last night from the shadows as she spoke to the gaians, explaining her vision of the future and converting them to her way of thinking. She didn't need him anymore. She had become a leader, only where she was going, he couldn't follow.

It was time to leave.

The door to the cabin squeaked open and Silas came out. He'd been checking on the obeah who was still imprisoned in the underworld. They had moved the man inside for protection. Silas had already released all the others and they were now down by the lake, at the gaians camp.

"What are you going to do about him?" he asked Silas, nodding at the cabin.

Silas shrugged. "I'll keep talking to him. Try to show him the error of his ways."

Gautier thought for a moment. "You're as much a prisoner as he is, then."

"He'll eventually come around."

"What if he doesn't?" asked Gautier. "You could be here forever." Beautiful as the day was, winter was on its way. He could
smell it on the wind. The old man couldn't spend the winter here.
Not alone.

Silas shrugged. "I'll set him free."

Gautier hesitated. The obeah in the cabin was much younger
than Silas. If he decided to attack the old man...

Silas shook his head and grinned. "I'll be fine, Gautier," he
said gently. "I'll only release him when I'm safe." He glanced down
at the lake, at the gaians camp. "You're sure you don't want to
wait?" His voice was soft with hope.

Gautier steeled his heart and shook his head. "You don't need
me."

Silas' eyebrows rose and he smiled slightly. "Self-pity, Gautier?
That's not your style."

Gautier sighed. He was right. Just because things didn't turn
out the way he'd hoped was no reason to feel sorry for himself. He
swung the backpack up over his shoulders and adjusted the waist
strap.

"Where's Lauren?" he asked. "I'd like to say goodbye."

* * *

Lauren sat cross-legged on a reasonably flat, sun-warmed
boulder and watched the sunlight playing on the water. It was
peaceful here. If it wasn't that their supplies were running out,
she could easily consider staying for a while. At least until winter
chased her out.

She sighed. Staying wasn't really an option. She had a lot of
work to do and all of it entailed getting out of here and back to civilization. So to speak.

Most of the gaians would come with her to Whitehorse. She
would introduce her friends and neighbors to their cousins. She
considered the people she knew and wondered if they would ever
accept gaians as part of their world. Charlie would be fine. Maybe
Mr. Chiang. As for the others... well, she'd have to see.

Maybe she should try to convince some of the gaians to stay behind when she moved on. Whitehorse was her trial run. If she could open up her home town for gaians—and convince gaians that her home town would accept them—she might be able to do this thing the Tree wanted from her.

"Lauren."

She jumped and turned to find Gautier staring at her. Her smile faltered when she saw the backpack.

"You're going?"

He nodded. She couldn't read his expression and he was downwind so she couldn't even smell him. She got off the rock and, dusting the seat of her pants, slowly walked up to him. As she got nearer, she took a deep breath. He had bathed in the last few hours but his clothes still smelled like him. His face was covered in a reddish beard that contrasted strangely with his brown hair, but that made his blue eyes even more startlingly beautiful.

She stared at him for a long moment, drinking him in. She wanted to touch him, touch his face, his hand. Kiss him. Try to convince him to stay. But she stood where she was and made no move toward him. She had seen the look in his eye when she finally emerged from the Tree.

He wanted no part of what she was or what she had to do. And it wasn't fair of her to expect him to stay. He had done enough for her. For gaians.

"Where to?" she asked, and was surprised that her voice sounded so normal.

He shrugged and looked away, to the distant mountains to the east. "Ontario. I'm fixing up a house there."

Her throat constricted suddenly and she looked down at the ground, trying to control the tears that threatened. Finally, when she could speak again, she looked up. He was looking at her intently.

"Have a safe journey," she said softly.

He nodded abruptly and turned away.

"Gautier!" She called him back. When he turned back to her, she hesitated, her heart warring with her head.

Finally, she smiled at him. "Thank you."

His gaze roamed her face as if he was committing it to memory. Then he smiled crookedly and walked away.

* * *

She was still sitting on the rock when Silas tracked her down. Her grandfather glanced around the shore, then at her face. She had wiped the tears from her cheeks when she sensed his approach, but knew he could sense what she was feeling.

"Why did you let him go?" he demanded.

Surprised, Lauren looked at him. "Because he didn't want to stay."

With a look of complete exasperation on his face, Silas threw his hands up. "Young people!"

What was the matter with him? "Are you all right, Grandfather?" she asked gently.

He frowned and she had the sudden sense that he was disappointed in her. "Have you spoken to your mother yet?"

Lauren shook her head. She had been too busy. *Oh, be honest,* she told herself abruptly. *You're afraid to see her again. Afraid she'll be disappointed, too.*

"She's expecting you," said Silas. "At home." He crossed his arms as if he was prepared to wait.

Lauren swallowed a sigh. Maybe her mother could give her pointers on how to deal with the old man. Without another word, she got off the rock and walked down to the sandy shore, where she lay down. The sunbaked sand warmed her back even while a cool wind played over her face.

She closed her eyes and suddenly she was in the underworld. Still marveling at how easy the transition was, she looked around. The spruce and aspen trees looked familiar and her gaze caught on the familiar lines of her cabin. In spite of everything, her heart filled with happiness. *Home.*

She walked toward the cabin, following the familiar path at the back. Smoke came out of the chimney and beneath it was the smell of bread baking. Someone was home.

The smile on her face froze when she came around the front of the cabin. There, not fifty feet away, was a lake with a dock on which stood two Adirondack chairs, painted bright red. And sitting in one of the chairs was a familiar figure.

Meridy looked up from the book she was reading and waved. Hardly daring to breathe, Lauren approached the dock. Meridy put down the book and stood up. She watched Lauren walk toward her, the look on her face a mixture of pride and sadness.

Lauren stopped within a few feet, drinking in the sight. Meridy looked barely thirty. Her chin-length black hair was held back with the familiar beaded hair band. Lauren's hand fished in her pant pocket and found the band. For a moment, everything felt surreal. Then she let go and accepted.

"Hello sweetheart," said Meridy softly. Her eyes were full of love.

Lauren took a deep breath, refusing to burst into tears. "Hi, Mom," she finally managed.

Then Meridy stepped forward and gathered Lauren into her arms. It felt weird at first—she was taller than her mother and Meridy looked barely ten years older than her—but then the tears came and she hugged back with all her might.

They spent the next few hours talking and it was the happiest time of Lauren's life. At one point, Meridy got up and went inside the cabin. She came back with slices of still-warm bread with butter melting on them and they ate in companionable silence, watching the water.

Finally Lauren had to ask.

"What's with the lake?"

Meridy sat back contentedly and studied the lake with Mount Lorne in the background. "I always felt that's what the place needed," she said. "We had mountains and forest, but I missed having water around."

Lauren smiled. "So what's it called?"

Meridy's face grew still. "I called it Lake Zack," she said softly.

Lauren's smile faded. Was there an underworld for sapiens, she wondered? Or had her dad's death been final? She glanced at her mother and saw the sadness on her face. Even after all these years, she still grieved for her husband.

"That's because we loved each other very much," said Meridy. She glanced at Lauren. "I had hoped you would find a love of your own."

Gautier's smell sprang unbidden to Lauren's memory, as clear as if he stood in front of her. She looked away from her mother, unwilling to reveal her pain.

"I'm going to be too busy," she said. "There'll be no time for love."

Meridy's voice held a trace of laughter. "Too busy? Do you think it's something you can put off?"

Lauren turned to her mother, unable to keep the misery from showing. "Mom, you know what I have to do. It's unfair to love someone who will always come in second to my mission."

Meridy reached across the arm of her chair to hold Lauren's hand. "Sweetheart, you're off balance," she said softly. "Maybe he's *part* of your mission."

* * *

It took her three hours to catch up to Gautier. By then it was lunch time and she was hungry, sweaty, and tired. Not to mention grumpy. The man was certainly moving fast.

She found him squatting on a gravel bed by the side of a river, boiling water for drinking. He stood up in surprise when she stepped out of the woods.

"Lauren!" His gaze traveled from her flushed cheeks and damp hair to her sweaty shirt. His gaze lingered on her shoulders, noting the absence of a backpack.

He abandoned the fire to stride toward her. As he walked, he pulled his knife out of its sheath. "What's the matter?" His gaze searched the woods behind her as he placed himself between her and the trees.

She smiled, feeling suddenly much better.

"Nothing's the matter," she said. He turned back to her, a puzzled look on his face. "I came looking for you," she added.

He was less than a foot away from her. As he looked down at her, she saw his blue eyes grow darker as he became aware of her nearness. He cleared his throat. "For me?"

She nodded.

His gaze lingered on her lips for a moment before he dragged it back up to her eyes. "Why?" he asked.

She smiled and stepped close, breathing in the scent of him—wood smoke and sweet hay and something like cloves. Only yearning and a breath of air separated them now.

"I wanted to ask you something," she murmured.

As if hypnotized, he stared at her lips. "Ask me what?"

Her hand reached for his neck and urged him down and she kissed him. He tasted as good as he smelled. When she finally pulled away, she was having trouble breathing.

"I wanted to know just how attached you are to that house you're building."

He looked at her for a long, long moment. Then he pulled her close and bent down to her lips. With his warm breath fanning her cheek, he asked, "What house?"

Then *he* kissed *her*.

THE END

ABOUT THE AUTHOR

After 35 years in the Yukon, Marcelle Dubé now lives in small-town Alberta. She has published 16 mystery and fantasy novels, including two series. Her short stories appear in a number of anthologies and magazines. Her work has been short-listed for the Derringer Award and the Crime Writers of Canada Award of Excellence for Best Crime Short Story, which she won in 2021 and 2024. She is best known for her Mendenhall Mystery series.

Find out more at www.marcellemdube.com.

NOVELS BY MARCELLE DUBÉ

Mendenhall Mystery Series:
The Shoeless Kid
The Tuxedoed Man
The Weeping Woman
The Untethered Woman
The Forsaken Man
The Wronged Woman

A'lle Chronicles Series:
The A'lle Murders
The A'lle Mutation

Standalone:
Ghosts of Morocco
Identity Withheld
Jilimar
Kirwan's Son
Obeah
On Her Trail
Shelter

A Little Strangeness (collection)

www.ingramcontent.com/pod-product-compliance
Lightning Source LLC
Chambersburg PA
CBHW060601030726
47498CB00005B/1485